Penguin Books
A Story Like The Wind

D1139698

Laurens van der Post was born in Africa in
1906. Most of his adult life has been spent with
one foot there and one in England. His
professions of writer and farmer were
interrupted by ten years of soldiering – behind
enemy lines in Abyssinia, and also in the
Western Desert and the Far East, where he was
taken prisoner by the Japanese while
commanding a small guerrilla unit. He went
straight from prison back to active service in
Java, served on Lord Mountbatten's staff, and,
when the British forces withdrew from Java,
remained behind as Military Attaché to the
British Minister. Since 1949 he has undertaken
several official missions exploring little-known
parts of Africa. His independent expedition to
the Kalahari Desert in search of the Bushmen
was the subject of his famous documentary film
and of *The Lost World of the Kalahari*.
His other books include *The Face Beside
the Fire, Flamingo Feather, The Dark Eye in
Africa, The Seed and the Sower, Journey into
Russia, The Hunter and the Whale, A Portrait
of Japan, A Far-Off Place* which is a sequel
to *A Story Like the Wind, A Mantis Carol* and
Jung and the Story of Our Time. Colonel van der
Post, who is married, was awarded the C.B.E.
for his services in the field.

Laurens van der Post

A Story Like the Wind

'The story,' the Bushman prisoner said,
'is like the wind. It comes from a
far-off place and we feel it.'

Penguin Books

Penguin Books Ltd, Harmondsworth,
Middlesex, England
Penguin Books, 625 Madison Avenue,
New York, New York 10022, U.S.A.
Penguin Books Australia Ltd, Ringwood,
Victoria, Australia
Penguin Books Canada Ltd, 2801 John Street,
Markham, Ontario, Canada L3R 1B4
Penguin Books (N.Z.) Ltd, 182–190 Wairau Road,
Auckland 10, New Zealand

First published by the Hogarth Press 1972
Published in Penguin Books 1974
Reprinted 1976, 1977
Copyright © Laurens van der Post, 1972
All rights reserved

Made and printed in Great Britain by
Hazell Watson & Viney Ltd, Aylesbury, Bucks
Set in Linotype Times

For
Emma-Clare Crichton-Miller
and Rupert van der Post;
David James Laurens Crichton-Miller
and Rebecca van der Post,
in order to redeem a promise
made to them far too long ago

As well as to my wife,
Ingaret Giffard,
for keeping me up to it

Contents

Introduction 9

1 Hintza's Warning 13
2 The Coming of Xhabbo 49
3 Hunter's Drift 77
4 Foot of the Day 115
5 Mopani 166
6 The Gates of Distance 202
7 James Archibald Sinclair Monckton, K.C.M.G.,
   D.S.C., B.A. (Cantab.), and daughter 254
8 The Birds Change Their Tune 316
9 Lady Precious Stream 362
10 Finishing School of the Bush 397
11 And So to the Washing of *u-Simsela-Banta-Bumi* 428

Testament

Ákẹn ╪ẽnnă, tĭ ē, n̆ ǃkã sshŏ aŭ ǃχŏë-sshŏ-ǃkuĭ,
ssë ǃχuŏnnĭyă, kkẽ, n̆ ssẽ ǃkúïtẹn n̆-kă ǃχŏë, n̆ ssẽ
ttumm̄-ă ǃkẽ-tă-kŭ kă kkŏ-kkŏmmĭ . . . .

Tă, n̆ ǃkŭ ǁhă;
n̆ γáukĭ ǀkĭ kkŏ-kkŏmmĭ
N̆, ǀkŭ-g ǀnĕ ĩ, ( ) ttumm̄ă ǁgáuĕ kkumm̄, hă n̆ kă
ttŭ hă; aŭ kă ǀnĕ ǀkă ǃkã sshŏ, ã; hă ssẽ-g ǀnĕ

áu kă tătĭ ē, n̆ ǀkẽ
ssin̆ ǃgwẽtẹn ǀuhĭ hhŏă ǀχárră; hĭn ǃgwẽtẹn ǀkạm̄
ǁã n̆-kă ǃχŏë; n̆ ssẽ ǁã ssuẽn̆ hĭ; n̆ ssin̆
ttumm̄ttumm̄ kĭ ǀyặ ǁẽ; aŭ n̆ ǃnɡ̊ă ǀkŭ, ē n̆ ssin̆
ǁa ĩ; aŭ kă tătĭ ē kkọmm̄ ǁkuặn ē ǃkhwẽ.

'Thou knowest that I sit waiting for the moon to turn back,
that I may listen to all the people's stories ... For I am
here – in a great city – I do not obtain stories – ... I do
merely listen, watching for a story which I want to hear;
that it may float into my ear ... I will go to sit at my home
that I may listen, turn my ears backwards to the heels of
my feet on which I wait, so that I can feel that a story is
in the wind.'

Introduction

I begin with the extract from a statement made by a Bushman convict a hundred years ago, which appears as my Testament on the page opposite because it shows that he was sick even more for stories than for home or people. One of a doomed fragment of the first people of Africa, he had been sentenced to work on the breakwater in Table Bay which, at that time in the Cape of Good Hope, was considered the heaviest punishment for crime, short of death. He had been sentenced thus because when hungry he had taken a sheep from the flock of a man of a race who had stolen all his own people's great land.

The statement from which this extract is taken is for me one of the most tragic and significant utterances to come out of my native country, but I have given only this much because it is enough to show, as nothing else I have encountered in the literature of the world, how the living spirit needs the story for its survival and renewal. It was this universal consideration which made me take up the story that follows. But I had another reason as urgent to me personally, for writing it.

Men have written a great deal about the history of Africa: the horror of the past, the racial, social and economic problems; the dirt, the dust, the heat, the fever, the mosquitoes and many other painful and enigmatic aspects of the land. But no one, as far as I know, has ever recorded the aspect of Africa with which this story is concerned. It is an aspect which cannot be rendered by any purely rational means or any merely documentary or factual processes. However imaginatively written, it cannot even be rendered just as history. It can only be done in the way in which Africa itself excelled and transmitted it from unrecorded time to the present day through stories, myths and legends. They alone can reflect what I can only describe as the magic which

9

life in primitive Africa seems to me to have possessed before we arrived from Europe to spoil it.

I was lucky enough to be born just in time to experience some of this ancient Merlinesque world of Africa. I was so close to it as a boy that all I had to do was sit and listen for the heroic dead and their magical age to live again on lips of living men who had experienced and even made it. As a result, all the fairy-tale characters of my childhood were not the pale faces of the breed to which I and my family belonged but the yellow, copper-coloured and black indigenous peoples of the land. They were so for all members of my family. I was one of fifteen children. When the few of us who are left alive of what was once a large pioneering family meet and recall our relationships with the despised coloured peoples of our childhood, I am struck how warm our voices become, how lively the conversation and quick the imagination.

For example, we had a man, half Bushman, half Hottentot, who worked for us and first came to us as a boy, already dismissively named 'Vet-Kop' (Fat-head), since his first employers, when they took him away, did not think it necessary to ask him what his parents called him. The amputation from his own society was so brutal that he himself lost all memory of his original name.

He was always in and out of our local gaol for minor offences against a one-sided code of law and always came straight back to us. There would have been a mutiny in the army of children in my home had my parents turned him away. Fortunately, they loved him as we did and he had an influence on my imagination that no minister of the Dutch Reformed Church could equal. To this day I grieve that he is not alive in this grey moment of time to colour it for me as he coloured my childhood with his rainbow spirit.

The truth is that children like ourselves were lucky enough to be in touch with this past through such people as Fat-head, before the slanted Calvinist spirit of our society could convert us into sour creatures of disapproval and acid judgement. We were therefore wide open to the wonder of Africa. As a result, this flow of a primitive world into my imagination was so rich that even I have been surprised by its wealth. I constantly turn

10

to it again and again as a person might on a cold winter's night to a fire for warmth. The older I have become, the greater has grown my awareness of the debt I owe to this fast vanishing world of Africa and the greater my conviction that somehow it must be recorded, so that it should always be there to help thaw the frozen imagination of our civilized systems so that some sort of spring can come again to the minds of men.

The recording seems all the more urgent because the ancient way of keeping alive this aspect of life has itself been lost in African societies and it is no longer passed on from generation to generation in the shape of stories. Africa, when I was a child, had at its disposal for this purpose an immense wealth of unwritten literature. But we, just through the radioactive fall-out of the nuclear split in the European spirit, have killed contemporary Africa's respect for its own great spoken literature of the past. Modern African societies, I regret to say, have so lost their own natural way that they even tend to distrust anyone who tries to redirect them, as I have tried to do, to what is valuable in their own beginnings. To tell them that the balance has never been fairly struck between the primitive and the civilized in any society as yet is believed, by many in Africa, to be just a form of intellectual paternalism, if not a trick, to keep them in a 'backward state of mind' for selfish European ends. One of the most reprehensible things we have done to the people of Africa is to make them ashamed of the working of their natural imagination. We have made them like children who are ashamed of their own mothers; ashamed of the natural spirit that gave birth to their unique character and once made them so vivid.

Part of the complex of personal reasons that made me try to preserve in the form of a story something of what was wonderful and honourable about primitive life in Africa, is the hope that it may help to restore the self-respect to African imagination, of which it should never have been deprived. Another is the belief that this story may, even at this late hour, awaken some awareness of how much the despised primitive values deserve to be honoured by the most civilized of men, not only for their own sakes, but so as to help them on the way to honouring African man in their societies as they wish to be honoured themselves.

Finally as a story, its setting is not photographic. It is a painting of only part of an immense landscape, and even in part is not complete because, like all paintings, it chooses for its canvas only what the painter finds significant in the scene. For example, the Matabele people in this story are not representative and are described only in so far as they carry a particularly electric charge of what is representative in African man. They were chosen as conductors, because a Matabele clan, almost untouched by our own time, still inhabited the 'far-off place' which is the raw material of this story, when I rediscovered it some years ago. I found them still telling their stories in the ancient way. Theirs was one of the voices I had in my ear as I wrote, compelling my story to be a thing not so much of pen and predetermined pattern, as of the spoken word I once had direct from their burning imagination.

1 • Hintza's Warning

Something happened to François when he was barely thirteen, without which the story that follows would not have been possible. He was fast asleep in his bed in his own room at the far western end of the farmhouse at the time, when a tense, high-pitched whimper from Hintza sounding right in his ear woke him.

Hintza was François's own special dog and one of the most important characters in his life. It had been given to François by his father when he was eleven years, six months and seven days old. Life at Hunter's Drift was always so packed with interest for François that he did not measure it just in years, or even half-years, as the time-weary grown-ups of his world did, but in days, if not hours. For instance he would never have a birthday or experience a Christmas without wondering how he could possibly endure the strain of having to wait twelve months before it came round again. He always remembered the shock that went through his system when he heard grown-ups exclaim, as they seemed to him more and more inclined to do, that it was fantastic how quickly Christmas came round again. It struck him as so grossly inaccurate, if not incomprehensible, an observation that he secretly regarded it as a downright lie.

Hintza was a magnificent young ridge-back. It was the finest puppy in a litter of six born to a couple of the most famous hunting dogs in southern Africa; a bitch called Nandi and a dog called Dingiswayo – 'Swayo for short to his friends. Both mother and father had received their names from the man who owned them – the chief ranger of one of the greatest game reserves in Africa. This reserve lay to the west, some fifty miles beyond the crescent of hills that enclosed Hunter's Drift to the east as a half-moon does a star between the tips of horns. It declined into two sharp points of sheer cliff that cut into the banks of the river near which the homestead of the farm stood. This ranger, before he took up the work of preserving the vanishing game of Africa, had been one of the greatest hunters Africa has ever known. He was the son of the legendary hunter whom John Buchan made, thinly disguised, into the hero of two of the stories which François found by far the most exciting of all the many books he wrote. He was known all over Africa as Mopani Théron, although he had Christian names of his own which he kept to himself – but more of that later. He appeared in François's life as Mopani Théron and was just called Mopani by everyone who was his equal, or a polite 'Oom' (Uncle Mopani) by young persons like François.

Mopani Théron was seldom seen without one or both of his dogs on the patrols he was constantly carrying out against the poachers of ivory, rhinoceros horn, leopard and other valuable game skins. The poachers, from hideouts skilfully concealed in the dense bush that covered most of that remote country, were for ever raiding Mopani's reserve, which was almost the size of the France from which his ancestors had come. One of François's earliest and most vivid memories was his first glimpse of Mopani riding up the stoep of Hunter's Drift in the heat of a summer's day, his long legs dangling loose in the relaxed, natural stirrup that all long-distance riders used in Africa, and the lively little Basuto pony on which he was mounted, looking much too small for its tall rider. The right image for describing the effect he made on François at that precise moment did not come until some years later when he saw, in his father's illustrated edition of Cervantes's great work, a reproduction of a Daumier painting of the elongated Don Quixote. Mopani Théron, François was to realize then, with his long, wiry frame, ascetic features and neat pointed beard, had looked like another Knight of La Mancha come to tilt against evil in the bush of Africa. The parallel was most marked that same evening long ago when he had galloped away to ambush some poachers, who moved mostly at night, his tall sunset shadow, dark as ink, travelling in the scarlet dust at his side. Only unlike the Spanish Knight, he had two superb alert and highly dynamic dogs trotting at the heels of his horse as easily as any of the wild dogs

14

who never know what walking is. They were, of course, Nandi and 'Swayo.

When he noticed how interested the boy was in the dogs Mopani Théron had told François that he had called the bitch Nandi after the mother of the greatest warrior Africa has ever produced – Chaka, the king of the Zulus, whose general 'Mzilikatze had founded the Matabele nation on the perimeter of whose lands both Hunter's Drift and the game reserve lay – because he was certain the bitch would be the mother of great fighting dogs. He called the dog after Dingiswayo, the founder of the Zulu nation and therefore ultimately also of the Matabele, for he was equally sure that 'Swayo would be the begetter of more great dogs.

It must not be imagined from all this, however, that Nandi and 'Swayo were black. Like all ridge-backs they had coats like lions, so much so that when out hunting in the bush that crowded in on Hunter's Drift as it did on the great game park, one had to be always on guard not to let a partial glimpse of their tawny electric colour flickering in the undergrowth trick one into the assumption that they were indeed lions about to attack.

Hintza, one of the couple's fourth litter, was a superb blend of his father's and mother's best qualities. When François first saw him as a puppy, he glowed like one of the nuggets of virgin gold occasionally found in the dried-up banks and beds of the rivers, which cut deep through hill and bush to join the powerful Zambezi far to the north.

It had been a cold winter's evening when François's father brought Hintza home. The sun, red in a turquoise sky, was just going down over the immense desert which started abruptly some fifty miles beyond on the edge of the bush to the west of the farm. At one minute a person was apparently deep in bush country, the next stepping out of it on to a desert stretching for close on a thousand miles to where it ended in a swell of dunes of piled-up sand, so fine that the lightest wind raised a spume of dust like smoke from their curling summits, moaning faintly in the process, until the sound was lost in the reverberation of the great breakers of the cold South Atlantic, levelling out a satin-yellow beach at their feet.

François and his mother had begun to give up hope of his father's return that night. They were not unduly worried because no one could tell precisely how long any journey from the capital, some four hundred and twenty miles to the east, would take. It was merely that they were both disappointed because, with luck, François's father could have been home two days before. Indeed, for two afternoons François had repeatedly climbed the highest point in the hills at the back of the homestead to look out for any sign of dust on the track of crimson earth that wound in and out of the bush. This third evening had been no exception. When there was only half-an-hour left before the sun would plunge swiftly below an horizon, dark blue and from the hilltop a circle perfect as a ripple, travelling rhythmically out over the surface of a deep, still pool, and there was yet no spurt of dust on the track, François climbed down the hill and started home despondently. He was more disappointed than he would care to admit, because he had woken that morning with a hunch that his father would definitely come home that day. But no sooner had he found the footpath at the bottom of the hill when he was startled by an outbreak of barking from the five large mongrel watch-dogs they kept on the farm.

He knew at once that something unusual was happening and went up the narrow path to his home at the double, carrying his ·22 rifle like a light-infantryman at the trail. He arrived at the edge of the vast clearing on which the homestead stood near the banks of the river, to see his father already dismounted from his horse, the bridle over the crook of his right arm and his left round his wife who had rushed out to greet him.

His father, he learned, when his own excited greeting was over, had come home not on the normal road from the railway, a distance of some ten miles, but on a back trail through the bush leading past Mopani Théron's base camp, fifty miles further away.

And what had he been doing at Mopani's camp? He asked the question of François with a mysterious air and the note of teasing which he always seemed to use towards his only son when he needed a counter for the uprush of feeling that came to him when his affections were deeply engaged. François remembered this aspect of their meeting particularly, because it seemed

16

to him at the time that never had he known this paradoxical trait in his father's character as lively and pronounced. So much so that it made him oddly uneasy, almost as if it had another purpose, that red sunset evening, than its normal one of preserving the proportions of male restraint and deep-felt emotion at any given moment in his father's Spartan state of being. Anxious as he was to know what lay behind it all, he was to remember that he instinctively connected his reaction with the fact that he had never seen his father looking so tired after a journey, nor suddenly so thin and so much older.

However, all trace of unease vanished when his father explained why he had come the long, round-about way just to spend a night with Mopani Théron. He said that all the while he had been away he had been thinking that although François had a gun of his own (he had on his tenth birthday been presented with a new ·22 repeating rifle and two hundred rounds of ammunition), he still needed something more before his equipment as a hunter was complete. Could François guess what that was?

François had a very good idea, not of what it was but of what he would like it to be. Yet so much beyond all reasonable expectation was it that he quickly pushed all thought of it aside, because, young as he was, he already knew what agonies of disappointment over-expectation could produce in people and, as a result, had determined that the beginning of wisdom in any young person in the power of unpredictable grown-ups, was to take every possible precaution against excess of hope and anticipation.

Couldn't he guess? His father went on in that new, rather tired voice which he seemed to have developed on the journey just behind him. What was it that François secretly wanted and yet was so small that it could be concealed on his person? Yes, let François look at him. He had something on him for François at that very moment.

The emphasis convinced François that it could not be what he longed for, and made him glad in a sad way that he had not indulged his expectation. He could not imagine how what he would have liked as a present could be concealed on his father's person. Examining his father as he stood there, tall in front of

François, his arm about his wife, who seemed to be, in the unfair way of grown-ups, already in the conspiracy, and the brilliant dying light of the winter's day like a halo round them, François could detect no bulge in his clothes, nor any other evidence that his father might have brought him anything of importance. He tried not to give any sign of the involuntary inrush of disappointment, but he found himself silently imploring Providence with a quick, strong wish: 'Dear Lord, please not another hunting knife.'

Both parents seemed to have realized that teasing had gone far enough because, at a nudge from François's mother, his father lifted the flap of the wide, deep pocket of his old military great-coat, put his right hand inside and when he pulled it out again joined it with his left. With both hands cupped together he held out to François something of a deep golden colour.

Although it took him some time to believe it, so great was his surprise, it was of course exactly what he had secretly wanted; perhaps somewhat smaller than he would have liked but none the less a puppy and a dog of his own. It could not have been more than a fortnight old and was fast asleep, no doubt exhausted by its journey and from the shock of suddenly being alone. Its eyes, fringed with unusually long lashes for any dog, however well-bred, were tightly shut and creased at the corners, like the lines round eyes that have looked far too intently and far too long at the African sun.

As François's eyes came out of their trance of unbelief, they saw the cold evening air send a shiver through the glistening coat of the tiny yellow bundle in his father's hands. He reached out and took it carefully into his own. He felt with a great flush of pleasure that it was as warm as his breakfast toast. As he thought this, the puppy suddenly opened its eyes and looked up into his own. He was startled to find that they were a deep dark blue. He had never seen so charged and human a colour in any animal's eyes, particularly an animal so small, tired and bewildered as the little puppy between his hands. Looking into them, his sense of wonder grew because all bewilderment was vanishing from the puppy's eyes. They seemed to be recognizing in François their destined home. A quick whimper of greeting broke from the puppy; it began to wriggle in his hands and the little yellow tail started to vibrate against the palm which held it, in an effort to wag. At the same time it tried to heave itself nearer to François, so that he had to clasp it against his chest or it might have fallen. François put his face down to make a noise of welcome to the puppy and at once the cold, wet black nose, the incontrovertible sign of good health in any dog, came up to meet him and a tongue, pink and smooth as the petal of one of the finest of his mother's bright cannas, which grew in the flower garden in front of the house, glistened in the evening light and reached out to lick François's cheek.

'What's his name?' François asked his father, his voice almost incoherent with pleasure, gratitude and surprise, all churned up together.

'He has no name yet,' his father replied in that studied, meticulous way of speaking that years of work as an educationalist had inflicted on him. 'As he is yours, you must name him and I am certain you will name him well and accurately. But before deciding just remember what distinguished stock he comes from and that he has a mother called Nandi and a father named Dingiswayo – great names both, as you no doubt know.'

François's father had been born in the far south of Africa among the great Amaxosa people and spoke their language as he did English and Afrikaans. François had been brought up knowing Amaxosa fairy-tales, myths, legends and history perhaps better than those of the remote Europe from which his people had come some three hundred years before; and almost, though not quite as well, as those of the Bushman people to which his old nurse, Koba, who had died a few months before, had belonged.

Everything his father had told him about the Amaxosa had made them, second only to old Koba's Bushmen, a favourite people. He had been particularly impressed in their history, as his father taught it to him, by one of the Amaxosa paramount chiefs, a dashing, spirited person called Hintza, who had figured in the long War of the Axe, and as his father spoke, François knew suddenly what he would call the puppy. Without doubt or hesitation now, in a clear voice which surprised even himself with its firmness, he announced as if it were a self-evident fact, 'His name please is Hintza.'

At the sound of the name Hintza the puppy against his chest became surprisingly alert, for a reason that was to become clearer much later. It wriggled all over and pressed closer against François, and a small noise of contentment broke from it like a sign of confirmation that it had known well in advance what its name was. Then it once more relaxed, shut its eyes, sighed profoundly and resumed its sleep.

'Now I wonder,' François's father was teasing him again, 'did he put the idea into your head? Or did you really think of it yourself?'

But François felt there were more important things to do then than to engage in a bout of teasing with his father. There was the question of arranging proper accommodation for Hintza in his own room, as well as the problem of seeing that it had food and drink after so long a journey, both matters the urgency of which grown-ups, with their slack attitude to time, were inclined to overlook when dealing with the immediacy of the young. Without answering he turned about and once more at the double, dashed to the house, straight up the wide steps of the broad stoep and vanished inside, hastening for his own room. There he took an old winter coat from the cupboard, arranged it rather like a big bird's nest on the foot of his bed and placed Hintza gently in the middle before covering him over with the end of one of his own woollen blankets. Clearly all this was very much to Hintza's liking because not once did he flicker so much as an eyelid and appeared to be sinking deeper than ever into his sleep.

That done, François hurried out to the big kitchen at the back of the house, snatched a small milking can from a shelf and ran out to the milking sheds a quarter of a mile away at the end of the great vegetable garden and orchard, which stood on the fertile black soil between his home and the hills. The Matabele herdsmen there were just finishing off the evening's milking and already there were a dozen large gleaming metal pails filled to the brim with milk, standing on the stone floors against the wall near the entrance. As always there was something magical about the milk for François because not only did it glow white as snow in the twilight air, but was topped with a mound of foam caused by the vigour with which the skilful Matabele drew it in quick jets from the cows, making a sound like rain in the shed. This foam, glowing gardenia-white in the brown air, rose high over the silver rims like a Muslim dome.

Snatching the burning copper dipper which hung from a rail above the pail in the company of other dairy utensils, he began filling the little milking-can with such haste that he spilt some of the milk. He was solemnly reproved for it by the chief herdsman, a tall, broad, grey-haired old Matabele gentleman (old that is by François's standards), of whom François was very fond. His name was 'Bamuthi, which meant 'He of the Tree'. He was said to have been born unexpectedly under a sacred tree while his mother was hiding from their hereditary Mashona enemies. The latter had attacked their kraal while the men were away on a hunting expedition. He had been at Hunter's Drift ever since François could remember.

'*Gashle!* Slowly, Little Feather,' he said in his deep bass voice. '*Gashle!* He who wastes food will bring famine upon himself. And what has happened that you should want to spoil your appetite when the evening food is nearly cooked?'

'Little Feather' was the Matabele nickname for François. Like so many of the African peoples, European names had no meaning for them and they insisted on giving all white people with whom they came into contact, special African names that symbolized for them their main characteristics. So widespread was this practice that Europeans were only remembered and referred to among the Africans by these special names and, from the beginning, their name for François had been Little Feather.

They had called him this simply because they called his father (although never to his face and they thought it was a deep secret), The Great Bird. François, who was in the secret from the start because his old nurse had told him of it, knew that this was a name full of instinctive respect. Birds, for the people of this great bush country, had many magical properties. For example, they were thought to know the secret of all living things, to have great foresight and to fill with wisdom the hearts of those who took the trouble to learn their language and listen. That was why African chiefs in the old days had always worn a long black and white tail feather of the *um-Xwangbe* (sacred ibis) stuck in the metal bands around their heads, as a sign for all their people to see that their heads were full of natural wisdom and inspired thought.

Now François's father had been the chief inspector of African education in that vast territory before he so unexpectedly turned to farming. His reputation as a man of great wisdom and learning had spread so widely through the territory that it was even known on the remote frontier where he had carved Hunter's Drift out of the virgin bush. From the moment he appeared among them, both the reputation and manner of his coming seemed to make it inevitable that only the image of a great rare new bird, suddenly alighting from the sky, could serve the impression he made on the indigenous peoples. In this, for once, they had the full approval of old Koba. She resented and hated the Matabele, like all other black African races, for having played so terrible a part in hunting down and destroying without pity the last remnants of her race, which once had been the masters of the whole of southern Africa, if not the entire continent.

Birds, as François knew from the many wonderful stories Koba told him at night before he went to sleep, had even greater magic for the Bushman than for the Matabele, the Barotse and the Shangaans. So he had not been surprised when Koba, pledging him to secrecy, told him his father's Sindabele name and confessed that she thought that the Matabele, in naming him thus had, for once, not done too badly.

It seemed logical, if not utterly natural, therefore, that when François was born, he should have been thought of as a feather of the bird that his father was. He had happily accepted this name for years from the Matabele, particularly because invariably they spoke it in a tone of rare protective affection, as if thereby claiming him as one of their own. Moreover, as Matabele children were supposed to be terrified of feathers, he thought that the name implied a certain courage in his own character.

Yet recently, the 'Little' in front of 'Feather' had begun to irk, as though something in François was beginning to feel that it was high time the 'Little' was dropped and he was promoted at least to a full feather, if not another bird in his own right. On this particular occasion the 'Little' smarted more than ever, perhaps because the fact that he had just become the owner of a puppy of his own – and a puppy that would soon be a hunting dog – might have started in him a feeling of crossing a frontier, leaving his childhood for ever behind, and taking the first step towards a new world of full male responsibility.

He was, therefore, uncharacteristically sharp with 'Bamuthi. Indeed, so sharp was he in his reply that if his father had heard, François would most certainly have been severely reprimanded. François's father always insisted on his household showing the utmost courteousness to people who themselves were naturally courteous, and attached much importance to good manners, as did the Matabele.

'Those who judge before they know the facts will learn to string the beads.' He hurled the Sindabele proverb back at 'Bamuthi with the automatic pompousness proverbs tend to bring to the tongue of those who use them, even one so young as François. The reference to 'stringing the beads' was a Sindabele image for the tears, bright as beads, that human beings shed in moments of great grief.

Pressed and preoccupied as François was, he had snapped it out unthinkingly. But he did have a sneaking sense of shame realizing that, perhaps for the first time, he had not preceded his sententious remark with the 'Old Father' that good manners demanded from a youngster like himself when addressing so old and fine a Matabele gentleman.

He felt it all the more when 'Bamuthi replied lightly, without a trace of resentment: 'And even the greatest bird, Little Feather, must come down from the sky to find a tree to roost upon.'

This was another proverb implicit with the simple reproof that François could not fail to feel, since it meant that no human being, however old or great, could live high and mighty with his head for ever in the air.

But by this time his little can was full, and snapping the lid firmly into position, he doubled back without another word to his room and Hintza. Hintza was still fast asleep, but François only had to put the bowl of milk, still warm from the cow, near its face to see the shining little nose come alive and the smell of milk make it quiver in scores of the finest magnetic little creases.

A second later the large blue eyes were wide open. Hintza was struggling out of the blanket and on to its feet, so unsteady and trembling that François had to support it under its stomach with his hand, while it fell to lapping up the milk as if it had not fed for days. 'Gosh,' he remarked to himself, 'his stomach is as warm as one of Lammie's hot-water bottles.'

From that moment on Hintza spent every night of its life in François's room. This was not an unusual arrangement. One of the facts to be faced in a dog's life in the wild country where François lived, was that an enormous number of dogs all the year round were killed by leopards. Leopards, who were great gourmets, loved two kinds of food above all others: dogs and baboons. Already in François's own life, seven of his father's favourite ridge-backs had been killed by leopards.

The trouble was that no self-respecting dog could ever see any reason why it should be afraid of a leopard. A leopard was hardly any bigger than itself and, in any case, was a species of cat which no dog could be expected to respect. When they had found themselves faced with a leopard, the dogs had had no hesitation in rushing to the attack. Unfortunately, leopards not only had teeth that were sharper than dogs' and jaws that were just as powerful, but they were also armed with four sets of long, sharp claws, as tough and piercing as steel. Dogs could not hope to match such heavy armament. No one in François's world had ever heard of an encounter between leopard and dog where the dog had won the battle.

So it had become the custom in François's home to keep their ridge-backs inside at night. The duty of guarding the homestead was left to five large mongrels because, although François now would hardly admit it to himself, the mongrels of Africa were far more intelligent and capable of taking care of themselves than well-bred dogs like Hintza. Hintza and his breed were too proud to put intelligence first. They needed men, as men needed them, to be at their best in the bush. When faced with any challenge from wild animals, even leopards, they felt it a point of honour to take up the issue without hesitation. It had accordingly become a fundamental principle in the training of all

24

pure-breed dogs at Hunter's Drift, to make them so obedient to their master's instructions that they would never attack any game, let alone leopard or lion, unless ordered to do so.

Somehow the mongrels were different. Born to make their way in life without any automatic privileges, they developed their sense and intelligence to an extraordinarily high degree. Moreover they were never troubled by any consideration of honour, self-respect or what some call the bourgeois compulsions of 'keeping up appearances'. They could, when confronted by wild animals, fight as fiercely and perhaps even more intelligently, than any ridge-back. But they fought only as a last resort and, at the first hint of any danger, much preferred to give tongue and bark and, at times, or so it seemed to François, at night even to scream their alarm. So it was quite natural, and with his parents' full approval that Hintza, from the start, shared François's room.

For some eighteen months Hintza was trained to be a hunter's dog with all the dedication and natural patience born of affection that François, single-minded as only a lonely boy can be, could bring to the task. In these crucial matters he also had his father's great experience, willingly shared. But perhaps most important of all, twice a year in the spring and early autumn, François was allowed to go on holiday to Mopani Théron's camp. On these occasions Hintza, of course, went with him. There they were constantly taken out on routine patrols in the bush by Mopani, so that both François and the rapidly developing Hintza had the finest teacher in these matters that Africa could produce. Also, Hintza had the constant example of his own parents, Nandi and 'Swayo.

Unexpected as it was to François, it was not really surprising, therefore, that at the end of his third holiday in the bush with Mopani Théron, sitting by their last camp fire the night before he had to go back to Hunter's Drift, that the old hunter admitted to François with a certain whimsical reluctance: 'Little cousin' (that is how he invariably addressed François in the intimate manner that people of his generation reserved for the young) 'Little cousin, it was a bad day for me and a good day for you, when I allowed that "slim" [clever] father of yours to talk me into giving Hintza to him. I am afraid he is going to be even better than his parents. It just shows you how much breeding counts in life.'

Pleased as François was with Mopani's verdict, and much as he admired Nandi and 'Swayo, François secretly felt that there was more to it than mere breeding. A great deal, he believed, was due to the fact that Hintza had been trained largely by a young person. He was convinced that no grown-up could have done the job half as well. He had only to think how incomprehensible grown-up people could be and how often they failed him in matters that seemed of the utmost importance, to be sure that the same gulf would exist between people like his father and Mopani, however well-meaning, and the little puppy.

He remembered, as an example, that first morning when he had taken it, after its long night's sleep, into the breakfast room to show it to his parents. Ever since it had woken up the puppy had been just one long intensive wriggle of playful energy. But at the first glimpse of François's parents it had gone instantly still and rigid, staring at them in sheer unbelief. Then it had suddenly given a sharp, apprehensive yelp, whirled about, and made straight for reassurance to François, who was kneeling on the rug near the wide open fireplace. The moment its eyes found François the bewilderment vanished.

Although he had only known Hintza for one night, François felt sure that Hintza's behaviour was due to the fact that his parents somehow were just too big for him to take into his understanding; their eyes too big and bright with predetermined grown-up judgement. The puppy, indeed, was having the same sort of difficulties he himself had experienced when first confronted with the concept of giants and colossi in fairy-tales and legends. Only he, François, was of a size that Hintza's young senses could grasp.

The parallel made him realize that he must act as a bridge between Hintza's uninitiated capacity for understanding and this world of tall, confident grown-ups, with loud voices and heavy footsteps, that made the floors vibrate and the ground shake under the purple pads of Hintza's sensitive paws. For months François was to notice how Hintza, when faced with adults, would inevitably turn to look to him first, before venturing another glance at the outsize shapes that bestrode the world of Hunter's Drift.

But there was one other reason for François's success with Hintza. It was, he was convinced, because he hardly ever spoke to Hintza in Afrikaans, Sindabele or English, the three languages most commonly used in his world. He always spoke to him in Bushman. He had learned Bushman from Koba who had, from as early as he could remember, always talked to him in her own language, when they were alone together. Indeed, his first clear memory was not even of old Koba's wrinkled magnolia skin and somewhat Mongolian face, but rather of the peacock light of brilliant Hunter's Drift sunsets playing on a necklace of heavy dark blue and red glass beads that she always wore, and the sound of her voice singing a Bushman lullaby to coax him, against his will, to sleep.

Bushman was a most difficult language to speak because almost every other consonant in it was a click of some kind. François's mother, who knew only a few words which she liked to use from time to time as a token of respect when speaking to Koba, would flush with the effort of pronouncing them. François therefore could easily have been discouraged from going on with it, if it had not been for four things. First of all, he possessed a child's supple tongue. Then there was his great love for Koba. Also there was the attraction, that appeals to all young people who are compelled, out of the need of protecting values which the grown-up world have forgotten, to lead in a sense a disguised life, of having his own secret language. It was almost as if an important part of himself felt it were on enemy territory, where it was safer to use a code for communicating with those who shared its secrets. Bushman seemed the perfect answer to this need. Finally, there was the overwhelming fact that Koba had assured him that all the animals, birds, reptiles and insects of Africa, and also the plants, understood the onomatopoeic Bushman tongue.

She told him many stories of how in the beginning the people of the early race, as she called the first Bushman, lived in complete harmony with all living things and plants on earth. She explained that it was only when the people of the early race snatched the first fire from underneath the wing of the great ostrich ancestor of all ostriches and started using it for their own selfish ends, that the animals took fright and ran away from human beings. But even though they fled, they never forgot the meaning of the sound in which they had first conversed in harmony with men.

François thought that from his own short experience of life he had already some intimation that old Koba was right. Even from the start Hintza had seemed to bring evidence to support her. One day François was playing with his puppy in the sun on the stoep of Hunter's Drift and the puppy wandered off on his own near the edge of the high stoep.

François, afraid that it might fall over, called out loudly to him in Bushman, 'Here, Hintza! Here!'

In his shout he had put the emphasis on the *tza* and to his amazement his puppy, instead of turning around and coming back to him, had leapt forward and vanished over the brink of the stoep. Alarmed, François dashed after the puppy and saw that it had picked itself up out of the dust, fortunately unhurt, but weak at the knees with shock and a strange, inner excitement, while it stared about wildly, the hair of its coat bristling and its mouth open, growling at the vacant day which was trembling with light and heat, as if expecting to see some kind of enemy ahead.

At once revelation came to François. Koba had long ago explained to him why the two most important words of command for hunting dogs were *tssisk* and *tza* – used by everyone from the Cape of Storms to Broken Hill. *Tssisk* was used when one wanted a hunting dog to go into the bush and flush out whatever one's quarry happened to be; *tza* when one wanted a hunting dog to go as fast as possible after the quarry, once it was flushed. His father, Mopani Théron and even the Matabele unfailingly used no other words for these precise purposes.

Accordingly François realized instantly how the 'tza' in Hintza had been taken instinctively for a word of command by the puppy. He knew that, henceforth, he would have to be most careful to use Hintza's name differently, or serious and even dangerous confusion might arise between them. So from then onwards Hintza became 'Hin' not only to François but, at his request, to everybody else at Hunter's Drift. The Bushman 'Tza' was added only when one really wanted the dog to go after live game.

These two words were so effective, old Koba had told him, because the hunters of the people of the early race got them straight from the stars. The stars, Koba said, were the greatest hunters of all and if François would come with her one night and walk out away from the sounds of the house into the darkness, she would give him an example of what she meant.

So he had gone with her on a very cold, clear and still winter's night and waited until there was not even the sound of a lion, jackal, hyena, bush-buck, owl or night plover to be heard. Then, as they stood beside the thick hedge of massive fig-trees which lined the orchard and looked up deep into a sky bursting at its black seams with the weight of the stars, François had become aware of a far sound rather like that in the great mother-of-pearl shell in his father's library when held to the ear.

'Now listen, Little Feather,' Koba had said, 'listen and hear the sounds they make hunting up there in the bush of the night.'

Obediently he had turned his right ear, already alerted, to the stars. At once quite clearly he had heard the stars, faintly yet distinctly, crying out: *'Tssisk!'* and a host of others crying out: *'Tza!'*

With this proof from the universe itself of the effectiveness of Bushman in communicating with natural things, François had used no other language between Hintza and himself. Soon he was convinced that there was almost nothing spoken in Bushman which Hintza, or Hin as he was now called, did not follow.

Within three months, Hintza knew the Bushman names of all the most important animals, reptiles, and birds in the bush and the words of command that François was likely to use in their connection. For instance, François had only to say 'snake' in Bushman and it was quite unnecessary for him to add the command 'stand and watch', because Hintza knew already that it was absolutely forbidden for him to tackle any snakes, much as he would have liked to. This too was an inexorable law at Hunter's Drift because the bush was full of poisonous snakes of all kinds and many dogs, even the mongrel dogs, had been lost through snake-bite because out of a natural aversion for them they would insist on challenging every snake they saw. The result was that they invariably got bitten in the head and even though they might kill the snake they would die themselves of the poison from the fangs of the serpents.

From an early age, therefore, like his father and mother, François was made to carry in a leather pouch attached to the leopard skin belt which he wore round his tough green whip-cord bush jackets, a complete anti-snake-bite outfit that consisted of a small scalpel, a hypodermic syringe, and an antidote of serum specially prepared in the capital and renewed every six months. This serum was most effective against snake poison and if immediately injected just above a bite into the blood stream of a snake's victim, counteracted the poison so effectively that within a day, the person or animal bitten could continue their lives as if nothing had happened.

In fact François himself had saved 'Bamuthi's life thus on one occasion when they had been out in the bush looking for a lost cow and calf. 'Bamuthi had been bitten on the ankle of his bare foot by a black mamba, the most poisonous of all the snakes in the bush. Unfortunately, 'Bamuthi, wise and experienced as he was, like all Matabele and Zulus, was extremely superstitious about snakes, particularly black mambas, because they all regarded them as reincarnations of their ancestors which had either come to warn, comfort or punish them for some neglect of tribal ethics. 'Bamuthi accordingly had immediately assumed that he had been punished thus by the spirit of his ancestors for some unwitting transgression of the Matabele code and was quite prepared to sit down on the track, there and then, and die.

However, François had immediately produced his snake-bite outfit, tied his handkerchief tightly above the spot where 'Bamuthi had been bitten, put a stout piece of wood through it and twisted it as tightly into the version of a surgical tourniquet as his father had taught him, to prevent the poison from speeding up along the arteries to 'Bamuthi's heart where it would immediately be fatal. He had then injected the serum thrice into 'Bamuthi's leg at different places, one above the other.

While doing this he tried to comfort 'Bamuthi by saying: 'Please don't worry, Old Father, this is powerful medicine, far more powerful than that of any snake. Soon you will be well, I promise you.'

But old 'Bamuthi had just shaken his head sadly and replied: 'Little Feather, when the spirits call as this great black spirit has called me now, no medicine of man can stop me from having to follow and lose my shadow.' This last phrase was a Sindabele image of dying.

François had gone on doing all he could to comfort 'Bamuthi but 'Bamuthi had just said: 'Thank you, Little Feather, but please say no more because I must now sit here and prepare myself for the long journey.'

From that moment until nearly two hours later he had refused to speak, and just sat there, still as black marble, his wide dark eyes so sad and remote that they almost made François cry. He did not even seem to notice that François, every few minutes, was unwinding his improvised tourniquet so that the blood could flow again and then tightening it up again to control the circulation for a while longer. This François was doing, as he had been taught, in order to prevent gangrene.

When finally he had removed the tourniquet and noticed that apart from 'Bamuthi's state of mind, there was nothing seriously wrong with him he had urged. 'Come, Old Father, you see the medicine has worked. There is nothing wrong. Let us leave the cow and calf and go home to rest.'

But it had taken some hours more before 'Bamuthi was convinced. Then he had allowed François to lead him home, walking more like a somnambulist than a person fully awake. But this episode had created an even greater bond between them.

The real point of the experience, François was soon to learn, was that the snake-bite antidote worked well only when applied against bites inflicted on the extremities of human beings and of the bigger animals like cattle and horses. But when the bites were inflicted as they invariably were, on the heads of the dogs it was impossible to put a tourniquet round the head of a dog and, although one could inject any amount of serum above the snake bite itself, the wound usually was too near the vital nerve centres of the brain for the antidote to disperse the poison in time.

Thanks to Hintza's grasp of Bushman and his confidence in François, this lesson was quickly and absolutely learned. It became the cornerstone, as it were, for the whole complicated edifice of Hintza's education in all the many matters of life and death in the bush. He learned to stand still, silent at François's side, pointing with nose and tail in the direction in which his keen senses had located the enemy, until commanded otherwise. Moreover Hintza had been skilfully helped by François to cultivate a kind of urgent, almost supersonic whisper to be used in moments of acute crisis for communication with François.

This was perhaps the greatest triumph in François's relationship with Hintza because Hintza was, even for a dog, a prodigious and most inspired barker. Indeed in the beginning his gift and love of barking had been highly troublesome because at one time even François had begun to despair whether he – I say he from now on because by now Hintza had ceased to be an 'it' at Hunter's Drift and was very much a 'he' – could be taught to restrain it. Barking at Hunter's Drift was something only encountered in the mongrel watch-dogs. Dogs kept inside like Hintza were supposed to be above such crude methods of communication. They were, one could say, the intelligence officers of the night, who had to monitor all the sounds outside, particularly the barking of the watch-dogs, interpret their meaning, and only when certain that the meaning was most immediate wake up superior officers like François or his parents, and communicate it to them in sounds not audible beyond the walls of the room in which they were sleeping. It took François months to get Hintza to behave accordingly.

The trouble was that for Hintza, barking was a form of singing. François was convinced that he was the most musical dog the world had ever seen, and this gift had been revealed to Francois within a month of Hintza's arrival.

He had been giving Hintza a last run-around in the twilight before taking him inside to put him to bed. Hintza by now had grown so fast and was so much stronger that he bounded easily up the broad steps on to the stoep to join François who was holding the great stinkwood door open for him. But instead of dashing inside as he normally did, Hintza suddenly turned about and faced the east, standing very still and silent.

François immediately thought that Hintza had noticed something unusual stirring in the deepening brown of the evening in the bush beyond the homestead. Curious, he followed the tense puppy's example but could detect nothing at all unusual in their surroundings except that the rising moon, although itself still invisible, was beginning to fill the dark air over the bush with a yellow mist of light. Against this light he could occasionally see the black zigzag streaks of the flight of the great bats who were emerging from their homes in the holes and caves in the hills down by the river. He was inclined to think that the bats were responsible for Hintza's attitude of intense concentration for the puppy was, from the start, obsessed with creatures on the wing, as if jealous of their capacity for flight. But as the lightning graph of the bats' flight became clearer and blacker against the rapidly spreading light of the moon, and still Hintza showed no sign of relaxing, nor of launching himself into the air as he normally did whenever he saw anything on the wing, and when even the first bark of a jackal setting out on the prowl for food, and a sarcastic retort from a laughing hyena bound on a similar mission did nothing to rob him of his concentration, François knew that there must be another explanation. But what?

Inwardly proud that Hintza even in this way was unique and so different in his reactions from other dogs, François was more than content to watch and wait for the answer. It soon came when the moon, heavy and sullen with gold, full, swollen and overflowing with light as only a moon in the clear bushveld air could be, lifted itself ponderously above the last ink-stains of leaves and scribbles of branches of the fever trees on the fringe of the bush to show itself at last, round, perfect and immaculate in the sky.

The moment it appeared thus, Hintza threw back his head and began to serenade it with a strangely mature sound that François had never heard before. It came not from his tongue and throat so much as from somewhere down near his solar plexus, with a passion that made him quiver all over. It was obviously the most deep-felt howl of which he was capable and although François, interested and somewhat impressed that so small a body could produce so large a volume of sound for so long, was prepared to give Hintza every reasonable opportunity for expressing himself on so poetic a subject, even he knew that in the end he would have to put a stop to Hintza's *aria bravura* performance, not only out of fear of his parents' reaction but out of anxiety for Hintza himself. For if, it seemed, he was allowed to continue at this passionate rate much longer he would be in danger of losing both voice and reason.

François had therefore ordered him in his most imperative Bushman first, to stop his serenade, and finally to 'shut up'. But in vain. He even tried pleading with Hintza in his most eloquent Bushman to desist. But, for once, Hintza seemed utterly indifferent to his words. He was driven in the end to picking up Hintza and carrying him into the house while Hintza, utterly unrepentant, continued to look back at the moon over François's arms, no longer barking praises because of the restrictions imposed by this ignominious form of carriage, but maintaining a fervent drone in the moon's direction. He did not break off droning and murmuring until François had him in his own room, closed the heavy shutters against the gold translucent night, and lit his bedside candles to repel the faintest intimation of the magical and magisterial expansion of moonlight that was proceeding outside and might seep through the bars of the shutters.

From then on any glimpse of the moon, whether full, or otherwise, was enough to set Hintza off on his singing. In the process he became such a nuisance and was such a contagious example to the five mongrels that they too considered themselves free to appoint themselves an impromptu Greek chorus to Hintza's impassioned recitals. Soon the prolonged dog-din was so great that François's father, 'Bamuthi, the other herdsmen, and all the many servants at Hunter's Drift were in an open revolt and Hintza, far from being the popular little figure he had been in the beginning, was rapidly falling into extreme disfavour.

François found himself more and more assailed from all sides by advice as to what he should do to put an end to Hintza's indulgence in moon-music. He was told to lock him up the moment he as much as opened his mouth to the moon. This was something that François was most reluctant to do for it meant depriving Hintza of valuable hours of education in the behaviour required of ridge-backs in the twilight and critical early hours of the night. The most popular school of thought among the opposition went even further and suggested that there was only one thing to do when Hintza refused to listen even to instructions given in Bushman, and that was to beat the habit out of him.

Even old 'Bamuthi, inclined as he was to spoil François in all things, took him aside and exhorted him again and again to take a tough disciplinary line with Hintza, ending with the ominous adage: 'Remember, Little Feather, soft-hearted witch-doctors do not heal but merely make stinking wounds.'

However, François could not get himself even to contemplate either locking up Hintza, or beating him. To him these alternatives were typical examples of the adult world's bankrupt imagination that drove them always to look for short-cuts to cure problems – as he knew to his cost. He obstinately clung to the belief that there must be some more constructive answer to the problem. But even he began to despair of holding out indefinitely against the pressures building up to compel him into violent repressive action. Then, quite by chance, a possible alternative presented itself to him.

François's father had in his large study a very good but old-fashioned gramophone, fitted with an enormous metal trumpet for amplifying its sound, and François had been introduced to the world of music by records played on this redoubtable instrument. The first record that he clearly remembered was one called 'The Whistler and his Dog'. The whole of the record consisted of a rousing tune whistled most compellingly by a man. When the final nostalgic whistle died away, a dog took over and barked clearly and long his appreciation of the whistler's performance. Remembering this record, François thought it could do no harm to introduce it to Hintza, who he was now firmly convinced, was highly musical. He could then watch his reactions and see what he himself could learn from them.

Hintza, who already knew quite a bit about whistling, though in a more prosaic fashion, from François's use of it in his training, was clearly entranced by this poetic extension of the whistler's idiom. When it came to an end and suddenly a dog's clear-pitched barks poured out into the room, Hintza's delight

35

at this evidence of an invisible dog-spirit was almost more than he could bear. He started barking back, running round and round the study as fast as he could and François had to run after him, catch him and gently close his mouth in order to stop this ecstatic display of joy.

As he did so, he had the relevant inspiration. With Hintza once more still and calm, he put the record on the gramophone again. Hintza immediately recognized the whistling tune, placed himself in a strategic sitting position hard by the wide open mouth of the trumpet, and waited with an air of agonized expectation for the applause of the invisible dog at the end. But just as the last whistle died away, François lifted the arm of the gramophone from the record . . .

At that moment Hintza was already poised to pounce into the air and let out his greetings to his invisible companion. When no sound came out and the music ended, he stared in utter bewilderment at François.

François immediately told him in Bushman that unless he stopped his own barking on this occasion he would not hear the other dog again. To illustrate the point he put on the record all over again but on this occasion allowed the whistler's dog to begin its barking. Instantly Hintza bounded into the air and started to bark in reply. As instantly François immediately lifted the arm and stopped the record.

Disconcerted, Hintza too went silent, and started prowling about the machine to search for the dog which had barked from within. He not only snuffed the machine all over, nudged it, licked it pleadingly and in the end, profoundly frustrated, was about to lift his leg and treat it as a gate-post, when François pulled him away by force and reproved him with the Bushman's most resounding, 'No, Hintza! Don't you dare!' A command which, uttered with all its many Bushman clicks, crackled like lightning in the room.

Dismayed and feeling trapped, Hintza had stopped, turned on François two large blue eyes full of reproach and tragic with a longing for elucidation.

'Now *that*,' François told him with clear, firm deliberation, 'is going to happen to you every time you interrupt anything with your barking. No music, see?'

It took François only half-a-dozen rehearsals that night to get his meaning through to Hintza. From then on Hintza knew that if he were to remain in touch with his invisible friend concealed at the end of that enormous funnel, he himself would have to keep silent. François followed this up with at least one daily rehearsal for three weeks. At the end of that period he was convinced that Hintza was beginning to have a firm concept of how and when it was in his own interests not to bark.

From this experiment, it seemed to follow naturally for François to take Hintza, the moment he found himself compelled to begin barking at the next full moon, immediately inside to his father's study and there to play the record to him. He followed this the following night by exposing Hintza to the moon and when he barked by putting him straight to bed without his daily dose of 'The Whistler and his Dog'. In this way he rapidly established in Hintza's mind a realization of the connections between cause and effect. In particular he concluded that if he ceased to bark at the moon, he would be rewarded with a session of his favourite whistler and dog on the gramophone. And soon, other records were introduced to extend Hintza's repertoire. It was astonishing how he developed and responded, and it seemed that this phase of his education was complete.

Then there came a night that held so full and provocative a moon that even the lions on the far side of the river were moved to roar at it in their most imperial manner. The night plovers too filled the gaps between their roarings with wind-rush outpourings of their flute-like voices always so charged with nostalgia for the night.

François, feeling that such a magnificent display of light was an unfair temptation to Hintza's self-restraint, gathered him up quickly and rushed inside to his father's study. It happened to be an evening when his father was sitting there at his desk writing.

Knowing instantly why François had burst in on him, he had remarked in his teasing way: 'You don't mean you've come to show me that already, on such a night as this, this lunatic, moonstruck hound of yours has graduated for a session with the Moonlight Sonata?'

François, who was hyper-sensitive about all matters concerning Hintza, was trapped into a reckless display of bravado by what he took to be the sarcasm in his father's voice.

'And why not?' he said, with the coldness that comes to boys only in hot moments of anger, 'I'm certain that'll be kindergarten stuff for him by now.'

He immediately took out the record of the Moonlight Sonata with a silent prayer to Providence to help Hintza succeed. To his delight when the first slow ripple of notes came rolling out of the bass to be followed by the first deep authoritative, transfiguring chords, he saw Hintza sink to his knees and then, stretching his front legs out in front as far as they would go, place his chin on the rug between them. At the same time he pushed out his hind legs as far as they would go until he lay there stretched, almost like a martyr in a state of religious ecstasy, about to achieve ultimate transfiguration. From that evening on, there was no more trouble. Hintza was moon-proof for good. 'The Whistler and his Dog' and the Moonlight Sonata together seemed to have provided Hintza with the perfect alchemical method of sublimating his musical aspirations.

It is true that, at times, at the end of 'The Whistler and his Dog' he would prowl sensitively, snuffing and soliciting the gramophone as if hoping still to induce his invisible companion to step out of it and play with him. When his quest failed he would look so wistfully at François that he would hasten to comfort him and talk sympathetically to him in Bushman, saying what 'Bamuthi in another tongue had often said to François when he himself was bitterly disappointed: 'Remember, a man could not value the cattle he owns so much if it were not for the cattle he could never possess.'

More of the developments which enabled Hintza to become a singularly mature and wise hunting dog will emerge as François's story progresses. This is enough to show what an ally he was that eventful early morning some eighteen months after his coming. It explains also why he used such a subtle manner of informing François that something strange was happening – or about to happen, in the world without.

François, for all his youth and its capacity to sleep profoundly, had long since learned the frontiersman's secret of

38

sleeping like an animal that has to be perpetually on guard. He had acquired the habit of waking up at frequent intervals of his own volition and, just briefly, but with all his senses alert, would listen to the noises of the bush for any news of the life of the night that might be important and, if all were normal, would instantly relax into sleep again.

Therefore, he was wide awake immediately the moment Hintza stirred. Putting out his hand he stroked him, both as a sign of approval and of communication. As his fingers moved gently along Hintza's back, he was startled to find that all the normally soft tawny hairs along the ridge were erect and stiff. This ridge of hair, which in the beginning had been to François one of the most attractive features of Hintza's appearance, had long since become for him a means of judging the importance of the unseen realities of the bush which Hintza's acute senses had apprehended. The golden hair on Hintza's back responded to the urgent life within the young dog as if it were a magnet which drew the hair into a meaningful pattern. Now the hair along the dog's spine stood stiff and erect, quivering to attention. Indeed, only on the night when a lion and lioness had leapt over the walls of the cattle kraal beyond the garden and killed several of their best cows had François felt such a crackle of electricity beneath his fingers.

Immediately François jumped out of bed to bend down with his mouth close to Hintza's head.

'Quick Hin, quick,' he whispered. 'What is it? Show me quick.'

But Hintza, instead of making for the door or window as he had done on other occasions, had merely made a noise which seemed to say: 'I don't know what it is but something strange and desperately important is happening outside.'

As François lit his bedside candle, propped on the wide-open pages of *The Gorilla Hunters* where he had left off reading it the night before, he noticed Hintza making for the old Dutch tall-boy in which he hung his clothes at night, to reach up and place his paws against the knob of the door, which he could only just reach. He pawed at the knob again and again as if to say: 'Come on, hurry and put on your clothes. We'd better get outside as soon as possible.'

François lost no time. It did not take him two minutes to put on his green whipcord bush jacket and long whipcord trousers. For years now, ever since he had been allowed to go into the bush, he had been made to stop wearing shorts and always to dress himself in tough whipcord clothes as some protection against the thorns, insects like scorpions and bushflies with stings like wasps, and, of course, snakes.

On this occasion he only varied his normal routine by slipping on a woollen pullover, because the mornings could be cold and he did not want to spoil his aim by shivering, if it came to shooting, as well it might, judging by Hintza's behaviour.

As for shooting, that was perhaps the gravest problem of all facing François at that moment. He had no idea what sort of trouble might be awaiting him in the bush except that, judging by Hintza, it could be the most critical he had ever had to meet in his young life. If it were, for instance, a lion or a leopard, his own .22 rifle was going to be much too light to be effective, even if he shot as straight as he normally did. Unfortunately, he had only one other alternative in his room at the time. This was a heavy muzzle-loader which had been given to him some years before by his father. This muzzle-loader had belonged to his great-grandfather who had used it on the journey by ox-wagon on the trek he led into the interior some hundred and thirty years previously. It had been used in many a desperate battle against Zulus and Matabele, as well as for the protection of his cattle and sheep against wild animals. It was a superbly made gun with a long octagonal barrel, engraved with a Paisley pattern on the sides, and equipped with delicately made ivory sights. Indeed, François thought it one of the most beautiful weapons he had ever seen. He had had his first instructions in shooting with it from no less a person than Mopani Théron, who said that no man who wanted to be a good shot could start young enough. François had been so young at the time that because the gun was so heavy he had had always to find a stone, ant-heap or branch of wood on which to rest the barrel; otherwise it shook from the sheer effort of holding the long heavy weapon to his shoulder.

However, as he had grown stronger the gun had become easier to handle and he had used it quite successfully to hunt for food in the bush round about Hunter's Drift. One of the attractions of this gun was that by pouring a lot of lead pellets down the barrel it could be used as a shot-gun or, by ramming down the barrel an extra charge of gunpowder as well as a large solid ball of lead on top of it, it could be used as a formidable big game weapon.

Loaded with solid ball ammunition François knew that his grandfather had shot many a rogue elephant and man-eating lion and so had the fullest confidence in it as an ultimate weapon of defence. Above all, François always enjoyed the fact that with the gun he had a beautiful powder-horn which he wore over his shoulder on a sling of soft red impala leather. Also, with the gun there went a workmanlike kit for melting down lead and casting it into round bullets of the exact calibre of the gun, something which François did with great relish, feeling there to be an almost magical quality in the process. He always kept his gunpowder dry, the horn full, and a supply of a hundred balls of lead in his room.

So, the decision now facing him was whether he should take his ·22 rifle which had the advantage of being a repeater, with fifteen cartridges in the magazine; or the lethal octagonal muzzle-loader, which, although it carried a deadlier bullet in the spout had the disadvantage that if he missed his target, it would take him at least a minute to reload it with gunpowder, ram down the wad to keep the powder in and force a new lead bullet after it. All that might be much too long for his own and Hintza's safety.

For a moment he was tempted to go and wake his father, but he was not well and needed all the sleep and peace of mind he could get. So much had this fact recently been impressed upon François by his mother that he even rejected the temptation of going to the hall where his father's guns stood in a rack and extracting a more suitable repeating rifle of heavier calibre. He was afraid that even with the utmost care, the boards in the long passage between his room and the hall which creaked so easily might well protest enough to wake his parents.

Just for a moment François had an inkling of what life must be for a 'grown-up' like his father, who must be continually faced with the responsibility of taking vital decisions without anybody to consult. He had a clear but fleeting glimpse of what it meant to be on his own with nothing but such judgement and skill as he possessed for meeting an unknown reckoning with fate. A sense of such acute loneliness assailed him that even his heart beat faster. His courage seemed to be about to fail. His feelings at that moment were clearly beyond his power to understand. All he could sense was that since the arrival of Hintza time had seemed to accelerate so fast that it was pushing him into circumstances for which he was still far from ready.

Happily it was Hintza who now came to his rescue. While these tumultuous and confused feelings were going through him, Hintza was becoming more and more agitated. At the depth of this dark ebb in François's spirit Hintza began worrying him at the back of his knees as he often did when impatient for action. Clearly Hintza had neither doubt nor fear and the realization helped François into a decision.

More by instinct than by reason François chose the heavy old muzzle-loader which had never failed his ancestors and had the experience that both he and his repeater lacked. He quickly rammed an exceptionally heavy charge of gunpowder down the barrel, plugged the gunpowder securely into position, followed it up with a heavy round bullet which he plugged firmly down so that no amount of vibration or shock could dislodge it. Quickly he tested the trigger and hammer to see that they moved easily and noiselessly, which they did, since François spent a lot of his spare time keeping his own guns oiled and clean. Slinging the powder horn round his shoulder, and putting a handful of lead bullets in his pocket, he quietly opened the door leading on to the stoep and stepped outside with Hintza, quivering with excitement, at his side.

He noticed that the morning star, the Dawn's Heart, as old Koba had always called it, was already high in the sky. A red streak of light was drawn across the dark just above the jagged heads of the hills to the east. As he realized the dawn was just about to break he became aware of another extraordinary fact. The five mongrel watch-dogs up to now had been completely silent and given no indication whatsoever that there was anything unusual going on in the bush.

Indeed, the moment he stepped down from the stoep, all five

now came rushing up to François and started to nudge him in a friendly fashion, wagging their tails with pleasure at the thought that his coming showed their night's work was over and that soon they would be having their food and the human company they so enjoyed. This discrepancy between their behaviour and that of Hintza, struck François as so extraordinary that for the first time in his life he was inclined to distrust Hintza's judgement.

He stood there himself watching the streak of red widening over the dark hills and listening intently for any kind of unusual sign to explain Hintza's summons. Hintza, more and more impatient and apparently mystified by François's reluctance to come along with him, was beginning to give him a couple of highly suggestive, even painful nips just behind his ankles. Oddly at that dawn moment not any tell-tale sound but a strange silence had suddenly fallen over the bush.

At that hour, what François's father called the 'Dawn Symphony' should already have reached its crescendo. The full chorus of baboons, monkeys, little bush apes, and a hundred or more different kinds of birds should be singing Hosanna to the day. The cynical jackals and hyenas, who loved the night and now were in full retreat from the light would normally be raising their voices too in derision until silenced by the authoritative bass of some great old lion soloist who ruled a whole wide valley in the hills nearby. All these should have joined in the dawn music by now. But for once they were all silent. Only down by the river some lesser birds, not renowned for voice, diction or ear, started a hysterical sort of tone-deaf twitter. That, François knew, was not the bush's way of giving thanks for deliverance from the Bible-black night and uttering gratitude for the relief from fear brought about by the swift, invincible, bushveld day. Only something most unusual could have made so large a hole of silence.

His faith in Hintza completely restored, François bent down, patted him affectionately on the back and whispered: 'Good Hin, lead on, please. Lead on!'

Hintza immediately went off at a trot and François had to follow suit, not without difficulty because of the weight of the gun he carried. None the less he kept it up until they had gone well beyond the great garden and orchard, past the cattle-kraal and milking sheds where for once cows and calves were as silent as the animals in the bush, and so on to the far side of the round, beehive huts, protected by an enormous high and thick stockade of wood interlaced with deadly branches of sharp white thorns forming the kraal in which 'Bamuthi and the other herdsmen lived. So early was it still that as yet there was no sign of the women stirring to light the fires for the morning porridge with which the Matabele began their day. Even their dogs, no doubt tired from their long guard duty through the night, seemed to be taking a nap, for not a sound came from them as François and Hintza went by. This, François, intent on discovering what lay ahead, did not fail to notice and took as a compliment to Hintza's bushcraft.

However, when they came to the end of the vast clearing which surrounded the homestead, and Hintza veered away sharply to the entrance of a narrow and complicated track leading through the densest bush at the foot of the hills, where a deep cleft opened up and led for many miles straight on to the great game reserve placed in Mopani Théron's keeping, François thought the time had come to be more careful.

'Here, Hin, here!' he called out softly.

Immediately Hintza turned round and came to stand in front of him, eyes intent but, none the less, impatient on François's face. By that time the light was just good enough for them to read each other's expressions.

'Slowly now Hin, slowly,' François commanded, 'if we go on at this pace and have any shooting to do, I shall be so breathless and shaking that I'll miss, and that won't do because I've only got one shot at a time in this gun. Look, it's not our normal quick little barker [the Bushman name of the repeater], but this one-shot old-father-of-a-gun. So slowly and carefully please!'

Hintza seemed to understand at once, almost as if he had already reached the same conclusion himself. He led on into the dark, narrow track at a much slower pace, pausing to stand, look, listen and above all lift his nose high to smell the dew-dank air at every twist in the track before pushing on noiselessly ahead.

François had another reason for urging caution on them both at this moment. This track along which they were about to go was one of three tracks used by big game to come out of the vast uninhabited bush to the east, in order to drink water at the river. It was also invariably used by lion and leopard when they raided Hunter's Drift as they often did, in the hope of catching cows, calves, goats, sheep or even hens and geese, for food.

For years therefore it had been the custom to protect these tracks at night with large steel lion-traps, skilfully concealed and securely held by a thick chain pegged with a long iron spike driven deep into the earth. These traps were constructed exactly on the same principle as mouse-traps, except of course that they were many times bigger and heavier, with the saw-like teeth in their wide jaws both longer and sharper. Also, when a lion or leopard tried to get at the meat which was suspended just above the trap for bait, the great tense spring which released the trap was so powerful that it had been known to snap through the leg of a bull which had trodden upon it, and also to break the necks of powerful striped hyenas. The traps weighed close on twenty pounds each and they were moved into different positions every day and the bait renewed. Immediately after milking, one of 'Bamuthi's first duties was to set out armed with his great fighting shield and longest assegai in order to inspect each trap. If anything dangerous were caught in them he would hasten back to Hunter's Drift and summon François's father to come and shoot it.

François himself did not know the exact location of the trap set in this track the night before. But he was certain it could not be more than a mile from the edge of the clearing. Naturally he did not want Hintza and himself either to tread on it or walk casually into anything which the trap might have caught. And now he began to have an uneasy feeling that in some way the trap was responsible for the strange silence which ruled over this part of the bush.

Luckily the light, as they proceeded, got so much better that soon François could distinguish all the details of the bush and the course of the scarlet track ahead. Consequently he began stepping out more confidently in the wake of Hintza who, obedient to the manner in which he had been trained, whenever he came to a turn in the track, turned round first to see that François was near, before he moved on again.

They went on like this silently for about ten minutes and, much to François's relief, passed safely through the narrowest and most dangerous part of the cleft in the hills. Just beyond, the cleft broadened rapidly into a wide valley and there the first thing that François noticed was an enormous baboon 'look-out', perched high on a boulder of the purple crown of *krans* of stone around the head of the hills above him, its auburn coat already on fire with the first rays of the sun. This baboon, in-stead of setting about his duty of getting his fellow cliff-dwellers marshalled and out on their business of collecting food before it got too hot was looking intently to the east in the direction of the track which François and Hintza were following. As if that were not enough, on top of the hill on the other side of the track, on a vast saffron boulder, another old baboon was being equally neglectful of his tribal duties and was looking intently up the valley in the same direction.

More significantly still, Hintza had suddenly come to a halt, and was staring ahead. François hastened to join him. With a brief, low and perhaps unnecessary: 'Stand Hin! Stand!' he himself stood at the dog's side while his own keen eyes searched bush, hills and sky ahead.

It didn't take him long to discover what held the baboon's attention. About a quarter of a mile away the branches of a grove of some of the tallest marula trees in the bush were shaking as if caught in a whirlwind. François stared at the heavy branches while the sunlight crept so far down the flanks of the hills that it touched the tops of the trees. Then he realized that all that intensive agitation of leaves and branches was being caused by the excited gathering of some of the biggest vultures he had ever seen. The fact that the vultures were massing in this way in the top of the trees was proof to him of their uncanny instinct for knowing when and where some living thing was about to die.

'What do you think it is Hin, *Xkha*?' [lion]

Hintza, who knew the deep, explosive word 'lion' well, gave him a steady, negative look in reply.

'*Xkāuëyāken?*' [leopard] François asked, using the Bushman

46

word again. Hintza's look was, if possible, even more negative than before.

'Well, what is it then, Hin?' François pleaded.

A faint whimper of uncertainty was all that he got out of Hintza, before he whirled about swiftly and started off again.

This, however, was far too precipitous and reckless a procedure for François's liking because obviously they were near the climax of their ventures.

'Heel!' he called out softly but clearly.

To Hintza's great credit he came back, however reluctantly, and for the first time took up his position close behind François. François then silently and slowly cocked the hammer of his muzzle-loader, made sure that the firing cap was firmly in position and, with the gun now at the ready, the butt firmly resting in his right arm, the blue eight-sided muzzle on the left, he noiselessly pushed forward, step by slow step. Hintza followed so skilfully that François was quite certain that he would arrive unobserved at the foot of the marula trees where by the minute the vultures were getting more impatient and demanding. But one old vulture perched high in the sun, its long neck erect and naked, with a large, scraggy Adam's apple prominent and red as a piece of raw meat in the sun, looked down and saw a glint of light on the barrel of François's gun. It squeaked a curse of warning like an old witch, before taking ponderously to the air on broad, clumsy wings, to be followed by the others, until some fifty of these enormous birds were circling the gold and green bush with shadows of crepe, and robbing the morning instantly of all its innocence.

More carefully than ever, therefore, because of the alert the flight of vultures must have proclaimed to all and sundry in the bush for miles around, François went forward bent nearly double in order to get into position where he could sink on his stomach and crawl closer to the trees.

He was on the point of lowering himself into a crawling position to wriggle forward when almost at once the three sounds of a twang, a swish and a dull plop hit his ear. His bush hat, which he wore only in the cool of the morning and dewfall of night, flew from his head. As he fell flat on his face, before turning quick as a cat on his back to check the mechanism of his gun in the shelter of the brush, he noticed his hat stuck on a thorn bush above him with an arrow through its crown. Hintza, bristling with apprehension and irritation, was looking down at him as if to say: 'Now that is just the sort of thing that will happen if you do not allow me to lead.'

2 • The Coming of Xhabbo

One glance was enough to reassure François that his ancestral gun had come to no harm and no dust had gathered around the hammer or trigger in the shock of his fall to the ground. All that was reassuring in a way but what was most alarming and utterly inexplicable to him, was the arrow through his hat. Obviously somewhere near at hand there was somebody who, to put it mildly, wished neither him nor Hintza well. Such a thing had never happened to him or anyone else at Hunter's Drift before. Who could it be? And why?

Unusually mature because of the independence thrust on him at so early an age by his lonely life in the bush, François searched his memory for some fact or fragment of knowledge that could explain the arrow, let alone the kind of person who could be using a bow and arrow even in that remote bush, at so late a period in time. The answer to all that, he was certain, was vital before deciding their next move.

None of the members of the many various tribes who had worked at Hunter's Drift from the time he had been born had ever in their history used bows and arrows. After all, he had spent enough days and evenings sitting with them all in their huts, listening to the stories of their past to know that. He knew, as well as any African child, how they had protected themselves against wild beasts and defended themselves against many enemies throughout long and, for him, Homeric histories. For instance, he even knew the secret names supposedly charged with invincible magic which the Matabele at Hunter's Drift gave to their favourite weapons, and would on no account have disclosed to their most intimate friends, let alone the 'red strangers' as they called the white people who had conquered their land.

Much of this François owed to his rare relationship with

'Bamuthi. Not only was he a Matabele aristocrat but head of the clan from which both their herdsmen and watchmen came.

Once, years before, in the course of telling François the story of a battle in which his own great-grandfather had fought in one of 'Mzilikatze's impis against the Baganda on the shores of the great lakes in the far north, and noticing how profoundly François was identified with him and his story, his last reserve of secrecy had melted away in an upsurge of affection. He had broken off his story, produced his great ox-hide shield, placed all his spears, his assegais, and his clubs upon it, and told the entranced young boy, on the pledge of secrecy, what the role of each had been in the fighting; and how they were addressed before the battle.

Spears and clubs, he said reverently, were living things, and unless properly named, would not know how to come when called and do their duty; just as they themselves had to know the name of him who called them, otherwise they could help the wrong person. So he, 'Bamuthi, in this regard, had a special name. He was called *u-Nothloba-Mazibuka*, which means 'He-Who-Watches-the-Fords'. This was his hereditary title and function because his family had originally been placed on the river just there by the great 'Mzilikatze to do precisely that, as the name Hunter's Drift implies. 'Drift' is the southern African name for a ford, and the ranch had been called thus because it stood opposite the place where for thousands of years the vanished legions of Africa and perhaps even of Sheba and Babylon had crossed the powerful stream in their fateful comings and goings between north and south.

'Now, mark well, Little Feather,' 'Bamuthi had told him as he held up a spear with a long silver-white blade. 'This assegai is *u-Simsela-Banta-Bami* [He-Digs-Up-For-My-Children], since it was made for my great-great-great-grandfather by a magic maker of spears who forged it beyond the forests of the night on the far side of the great waters and the Mountains of Smoke and Fire in the north. It has been the best hunting spear of my people and kept many hungry generations in food. This one,' he went on, holding up a shorter spear with a much stronger and thicker shaft and a broader blade ending in a long, narrow and gleaming point, 'is *Imbubuzi* [The Groan-Causer], because when it goes into action many groans are heard far and wide. This club,' he held up an enormous knobkerrie made of dark red ironwood, so heavy that when thrown into the water it sank, 'is *Igumgehle* [The Greedy-One], because when he is used in fighting he destroys the enemy as quickly as a glutton swallows food.' Then he held up the longest and most slender spear of all, obviously for use as a throwing lance. 'This assegai is *u-Silo-Si-Lambile* [The Hungry Leopard] because it will throw itself at the enemy, as does a hungry leopard at a baboon, and at once kill.'

Finally he held up a knobkerrie so big and heavy that François could hardly lift it at the time. 'And this one is *u-Dhl'-Ibusuku* [The Eater-In-The-Dark], because it is used best for things of evil that come at human beings by stealth at night.'

All of this François had absorbed and had not been astonished because it drew his beloved 'Bamuthi's people into the ranks of all that he had read of the heroic past from Hector and Achilles to the story of Arthur and his Knights of the Round Table and the sword Excalibur. But what had puzzled him even then was that so intelligent a people as the Matabele made no mention, and showed no signs, of using bows and arrows.

Caught up as he was in 'Bamuthi's story, he had interrupted and exclaimed: 'But Old Father, surely you used bows and arrows too, to kill at greater distance than even you could throw a spear or club?'

'Bamuthi had looked at him in pity that he should be so ignorant of the fact that a man's honour decided such matters, and answered scornfully: 'Little Feather, such things are only for cowards and cattle thieves, like the Massarwa.'

Massarwa was the Matabele word of scorn for the Bushman who, in the far past, they had hunted down like wild beasts. François's own ancestors had committed similar crimes as François knew only too well from Koba and his history lessons.

All this went through François's mind like lightning because of the danger which now confronted him. Then the thought hit him: 'Dear God, could there be a Bushman hiding behind the trees ready to shoot with bows and arrows at anybody who comes near him?'

But even as he thought it he dismissed the idea as highly

improbable if not impossible. All the great hunters, travellers and explorers who had been passing through Hunter's Drift ever since he could remember, had assured him that the Bushmen all over Africa had been exterminated by both black and white races. Only a tiny fragment of Koba's gallant little people had survived, deep in the heart of the desert which started on the far silver edge of the bush, many miles beyond the river, trembling there with light and heat like a tuning fork with sound.

Even old Koba, before she died, had often told him sadly how, since the age of fifteen, she had never set eyes on any other member of her kind except a few tame ones like herself. The word tame was used to describe those few Bushmen who had sadly accepted the fate of living as helpless domestics attached to European or Bantu overlords. Most of these were survivors of massacres, or children kidnapped by hunters and raiders on excursions into the desert, beside a few decadent ones, corrupted by mixing with the less reputable Bantu clans who lived on the better-watered fringes of the great desert.

Never had François heard anything to suggest that in the vicinity of Hunter's Drift there were any wild Bushmen – as the few surviving and truly independent ones were called. And if, indeed, a Bushman had been responsible for shooting the arrow which had lifted his hat from his head, he would have to be very wild indeed.

The thought made François's blood go cold. He realized that a Bushman arrow would merely have had to scrape his skin to prove fatal because, as everybody knew from history, the heads to such arrows were always dipped in deadly poison.

He had just reached this conclusion when, from close by in the direction of the marula trees, he heard a low moaning, and a pitiful sound as of a human being in unbearable pain. Hintza heard it too because all signs of bristling vanished from his coat, an indication that he no longer felt any sense of danger. He was still lying crouched beside François, ready to attack but with ears erect and cocked in the direction of the sound, as if already aware of its meaning.

François, therefore, immediately turned over on his stomach, signalled with his hand to Hintza to stay still and started with the utmost care to crawl towards the sound. Crawling, he took the precaution of first moving the gun silently in front of him and placing it on the ground within reach of his right hand so that he could pick it up at the first indication of danger.

They did not have far to go but so well had François been trained in these things by Mopani Théron and 'Bamuthi that he took the greatest and most patient care over the last stage of his stalking. He remembered in particular one of 'Bamuthi's favourite sayings, so often directed at him in the past: 'The buck sometimes gets out even from the pot,' the Sindabele way of warning that there was many a slip 'twixt cup and lip.

In this slowest of slow-motion fashions he came to a twist in the track close to the marula trees where he could see through the brush and look on the thrashed and trampled grass at their base. There he saw a small yellow man, his leg held fast in the heavy lion trap, making desperate efforts to free himself. He obviously had been struggling for hours, for the grass everywhere was not only flattened by the trap and chain as he had dragged them back and forth and about with him in a wide circle, but it was also stained with his blood.

It was not at all surprising to François that the little man was groaning. He would not have been astonished if he had been screaming in agony. But he knew from Koba how brave and stoical a true Bushman had to be. As well as compassion for the little man's plight, relief came to François when he saw a bow and quiver full of arrows lying in the dust beside the man, who must have assumed that the arrow shot at François had found its mark. His spear too lay there but within reach of hands now tugging so desperately at the iron of the giant trap.

François knew that if he showed himself without warning, there could be great trouble. In great pain, and on the point of fainting with loss of blood and exhaustion, the trapped man would be compelled by the terrible history of his kind, at the worst to seize his spear and hurl it at François and Hintza, probably with fatal effect, for now they were so close to him.

Yet, despite the obvious danger ahead, François had no feeling either of fear or resentment. He felt only pity for the little yellow figure caught in a trap which, in the past, had held seventeen great lions throughout long nights until the moment came when they would be shot. Moreover, the little man personified, physically, all the many characteristics of the people old Koba had described to him in such loving detail that they had become, for François, almost dream people, and he grew up heart-broken that these little Bushmen hunters with their child-man shapes and bows and arrows had vanished for ever. As a result, his first astonished glimpse of the man in the trap evoked deep preconditioned sympathies to add flame to the fire of pity.

His only instinct now, therefore was to rush out and try to rescue the trapped Bushman without delay from his terrible, if not already fatal, predicament. But how?

Suddenly he remembered how Koba had always impressed upon him that if her people were greeted in the correct manner they would always respond in the friendliest fashion, no matter how unpredictable the situation. The most important point of this greeting was for it to make the Bushman feel big and strong. They were, according to Koba, extraordinarily sensitive about the fact that they were so small, seldom more than four foot ten inches in height and they resented the fact that fate had made black and white both taller and bigger and consequently more powerful.

So by way of some sort of compensation for this injustice of biology, the soothing thing to do when one met a wild Bushman, Koba had told him, was to call out: 'Good day, I saw you looming up from afar and I am dying of hunger.'

Accordingly without showing himself and keeping flat on the ground to make himself as difficult a target as possible François called out, in Bushman, trying in vain to prevent excitement and apprehension from adding a tremble to his clear voice: 'Good day, I saw you looming up from afar and I am dying of hunger.'

At the sound of a voice addressing him in his own language, the Bushman stopped struggling, sat up rigid with apprehension. He looked wildly around him as if he could not believe what he had heard. Indeed he seemed almost immediately convinced that the pain and anguish of his situation had made him delirious and he was hearing voices from within himself.

He started again to wrestle with the trap more desperately than ever, groaning to himself as if groaning helped to relieve the pain. François at once called out the greeting a second time, louder and more confidently. This time the little man seemed to be convinced. He looked in François's direction. François could hardly bear to look in the little man's eyes, so dark were they with suffering. Yet he gave François slowly, in a voice hoarse with pain, which came out of him not consciously so much as if by a kind of reflex of history, the proper response that Bushmen had for this kind of greeting throughout their thousands of years in Africa:

'I was dying, but now that you have come I live again.'

At that, François stood up, ran forward quickly. Half ashamed of himself, he first snatched up the bows and arrows as if still afraid the Bushman might try to use them when he saw a red stranger, even a young one, confronting him, before saying, 'Please do not be alarmed, we want to help you all we can.'

Murmuring words of gratitude so blurred and low with pain that François could hardly hear him, the little man's wide dark slanted eyes suddenly seemed to lose their light, the eyelids to close over them and his body to relax, before he fell back in a faint to the ground. François somehow had a hunch that this reaction of the trapped man might be a vote of confidence in him and Hintza. Only a feeling of certainty that he was about to be rescued from fatal peril could have allowed him the luxury now of giving in so completely to pain and exhaustion.

Nothing could have suited François better. He could now tackle the trap without the twisting and jerking of the man's body to hamper him. He knew from past experience how difficult it was going to be to get the tough giant spring of the trap suppressed sufficiently for its jaws to open, since it normally took two grown men to do so comfortably. He had often tried it before in calmer circumstances by standing on the spring or pushing it down with his hands with all his weight behind them. But he had always failed. His only hope now he knew, was to get a long, stout piece of wood and use it as some kind of lever to suppress the spring. Luckily, there was plenty of such wood near at hand in the bush.

Ordering Hintza to mount guard over the unconscious man, he quickly found the stout, straight dead branch of an assegai

55

wood tree. He hurried back to look among the stones, which there, so close to the hills, were abundant. He selected two very large ones and carried them back to the trap. He wedged the jaws of the trap securely between them so that they could not shift when he started his levering and so further injure the mangled leg. Placing the end of the wood firmly underneath a jagged ledge of rock which protruded over the track just where the trap had been set, he pressed down on the spring with all his thirteen-year-old strength and weight. The spring flattened out far more easily than he had expected and in the midst of his relief he had time for a fleeting feeling of gratitude that his father had insisted on teaching him the science of Archimedes which had been his least favourite subject of study. More, he found that once the spring was suppressed he could keep it down by holding the wooden lever firmly in position with his right hand alone. Doing this, and as an extra precaution adding his own weight to the pressure on the spring by sitting sideways on the lever, he gently lifted the leg clear of the spring.

He had hardly done so when the wooden lever, tough as it was, snapped with the strain like a pistol shot. He had to leap clear to escape being caught himself in the jaws of the trap. They shut with a clang so loud that he was afraid it would be heard at the milking sheds a mile or so away.

The leg of the still unconscious man was fearfully gashed; the wound wide open. It looked almost as if it had been caused by a leopard, no doubt because of the night-long struggle of the Bushman, tugging to get his leg out of the grip of the saw-like teeth. To his dismay the wound, the veins no longer restricted by pressures of the trap, started immediately to bleed badly again. Happily, François knew that a vital artery could not have been cut because if so, the man would have long since bled to death. His greatest fear was that the leg might be broken. He felt it all over as gently as he could and was profoundly relieved that injured as it might be in flesh, sinew and muscle, the bones themselves miraculously had not been fractured.

It was a significant illustration of how deep Koba's picture of her people lay in his imagination that despite concentrating on his examination of the wound, he could not help marvelling at the shape of the injured leg. What a lovely muscular calf it had!

56

What delicate, slender ankles like those of the *tssessebe*, the fastest antelope in Africa whose name, given of course by the Bushmen, conveys the sound of the wind created by its own speed whistling through its shining coat of titian hair. And how small and well-shaped were the feet! It was almost as if he could hear in the midst of his urgent preoccupations the voice of old Koba in his ear saying: 'You see, as I have always told you, you will know the true men of my people by the smallness of their hands and feet and the beauty of their legs. He is one of my own – help him as I helped you!'

However, the problem was too pressing to leave time for pursuing the luxuries of imagination. The terrible wound was bleeding far too much for any further delay. Somehow he had to stop it and use all the first-aid knowledge that everyone at Hunter's Drift, in a world without doctors, learned from early childhood. He thought at once of the handkerchief in his pocket, the red cotton kerchief he wore round his neck in the early hours of the morning and evening, and the white woollen vest underneath his bush shirt. Discarding his shirt, he pulled off the vest, made a soft pad out of it and placed it around the wound, tied his own handkerchief and kerchief together and used them to wind around the pad firmly enough to keep it in position for the time being.

He had hardly done this when the man opened his eyes to speak again in a blurred, gasping voice which frightened François into thinking that he might be dying. But all that he was doing was trying, in broken sentences, first to warn that there was a leopard about and to say that all night long he had been threatened by the animal; and then to plead with François not to let him fall into the hands of any black man or other strangers.

François quickly reassured him on this last point because he shared the man's fears himself in that regard. Then immediately he took precautions about the leopard, perhaps just in time, because he noticed that Hintza was already aware of something dangerous creeping up on them under cover of the bush near at hand. He was indeed trying to attract François's attention, pointing with his head and tail a-quiver in the direction of the grass and shrub beyond the marula trees.

'Good Hin,' François whispered to him. 'Watch! I'll get the gun at once.'

Quickly reassuring the Bushman that he would never let him fall into strange hands, he stepped over the trap, picked up the gun and joined Hintza. The dog by this time was standing beside the Bushman with the ridge of hair along the supple and tawny back erect and electric, while there came from him an angry murmur of protest at the self-restraint imposed upon him by his training, preventing him from dashing into the bush to grapple with the invisible enemy.

'Beware, it's *Xkāuëyāken* [the leopard] coming back again. Take care!' The Bushman, obviously an experienced hunter, exhorted François in words fainter and uttered with greater difficulty than before.

This was a complication François would have given anything to avoid at that moment. He could hardly have thought of anything more dangerous. He would even have preferred to meet a lion just then, not only because it was easier to hit, but also because as a rule at that hour of the day it was capable of being discouraged from attack. Lions, unlike leopards, felt more relaxed in the day than at night and consequently were more placid and also lazier.

Leopards on the other hand were essentially nocturnal. They did not see at all well by day and accordingly felt insecure. Brave as they were they were inclined to panic in daylight and became more aggressive than at night, for which their senses were so superbly attuned. This applied particularly when hunger drove leopards, against their instinctive preferences, to search for food by day. And obviously this leopard, of which the Bushman had warned him, would not have contrived prowling around the trap all night and into the first light of day, if it were not extremely hungry.

François clearly had to be ready for the worst. Even so, he might not have been ready if it had not been for Hintza. The dog's attitude suddenly had changed significantly. Instead of looking deep into the bush in front, his head was slowly tilting upwards, his tail sinking into line accordingly, until tip of tail and point of his quickened nose, creased and quivering with apprehension were aligned, like the needle of a compass, on the middle of a particularly dense spreading tree which stood ahead of them with an enormous branch thick in leaves leaning over the track just in front of François's head.

The play of light and shade among the leaves upon the tree was itself as dappled and spotted as a leopard's coat. No leopard could ever have chosen better camouflage for a line of attack. Alternatively watching Hintza and then the tree, François's eyes were ultimately rewarded. Suddenly a substance too solid for either leaf or shadow moved. The outline of the back of an animal chequered with sun and shadow, emerged crawling slowly along the branch towards them. As François identified it, the animal suddenly halted, crouching so low that its head appeared resting on the branch. Watching it so intently François's eyes had become more accustomed to the nuances of shapes, shades and colours of the bush in front of him. The leopard was enormous, his coat now a flicker of lamplight among the black leaves. He was obviously gathering himself to spring.

Knowing he did not have a second to lose François brought the great old muzzle-loader, held all the while at the ready, to his shoulder. As Mopani Théron had so carefully taught him over the years, in the circumstances he wasted no time on careful aiming but shot by instinctive pointing, his eyes not on the gun but on the head of the leopard, knowing that the aim of the gun would automatically follow his eyes.

Before setting out at dawn he had rammed so big a charge of gunpowder down the gun that the recoil of the shot sent François reeling backwards with such force that he nearly fell over. However, he recovered his balance and quickly reloaded the gun with the sound of the shot, which had boomed out in the early morning silence like a cannon, still reverberating in his ears, and a dense cloud of blue gunpowder smoke drifting between him and the trees. All the time he kept his eyes fixed on the trees ahead, particularly as Hintza appeared to have vanished. His sense of danger was still so acute that he felt that he was re-loading his gun with nightmare slowness, although he realized later that he had never done it faster.

By the time the gun was reloaded and no leopard had as yet hurled itself at him, he moved carefully forward through the

59

haze of smoke. There, not fifteen yards away, was Hintza with his teeth in the throat of an obviously dead male leopard, holding it down unnecessarily to the earth. François had never seen a bigger leopard nor, indeed, one with so beautiful a coat.

Calling off Hintza, he returned immediately to the Bushman because he was certain that the sound of the gun would have been heard at Hunter's Drift and that by now 'Bamuthi and perhaps several of the other herdsmen, would be alarmed and already on their way with assegais at the ready, to see what had caused the shot.

If he were to keep his promise to the Bushman (and he knew how vital it was for the little man that he should do so) he had to get him out of the way at once. He had no time to explain. He just ran to him and said: 'You must please trust me and try to stand on one leg and come with me, quick.'

The Bushman, weak as he was, immediately allowed François to help him to his feet. The quality and texture of the indomitable spirit of the man showed in the fact that he did so without even a whisper of a groan. Obviously he had caught the note of danger in François's voice and was anxious to do his part. François's arms about him, he hopped on one leg down the track for about fifty yards, although each hop must have caused him acute agony. There, as François knew of old, he would find close to the track a deep ledge of rock protruding from the foothills down into the floor of the valley. Once at that place, he led the Bushman quickly away from the track into the bush, found the ledge and there made him lie down on the ground, right at the back of a deep and dark recess.

Exhorting him to wait and stay absolutely quiet until he could return, François doubled back to the leopard with Hintza at his side. Though he never knew how he managed it, he dragged the heavy carcass all the way to the trap, found another stout lever of wood to suppress the spring, inserted the front leg of the leopard into the jaws of the trap, removed the lever and allowed the jaws to snap back firmly. He then quickly rolled the boulders away, threw the wooden stump deep into the bush, tore off a branch of a broom-brush, swept away the smear left by dragging the leopard along the track, threw the branch away and ran down the track towards home as fast as he could.

It was just as well that he did so because not a quarter of a mile down the track came 'Bamuthi, shield on his arm and his great hunting assegai, *u-Simsela-Banta-Bami*, at the ready, trotting towards him with three other Matabele herdsmen similarly armed in single file behind him.

The relief on 'Bamuthi's face, seeing François and Hintza coming safely towards him, was most moving. The reaction, however, vanished when his relief changed to anger because of the fear aroused by the gun-shot and the realization that François must have set out alone into the bush at so dangerous an hour.

'To play at the man, Little Feather,' he admonished François, his dark face for once grey with emotion, 'before one has ceased to be a boy, is a black deed indeed.'

'Black' has the same symbolic meaning for Africans as for Europeans, and François knew that 'Bamuthi used it here to indicate in the strongest way possible that he had done a misguided, if not wicked thing.

François had been feeling rather pleased with himself. Perhaps understandably, he thought that he and Hintza had acquitted themselves rather well and deserved congratulations rather than condemnation. He was ready, therefore, in his high-spirited fashion, to give 'Bamuthi back as good as he had got.

But 'Bamuthi gave him no chance. The dark, grey-haired Matabele was following up his remark not in mere anger but also with scorn. Standing, and resting with his arms on his great ox-hide shield, somewhat out of breath because he was no longer young and had come faster than he cared for, he looked down at François and said in his most biting manner: 'And now, having interrupted our morning's work, I suppose all you have to tell us is news of the death of some miserable old baboon?'

Had François not been so young he would have been able to explain to 'Bamuthi what had happened. But now, wounded in his self-respect, and also anxious to get on with his mission of helping the Bushman as soon as possible, he answered scorn with scorn:

'If you are all so anxious to get on with the mere milking of old cows,' he said tartly, 'send the others back to do what children can do as well as men. And you, Old Father, come with me to see just what sort of baboon we have killed.'

François's tone immediately made 'Bamuthi aware of the fact that there was more to this than mere youthful irresponsibility. He took the hint, sent his followers back to get on with the milking and followed François back along the track towards the marula trees, wishing only that François was not in quite such a hurry compelling him to trot when he himself, now that the crisis appeared to be over, would have preferred a more dignified and stately approach.

He did not know of course that François had a secret, all-compelling reason for hurrying as he had never hurried before. Soon they were back at the trap where silently François stood aside, leaning on his gun without even deigning to indicate the great leopard. He lay there, his coat of gold covered as in some ancient script of life with the ink of his own spots and the scribbles of shade penned upon it by the pointed thorn growing beside the track. 'Bamuthi was free to see it for himself.

He let out a deep, sonorous '*Yebo!*' – the Sindabele cry which combines astonishment with praise when confronted with an unexpected revelation.

For some minutes he stood staring down at the leopard, his eyes wide with praise and dark with new thought. After a while he looked at François and Hintza and back again at the dead leopard, until at last all the mixtures of contradicting emotions caused by the events of the morning were transcended in one generous overwhelming conclusion.

He reached out, put his arm affectionately on François's shoulder and said. 'Unwise as the deed was, Little Feather, I was wrong to call it black. Perhaps the man is already hastening to meet the child. Now please run back and tell them all what they will be glad to hear at home. I will stay behind, skin the leopard, salt the skin, peg it out in the shade and prepare it myself so that you could have it in your room for your children and grand-children to see how you crossed the frontier alone this day,' – the Sindabele phrase for becoming grown-up.

Glad as François was that once more all was well between them, this was the last thing that he wanted to happen. He was absolutely certain that 'Bamuthi's experienced old eyes would soon notice how contrived was the set-up of trap and leopard. Also how all round the track and grass, despite the precautions he had taken, were signs to show that far more than the trapping and death of a great leopard had taken place at the foot of the massive clump of marula trees, once more black and swaying with vultures.

'No, Old Father,' he said to 'Bamuthi. 'No. You and I will go back home together. I would like to finish this work which I began and do the skinning myself. I shall leave Hintza here to watch and see that the vultures gathered in the trees above do not spoil the carcass, while I hasten to get all that is necessary for the skinning. And you, I hope, will be good enough Old Father to show me afterwards how properly to preserve so great a skin.'

Luckily, feeling perhaps that he already had been rough enough with François 'Bamuthi gave way without argument. He allowed François just time enough to order Hintza to stay behind and keep guard over the leopard. Then at a firm, long pace, full of the long, heavy grace with which a Matabele woodsman walked when his purpose was clear, 'Bamuthi led the way down the track towards the milking sheds and the homestead beyond.

François arrived home to find his mother in the kitchen talking to their cook, a redoubtable old 'Xhosa lady whom he always had to address most punctiliously as Ousie (Old Mother)-Johanna. (As a Christian she had a European name). To his relief neither of them appeared worried because the Matabele herdsmen who had brought in the first milk for breakfast had already assured them that François's absence was merely due to the fact that he and 'Bamuthi had gone to see to some old 'baboon' which appeared to have blundered into a lion trap. Besides, his mother was preoccupied with a far graver matter.

She was known to François, his father and every servant on the farm as Lammie (Little Lamb), the name given to her when a small child by the Amaxosa, and which had stuck to her ever since. No one ever called her by the formal 'mistress', much to the disapproval of European visitors who thought this far too familiar for the maintenance of white authority. François found

Ousie-Johanna scolding her affectionately, telling her not to worry about François's father. Ousie-Johanna was certain that he only had to eat more of her food, she assured her Lammietjie (Little, little lamb, as she addressed her mistress when particularly concerned for her), and he would soon be better. But all this obviously had not helped François's mother much because beyond an affectionate 'Good morning' she hardly asked him what he had been doing.

Picking up the breakfast tray laid with broad orange slices of the finest pawpaws of Hunter's Drift and some special milk food for his father, she merely remarked to François over her shoulder: 'Please remember, Coiske [pronounced *Swaske*; a diminutive of endearment for François], I shall want your help to prepare for our journey.'

The impending journey was in the morning to the capital, where she was taking her husband to see the most learned medical specialists in the country. So urgent did she regard the journey that for the first time she was leaving François alone at Hunter's Drift in the care of Ousie-Johanna and above all, of course, 'Bamuthi. François had just time to explain that he was just going back to the trap to help 'Bamuthi, a white lie he thought justifiable in the circumstances, and that as soon as they had finished there he would hurry back to help her.

That satisfied his mother, but not old Johanna. His mother was barely through the door when she went for François. She had been as alarmed by the heavy gun-shot as old 'Bamuthi had been, and when on top of that she had discovered that François and Hintza were not in his room, she had run to the milking shed to raise the alarm.

François accordingly had to endure one of the severest scoldings he had ever had from an old lady who was devoted to him. This was something difficult for a young person of his quick temperament, particularly when he could not explain his feeling that he had done no wrong and he might not have succeeded had it not been for the excitement of his important new secret mission working as an antidote within him. He felt he had no option but to sit down in the kitchen as he always did for breakfast and eat as even he had not eaten before, especially when feeling so little like eating, otherwise he would arouse suspicion and give away his new-found purpose. Ousie-Johanna moreover had cooked an enormous breakfast for him: porridge of mealie (maize) meal, served with wild honey and cream; home-made sausages grilled on coals of fragrant wood; hot crusts of bread fresh from the oven and filling the air with one of the oldest and most reassuring, life-promising smells in the world; fresh butter, a bowl of amber peach jam and a blue enamel pot of coffee.

In fact, he did not even dare refuse a large second helping, because experience had taught him that nothing mollified Johanna, whose nature like that of all born cooks, was touchy in the extreme where her cooking was concerned, so much as tangible evidence that her food was appreciated. Fortunately François was a gulper of genius. He could eat a meal that would take his parents perhaps an hour to consume in just under ten minutes. Then, pushing his chair away, he dashed up to Johanna who was mixing a cake for afternoon tea by her table, seized her hand, pressed it against his cheek and said: 'Thank you, Old Mother, that was super. Your food tastes better and better every day!'

Ousie-Johanna's eyes went bright and their corners wrinkled with pleasure. The natural artist that she was made her shy, sensitive and tentative as a child, though one would never have suspected it when one saw how large and Olympian her own cooking had made her. Now she was delighted to the point of embarrassment with the praise. Her cheeks went so hot that she put her hands to them and by way of self-correction answered gently: 'Little Feather, you were always a beautiful liar', the Amaxosa way of calling someone a gross flatterer.

But when François asked her if she could quickly prepare some sandwiches and a big thermos flask of coffee made with pure milk to take back to the trap, where he had work to do, she replied: 'Auck! I might have known, Little Feather, that you praised me only because you wanted something more!'

While Johanna was preparing the food, François ran quickly into the store room and helped himself from the large store of medical supplies kept there. He took bandages, first-aid dressings, three dozen M and B 693 tablets (the latest and reputedly infallible drug to prevent fatal poisoning from wounds and infections caused by no matter what agents, whether lion, leopard, or the thousands of unusual invisible microbes of Africa), some iodine, a dozen tablets of the latest painkiller, and some of the sleeping draughts which had been prescribed for his father.

He then rushed to his own room, exchanged the old muzzle-loader for his lighter ·22 repeater, snatched the large military water-flask given to him for day-long excursions into the bush, and went back to the kitchen where old Johanna had his food and thermos already packed beautifully into his haversack. A handful of dried raisins and apricots from the Cape had been thrown in, unsolicited, a sure sign that he was fully restored to Ousie-Johanna's graces.

Calling at the slaughter room at the far end of the wide court-yard behind the kitchen to select what he thought was the best knife for skinning, he stuck it into his belt at the side of his own hunting knife and set off to trot back towards Hintza and the dead leopard, avoiding the milking shed in case of further questioning but not forgetting on the way to stop by a water-furrow in the garden to fill his flask.

He got back to the trap none too soon. Hintza was foaming at the mouth and about to drop with exhaustion from his work of keeping the vultures away from the carcass of the leopard. With their usual cunning they had descended from the trees and surrounded Hintza and the dead leopard, in a thickly packed circle. As one segment of the circle moved in on Hintza and the dead leopard, Hintza would be forced into dashing at them to chase them away. They would do this with fantastic agility for such awkwardly-shaped and heavy birds, fluttering back-ward just fast enough to give Hintza the illusion that he might at any minute be able to catch them. While doing this, the seg-ments behind Hintza would close in, their long scraggy necks outstretched and their sharp beaks ready to strike.

No doubt they would have succeeded if Hintza had not been in similar predicaments before, although for never so long as on this occasion. He would know through his acute senses and ex-perience, exactly when he had chased the false, deceitful vultures far enough. He would then whirl about and dash back to the leopard just in time to scatter the advancing section of the rapacious rear-guard. Of course, no sooner had he got them at a safe distance from the leopard, than he had to whirl about to repeat the process with the other flank of the army of vultures. So the battle had gone on and on until now he was so tired and exhausted that if it had not been for the fact that he came from a long line of fighting ancestors he would have dropped, dead-tired to his knees and given up the struggle at least half an hour before François arrived on the scene.

François himself was so angry with the vultures and so pro-voked by seeing what they had done to Hintza, that without hesitation he shot five of them. Any pity that he might have felt for so excessive and hot-headed an action was cancelled by seeing the rest of the vultures fall on their dead kinsmen and devour them. They had not even the excuse of starvation be-cause in a world so full of game and carnivorous animals, they were always fat and well-fed.

Another cause for his anger was that the behaviour of the vultures had upset his priorities. He had fully intended to go first to the aid of the little Bushman. But with Hintza so ex-hausted he now had to set about the arduous task of skinning the leopard, or the vultures would devour the animal, skin and all, in his absence.

If that were to happen, 'Bamuthi would be so suspicious that it would not take him long to find out, from the many tell-tale tracks in the bush, that François had been up to something most extraordinary. He had no option, therefore, but to skin the leopard at once. He had been taught the art of skinning by so fine a craftsman as 'Bamuthi and had practised on goats, sheep, oxen, eland and even giant sable, ever since he was big enough to handle a knife. That, and the growing feeling of urgency to help the wounded Bushman, made him as quick on this occasion as any man could have been. The moment he had the skin cut away, unblemished, heavy and wet as it was, he rolled it in a bundle and hoisted it on to his shoulders.

Calling on Hintza to follow, he marched down the track to the place where he had hidden the Bushman. He found him lying awake, propped against the rock, an arrow in his bow, no doubt brought to the alert by the noise François had made shooting the vultures. Fortunately François had taken the pre-caution of announcing himself by once more calling out the proper Bushman greeting, before he showed himself at the entrance to the ledge.

The little man's relief at his coming was as obvious as it was gratifying to François. He crawled in underneath the ledge, threw down the leopard skin and sat beside the Bushman. Then he took out of his satchel the flask of hot, sweet coffee and made the Bushman drink its contents together with two tablets of pain-killer.

François followed this up with a third of the, as usual, over-generous supply of sandwiches Ousie-Johanna had made for him, reassuring the little Bushman as he passed the food to him that everything he was drinking and eating contained great magic to counter the harm the trap had done to him. He remembered from what old Koba had told him that there was for the Bushman magic in everything and therefore all their problems and complications had to have magic answers as well. Indeed he himself, strong and unusually mature for a boy of thirteen, was still young enough and so much under the influence of the people of the bush, from Matabele to Barotse and Shangaan, to believe secretly almost as much in magic as they or any Bushman had ever done. Although magic might not be all, he was convinced that it was not an illusion as his rational father, however dear to him, insisted, and he believed it still applied to life in the bush to an astonishing degree.

While he talked, he was happy to notice how quickly the pain-killer had taken effect and that the look of pain and strain was vanishing from the eyes and face of the injured Bushman. François thought that he had never seen so wonderful a pair of eyes. Although the Bushman was young the eyes had an astonishing light in them as if coming from so far back in time that it took his breath away. All this, of course, at the time was not an articulate observation so much as just instinctive feeling on François's part. As well as the vanishing of the look of pain, the hot coffee and food rapidly brought back the little Bushman's strength, which he showed in a new firmness in his voice and increasingly lively responses to François's efforts at making his idea of proper bedside conversation.

When at last he thought that the Bushman was, for the moment, out of pain and strong enough, he raised the question which was uppermost in his mind. He explained that he fully realized how the Bushman must not be allowed to fall into Matabele or any other strange hands, even European hands. But if he were not to do so, they would have to find a far better hiding place for him than the ledge under which they were sitting at that moment. They would have to do so quickly because unless François returned home soon, people would come searching for him and then the discovery of the Bushman would inevitably follow.

At this point the little man interrupted and explained that he himself knew the perfect hiding place near at hand.

François looked amazed. He could not help exclaiming: 'But surely you haven't been here before, how could you possibly have done so, in this enemy country?'

For the first time a delightful smile came to the Bushman's face and he nodded his rather Mongolian head vigorously. Quickly, in his own language, full of clicks so easily and lightly uttered that the words crackled like electricity on his lips, he explained to François. He had indeed been in this country once before, as a boy of about François's age. Here, close by, well hidden in the cliffs above the river was a deep cave, which from the time of the people of the early race had been the home of the little Bushman's clan. They had been forced to leave it when the coming of the Matabele, Barotse and Shangaan as well as the 'red strangers' had started the process of mercilessly hunting them down and exterminating his people. It had become impossible for them to hunt in the bush for food, although they were certain they could have kept the whereabouts of their great and ancient cave a secret indefinitely, so well was it hidden. So one sad day, long before he was born, his people at the dead of night had moved out of the cave and gone out into the great desert beyond where they already knew many others of their kinsmen had fled.

He himself had been born in the desert, but in all the Bushmen there was a hope that one day they would be able to come back to their home in this cave. The memory of it and the love of it was kept alive among them by the stories, poems and songs taught to them by their parents from the time they were born, and even in the great art of the dances they danced around the fire at least once a year in the desert, to express the joy they would all feel when the great day came and they could take possession of their cave, honey-pastures (they loved honey above all things) and hunting grounds again. Moreover, it was the accepted tradition among his people when the first-born son was about to become a man – here he looked at François and said, in other words when he reached the age that François appeared to have reached – for the father to lead the boy out of the desert·and secretly show him the way to the cave. There he would live with him for a week or two so that his memory of it, the magic spirit of the place and the sense of return which living in it, re-created, would remain with the son for ever. When the father died, as his had done, the son would have to return to tell the cave the sad news and make its new master known to it. He thought that if François would help him, the best thing to do now would be to make for the cave. He could lie up there safely, since the cave had never been discovered by any other race. When he was fully recovered, he could make his way back again to the safety of the desert.

François's excitement at this piece of intelligence was only matched by his relief that there was in fact a place nearby where the gravely injured man would be safe. His only doubt was whether the Bushman would be strong enough to get to the cave, and he unhesitatingly said so. But thanks to the pain-killer and the food, as well as his indomitable spirit and natural re-silience, the little Bushman at once illustrated how capable he was of setting out there and then. He stood up without any assistance on one leg, picked up his bow and arrows and spear, grasped his spear in his right hand and leaning on its shaft he hobbled out on to the track on his own.

François immediately offered him his arm to help as he had helped before but the Bushman would have none of it, only allowing him to carry his bow and quiver. For the rest, he just begged François to follow and slowly started through the bush northwards, in the direction of the hills. There was no track of any kind to follow, but the Bushman seemed to know every stone, tree, shrub and plant individually as if they had been intimate friends all his life. Indeed, he went straight without hesitation, as François had read in his books a homing pigeon would, still knowing the way back to the loft where it had been born, despite having been hooded and taken a thousand miles away.

What impressed François even more was that not once did the Bushman, handicapped as he was with that terribly mangled leg, step on a blade of grass or bruise a leaf thereby leaving signs behind him of their progress through the bush. So they climbed steadily upwards, with many a rest in the shade of storm bush and acacia trees, until at last they came to the top of one of the horns of the crescent of hills which enclosed Hunter's Drift. They stood there for a moment, hidden behind some black storm bushes and looked down five hundred feet into the swirling waters of the swollen Amanzim-tetse, the River of Sweet Waters. Clearly there was no way up the sheer cliff from the river and, what was far worse, so far as François could see there appeared to be no way along its face either. Yet still the little Bushman did not hesitate.

He turned sharply to the right, went down on his hands and knees and crawled forward slowly underneath the black storm bushes until suddenly they came to a narrow cleft in the rock face, blocked by an enormous boulder. Here the little Bushman signalled to François to be silent and come to his side. He whispered to François for help saying he wished to climb up the boulder. Instantly François assisted him and, on the top, the Bushman lost no time in sliding over it and vanishing down the far side.

François and Hintza followed quickly, just in time to see the Bushman once more down on all fours and crawling underneath some more bushes along the cleft. They all continued thus, took a sharp right turn, followed it away from the river for some fifty yards and came to an abrupt stop against another cliff face, with both trees and bushes of thorn as well as wild raisins growing thick and tall at its base.

Without hesitating again the little Bushman crawled on his stomach straight into this formidable undergrowth. François and Hintza followed. The undergrowth was so thick that after the broad sunlight outside François could hardly see his way ahead. But after a minute or two he found himself facing a round hole at the base of the cliff, just big enough to crawl through as the Bushman was doing. He followed, Hintza panting at his heels, and then stood up in one of the widest and deepest caves he had ever seen. The little Bushman was sitting back against a wall within, gasping for breath but obviously well content, as François could see, because some hundreds of feet away there were several narrow openings through which shafts of light struck into the cave, illuminating the yellow sandstone surfaces until they glowed like honey and making the level, soft sandy floor of the cave like an orange coloured mat.

But what really excited him was when he saw that the smooth walls of the cave were completely covered with the most wonderful paintings he had ever seen. One was of a whole herd of eland in full flight, running with such speed that watching them he felt he could almost hear the wind of their speed sing like violins in his ears. Another large slab carried a lovely conversation piece with a couple of tall giraffes standing tenderly over a baby giraffe crouched at their feet. Another had a painting of a lion with its claws in the back of a giant sable antelope which it was in the process of pinning down to the earth, and so on and on until most of the animals of the Africa he knew and loved were represented on the walls, in one characteristic role or another. But the greatest panel of all seemed to be reserved for something that had never been seen on land or sea as far as François knew. It was of an enormous serpent wriggling out of a gigantic shell, and a tiny Mantis with·a small mongoose at its side, sitting calmly in front of the serpent, as if telling it. 'Now you had better behave yourself or you will get into trouble.'

Over praying mantis, mongoose and serpent there was unmistakably the arc of a rainbow. Below the rainbow, as if belonging to it, was a delicately drawn and painted porcupine and beside the porcupine, two little hands obviously imprinted on the canvas of stone after having been dipped in red paint.

François could have gone on staring for hours at all this, feeling not only as if he were in an art gallery but in some kind of a church as well, but he was interrupted by the Bushman saying to him, in a voice blurred this time not with pain but with great emotion: 'This is my place and the place of all my people.'

François would have loved to have asked the little Bushman the many questions that were welling up in him, but the sound of a human voice had brought him back to immediate realities. He had already been over-long. He must lose no time getting home if he were not to be missed and people come searching for him. He hurriedly explained all this to the Bushman, made him lie down on his back, undid his improvised dressings of the early morning and explained that he was now going to apply the most magic of all medicines to the wound. He warned that it would hurt as even the trap itself had not hurt. He poured the iodine into the raw wound. Far from flinching, as François had expected, a great look of happiness came into the Bushman's face as he felt the iodine stinging like needle thrusts into his leg, the pain obviously convincing him that François's magic must be very good magic indeed.

François then bound the leg with proper field dressings and clean, sterilized bandages, made the Bushman swallow three tablets of M and B 693, and told him to take three more when the sun went down. He gave him three more pain-killing tablets and three more sleeping draughts to take at sunset. He placed the remainder of the sandwiches and the field flask of water on the ground beside him. Finally, he made the Bushman promise that he would not move until François came to him again the next day, which he assured him he would, although at an hour which he could not now determine. He was then ready to leave, and was about to turn and make for the entrance of the cave where the daylight shone like water on the surface of a deep well when, to his amazement the Bushman, hurt as he was, stood up and raised his hand half above his shoulder rather like a rough Roman salute and thanking him profusely, ended with the words: 'Until today Xhabbo was one; now he is two.'

François's embarrassment at so full an expression of thanks from the Bushman, because he had only done what appeared to him perfectly natural and obvious, was so acute that he doubted whether he could respond adequately. His knowledge of the uninhibited people among whom he had grown up told him he had to do so, unless he were to appear boorish, as Africans think all 'red strangers' are only too apt to be. But how?

He could only take refuge in the kind of expression Koba had taught him a well brought-up Bushman might have used on such an occasion and answered shyly: 'And now that you have come, I live again.'

Something else occurred to him that made him ask, 'I did hear right? Your name is indeed Xhabbo?'

'Because my father felt utterly that my coming was Xhabbo to him,' the little Bushman answered in the round-about manner of a language, which may lack logic and reason but more than compensates for them in feeling: 'I have come to feel myself also utterly to be Xhabbo and to feel not a little that there could be no other name for me.'

Xhabbo, as François knew only too well from Koba, meant Dream, and Dream, she had taught him, was a favourite name for all the first-born sons in eminent Bushman clans.

All this time Hintza, who had had his first experience of rock climbing on such a scale that he must have qualified as the first ridge-back Alpinist in southern Africa, had been lying with his head in his paws. After all, he had just about had the most exhausting and eventful day of his eighteen-month-old life, what with waking François before dawn, facing leopards, chasing away vultures and all the other tiresome chores a hunting dog has imposed upon him when accompanying human beings who are so deficient in the essentials of bush education such as having a proper sense of smell and hearing. His long pink tongue was fluttering like a canna petal in the breeze while he panted like a blacksmith's bellows.

François now called to him, 'Here, Hin!'

Hintza immediately controlled his breath, rose with all the slow dignity of sheer fatigue and went to François.

Pointing to Xhabbo, François said politely: 'Hin, shake. This is Xhabbo and Xhabbo, this is Hin, who will be yours as he is mine.'

Hintza, an expert in the art of shaking paws, gracefully held his out immediately, indeed so quickly that François had to explain, and beg Xhabbo to take it. Shaking hands, let alone paws, is not a Bushman custom, and any breach of etiquette could now offend Hintza's sensitive concept of what was fitting and set him against Xhabbo. Luckily, Xhabbo was as intelligent and quick on the uptake as he was brave and good-looking and to François's great joy the introduction went off without a flaw.

On that note François raised his hand and gave Xhabbo the Bushman farewell: 'Taixai-Xhum', 'May you rest well.'

Quickly, without looking back, lest he be tempted to stay longer, he crawled out of the cave. When he stood up outside in the daylight and saw that Hintza had appeared at his side, for the first time that day he could allow perhaps one of the most singular aspects of that singularly eventful morning to rise to the surface of his mind.

'Hin,' he asked softly, bending down and stroking Hintza affectionately. 'Tell me, how could you possibly have known that there was something unusual in the trap in the dark of morning, when not another dog either at home or at 'Bamuthi's kraal knew anything about it at all? Come on Hin, out with the secret! How did you do it?'

Hintza looked up at François, head cocked sideways as always when listening carefully to his words. He seemed to understand the question perfectly because immediately that sensitive damp, ink-black nose of his contracted in scores of infinitely fine little creases, vibrating with the effort of expressing their own extreme of concentration, while he re-enacted the scene in François's room as if he were sniffing the black morning air all over again, clearly indicating. 'I have not got this nose for nothing, you know. It was a scent we have never smelt at Hunter's Drift before and, of course, I had no option but to let you know.'

François himself was well aware of the fact that different human beings had smells of their own. The Matabele were as little inclined to like the smell of the Europeans as the Europeans liked theirs, and he remembered how that he himself had been struck by the acid, desert tang the little Bushman carried on his person when he helped him on his way down the track towards the first sanctuary.

Proud of Hintza as never before, he hurried back towards the ledge where he had left the leopard's skin, loaded it on his shoulder and carried it home in triumph. He arrived just as Johanna was impatient to serve the afternoon tea and where 'Bamuthi and all the others were gathered. At the sight of the skin they gave him, half in play and half in earnest, the royal Matabele salute. François felt almost like one of the legionaries of whom he had read, returning with a rare trophy of war from the far perimeter of the great and vanished Roman Empire.

3 • Hunter's Drift

The meal that followed François's return was one of the strangest he could remember. His father had insisted on getting up and was already in his usual place at the head of the table when François, after a quick wash, hurried in to join his parents. The signs of something indefinably but seriously wrong, which François had noticed in his father that memorable evening when Hintza had first come into his life, had not proved an illusion. Pierre-Paul Joubert, to give François's father his full name, had continued to deteriorate in health steadily over the past eighteen months. He was now so weakened and obviously seriously ill that his wife, despite all his protestations, was taking him on the long journey to the capital to see the best doctors in the country.

Most depressing of all, there appeared to be no name for the condition of François's father. If only one could put a *name* to it, François felt, one could do something about it. But without a name one was lost, like a hunter in a mist in the bush at night without even a star to guide him home.

'Bamuthi, the other herdsmen and servants and even Ousie-Johanna, who seemed to combine without spiritual discomfort a certain petit-bourgeois Christianity in the head and an active Amaxosa paganism at heart, were convinced that it was all due to some form of witchcraft. They had already tried to enlist François as an ally, and begged their Lammie to get their master to consult one of the most eminent witch-doctors who lived over the hills in another wide valley, in the midst of a well-to-do Matabele clan. People came from far and wide to consult him and, according to 'Bamuthi, if he were paid well enough he had never yet failed to cure the worst afflictions of Bantu man.

François, indeed, had already had several discussions with 'Bamuthi on the matter because he was not at all inclined, as his parents were, to dismiss witchcraft as the cause of his father's decline. Both his youth and a pagan environment which accepted witchcraft as a great fact of life, predisposed him to believe in magic. The great objection to this explanation was that he could not think of any human enemies who might have put a fatal spell on his father which, as one European doctor after another failed them, appeared to be more and more likely. Pierre-Paul, though by pagan standards a shade too austere, was so obviously a good man that as far as François knew he had not a single enemy in the world around Hunter's Drift.

He had indeed confronted 'Bamuthi and Ousie-Johanna with this obvious flaw in their theory that his father was bewitched, and protested indignantly. 'You cannot be bewitched unless you have enemies! Tell me, Old Father and Old Mother, who in this world in which we live hates my father enough to put such a spell on him?'

'Bamuthi and Ousie-Johanna had shaken their heads, saddened that François, even for one so young, could be so naïve. Of course, they told him, they knew his father had no enemies among Matabele, Barotse, Shangaan or Mashona, or any of the people who came and passed through the remote world of Hunter's Drift. No, he had a far more powerful enemy, though far away. He had the Government.

'The Government!' François exclaimed. 'But 'Bamuthi and Ousie-Johanna, do you know what the Government is, that you could say such a terrible thing about it?'

Of course, they knew perfectly well what the Government was, they replied. They were not inexperienced fools. The Government was a very tall, severe, old Red Stranger, a tyrannical person with a long white beard and a very clever head. Once every year he packed all his best clothes in a suitcase, took the train to the great water, crossed it in a 'water-wagon' and went to see the great white paramount chief on the other side of the water, to come back with his head full of ideas for strange new laws to inflict on people like themselves in the bush. Everybody knew that François's father had fallen foul of this formidable old gentleman, refused to go on in his service and had come to live here in the bush as far away as possible from him, to help people like the Matabele who needed it because, ever since the days of Lobengula, the Government had refused to listen to the voices of even the wisest and greatest Matabele Indunas, so that he ruled them no longer like his own children but still like troublesome impis of 'Mzilikatze who might rise again in rebellion against him at any moment.

François, young as he was, had a slightly more sophisticated idea of the complex institution that was modern government in the remote capital. Yet he immediately understood what had given them the idea. He himself did not know the full story. He only knew that his father, as Director of Education in that vast territory, had had such serious differences with the Government over their education policies that he had felt compelled to resign from the service before François was born. Knowing nothing of the details of his father's quarrel with the Government, he was aware only broadly that it was because his father could not stomach the official neglect of African education, although the Africans hungered for it and needed it even more than the Europeans.

Pierre-Paul Joubert had originally been appointed Director of Education when he was only in his late twenties because he had grown up among the Amaxosa, and so knew Bantu Africa as few Europeans did. Apparently all his life he had felt specially tied to them, and when he left the university in the far south he had gone straight to work as a teacher among them. He had done so in spite of the fact that he had inherited, right on the Amaxosa frontier, a rich farm which had been in his family for two and a half centuries, and had been expected, as had been all the elder sons, to carry on the family tradition of work on the farm. Part of him would have liked nothing better than to do just that because he loved the land. Few things gave him greater pleasure than struggling with the unpredictable African seasons and making beautiful and fruitful the difficult Cinderella earth of Africa. Yet, he was also a born teacher, a person of instinctive vision and utterly convinced that if the future of Africa were to be creative and not become increasingly destructive, as it showed signs of becoming already in his youth, it could be so only through a sustained process of education of both Africans and Europeans for a common non-racial destiny.

When he was prevented from carrying on the work of education in this spirit by the reactionary Government which came into power in southern Africa after the War, he left the Education Service in the south and turned to the world north of the Limpopo. There a more liberal approach in these matters still seemed the rule. All the signs were that a person with his academic qualifications, with knowledge of a key African people like the Amaxosa, and already a reputation that would not have disgraced an educationalist at the end of his life, let alone a youngish man, would be made most welcome. So he had sold his farm, and he and his young wife, who felt about these things exactly as he did, had gone north, deeper into the interior of Africa.

They had arrived there full of hope, plans and abundant energy and within a year all their expectations appeared confirmed when he was put in charge of African education. But within a decade he was faced with a repetition of the discredited pattern of racial policies that had made him leave his native country. He fought hard to change it all in his new sphere of activity. But when it was clear that he could no longer do so, and was becoming in his own eyes an accessory both before and after the fact of what appeared to him another disastrous trend of discrimination, he resigned from the service.

Using the gratuity which he applied for instead of a pension and, of course, the considerable sum he had received from the sale of his family's valuable farm in the south, he had moved to the western frontier of his new country. There, on the Amanzim-tetse river, he had established Hunter's Drift. He had chosen this particular part of the country for many reasons. One was because here, where the hills came to an end and the land began to level out towards the great desert in the west, there appeared in the bush natural wide open spaces covered with rich veld grasses, that made them ideal grazing areas for cattle. He had already proved this to his satisfaction on one of his regular vacations one year before with Mopani. Once a year he accompanied Mopani, who was an old friend of his from the War, on his patrols in the immense bush. On these expeditions he had been deeply impressed by the vast herds of eland, hartebeest, tssessebe, roan antelope and sable, who made their home in those remote and sheltered pockets of grassland, because they all had the same feeding habits and needs as any civilized old cow. Indeed, nowhere else in all his many travels in the course of his service throughout that great territory had Pierre-Paul seen more natural country for cattle.

In addition there were, close by, the sweet waters of the Amanzim-tetse river. Water, as even the tiniest African child knew, was the greatest problem for everyone, white, yellow, red or black, in that part of Africa. Where these animals did so well he knew that cattle with such abundant water, with care, could do even better. As these facts, which appeared unknown to others, settled deeper in his imagination, the thought that he would like to end his days there had by the year become more compulsive.

Another reason was that he had already discovered a clearing and an ideal site for a homestead. This was due to the fact that one of these open pockets of land faced the broad ford over the Amanzim-tetse which gave Hunter's Drift its name. It was precisely there that the *Punda-Ma-Tenka* road (literally the Lift-and-Carry road, obviously so-called because the people who first used it had had porters to lift and carry their baggage for them) crossed the river. This was one of the greatest tracks in the history of Africa, older by far than any tribal memory. It ran from the Cape of Good Hope in the far south, by places with names which were full of romance: Molopo, Mafeking, Lobatsi, Mahalapye, Bushman Pits, Old Copper Mine, Francistown, Makari-Kari, Nata, then on by desert fringe and through densest bush until it crossed the Amanzim-tetse at Hunter's Drift. Thence it went north, past *Msuyhi-tonyi*, the Smoke-that-Thunders, as the Africans called the Victoria Falls, on to Kazungula on the broad reaches of the Zambezi, where this great river again could be crossed and the track on the far bank branched out and away in all directions: west to the swamps and mountains of Angola; north through the bush to Broken Hill, so on beyond to the Mountains of Fire and Smoke; cast by way of the Bangwelo swamps, between the great lakes of Malawi and Tanzania on to the Indian Ocean, there to meet the great Oriental world at harbours like Tanga, Dar-es-Salaam and Kilindini.

It was, in fact, the very route that all the great explorers and hunters in African history had followed on their way into the interior and which appeared marked 'Hunter's Road', on British maps. Men like Livingstone and Selous had used it when leaving the civilized world of the Cape for the unknown interior. The coming of the railways and, since the war, aeroplanes, had put an end to much of the usefulness of the road for Europeans. But it was still, despite all its appearances, the main road for Africans as they continually travelled in thousands from the under-developed and impoverished north to look for work in the rich, developing south. This fact had counted a great deal with Pierre-Paul. He knew he could always keep in touch with the civilized world by reading newspapers and through extensive correspondence by letter. But here he could also keep in touch with the Africa of the interior that he loved. Here, at Hunter's Drift, news could be gathered from the lips of living men to keep him close to this other greater Africa that he had tried, in vain, to educate into the modern world.

But the last and greatest practical consideration of all, how-ever, was the fact that the railway which travelled from the Cape by way of Bulawayo and the Victoria Falls to the rich copper belt in the far north, made a wide curve through the hills which brought it within nine miles of Hunter's Drift. On its way it also passed the greatest coal mine in Africa which had pro-duced a large, modern industrial centre in the heart of the bush. This centre had coal and minerals to spare but no earth worth cultivating and no grass for grazing near at hand.

Pierre-Paul decided that if only he could persuade the railway authorities and the mines to make a train stop at the point nearest Hunter's Drift, he would have almost on his doorstep, an immense and rich market for all his cattle and produce. And this, indeed, proved to be the case. So great was the centre's need for fresh supplies that he had no difficulty in persuading the mines to put pressure on the railway authorities and within a few years the train stopped every night at what became known as 'Hunter's Drift Siding', to be met by mule-wagons loaded to the full with fresh vegetables and fresh meat for the mines.

He was convinced, further, that if only he could make Hunter's Drift an ideally self-supporting farm, the men coming and going through it, camping at the old 'outspan' by the fords and seeing it for themselves (while being made thoroughly welcome in the process), would begin learning how to live in the modern age, since they, like himself, were all at heart farmers and cattle-men, however primitive their methods appeared to be. Moreover near and all around Hunter's Drift, to the north and to the east, in valleys and isolated clearings in the bush, there were already numbers of Bantu outposts. He thought that if he recruited as many of these as possible, they could share in the development of Hunter's Drift, not just as servants but as partners, who would find security and receive regular wages as well as a share of the profits, which he hoped to make out of his ranch. In this way he could create, in miniature, a tiny model of the non-racial Africa that he had visualized as an educationalist. This hope indeed was so compelling that he and his wife felt no resentment for their personal defeat by the Government. Was there not after all the Sindabele proverb: 'The greatest and sweetest of marula trees grow out of only a single little stone?'

With all this in mind, Pierre-Paul Joubert had gone first to *u-Nothloba-Mazibuka*, the traditional Keeper-of-the-Ford.

He had already, several times before, met the old gentleman and he now spent a week with him in his kraal, *Osebeni* (On-the-River-Bank) in another clearing by the Amanzim-tetse. He took a week because he knew the deep mistrust that all Africans had of doing things in haste. From dawn to dusk he waited on the old Matabele gentleman who wore like a halo around his grey head the metal ring which was a badge of his rank as an Induna, Great Counsellor and Advisor of Kings. Without the least temptation to impatience, Pierre-Paul had explained elaborately to the dignified old gentleman all that he had in mind. He had answered a thousand and one penetrating questions with the meticulous sense of the importance of detail natural to an inspired teacher. At the end of the time, the old man had given his answer in a way far more convincing than mere words could have been. He had just summoned his eldest son, 'Bamuthi, and in front of all his clan called to meet Pierre-Paul, he had told 'Bamuthi that he was to go and henceforth make his home with him.

Soon, Hunter's Drift had as fine a collection of herdsmen and other servants as perhaps that part of Africa had ever seen. They were persons all the more committed because the concept of the enterprise basically was of a pattern dear to so communal a people as the Bantu, and one they had followed in essence for millenniums.

It was indeed significant how all visitors to Hunter's Drift felt it was more a family affair than the usual servant and master set-up. Accordingly many disapproved of it strongly, roundly declaring behind Pierre-Paul's back that he was 'spoiling everything' for others; 'letting the side down' and so on and on. Even worse, there were the occasional high-minded idealists from overseas who, after enjoying Hunter's Drift's hospitality to the full, would dismiss it all as too 'paternalistic' – the favourite term of abuse of the intellectual of the day – and would even write letters to the newspapers to that effect on their return home. That hurt Pierre-Paul far more than the Government, because they did not have the excuse of being caught, as he often put it, 'in a trap of their own history, as my people are'.

The news of Hunter's Drift's success spread throughout the territory. European ranchers came from far and wide to try and follow Pierre-Paul Joubert's example. But he had already taken the precaution of seeing that all the free land in that part of the world had been claimed and registered for ever in the names of his neighbouring Bantu friends. There was only one irritating exception. A large area between him and the railway nearby had already been bought, apparently some years before Pierre-Paul came to Hunter's Drift, by some mysterious European called Monckton.

Pierre-Paul had tried in vain to find out all he could about this person who was apparently even more far-sighted than he had been, but all he learned was that Monckton had once been a very junior District Commissioner in the Colonial Service, responsible for keeping an official eye on that part of the bush, over a term of three years. Since then he appeared to have vanished on other duties into the British Colonial Service, which in those days was still immense. All Pierre-Paul knew was that there, almost within reach of his hand, was a piece of land perhaps finer than his own and strategically even better placed, with an owner apparently so indifferent to it that he never even bothered to visit, let alone develop it.

As the years went by, Hunter's Drift prospered so that it merited expanding to double if not treble its size. The whole of the clearing around the homestead became a precious emerald green from vast vegetable gardens and orchards watered by irrigation from the river. The homestead, an exact replica of the graceful gabled old Dutch farm with green shuttered windows and half-doors, complete with bronze latches and knobs shining like gold, which the original Jouberts, fresh from Huguenot France, had built in the far south, began to look as if it had grown out of the soil rather than been imposed upon it. Its elegant white walls, rising above the wide stoep of yellow stone, looked more and more inviting as their dazzling surfaces were increasingly brindled and dappled with the shadow of the rapidly growing trees, creepers and vines planted around it. Seeing thus what could be done, François's father became so irritated by the vision of the great tract of Monckton country lying unused next door that he conceived a powerful prejudice, if not active hatred for a man he had never even seen. However, there was nothing that he could do about it except to cultivate his own garden with even greater vision and energy than before.

Into this world François was born. His parents had already been married for twelve years and his coming was not only unexpected but, coming so late, inevitably produced an unusual relationship between the three of them. His parents were profoundly attached to each other. Their relationship in fact was so complete that they were utterly content in each other's company. The arrival of a child in their lives, unlike those of normal married couples, could have appeared irrelevant, if not perilously near to an intrusion, had it not been for the fact that they were both unusually loving, caring as well as sensitive and imaginative persons. They were absolutely delighted with François from the start but delighted in a way which was suspect in the prevailing concept of parent-child relationships in the European Africa of the day. They never defined their attitude for their own benefit or that of their friends because it was for them a matter of personal feeling and a groping after a process of growth rather than of reason and preconceived theory. Yet their actions implied in all sorts of ways, right from the beginning, that they had no marked parental attitude in the conventional sense of the term, to their son. In fact Lammie unintentionally made this only too clear at the time of François's christening in the capital.

She did so by asking her friends to attend the christening party so that they could meet 'the other little person' who had joined their lives. Those who were truly close to the couple knew that this phrase 'the other person' did not imply any coldness or lack of love for François. They saw it clearly as an expression implying that their child was not going to be merely an egotistical extension of their parental personalities but rather someone with a unique nature and personality of his own. Both Pierre-Paul and his wife had an instinctive horror of the way many parents tried to compel their children to live a life they would have liked to live themselves; but had failed to do. Pierre-Paul had seen enough casualties from this approach in his own schools.

This of course did not mean that François was not brought up with discipline. His father, in particular, was too good a teacher to be ignorant of the importance of discipline. As he so often had put it, no true self-expression was ever possible without discipline. So François, from his earliest memories, was subject to a strict upbringing designed, as Pierre-Paul put it to his wife, when her tender heart was disturbed by some unusually severe line taken with François, 'not to blur the edges but to give shape to the personality'.

She would accept this with a nod of her beautiful head. Nevertheless the last word was always hers. 'All the same, whatever we do, we must never drive this urgent little spirit underground, as we see parents doing all around us in this terrible Calvinist world of ours.'

It was not surprising, therefore, that François could not remember a time when he had addressed Pierre-Paul as 'father' and Lammie as 'mother'. He did so only when talking about them to others. Although there may have been a time in his cradle when he had made noises like 'Pa' and 'Ma', the moment he was capable of uttering proper words his mother had always been Lammie and his father 'Ouwa'.

This last was the name he took over from old Koba. She unfailingly called Pierre-Paul Ouwa because this apparently was the name by which he had been known to her and her people in the far south. It meant, literally, Old Wagon, 'ou' meaning old and 'wa' wagon.

When François, at a more analytical period of his growth, asked Koba why they had chosen so odd a name for Pierre-Paul, she said that it was because 'like a wagon, he carried many people and their troubles with him through life'.

'But why *Old* Wagon, Koba?' François piped up, not without a twinge of indignation, because to him his father was young and handsome, unlike the many flabby and florid fathers of others he had met.

'Because old, my Little Feather,' old Koba had answered, so amused by his touchiness that her smooth yellow Mongolian face creased finely all over with smiles, 'because old is our greatest Bushman word of respect.'

This absence of formalities between parents and son may have been their own private affair but it did not prevent Pierre-Paul's official enemies from making a note in their dossier of his failings to calm their guilt-ridden consciences, and strengthen the feelings that they had done well to rid themselves of so non-conformist a civil servant.

This aspect of François's relationship with his parents has been described in some detail, because it helps to explain why he was not sent away to boarding school. Obviously, his parents cared more than most that their son should be well educated. Yet they had not just a fear but an absolute conviction that the sort of schooling at even the best schools available in the country would be so unaware of 'the other person' in children that François would be cut down to a common pattern and leave school like the human equivalent of a machine coming from a remorseless conveyor belt in a large factory, exactly like thousands of others.

Although the law of the land made education compulsory for all European children, François's father decided not to send him to school. The authorities, the moment they became aware of the fact, did their utmost to force him to send François to what they called a recognized school, but Pierre-Paul was able to resist them successfully. He may have ceased to be official Director of Education but his professional qualifications as a schoolmaster remained and could not be denied. There was, he was able to demonstrate, no law against private schools. So all Pierre-Paul had to do was to claim that he had opened a private school at Hunter's Drift. That it had only one pupil was no fault of his. If any other parent would like to send their children to his school, make arrangements for their board and lodgings and were prepared to pay the requisite fee, he declared that he was prepared to receive them. No one, of course, was either near enough or sufficiently in love with Pierre-Paul's attitude to take advantage of his offer.

However in law his claim was held to be valid, to such an extent that once a year an official inspector was compelled to undertake the long and arduous journey from the capital to Hunter's Drift, just in order to verify that François was receiving a proper education within the meaning of the Education Act, and to put him through the prescribed examinations. To do the inspectors justice, they enjoyed the break in their dreary and monotonous routine enormously, and would look back upon the week which it took them to accomplish their duties at Hunter's Drift with delight. Some of them were even known to have admitted, over their whiskies and sodas in their clubs in the capital, that 'there was some wisdom in that Joubert fellow's madness'.

But none of them enjoyed it nearly as much as François's parents, who were human enough to feel satisfaction in getting their own way, as well as a windfall of, for once, having the joke on the Establishment.

Still, one has to wonder whether François himself might have been as happy in his family situation, had he been able to compare his life with the lives of children in other European families. May he not in his secret heart of hearts have experienced a greater sense of belonging, if the attitude of his parents had been more proprietary, and he were privately treated and addressed more emphatically as their son? There was no doubt that in the order of their trinity, his father came first for his mother, equally Lammie came first for Ouwa. None of the displacement of emphasis in affection from husband to child, which is commonly supposed to take place in a woman when she becomes a mother, had occurred in Lammie. Pierre-Paul remained her sun; she and François were satellites and no one could suspect that the priorities of Pierre-Paul's affection were not exactly the same.

So it is just possible, one believes, that there may have been at work in François's disposition an unacknowledged longing to come first with both, producing in the process a certain degree of isolation and aloneness too early in his life. One suspects something of this from his reaction to the coming of Hintza. There could be no doubt that François found more reassurance and comfort from the fact that he, and he alone, came first with Hintza, than he or anyone else would have thought possible.

Was this not then the secret of his great love for old Koba? There was no doubt that she had put him first and had been known to round on his parents like a leopard when she suspected them of being more just than loving with him. Perhaps the trouble was that there was no disproportion or flair in relationship with his parents. There was undoubtedly a great protection for him in that exact balance of love and reason. But does anyone, let alone a child, want perfection? Do we all not secretly long for more love than reason, more pardon than justice, more impulse than calculation, more heart than head and altogether for an asymmetrical slant in our favour in our lives? One asks these questions not in a spirit of criticism of Lammie and Pierre-Paul, but because they are believed necessary for understanding why François became what he was so early in life and why he behaved as he did in the series of desperate events that he was to encounter.

He himself was superficially unaware of any such reservations, happier by far than the most claimed and spoilt son of any other family. None the less at heart there lay the shadow of an intimation that he may have been called upon to play the man on his own perhaps a shade too soon. There were no other European families within a hundred miles or more of Hunter's Drift. He hardly ever went to the capital or the nearby mining city with his parents. So he had no standard of comparison in these matters except with those of the children of 'Bamuthi and the other herdsmen. They were his only playmates. But in that wild and savage environment he found their company so stimulating and enjoyable that he did not consciously long for companionship of children of his own kind. He was a frequent and welcome visitor in their kraals, particularly in 'Bamuthi's kraal.

Compared with them he seemed to be singularly undisciplined. All he had to do was to work for two hours in the early morning before it got too hot, at the lessons set for him by Pierre-Paul, who had always maintained that the normal school hours were far too long. He was convinced that teachers made far too great a mystery of what they had to teach; and that intelligent children could do the work in a third of the time they were given for accomplishing it. Once his lessons were learned, François was always free to join in the life of the ranch until the evening, when he had an hour of homework to do for the next day's schooling. Even Pierre-Paul was astonished how his theory was confirmed in practice, and what a rewarding process teaching his son became for both. But once school was over, François would make straight for the Matabele kraals.

The contrast in living was particularly stark in 'Bamuthi's own kraal. Old – that is, old by François's exacting measure – 'Bamuthi had installed his fourth and youngest wife in his kraal at Hunter's Drift; the other three had been left with the grown-up children at Osebeni to look after his land and cattle there. Within the stockade of thorn which surrounded the huts in a wide circle to protect their cattle against lion and leopard at night, it was a world where 'Bamuthi was king. His wife and children, even his own mother who visited him from time to time, were his obedient subjects. He ruled them sternly according to a tribal law passed on, by example, over thousands of years of forgotten history. The assumption was that fear and authority, above all male authority, were both the beginning of wisdom, and the basis of all law and order in a Bantu community.

This was not fear in a negative sense but a kind of holy awe expressed in the impressive word, *Ukw-seba*, uttered far down in the throat in a sonorous bass tone. This awe was instinctively accepted as a bridge between the spirit of children and parents; parents and grandparents; grandparents and Indunas; Indunas and sub-chiefs; and so on up to Paramount Chief. Finally it existed between the Paramount Chief and the great *Umkulun-kulu*, the first spirit of all things.

In this world from the moment a child could walk, the only school was one of practical work according to capacity. After sunset it was one of an imaginative recital of colourful stories, myths, legends and the lip-to-lip history of the Bantu peoples. Any failure on the part of a child to fulfil his share of duty in this prescribed pattern of tribal behaviour was severely punished by 'Bamuthi and his wife.

In fact François was often amazed that 'Bamuthi who was so obviously a man of feeling could also be so ruthless when a mere child in his kraal did not measure up to his idea of tribal etiquette and expectation. Little as François had seen of the world of his own people outside, he had seen enough to realize how ludicrous were its conceptions of Bantu life, and how vast the ignorance on which they were based. There was no nuance of life in the kraal that was not determined by tribal etiquette; every child knew exactly how it was expected to behave towards older people; how to conduct itself at meal times; how to respect the belongings and dignity of others. The overwhelming importance of courtesy, cleanliness, self-respect and constant work was reinforced in them by a routine of order and orderliness. The Matabele wife, like 'Bamuthi's, set the example, above all by treating the smaller children with the utmost consideration; and sharing whatever came their way with everyone else.

This sharing applied as much to hard work as it did to the humble gifts of the bush. François, indeed, was always amazed to find on his visits to the kraal, that ever since dawn each little black boy and girl had already been hard at work. The smaller ones who had only just learned to walk would be looking after the babies, since their mothers, who were the hardest worked of all, would be away tilling the fields. Their elder brothers were out herding and protecting the cattle, sheep and goats. The older girls would be busy cleaning the kraal, sweeping the hard-baked earth around the huts with hand brushes made of golden Aminzim-tetse reeds and sprinkling it with water. This they had to fetch and carry in buckets from the river so that the dust could be securely laid around the dwellings for the rest of the long, hot day. Some of them would be pounding corn or millet in the great wooden mortars that stood in each kraal like anti-aircraft missiles on their pads ready for launching into the air.

The melodious sound of the regulated pounding was always there to tap out the rhythm for the chorus of birds, turtle doves and sun beetles, singing in the bush with ecstatic voices and with an even greater and more quicksilver intensity as the sun rose towards its peak. It was a sound that did to the human ear what a glimpse of fire does to the eyes of someone wandering lost in some wilderness at night, signalling beyond all possible doubt that there was order, home and organized sanctuary for life in that savage, chaotically abundant world of nature.

Very often François would see 'Bamuthi's oldest girl, barely ten, combining pounding with the care of her baby brother. She carried him securely, tied to her slim, long back in a shawl, while she lifted the enormous wooden pestle, almost twice her own height, high above her head to crush and recrush again and again the purple millet in the mortar. So at home would the black baby be there that although its head wobbled in the process as if it would fly from its neck, its eyes remained shut in the happiest of sleeps. No child was ever too small to be included in the life of family and tribe, and François never saw an infant excluded or left to its own devices, no matter how early the morning or late the night. Everybody belonged absolutely to everybody else in a way that passed all European understanding, until one is compelled to wonder whether the sight of all this did not cause François, in the depths of the unknown in his own heart, to feel some kind of envy, a twinge perhaps of having been left out of some subtle but essential scheme of things, despite all the manifest good fortune of his own up-bringing.

Compared with the girls, the boys of François's own age appeared on the surface to have an easier time because, when they were barely old enough to walk, they had to join in the task of herding the cattle, sheep and goats. This gave them opportunities for a great deal of play which disguised the exacting and responsible nature of their work so well that it was only when something went wrong and they failed in their duty that François saw it for what it really was. Indeed he had gone for some years fancying that, compared to his own life, 'Bamuthi's boys and their friends had nothing but fun herding the cattle in the bush. It is true that one of the older boys had to be continually on watch for wild animals about to raid their herds, as they so often tried to do. For this purpose the look-out and all the boys with him had to learn from an early age to read all the signs of life in the bush as François had to learn to read his father's books at home.

There appeared, he soon discovered, not a movement or a sound of a bird or insect that did not have its own special meaning for his black companions. Yes, the bush was another great book to them; its vocabulary the sounds of birds and insects; its script the movement of animals, from scorpions, centipedes, lizards, chameleons, snakes, rock rabbits and the smallest gazelle of their world, the graceful little flickering steenbuck (adored by 'Bamuthi's clan because it was supposed to be a bringer of rain), to the most imposing of antelope, such as the sable and eland.

It was all like some hieroglyphic code of which the Europeans had lost the key. So François just had to sit down as humbly as he did in front of his father during school hours and learn the archaic cypher from his friends. So good were they at reading this script of nature that François was never tempted to feel superior to them, as might perhaps have been expected of a son of the man who was the acknowledged chief of them all. On the contrary, there were times when he came near to developing an inferiority complex because he had consistently failed to read a message of the most immediate importance in the sounds and movements of the bush which had been perfectly obvious to the youngest among them from the start. It had continued thus to appear only too easy for them until one bright spring afternoon, when François was barely nine.

The sun was just on the edge of its long, steep slide down its shining blue slope to the flawless horizon of the great desert in the west. He had joined his friends some hours before at noon, when a dozen different groups of boys had come together in the process of watering their separate flocks by the river. It happened to be a place where the river was joined by a tributary that ran only in the rainy season but was dry at the moment. The eroded banks of the tributary consisted of thick layers of the red potter's clay which the women from the kraals used for the making of water jugs, milk jars, pots and other domestic utensils. The boys, however, would use it for modelling armies of miniature fighting men, ochre-stained Matabele warriors of the vanished Impis of 'Mzilikatze and Chaka, or herds of cattle and flocks of sheep and goats. Meeting in such unusually large numbers at this place of all places seemed a natural opportunity too good to miss, since they were all within reach there of the material needed for one of their favourite games.

Once each group had fashioned its own herd of miniature cattle, the animals would be drawn up in a crescent, in front of which a bull of Mithraic power would be placed to be manipulated by adroit hands into challenging the bulls of the other herds for the right of grazing near that part of the bank of the river as well as for possession of the cows of the others. The bull whose horns and legs crumpled first in the battle of horns which followed, was declared the loser and the winner entitled to have all the cows of the vanquished assembled to swell the crescent of clay cattle at its back.

As François had learned to his cost, a great deal of thought, experience and natural art went into the making of a bull which would stand up best to this kind of make-believe fighting. Indeed the favourite subject for argument and discussion between the boys, as they sat by their fires in the kraal at night waiting for the closing meal of their long day, would be precisely about the best means of constructing a champion bull. For instance, was it better to use spit or water in mixing the clay? Which cemented clay best, saliva, river water or a combination of the two? And did the addition of grass, or even some thin pliable twigs to the clay, help to make the body of the champion less brittle and more resistant to shock, not to mention the reinforcement of horns by a piece of European metal wire, which some cad in a neighbouring kraal – of course such a thing at Hunter's Drift or Osebeni would have been unthinkable – was reputed to have used once against a team matched against it by a generation of their older brothers? Whatever the method used, it was extraordinary to François with what art these black boys shaped cows, bulls, calves and armed warriors. He tried hard himself but he never did it half as well. In that fact, was another stimulus for preserving a wholesome sense of proportion to prevent him from feeling himself a cut above his companions.

On this placid, shining, yellow afternoon, owing to the exceptional number of herds and bulls involved, the fight for the championship lasted longer and was far more exciting than any that François had ever seen before. In fact, it became a little too exciting for the older boy, the look-out, who had been left high up on a boulder to watch over all the herds while the battle of the bulls was being fought out on the river bed below. He became too interested in the game to do his duty properly. This was not surprising, because as the game approached its climax, both the movement and din down below were terrific. Onlookers and participants were making the contest more realistic by shouting out challenges to one another, lowing like cows and roaring like bulls, pawing the earth, and throwing up handfuls of dust behind them to make the exercise more realistic.

When it came to the decisive battle, with only two bulls left in the contest, the look-out's curiosity became too much for him. He jumped from the boulder and hurried down the slope to join in. The two bulls, after a great deal of skilful feinting, each trying but failing to get his horns into the flanks of the other, had just been compelled to meet in the classical manner, heads down and horns locked together so securely that simultaneously the dread shout had issued from the throats of all the onlookers, soaring up in one great glittering cry: 'At last, the washing of the horns!'

That cry meant that the moment of truth in the spectacle had come. The horns of one of the bulls were about to be washed in the blood of the other. This shout would no doubt have been repeated on an ascending scale if two other sounds, far more fearful and imperative, had not broken in on the game. First, there cut through the noise of the battle, killing it instantly, the high and razor-sharp bleat of a goat, quickly dying away into a strangled cough from the river bank just beyond the boulder. It was followed by the characteristic snorting of a lion just as it pounces, to be followed by the drumming on the earth of the hooves of cattle scattering in a panic.

All the boys stood, grimly silent, looking at one another in horror. Then in the direction of the bush they saw spurts of red dust rising into the air, unmistakably from the death-kicks of a cow no doubt pinned to the earth by a lion. The sight of the fateful dust brought the boys out of their trance of shock. Quickly snatching up the hunting sticks and staves which each boy had laid on the earth beside him while he watched the game, they forgot all about their clay cattle and hurtled over shrub and thorn to the rescue of the real animals. Splitting instinctively into two groups, shouting and crying out now not in pretence but in real fury, they left François well behind.

It all happened so quickly and confusingly that he himself made first of all for the boulder. Having climbed up it, quick as a rock-rabbit, he looked round him fearfully because there had been no mistaking the intent to kill in that lion's roar. He was just in time to see the smallest group of infuriated little boys fearlessly beating a huge, armour-plated crocodile over the head in order to force it to let go of a goat which it had by the throat and was slowly dragging backwards towards the river. At the same time another and larger group of boys had just reached the far end of the clearing and were beginning to pelt a huge, titian-haired lion with stones and sticks, shouting curses and challenges as it lay growling over the limp neck of the cow it had just savaged.

Soon the crocodile was so bewildered that it was forced to loosen its grip since its jaws, as all Bantu boys know, are in any case not very strong. The little black boys, who had the goat firmly by the hind-legs, were able to pull it clear. They were not in time to save its life. Even François, at a distance, could tell that it was dead. But they could preserve it for their own, rather than the crocodile's larder.

The lion, however, was a far more serious matter, as everyone knew. Once the goat had been dragged back into the clearing at a safe distance from the crocodile's hiding place in the river, the boys all rushed to the aid of their friends who were engaged in scaring away the lion.

Unfortunately the lion was refusing to be scared. Whenever a stone hit him too hard, or any of his tormentors came too near, he would charge, snorting, claws bared and pawing the air in a frightening manner in order to drive them away. It was François's first demonstration at close quarters of the extra-ordinary speed and power of the lion. Indeed, as he was to hear later, its speed is so great that over short distances it is one of the fastest animals on earth. In consequence the little boys, agile and athletic as they were, had to run as never before when it made one of its lightning rushes at them. Even then they might not have succeeded in getting clear if the other flank of their little army, which had infiltrated the clearing at the back of the lion, had not come rushing after it, pelting it from behind with stones and hurling sticks, staves and high-pitched abuse at it. The lion would then be compelled to whirl about and face this new threat in its rear.

They were helped, too, because the lion was just then not interested in killing any more. It was just waiting to enjoy its supper, and merely resented this unwarranted intrusion into its business and comfort. Indeed, François might have found the expression of outraged dignity which the lion wore on its face almost comic, if he had not feared so greatly for the safety of his naked companions. But they seemed to have gone mad with determination to prevent the lion from having his kill.

François's fear increased as his companions steadily became bolder and more reckless when the lion continued to fail to catch, let alone hurt any of their number. One little boy charging from behind the lion even appeared to François to be on the verge of reaching out to try and snatch at the lion's tail, presumably in order to twist it. From all that François had heard about lions he was certain that this would be the last indignity and most certainly change the lion's mood from one of outrage to one of implacable retribution. Fortunately the lion whirled about just before this became possible so fast that the reckless little black boy half stumbled in the quick side-step he was forced to take in order to evade the lion's retaliation. The stumble was providential because it spoilt the aim of a lightning thrust from the lion's left paw, the claws just missing the exposed naked flank of the boy by a razor's width. Had the lion swerved aside after the boy, François had no doubt that he would easily have overtaken him, so much had the boy been thrown out of the rhythm of his long stride, but the lion obviously had no taste for minor issues and was concentrating on the bulk of his enemy fleeing straight in front of him.

It seemed to François that the climax of this episode had arrived and that the lion had reached the limits of what passed for patience in him, and he was about to attack in earnest. He pursued the little boys at this moment far longer than before and at such speed that they were forced to take to the trees. They would not have achieved this successfully were they not as adept as monkeys in leaping for the nearest branches and swinging themselves clear of the ground, and had not the lion, on the critical point of launching himself full out at the nearest enemy, been distracted by the most determined attack of the afternoon in his rear. Yet already the change of mood had made itself manifest in the deepest growl and quickest turnabout of the whole afternoon. François knew it could not go on much longer like this without one or more of his companions joining the dead goat and cow. The little boys did not have it in their power to kill the lion. Equally, the lion did not possess the patience to endure indefinitely this intrusion into what was to him legitimate business. He was clearly just as determined not to be scared away from his meal as the little boys were determined not to allow him to enjoy his kill.

So perturbed was François by all this that he was thinking of jumping from the boulder and running the three-quarters of a mile to Hunter's Drift for help. Luckily he was spared so desperate and foredoomed a mission, since he could never have run that distance in time to save the situation for his companions. At that precise moment a great shout of deep bass voices, joined as one, went up from the bush.

The words of the shout were uttered with a passion and force that blurred their shape for François, but their meaning was clear: 'Kill the wizard, kill!' it commanded with all the authority with which freedom from fear invests the voices of the men of Africa.

All this made strange sense to François. It was one of the firmest beliefs of the pagan world at Hunter's Drift that wizards often assumed the shapes of lions for hunting when they felt like having roast beef for their midnight supper. Whatever the precise meaning of the words, however, their intent was clear and became clearer when suddenly 'Bamuthi burst through the bush, his ox-hide war-shield on his arm and his great spear *U-Silo-Si-Lambile* (The Hungry Leopard) in his hand. He was followed by half a dozen other herdsmen similarly armed.

Obviously the noise of the contest on the river bank had reached them, even in their kraals. Reading its urgent meaning at once they had rushed to the scene. The boys promptly withdrew to the edges of the clearing as if knowing that they had done as much as they could do and from now on would only get in the way. They resumed their role of spectators, unaware of how deep and how fast they were breathing from their desperate labour and how near to collapse they were with fatigue. They just stood there, their dark supple bodies shining like silk in the sun from the sweat running down them, their wide eyes bright and intense, watching the last act in this afternoon matinée of a classical theatre of fate in the life of the bush.

Led by 'Bamuthi, the herdsmen began manoeuvring to try and surround the lion. Instinctively the lion knew that any element of license there might have been in the afternoon was gone as far as he himself was concerned. From now on all would be a matter of life and death. Accordingly he sunk down low on his haunches beside the dead cow. His claws tested and re-tested the earth beside him as the toes of a runner would an Olympic track just before the starting pistol, in order to be certain that he had the right stance and grip for launching himself forward when the real danger came. All expression of anger and outraged dignity had gone from his broad brow and topaz eyes. His features and bearing, so like those of a great elder statesman of the bush, were joined in a tightly-strung mood of intense watchfulness.

First 'Bamuthi approached the lion slowly, a foot at a time, from the front, crouching behind his shield with the long spear at the ready, to give the impression that he was coming in for attack, so convincingly that all the lion's attention focused on him. Meanwhile, equally slowly, the other herdsmen began to close in a rough circle around him. The lion must have been aware of this because a sudden uncertainty showed on his face. His tail started beating the ground in a passion of unease and with such force that the red dust rose in the air and with it a noise that put fear into François's pounding heart. For a moment the lion looked as if he would whirl around to have a quick look behind him. But at that moment, 'Bamuthi raised himself to his full height, as if about to hurl his assegai. Taken in by so convincing a performance the lion appeared to gather himself for charging 'Bamuthi. He was about to spring when two of the herdsmen dashed in from behind and stabbed him in the flanks. Immediately the lion turned about with such speed that an assegai was wrenched from the hand of a spearman and left sticking in the lion's side. His yellow coat stained red with blood, deeply wounded, and with the assegai waving over his back, the lion yet managed to throw himself at his treacherous attackers with undiminished power and speed.

As he did so 'Bamuthi and two other men rushed in and stabbed the lion again and again, forcing it once more to whisk about. From then on the lion was whirling about with such speed, and his attackers dancing about him with such fury, that he vanished from François's sight in the clouds of dust sent up from the earth. The lion was clearly doomed, yet, with the characteristic courage of its species, he refused to accept defeat and went on rounding on his attackers with undiminished tenacity. As a result, judged by any standard of time, the battle between 'Bamuthi and his men and the lion lasted long. To a heart as anxious as François's it seemed to continue for ever.

Finally, a silence fell on the scene and 'Bamuthi and his companions walked out exhausted from a vortex of dust. One of them had the calf of his leg flapping like a red rag where the lion's claws had torn it; another had his buttocks streaming with blood. When the dust finally settled, François and his companions went forward fearfully to gather round 'Bamuthi and his six herdsmen all leaning on their shields, their broad chests heaving, as they silently and solemnly looked down on the dead lion with five spears in its body, lying beside the cow it had just killed. A snarl of defiance was still on its face where it had been arrested by death. They all stood looking at the lion with admiration as the men of some vanished Homeric age might have looked on the body of an heroic enemy. Then the birds in the bush could be heard once again, taking up evening song. A night plover or two piped up-river to show that the sunset hour shadows were lengthening and darkening the illuminated bush. It was all a little too much for the eight-year-old François. He could not have prevented himself from bursting into tears if 'Bamuthi had not done something to distract his attention.

'Bamuthi had turned his black marble back on the dead lion and was surveying the concourse of little black boys around him. Then he spoke in that deep, solemn voice that always came to him when a feeling of traditional authority and tribal responsibility claimed his mind and feelings.

'Our little brothers called us and we came,' he stated with massive deliberation. 'But why was it necessary to call us and for us to come?'

François knew instantly from the tone and the rhetoric of the question that another kind of moment of truth in the long afternoon had arrived.

None of his black companions answered. Free for the first time in their minds and emotions to give thought to their share of responsibility in the events of the afternoon, they seemed overcome by the magnitude of it all. They looked at 'Bamuthi with an unconscious plea of pardon as if they knew already what the final judgement of their conduct was going to be. But not even the oldest boy among them seemed to have the courage or the wit to speak.

'Judging by the sound that brought us from our kraals,' 'Bamuthi reprimanded them, not without scorn, 'you had words enough for the lion and one another. How is it that you have none for me?'

Even this brought no response from his hearers, who seemed shocked and hypnotized by their sense of guilt. In the end 'Bamuthi was forced to observe ominously: 'It is perhaps as well that you cannot talk of it now because so grave a matter will have to be discussed by all the clan in order to know what to do. Besides, there are the scattered cattle and sheep and goats to gather from the bush before it is too dark. Go to it at once!'

Preferring action to words just then, the boys immediately broke up into their original groups and dashed away into the bush where their herds had vanished. For a long while François could hear them calling out pleadingly to their favourite cow or goat to come to them. He himself stayed behind, physically and emotionally exhausted. He watched 'Bamuthi and the others deftly skin the dead goat and cow, cut them into pieces, place the best of the raw meat on their shields, and leaving one man behind to protect what they could not carry away, start back for their kraals at Hunter's Drift, bowed down with the weight of their burden.

Yet, loaded as he was, 'Bamuthi had strength enough to extend the little finger of his left hand to François and say, 'Come, Little Feather, it's been a long, black afternoon for us all.'

François took the finger willingly and, encouraged by this sign of solicitude from 'Bamuthi, asked out of fear of his companions, 'But what is to happen now, Old Father?'

'That will be for the *Indunas* [counsellors] to decide,' 'Bamuthi replied, as if he preferred not to talk about the matter at all.

François did not like his tone at all. He found himself stirred into defending his friends, saying, 'But it was not their fault, Old Father. It all happened so suddenly. Everyone did their best to save the cattle. Honestly, you should have seen how brave they all were!'

He got no further, because 'Bamuthi cut him short with unusual severity, no doubt because he himself was divided at heart.

'Enough for the day, Little Feather. All this must be properly investigated before more is said. You too can speak at the *Indaba* [tribal council] if you wish. But more talk now will just be wandering in the belly of a bullock' – the Sindabele for groping in the dark.

So urgent did 'Bamuthi consider the incident that the inquest, to give it its European equivalent, started that very night. From a talk with boys from his own kraal, 'Bamuthi gathered that they were taking refuge in a plea that they had been bewitched and would not have been caught out as they were if not under the most powerful of spells. They themselves put this forward all the more convincingly because it was not just an excuse but something in which they now, with hindsight, profoundly believed. This was clear from the note of awe in the voices with which they presented their case to 'Bamuthi. If no magic were involved, they asked him, how was it that a lion and a crocodile could have been brought to attack their herds at one and the same moment? Had there ever been such an overwhelming coincidence in the history of herding cattle among the Matabele?

'Bamuthi had to admit to himself that he knew of none and felt, as a matter not just of fairness but of the welfare of his clan, that he should make absolutely certain that no enemy of his people had enlisted the help of black magic to bring disaster to their cattle. Accordingly a messenger, with suitable gifts, was dispatched that very night over the hills to the rich valley a day and a half's walk away where one of the greatest sorcerers lived. In fact he was more than just a sorcerer; he was considered a seer and a prophet as well. His name was uLangalibalela. This name possessed a hint of a Sindabele honorific appropriate to the ancient nature of the man's high calling which one can only roughly translate as The Right Honourable Sun-is-Hot.

Despite his paradoxical name, The Right Honourable Sun-is-Hot had already helped 'Bamuthi's people, it was firmly believed, by making rain for them on much needed occasions as well as in the interpretations of strange omens, so that they could correct destructive trends in the pattern of their private and communal life. François had never seen him, but all he had heard filled him with awe. So, like his black companions, he waited in a state of almost unbearable suspense for the return of 'Bamuthi's messenger.

The messenger was not back an hour before it was made clear that uLangalibalela had not interpreted the event in a way which was going to help François's friends. It was true that as far as the goat was concerned, uLangalibalela supported their plea. He judged that it was obviously the work of some wandering Bakwena whom he divined had been in the vicinity of Hunter's Drift on the fatal afternoon. One of their number, he declared, had assumed the shape of a crocodile to snatch a fat goat for food; a disguise to be expected from them since, as their name denotes, Bakwena meant Men of the Crocodile, because the crocodile was their protector and totem. This pronouncement established uLangalibalela's credentials as nothing else could have done, because everyone in 'Bamuthi's kraal knew that a party of Bakwena on their way to work on the copper mines in the north had camped at the outspan by the ford on the day of the disaster.

But the lion was quite another matter. The lion, uLangalibalela judged, had acted entirely on his own behalf. The boys, he ruled, had reacted to his presence in the bush most irresponsibly (the word sent a shiver of apprehension through François) for they should have known, as every child should know, that the lion possessed powerful magic of its own. Ever since there had been Bantu men, they had had to beware of the ever-present danger, namely, that all the animals they hunted protected themselves by creating either a desire to sleep, or a decline in the watchfulness of the hunter. The greater and the more dangerous the animal, the greater its power to destroy the concentration of the men pursuing it. In the case of children and little boys this effect could be overwhelming unless, of course, they had been forewarned and equipped with powerful charms — especially, naturally, charms obtained from uLangalibalela.

Either, uLangalibalela continued, 'Bamuthi and the older people in the kraal were to be blamed for not having warned their children sufficiently, or the boys were delinquent in not recognizing instantly, when so great an excitement arose in the dead hour of the afternoon, that it was not a natural emotion at that time. It must, therefore, be the result of a powerful spell which one would expect from an animal so powerful as a lion. Since 'Bamuthi and his fellow-tribesmen had continuously impressed this aspect of concentration in their duty on their boys, and even exhorted François to be aware of it, François, sick at heart, feared the worst for his friends.

The goat, he knew would be forgiven them. But the cow was a far more serious matter. Not only were cows bigger and more valuable but they were also a revered link between the living Matabele and their dead ancestors. François had been taught, at an early age, that the spirit of the ancestors invested the cattle and spoke to their descendants particularly clearly through the sounds that they made in their kraals at night. He had even seen funerals in the bush where the dead owner's favourite black and white stippled heifer had been brought to stand at the foot of the grave and look on her dead master's face for the last time so that she could receive his spirit for safe keeping and transmission before the body was finally covered. Therefore he knew that the death of the cow would not be regarded merely as a materialistic loss but as a sacrilege.

It says a great deal, however, for 'Bamuthi's and indeed for

104

the whole kraal's instinctive sense of justice, that uLangali-balela's judgement was not instantly accepted as the final word and the investigation continued by summoning all the boys to an *Indaba* with the *Indunas*. There, 'Bamuthi exhorted them to full and frank confession with the traditional injunction: 'Let the receptacle of the ear be filled,' after which everybody was closely examined and patiently heard. Even François was given an opportunity to speak up for his friends which he did badly, so over-awed was he by the solemnity and the importance of the occasion, although all these beautiful old faces, and imposing and experienced grey heads, listened respectfully to his quavering young voice.

The final judgement, however, was never seriously in doubt. One morning after the milking, just before the flocks had to be taken out to graze, all the boys concerned were gathered in 'Bamuthi's kraal and made to lie naked on their stomachs with their arms stretched out in front of them. The women and girls had been rigidly excluded, and only the men, boys and male children, whimpering with presentiment, remained. 'Bamuthi himself had then produced a whip of fine impala leather and given each of the boys a dozen of the hardest lashes of which he was capable. François was certain that he could not possibly have endured a whipping without a moan or whimper of some sort. Yet to his amazement, as stroke after stroke fell, neither a sound nor a tremor came from the little black boys stretched out so helplessly on the ground. The moment a boy was thrashed he leapt to his feet and stood there, to François's amazement, upright, without a quiver and dry-eyed, looking straight ahead until all the whipping had been done and there was a line of some twenty little boys and still not a whimper or a tear from one of them.

François thought it one of the most impressive experiences of his life. He was aflame with pride for his companions. He was prouder still when he noticed that there was no sign of bitterness in the expression on their faces but only one of intense relief, if not actual achievement. They stood while 'Bamuthi and the other *Indunas* walked down their line, closely inspecting their eyes and faces and, at the end of the line, putting their heads briefly together to exchange words with one another before sending 'Bamuthi forward to announce loudly, with great satisfaction to all, 'Not a wet eye among them. A fierce lot of men are they.'

This, François knew then, was the test the boys must have feared even more than the punishment. It was astonishing how their faces shone when they heard the word 'men' conferred upon them because they knew as François did that the terrible matter was transcended and done with for ever. Indeed, the women and girls outside must have been waiting for just such a sign because hardly had this final verdict been pronounced than there went up one of the most exciting sounds in François's experience of life in the bush – the sound of glittering feminine Matabele voices making the quick vibrating sound of praise and welcome at the back of their palates which Europeans inadequately call ululating, but which is as near to the ringing of silver bells as the human voice can get.

It was the final sign that the boys had been restored fully to the grace and love of the clan. It was all very impressive and moving, and left François feeling curiously the odd person out as well as strangely inadequate. When he was older, thinking about it all as he often did, he was not at all certain that he could have carried such heavy responsibility as these friends of his, nor survived in so manly a fashion the feeling of guilt, the ordeal of trial, condemnation, and severe physical punishment by their elders.

François could not but feel glad that he himself had never been tested likewise. He remembered how close to one another this had brought all the kraals, how everyone in them, from the smallest baby to oldest grandmother and *Induna*, presented a great transcendent unity thereafter and how completely punishment had redeemed error. He remembered above all, how on the evening of the same day he had seen the boys comparing their scars as if they were war ribbons and a couple of the older lads nearly coming to blows because one claimed his scars were more pronounced and worthier than those of the other, and, as a result he was not certain that unwittingly the sum of the experience for him had not been the planting of a tiny, secret seed of envy deep within him. It was as if he would have liked not only himself but Lammie and Ouwa to be not the little outpost of estranged lives they appeared to be, but also incorporated into some such firm, definite and passionate a design of living.

The evening of atonement, as François came to think of the end of this day later on, was also memorable in another way. He was asked by 'Bamuthi to take the evening meal with him and his kraal in his principal hut. François did that often. His parents not only had no objection but encouraged it. François loved the occasions for the rewarding and exciting company and wonderful conversation. Besides, there was the food. There were two things 'Bamuthi's wife and daughters seemed to cook even better than Ousie-Johanna, though he would never have told the old lady so for fear of hurting her sensitive feelings.

They cooked a porridge of maize, or mealie meal, as they called it, far better than anything he got at home. They cooked it until the water was boiled away and it was a firm substance which one could take between one's fingers, roll expertly into a round ball and swallow with a wooden spoonful of curds and whey, and at some rare moments of perfection also with a lump of fierce black wild honey. At his age, eating with his fingers seemed a far more exciting business than with awkward utensils like knives, forks and spoons that continually tended to slop over and got one into trouble with fastidious spirits like Ousie-Johanna and Koba.

But the greatest of all foods to him was the porridge which he only got at 'Bamuthi's. It was made out of the millet, the grain the Matabele had brought down with them on their centuries' long march from the north of Africa, and which their own girls and wives pounded fresh daily in their tall wooden mortars as long as the year's store of grain lasted. They called it mabela and François was to remember nostalgically that it had an ancient flavour as if it were one of the first foods ever grown by man. This evening there was not only mabela, but tender wood-grilled goat's meat and some beer made from the same millet as the mabela.

Moreover, François was seated beside 'Bamuthi. 'Bamuthi and the boys had entered the hut first to see the huge, cast-iron pot set on its tripod over a ruby red bed of wooden coals, with a head of fragrant steam standing above it in the blue smoke-filled atmosphere of the hut. Clean wooden spoons, with long handles, had been placed against the iron pot, the amber ladles projecting high above the rim together with the steam and smell emanating from it. They immediately picked up the yellow mats woven from the finest Amanzim-tetse reeds and piled beside the entrance, unrolled them, and sat down in their centre; it was considered rude to sit otherwise in well-bred company.

The moment they were seated the women had come in with earthenware bowls of water for them to wash their hands, and then had unrolled mats for themselves until the hut was so full with people that an outer circle of young eaters had to be formed. The conversation, the wit, the repartee, the jokes and the stories which accompanied the eating were among the most entrancing François had ever encountered. There were times when he was so interested that he forgot to help himself to food and once had to be brought back to the outer world by 'Bamuthi exhorting him: 'Remember, Little Feather, that you must not forget to eat for two; the one that you are now and the one that you are to be.'

François had complied with such a will that some whey got into his nose and he sneezed violently. He could have done nothing better. Sneezing in the young was a good omen, and immediately all the people in one clear shout of approval called out to him: '*Tutuka*, Little Feather! *Tutuka!*' (Grow, Little Feather, grow!)

But for François the great event of the evening was a discourse of 'Bamuthi's at the end of the meal. He obviously had in mind the events of that morning but was careful to make no direct reference to them. Indeed, 'Bamuthi was so anxious not to be suspected of reviving the immediate past that he instinctively adopted the device of pretending to be speaking only for François's benefit. François, his lively imagination heightened to an extraordinary degree by recent events, took in every word. The gist of what 'Bamuthi said that evening was to become for him the definition of a Matabele 'gentleman'.

'You see, Little Feather,' 'Bamuthi had started at his evocative best, 'I remember when I was your age, sitting in the hut of my father at Osebeni on just such an occasion as this. The words he spoke to me then were the words that his father had spoken to him before; his grandfather before him; and so on back and back to the first man, who had them from Umkulunkulu. My old father warned me, as I say to you now, that a man-child cannot learn soon enough that life is not possible without a heart that knows no fear. Without a heart free of fear a man cannot protect either his cattle or his women and children and the life of the tribe, or that of the nation. He will not know how to speak the truth; how to protect the weak; and overcome beasts of prey and men with black hearts. Such men are fish-hearted and with their hearts of water are strangers from the truth. But, as you will have seen recently, some of the youngest of us are learning to find just such a heart.'

With a great effort of will 'Bamuthi prevented himself from looking at the boys he had in mind but a deep vibration of pride was unmistakable in his authoritative voice. Although the light in the hut was dim and François's own eyes were smarting with the blue smoke which now filled the atmosphere and hid the thatched roof of reeds above him, it seemed that the words started up such feelings of love in the boys concerned that suddenly their eyes shone like lamps in the shadows beyond him.

'Bamuthi had gone on from there at great length to expound how only after freedom from fear a man-child could start to learn how to defend himself against the physical dangers of his world, and learn how to endure pain and suffering without complaint. Above all a man-child had to learn to be patient because as Umkulunkulu himself said, 'patience was an egg which hatched great birds': even the sun which was bleeding into darkness outside was such an egg. For this reason the best that one Matabele could wish another was that life would allow him to 'Hamba Gashle'; that is, to go slowly. In the bush all bad things in life came out of haste since haste, too, was a child of fear, and he who hastened would surely stumble and know neither peace nor happiness nor prosperity. He, 'Bamuthi, knew that Europeans had many words for saying what he meant. But the Matabele had only one phrase, 'Hamba Gashle'. And if one observed this commandment all possible manner of other good things followed inevitably.

Yet a man-child also had to learn to fight against the hearts and minds of others who would deceive and try to destroy him and his people through treacherous words. For this reason a man-child must learn that he had to be well-spoken so that others could feel the truth as he felt it. Above all, he must defend the truth against the strangers who would come as they had always come, like locusts out of the north, to weaken first with their destructive tongues, before they moved in to wash their spears. He must be well-spoken also so that he could pass on the thoughts, names and deeds of his ancestors to his children from the days of Umkulunkulu onwards.

Being well-spoken, a man-child then would have to learn not to like his own words too much; nor to use them for his own ends. He must learn always to be truthful to the people of his own kraal and tribe. It might happen that there would have to be times when he would be forced to use his well-spokenness to deceive an enemy. But on no account was he ever to do so to his own people. Between him and his own kind, there could never be any secrets. That was the meaning of the saying that had come down from the ancestors, 'He who has killed in secret will hear it announced to all the world by the grass of the veld.' Secrecy was something that came out of fear. Until a man had learned to abolish habits of secrecy he did not have a heart free from fear.

Then a man-child also had to learn how to sing, and above all to dance; for dancing and singing were the best ways he had of showing gratitude for the good things of life. Song and, above all, dancing were the surest ways of helping a man to endure the great trials of his existence; they were needed at birth, marriage and before war to strengthen his heart. Also, after war, they were needed to exorcise the spirit of death in him, and at the moment when the final loss of his shadow was upon him and those he loved, to drive away the power of death and revive the desire to live. François, 'Bamuthi added, must have seen for himself how by dancing the magic circle with the sick, not in body but in heart, they danced back health into one another and made the divided person one with the tribe again.

Finally, the man-child had to become a man who, though he should never weep for himself, could weep easily for others. In order to do this he would have at times to go alone and sit apart at sunset by the Amanzim-tetse. He would have to go out into the kraal among the cattle and watch the stars for signs in the dark, and listen to the voices of the ancestors speaking through the sounds of the dreaming, contented cattle around him. In this way he would learn to ask in his heart for the things for which there were no words. Unless a person could ask in this way, he could not get the answers to protect him and his tribe from loss of spirit. This would mean, in the end, not only that the old praise names of Umkulunkulu would be forgotten: it would mean that the new praise names needed to promote the increase of spirit could not come. Thus the heart to endure, both in him and the tribe, would decline and die.

Here then is the final example of the great non-European influence that went into the shaping of François's imagination and contributed as much as the books in his father's study and his schooling to his education. When one considers his profound allegiance to the vanished world of the Bushman which had been implanted in him by old Koba, and one added to that the impact of the living example of the Matabele world provided by 'Bamuthi and the other kraals beyond the great hedge of fig trees at the end of the garden, it is difficult for one to think of him from now on just as a European child. Whatever the European influences were and however much they encouraged the sense of his European origin, the world of Koba and 'Bamuthi drew him deeper into a pattern that was the antithesis of Europe and to a significant extent made him uniquely of the earth and spirit of Africa.

There came a day, some years later, when a visitor, bolder than most, took it upon himself to upbraid François's father and remark: 'God man! How can you stand by and see your only son carrying on just like a white kaffir?' Unjustified as such an observation by a visitor to his host undoubtedly was, it must be said in fairness that François had played a certain role in provoking the outburst.

He had learned from his black companions by then also to play at clay soldiers and when his clay battalions, awkwardly made in comparison with those fashioned by his friends, were drawn up in the classical crescent formation prescribed by the highest Matabele military authorities, he would dance in front of them as a Matabele king was supposed to dance before leading his soldiers into battle.

He would think up his own words for the song which accompanied his dance, although there was ready to hand a traditional song thought to be very effective on these occasions. This song had been danced first long ago by a famous Matabele hero called u-Ndaba and it became famous not only because it meant that his enemies were invariably scattered but also at one time it had unfailingly brought on rain. The first time François had ever danced it by some curious coincidence it had brought down upon Hunter's Drift, when badly needed, an abrupt and violent thunderstorm, followed by a heavy downpour of rain. This coincidence immediately raised a superstitious suspicion in Matabele kraals that there might have been some connection between François's dancing and the fall of rain. Coincidences to them were never idle, and the consequence of this particular one was revolutionary, since they themselves had long since given up using this song and dance for the purpose of making rain fall, because for generations it had failed them and they believed their powers to have perished with the great u-Ndaba himself. Their original belief, however, was reconfirmed when some two years later, in another period of drought, 'Bamuthi provoked François into performing the same dance again. And again it rained the following night. 'Bamuthi's explanation to his tribe for François's success was simple. Since power clearly had passed from the black to the white man it was not surprising that the son of a Great White Chief should have the gift of making 'the long serpent of water' and other spirits concerned hear him, as they could no longer hear the weakened Matabele.

François himself had no idea why he was, from time to time, exhorted to give an exhibition of this dance. 'Bamuthi took great care that he should not know, not because he wished to deceive him but because he believed, as he told his kraal, 'It is better in these matters not to know how a person is being called, for often to know is to drive out the power to answer the call.'

The morning after the discourse then, François was subtly provoked into doing his dance. It was a particularly arid day and he started to dance close by the Matabele kraals just when the Matabele herdsmen and their male children had brought in the cattle in readiness for the evening's milking. All, however, broke off work to watch François's performance. They kept one

112

eye on the young boy as he leapt up and about and brought his bare feet heavily down on the earth to make it vibrate like a drum, at the same time emitting the dread sound that would put fear into the heart of the enemies of the Matabele. The other eye, of course, the herdsmen kept on a great formation of thunderclouds that were massing in the north-west as might a fleet of sail for battle.

His hair was burnt almost a platinum white by the sun, because François only wore a khaki bush hat when hunting, in order to provide shade and camouflage for his head and face which Mopani had taught him were features most likely to betray a stalker to his quarry. And also because Ouwa thought it unhealthy for boys to wear hats even under so hot an African sun. François, with his blue eyes and fair young skin, tanned and fresh as a peach, could not have been more obviously European. But the sounds that came out of his throat and the movements that shook his long legs and arms and a body, rather tall and broad-shouldered for its age, came from far back out of the savage and heroic Matabele past, with the sole exception that, instead of calling on u-Ndaba as tradition demanded, François had substituted his own name.

As his legs rose and stamped down on the earth faster and harder and he leapt higher and whirled about before his feet crashed down once more, he sang and shouted the refrain again and again with increasing force and volume, trying in vain to make his shrill young voice deep and strong:

'*u-François u-Inkosi!* (François is King)
Oho! O!
Ha! Oyeeh!
Jijidgi! Jijidgi!'

The *Oho!*, *O!*, *Ha!*, and *Oyeeh!* were utterances of scorn, sheer and unmitigated; the *Jijidgi!* an imperative to warriors to go in and kill.

This, of course, was a picture of gross over-simplification if considered out of context, as the visitor might have observed had he stayed on to see François instructing his companions at other times how to play Greeks and Trojans, or equipping them with glittering shields battered out of empty four-gallon paraffin

113

tins, and long lances made out of the straightest mopani wood. In their game of make-believe he made them into Knights of the Round Table in search of an appropriate quest in the bush, which was the nearest African equivalent to the dark medieval wood of the Malory he had discovered in his father's study. No passing observer could possibly have known therefore of this great heraldic influence in François's life, nor how Mopani Théron had captured as great a segment of his imagination as either 'Bamuthi or Koba had done, but more of that later. This must be enough to give a valid hint of the kind of 'other person' François had in essence become that day he and Hintza rescued Xhabbo from a lion-trap and he found himself late for the mid-day meal facing his ill and exhausted father at table.

4 • Foot of the Day

'Oh Coiske,' Lammie gently reproached François as he spread out his napkin on his knees, 'why do you choose today of all days to be late?'

Already made uncomfortable by being late, as well as by possession for the first time in his life of a secret that he could not share, François would have been unable to find an appropriate word of excuse. Luckily he was saved from having to do so by his father. For once Ouwa did not seem to find it necessary to support Lammie as he always did, even in the smallest things. It was as if his mind, through pain and sickness, was working in a dimension where things like 'being late' or 'in time' were no longer important. He merely looked up from his own cover and tried hard to adopt a certain ironic insouciance which was his favourite pose for containing his affection for François. He then started teasing him in that slightly pedagogic way that involuntarily came to him when confronted with anybody young, even someone so familiar as François.

'What of the bush, oh hunter?' he asked in a voice taut with effort and pain. 'Is it true, this enormous lie that has preceded your coming? Have you really succeeded in killing an outsize leopard?'

Grateful as François was for the question he was, as always, somewhat put out by his father's teasing. It made him feel small and rather self-conscious. None the less he was glad of it as a diversion and began his story of the day from the moment Hintza had woken him just before dawn. As he talked his confidence returned, particularly when he started describing Hintza's almost extra-sensory perceptive role. Encouraged further by the obvious look of interest that came to both Ouwa and Lammie, in the end he told his story rather well.

He was helped, too, by the fact that Ousie-Johanna seemed

to have cooked one of his favourite dishes as a first course to the meal. It was a Hunter's Drift speciality, a kind of milk soup made out of fresh milk and home-made noodles with black Natal sugar and sticks of fragrant cinnamon. The moment Lammie lifted the cover of the dish to serve them, there was a magical scent of milk and cinnamon in the cool air of the great dining-room, a spice with which François associated all the wonder and mystery of the far Far East.

It smelt particularly good to him on this day because he was exceptionally hungry. For a moment he had even the temerity to assume that Ousie-Johanna might have cooked it specially for him, because in shooting the leopard he had killed one of the worst enemies of civilized life at Hunter's Drift. But soon, in the midst of talking and eating, he was disillusioned.

From where he sat he had a view of the open door that gave on the passage leading to the pantry. When his own eyes were accustomed to the shaded noon-day light he saw within the frame the dark glowing eyes, the plump, creased, benign features of Ousie-Johanna. What on earth could she be doing there?

The answer came when he noticed that the eyes were not on him but fixed on Ouwa. She was obviously watching, in a state of great anxiety, to see whether this fragrant dish was to his liking. Unfortunately he only took a spoonful or two of the delicious soup before laying down his heavy silver soup-spoon as if he could not bear the effort any more. Leaning back in his chair, he half closed his eyes and just urged François not to leave out a single detail of his story, as if it seemed to relieve his mind from the oppression of the pain.

When that happened, François, out of the corner of his eye, noticed Ousie-Johanna quickly putting a plump hand to her eye and heard a faint: 'Oh no! Dear little Lord in Heaven, oh no!' break from her before she vanished into the shadows of the passage beyond.

He knew then that the dish had been cooked specially for Ouwa because it was the most powerful medicine in her long repertoire of dishes for making those who were not well better. In his own convalescence from afflictions like measles, scarlet fever, malaria and mumps, Ousie-Johanna, to his great delight, had never failed to see that not a day passed without liberal helpings of this rich milk food. But such occasions shrank to insignificance compared with that of the present with its scale heightened as it were by the acute sense of crisis for his father. As a result of this poignant gesture of solicitude and despair from Ousie-Johanna, he had from then on only to get a faint whiff of cinnamon and no matter how unlikely the circumstances or urgent the preoccupations of his own mind, he would be instantly transported back to the dining-room at Hunter's Drift and re-experience all as it unfolded about him now.

This dish was followed by another, not one of his own favourites, but one he knew both his parents loved, a fricassee of fresh calves' liver and bacon cooked in dry sherry, sent to Ouwa annually at Christmas by his cousins who made wine in the south. Again the face of Ousie-Johanna appeared anxious and hopeful at an angle of the door and again, when François's father had only nibbled at the dish, there came that little demonstration of despair that drove the grand old lady of the kitchen back into the shadows.

Meanwhile, François was being exhorted by Lammie at one minute not to forget his food, the next by Ouwa to get on with his tale. He was only once interrupted seriously in the telling, however, and that was when he described how he had had to choose between taking his ·22 repeater or the beautiful old muzzle-loader out into the bush. He found himself hesitating then because he realized that he could not be frank about the consideration which finally had determined his choice of the heavy old muzzle-loader; namely that he had decided against going to the armoury in the hall in case the wide wooden floor-boards, which creaked so easily and loudly, would wake his father from his much-needed sleep. This aspect had to be omitted. As a result he made his final choice of a weapon sound more impulsive and far less thoughtful than it had been.

His father, quick as always in his appraisals, at once broke in curtly: 'But surely the ·375 express rifle with its magazine of five would have been a better choice. Did you not think of that?'

'I did in a sort of way,' François answered awkwardly.

'Only in a sort of way?' his father asked sharply. 'Surely it needed consideration in every possible way?'

François could only repeat that he had given it thought but

117

decided finally that the muzzle-loader, considering he had had so much practice with it, would do as well.

'You disappoint me, Coiske. I thought you more mature.' Ouwa spoke with a mildness that made the rebuke all the more acute. 'You must forgive me but I don't think in the circumstances that was either a wise, necessary or useful way of looking at it.'

All this made François smart bitterly within. He would have loved to explain to his father what had really gone on in his mind: above all how he had been thinking of Ouwa's wellbeing, knowing clearly the risks to which he was exposing himself in settling for the muzzle-loader. But he knew that all the benefit of his forethought would be cancelled if he made Ouwa aware of how deeply he, François, was concerned about the state of his father's health. It might even perhaps make his father realize that everyone at Hunter's Drift was desperately worried about him.

So he went on with his story determined, but sadly philosophical at heart. He had often been in the position of experiencing a feeling of utter helplessness at his inability to make grown-ups understand his real motives in certain situations. He had, in a measure unusual for someone of his age, learned to make his peace with the fact that there were situations in which one just had to remain unfairly suspect by one's elders and betters. He could think of a dozen occasions when what was obvious to him had remained incomprehensible to Lammie, Ouwa and Ousie-Johanna. But, oddly enough, this had never happened with old Koba; probably because as a Bushman she herself had been exposed to injustice and lack of understanding too long not to recognize it instantly when they affected others.

But this difference between him and Ouwa, entrenched in the marked valedictory atmosphere of the meal, was the most difficult one of the lot to endure. Yet necessity made him accept Ouwa's reproof without further argument.

'Perhaps it was not a wise thing to have done,' he said deliberately appeasing, and hurried on to complete his account, leaving out only the part connected with the rescue of Xhabbo. But the fact that he had been unable to tell the truth about his choice of gun went deep and hurt so much that it became a milestone in his emotional development, as one will have cause to observe later. On the other hand, the fact that he could not reveal his secret about Xhabbo ceased to give him regret from now on. It seemed to him more than ever a matter of dire necessity and his own special responsibility, which could not be fairly imposed even in part upon Ouwa and Lammie, who clearly had so much to worry about just then.

Fortunately, the meal ended with handsome words of praise from Ouwa for the killing of the leopard, before he went off to his afternoon's rest. François could forget his sense of injury and felt himself free to hurry to the kitchen to have a word with Ousie-Johanna.

She was sitting at her wide table, made of plain whitewood, as always scrubbed so clean that its surface shone like satin. She sat with her multiple chin supported by both her hands, and the light of the vivid placid afternoon flaming against the wide white windows showed up every detail of her skin. François could not fail to notice the dark streaks where many tears had dried on her cheek.

'What's the matter, little old Ousie?' he asked, using all the endearments of which his native language was capable.

'It's just no be-damned good, Little Feather,' Ousie-Johanna replied vehemently, using the only swear word François had ever heard her use and one that only came to her when she was in extreme emotional stress. 'It's no be-damned good. Did you see, he didn't touch any of the food I have been thinking out for him all night long and spent the whole morning preparing, better than I have ever prepared food before? And he hardly touched any of it. It's no be-damned right. The man is blerrie-well (her idea of bloody-much) bewitched, he should go straight to uLangalibalela without any more waste of time. I am going straight to that Lammie of yours and will tell her so.'

Lammie always became 'François's Lammie' when Ousie-Johanna was indignant with her, just as she always became 'my Lammie' when Ousie-Johanna was pleased with her.

François tried hard to persuade her not to do so although his dismay was as great as hers, and his own secret inclination to believe that only a witch-doctor might have the cure for Ouwa's mysterious illness, was rapidly becoming as strong as her own and 'Bamuthi's. He might not have succeeded, had not a thought come to him that since witch-doctors were such powerful people they could perhaps cure people without the persons concerned actually being taken to them. Accordingly he interrupted Ousie-Johanna's third reiteration to have a 'smart, straight word or two' with 'his Lammie' in order to ask her:

'Tell me, little old Ousie, is it not possible for somebody to be cured by a witch-doctor without going to see the man? Can't others go on his behalf?'

Ousie-Johanna for a moment looked quite stunned by the thought, not so much because of its originality, but because it was so obvious and yet had not occurred to any of them before.

'You are a slim little skelm' – a phrase meaning an intelligent little rogue and, when used with the right intonation at the right moment, a term of both admiration and affection.

'By the living little Lord in Heaven, I think it is perfectly possible, but why don't you go at once and ask 'Bamuthi? He'll know for sure, that slim Matabele who throws so fine a shadow!' This was a great Bantu compliment to the reality of the person to whom it is applied.

François immediately went out to the kraals to consult 'Bamuthi. He was told without hesitation by 'Bamuthi, whom he regarded as the ultimate authority in these matters, that provided someone went armed to the witch-doctor with something of Ouwa's person like a nail clipping, or best of all a hair of his head, the witch-doctor could most certainly remove the spell cast upon him without Ouwa himself having to be present.

François was exhorted there and then to make certain that he secured a hair of his father's head. Then, if the doctors in the capital failed them he, 'Bamuthi, could arrange for the great uLangalibalela to deal with the spell which he was still convinced the Government had put upon Ouwa.

Encouraged by this ruling of 'Bamuthi, François hastened back to reassure Ousie-Johanna and continued for the rest of the day to help Lammie with her packing. He was lighter at heart than he had thought at lunch he could ever be, because for the first time now they had an alternative which they could try if the doctors failed.

Close beside this huddled another secret cause of warmth in

his spirit. The days between Lammie and Ouwa's going and their return would not now be so empty as he had feared because he had this great, exciting task which life had so unexpectedly thrust on him that morning: he had to heal, protect and set Xhabbo on the way back to his people in the great desert to the west.

There was only one further sad element in an afternoon which passed quickly with so much to do. It was when he carried out to Ouwa on the stoep a tray of coffee and some of Ousie-Johanna's best rusks and afternoon buns, brown as gypsies on top and below, and white as milk-foam in between.

This was almost a sacred ritual at Hunter's Drift. Ever since François could remember he, Ouwa and Lammie had always met on the stoep on the west side of the house, to watch the sun go down over cups of coffee, buns and rusks. They would sit there, happily exchanging the news of the day until the moment came when the sun was about to touch the horizon. At that point it was remarkable how they would always stop talking, and watch the sun vanish in a silence which seemed to François full of wonder and awe. No two sunsets were ever alike and François could not remember a single one which did not have an immense drama and splendour of its own. He himself would become so involved with these aspects of it that a sunset became not just an external event but something happening deep within himself. The time was to come when he would feel as if his imagination faced some profound mythological pronouncement in this daily event, for which no amount of familiarity could breed contempt, but only an increasing sense of wonder and, in some strange way, a kind of dependence of his peace of mind emerge from it. But for years he just read all sorts of stories into it and saw its final phase as the conclusion of some great epic, illustrated in the most wonderful of colours and accompanied by a feeling as of great music drifting up towards him from the other side of the world.

It was extraordinary how all three of them felt frustrated and jangled if something happened to interfere with this evening ritual, perhaps because, as Lammie put it once after a particularly moving sunset which had made her take his hand in her left and Ouwa's in her right: 'It makes one feel so belonging, we, the bush, the birds, all at Hunter's Drift, the animals, even the bats [she loathed them normally] all part of one another and all at one.'

The return from this mythological moment to reality always came when the evening was established, and they saw the bats emerge from the direction of the cliffs by the river and start their zigzag lightning darts through the brown air, staining the scarlet light dying in the west with streaks of Indian ink. Then an altogether new sort of conversation would start up and some of the best of François's childhood moments occurred, because the colourful fall of night seemed to compel the return of the imagination of all grown-ups to a resplendent past, which François to his regret had missed.

This afternoon was no exception. When he appeared Ouwa had tried to look up as if all were normal, thanked him with a brief, sardonic, 'You are indeed a scout', and then showed that his powers of observation were still keen by noticing that Hintza was not with François and observing with mock surprise: 'What, no faithful hound at your heel?'

François explained that Hintza, ever since his return from the lion trap, had been sleeping in the shade of the big flowering acacia tree in the centre of the courtyard at the back. He said this with some heat to justify Hintza's behaviour, in case Ouwa might think his resting was a sign of weakness. He was stressing at length the extraordinary exertions to which Hintza had been put that day, in particular the long sparring match with the mob of vultures, when Ouwa silenced him.

With a smile of ironic affection on his ascetic face, he observed with gentle amusement: 'You protest too much, sir! He who excuses, accuses. I was not casting aspersions on the capacities of your hound; merely registering surprise. It had just occurred to me that since I presented him to you on just such an evening as this, some eighteen months ago, this is the first time I have seen you without him.'

At that moment Lammie joined them, poured out the coffee in the traditional manner and together they prepared to watch the sun go down. It was a clear evening without a cloud, whisp of moisture, or veil of dust in the sky. François could follow the sun until its last segment was poised in a sliver of gentle orange on the dark blue line of the horizon. So clear was it then that there was a silhouette as of black lace above the far ocean swell of land, drawn Japanese-wise on a screen of silk light by the tops of the tall trees in the bush between Hunter's Drift and the western desert.

At that moment, for the first time that François could remember, his father broke the ritual of silence and exclaimed, not in English but in Sindabele. '*Langa, valela.*'

This 'Goodbye, sun' was uttered in such a final manner that it aroused all François's worst fears.

He turned from the words as if from the lash of a whip and pleaded, 'Please Ouwa, don't say it like that.'

Ouwa, of course, made light of it, because it was obvious that both the going of the sun and François's reaction, revealing such a depth of natural feeling for his father, had upset him more than he cared to admit.

'Why not, oh hunter,' he answered in as gay a tone as he could summon. 'What better way of saying farewell to the day? These moments are moments of long and ancient standing in nature and need ancient words to acknowledge them. What could be more ancient than the *valela* of the Matabele? For have you considered with the knowledge of Latin which I have tried too hard to instil in your teeming brain, that *valela* could well have come from the ancient Romans themselves, since it is just an orchestration of the Latin farewell, the *vale* of Rome?'

From there he went on at great length, hiding himself and his feelings in the smokescreen of discourse, to enlarge on one of the most beloved of his many theories which argued that since Bantu man had slowly come over the millenniums out of the far and mysterious north of Africa, he may at some Mediterranean moment of his history have had contact with the earliest Romans and acquired some of their vocabulary. *Vale* indeed was not the only evidence for such a theory. There were other words, like the *ene, bene*, the one, two, which began the Bantu system of counting. Even more imposing, there were great sonorous words like *innunadata*, the Zulu indication of a flood, to suggest a suspicion of influence from the Latin.

He argued all this eloquently and long, with many examples from 'Xhosa, Zulu and Sindabele, but François was not deceived. He went to bed that night firmly convinced that there was more to that farewell than just a classically appropriate salute to another great sunset. So convinced was he of this that he might not have gone to sleep had he not been in possession of an antidote to his disquiet ever since 'Bamuthi had ruled that they had an alternative method of dealing with his father's sickness. They had uLangalibalela whose name, significantly enough, was also connected with their great sun.

François was awake at four in the morning to see Ouwa and Lammie prepare to get in the lightest, fastest and best sprung of their mule wagons, which was to take them to Hunter's Drift Siding to catch the early morning express train from Livingstone and the Victoria Falls to the capital. Ouwa had already ruled a week before that François was on no account to come with them. Life, he said, consisted of a process of turning pages and when they had to be turned, they were best turned quickly and firmly. François had protested but in vain. Ouwa would not give in and one wonders whether in doing so he was not consulting his own emotional conveniences more than those of his son, for one cannot disguise from oneself the suspicion that it might have been easier for François to adapt himself to his first separation from both Ouwa and Lammie simultaneously if he had had the journey to and from the station with all its excitement, novelty and minor exigencies to occupy his imagination.

However, all François could do was to be in the dining-room in his place at the table, with a rejuvenated and wide-awake Hintza sitting beside him. Lammie and Ouwa joined him. François swallowed his coffee and rusks eagerly, Lammie did her duty by her own portion but no more.

What Ouwa would have done to his portion one shall never know because he was not given the chance. Ousie-Johanna was in no mood to give him the benefit of the doubt. She had her own ideas of what was most fitting, and the person who thought she could be denied in what she regarded as a moment of crisis in her duty and responsibility, would have underestimated the formidable queen of the Hunter's Drift kitchen. As Ouwa sat down, she appeared with a great blue china jug out of which the steam was rising and a smell of the utmost power emanating, until the atmosphere was so charged with it that the sensi-

124

tive Hintza was forced to sneeze violently. François was not at all surprised because it was not his favourite smell either. It was the aroma of the dreadful herb *buchu* – a sort of Bushman panacea for all the ills of the flesh and blood and one in which not only Ousie-Johanna but all Matabele and even Lammie believed. In Lammie's case it was confined to believing in it as a cure for colds and influenza in the winter. But Ousie-Johanna set no such limits to its powers. She produced the jug like some female Merlin with a magic brew, stood it firmly on the table, placed a large white mug beside it and announced uncompromisingly: 'You blerrie-well drink some of this *buchu,* Ouwa, or Ousie-Johanna will never speak to you again I may go on cooking for you and my Lammie for as long as I live but the Ousie-Johanna who had always looked after you, well, she just will not speak to you again.'

Somewhat astonished by Ousie-Johanna's behaviour and yet moved by the solicitude which ran like a thread of gold through her turbulent manner, Ouwa smiled his wry ironic smile, dutifully filled the mug and slowly raised it to his lips. But before touching it the powerful smell seemed to make even his experienced self shrink back.

'Come on Ouwa, you blerrie-well drink that down!' Ousie-Johanna, feeling he was about to fail her, exhorted him, 'you know that there's nothing in the world like *buchu* for protecting a man about to go on a journey in the cold hours of morning. You know how many times I have cured the three of you from serious illnesses with my *buchu* that I make better than anybody. There was my sister at death's door and I ...'

'My dear Ousie,' François's father replied, the mug at his lips: 'Would you please stop lying to me? I already believe you!' With that he put the mug to his mouth and drank down the *buchu* as fast as possible.

When he had finished he made a face at François and said: 'No greater love of woman has a man ever shown than in this ... I will give you three good reasons why I should not have touched the stuff. One, I detest the taste. Two, I believe it is utterly useless. Three, in so far as I have room left in my contracted stomach, I would much rather have given it over to some hot sweet coffee.'

But nothing that he could say, even in jest, could possibly dim the light of triumph and contentment that he brought to Ousie-Johanna's face; a light which perhaps warmed him more than the hot *buchu* had done. Ousie-Johanna's intervention too, had helped to introduce a certain element of comedy into the occasion, making the parting from his parents that followed soon afterwards easier than it might otherwise have been.

François now had to give his mind to Xhabbo. Dark as it still was, he would have liked to set out for the cave in which he had left the little Bushman as soon as the sound of the wagon wheels and the clip-clop of the hooves of the mules had faded away into the bush. But that was not possible without arousing Ousie-Johanna's suspicions. All he could do was to beg her to let him have his breakfast as soon as possible, saying that he intended to go off into the bush and see if he could not get some nice fat gum bustards, the wild peacock of his people, and birds that Ousie-Johanna always coveted. Ousie-Johanna obviously thought that François had the right sort of priorities in giving first thought to her larder in this manner, so she set about preparing one of his favourite breakfasts. She had, in any case, decided in the night to do this because she secretly feared what this first separation from Lammie and Ouwa might do to François.

While she was busy François was free to go to the great store-room on the other side of the courtyard, unlock it as he was now the official keeper of the keys at Hunter's Drift, go in and select three of the largest and best pieces of beef biltong, the sun-cured meat of his people, which were suspended in row upon row from the rafter. Biltong, in pioneering households such as theirs, played the same role as tinned meats in a modern home. It was the traditional stock against shortage of fresh food, since it kept almost indefinitely and was an essential element of provisions for journeys and expeditions into the bush. More important even on this occasion, biltong was considered to be meat in one of its most digestible and nourishing forms. Thinly sliced or grated it was always given as a tonic to invalids in convalescence.

At the same time François helped himself to a generous

amount of raisins and dried peaches, which they received regularly from their cousins in the south and which were a first-rate substitute for fresh fruit when their brief season at Hunter's Drift was over.

He carried all this back to his room unseen by an Ousie-Johanna who was in high spirits, humming her favourite hymn, 'Abide with Me', not sadly and solemnly but quite gaily, with a natural syncopated rhythm and urgency, as if it were some 'Xhosa song of innocence and joy. She did this so loudly that she could be heard all over the house. François quickly wrapped his supplies in paper, spread them at the bottom of the haversack that he always used when out in the bush for a day and prepared the old muzzle-loader which had served him so well the day before, by ramming not a solid lead bullet but a great handful of lead pellets down the barrel, transforming it into a shot gun. None the less he also took a supply of solid lead bullets with him just in case, though he thought it extremely unlikely he would need them at an hour of the day when the bush was, as everybody knew, exceptionally free of menace. Then, fully armed, he arrived in the kitchen and, despite his impatience to be off, ate the kind of huge breakfast which could not fail to please Ousie-Johanna and helped him to persuade her to make an extra large round of ham and cheese sandwiches and fill the largest thermos flask they had with hot sweet coffee. She saw him out of the kitchen with undisguised approval of the way he had reacted to her scheme for mitigating his parents' departure. Pausing only to equip himself with more medicine for Xhabbo, slinging an extra flask of water over his left shoulder, with Hintza at his side, he made off for the bush just after sunrise.

He had already decided in the night that he must avoid approaching the cave where Xhabbo was hidden always from the same direction. If he did so, he was certain he would arouse the suspicion of 'Bamuthi and the Matabele community, since he had never observed a regular pattern before, in his many excursions to the bush. Instead of going the short way past the Matabele kraal, he went off in the opposite direction as if he were going to look at one of the other traps set in the tracks to the west of the homestead. But once well hidden in the bush, he took an appropriate game track – there was not a track within a dozen miles of Hunter's Drift that François did not know by heart – and in a round-about way came to the horn of hills on top of which Xhabbo was sheltering in his cave. He also took great care to see that he and Hintza left no spoor in any of the main tracks they crossed and climbed the hills from stone to stone, avoiding breaking any of the branches and twigs or shrubs or trampling the long, yellow tasselled grasses.

He was amazed how much more difficult the climb was than he remembered from the previous day. He wondered more and more as they climbed how someone so severely hurt as Xhabbo was, could ever have made the ascent successfully. His admiration for Xhabbo increased the higher he went. When he was right at the top and could see the Amanzim-tetse's brown water churning at the base of the dark blue cliff, he thought for some minutes that he was not going to find the way to the cave again. Disconcerted, he looked around him to find that he had no clear idea how to proceed. It was a great blow to his pride, because he would have thought that by now his bushcraft was as good as anybody else's at Hunter's Drift and that said a lot, with so many experienced Matabele trackers about, and yet, good as it was it appeared to have failed him. He would have liked to excuse himself, pleading that he had been so concerned over Xhabbo's plight the day before that his mind had not been free to observe the way as closely as he should have done, except that he knew the plea was not good enough.

Had not his chief instructors in these things, 'Bamuthi and Mopani Théron, impressed upon him over and over again, that the most elementary lesson of security in the bush was always to make absolutely certain that one knew all the signs one would need to bring one back the way one had come. In his perplexity he turned to Hintza. Hintza was beginning to be impatient again and had started nudging him in the leg as he always did when he thought it was time that François both took notice of him and really got a move on when there was urgent work to be done.

François bent down, scratched Hintza fondly on the back of his ears and along the magnetic ridge on his back. Hintza raised his head appreciatively to François, and at the same time wrinkled and rewrinkled his beautiful shining black nose as it focused and refocused by reflex on some scent of meaning to him, clearly indicating to François: 'Can't you smell what I am smelling and do the necessary?'

François got the message at once. 'Lead on Hin,' he whispered to him in Bushman. 'Lead on. But not too fast! See that you keep close to me.'

Hintza at once led off carefully, stopping whenever he was in danger of losing contact with François; looking over his shoulder to see that François was keeping station close behind him. Soon they were back among the boulders and wild raisin bushes François thought he recognized from the day before. Still he was not absolutely certain, until he came to a particularly large and smooth boulder. Then he recognized it instantly as the one over which he had had to help Xhabbo climb the day before. But his recognition was due, he realized, not to the shape of the boulder, but because there was an unmistakable streak of blood across its shiny surface, obviously from the terrible wound in Xhabbo's leg.

Before climbing over the boulder, he unslung his flask of water, poured some of the precious liquid on his khaki bush handkerchief, and carefully removed all traces of blood from the stone. Then he scrambled up the boulder himself.

He was about to jump down the other side when he saw on the top of one of the highest points of the hill, directly opposite him, one of his favourite animals. It was a rare and a privileged glimpse of the smallest antelope of the bush, a little klipspringer ram. The klipspringer (literally, boulder-jumper), so called because of the prodigious chamois jumps of which it was capable was, both to the Matabele and the Bushman a beloved creature, gentle and beneficent. It was the hero of many an African fairy tale, a kind of princely and graceful Tom Thumb who always intervened in the stories told around the evening fire in the bee-hive huts all over the land, to enable good to triumph over evil, beauty over ugliness, and to save the unprotected and the weak from destruction by giants and other tyrants of the bush. François knew many of these stories and remembered one, above all, told to him by old Koba.

In her story the klipspringer was the favourite among all the creatures created by the Bushman god, Mantis. It told how Mantis himself had fed the little antelope and made it strong and beautiful with the sweetest wild honey: another way of saying that Mantis had devoted to the little animal all the sweetness of disposition of which he was capable. There was a particularly touching episode when Mantis once had to rescue the klipspringer from an elephant. The elephant in the Bushman world (unlike that of the Matabele) played the same role as one-eyed giants in François's Greek legends or wicked giants in his European fairy tales. It was always threatening the life of the innocent and small to which the little Bushman people attached such overwhelming importance. In this episode Mantis was deep down a hole in the side of the hills where some wild bees had made their nest. He was extracting one translucent comb after another of the sweetest honey for his beloved klipspringer, and throwing them up to it, singing out as he did so: 'Eat, my honey-child, eat and grow and tell me you are happy!' Whereupon the klipspringer would thank him in a lovely soft, reed-like voice.

Suddenly a great shadow fell over the hole. An elephant, long suspicious of Mantis's doings, and with a tooth as sweet if not sweeter than any other animal in the bush, had come down on the place determined to have the honey for himself. So greedy was this great bull elephant that he swallowed not only the honey lying on the grass outside but the little klipspringer as well.

The moment Mantis became aware of the shadow, he called back alarmed: 'You are eating and growing well, honey-child?'

Instead of a sweet call of gratitude the elephant, in vain trying to imitate a klipspringer call, replied gruffly and ungraciously: 'How can I grow, when you give me so little to eat!'

Instantly Mantis knew evil was about. In the fiery manner characteristic of him, he jumped out of the hole and, tiny as he was, snatched up a porcupine quill lying near at hand, jumped into the mouth of the elephant and forced it to swallow him. Once well inside the elephant's stomach, he proceeded to prick and tickle him so violently and regularly with the sharp porcu-pine quill that the elephant, overcome by cramp and nausea, was compelled to vomit up both the klipspringer and Mantis before any harm could come to them. Disgusted, he then went walking away from the place.

A similar little klipspringer François now saw was standing on the hill opposite him, its neat little black hooves delicately lacquered and above them the long slim legs, covered with short golden hair. Above the legs was a well-proportioned little body, also covered with golden hair which at this moment was so charged with the light of the early morning sun that it seemed to flicker with fire, up and along an erect neck to a proud little head, crowned with a pair of neat horns, black and polished, and flashing like mirrors in the clear morning light.

François thought he had never seen this little animal look so beautiful, nor so innocent and unafraid. Though aware of François and Hintza, it just looked, fascinated, in their direction. But, knowing itself safe on the peak on which it stood it spared them only a passing glance before it looked again straight across the river and over the bush as if it were indeed the prince of all that immense shimmering world, stretched out below it, its yellow and green cover resounding with birdsong, and scarlet, blue and vermilion with the multi-coloured multitudes of the birds of Hunter's Drift, taking wing above it. Seeing it there at that moment and in that still attitude, François found it a singularly good omen. However they could not stay there all day long admiring it. Calling both himself and Hintza back to their immediate senses, François went on until at last they came to the final boulder, crawled over it, went on their stomachs underneath the bushes, found the narrow hole to the cave and, side by side, crawled through it.

Xhabbo must have heard them coming from a long way off and though he must also have been reasonably certain who was coming, had taken no chances. Nor had François for that matter, because the moment his head was through the entrance, while still flat on the ground on his stomach he had called out Xhabbo's name and the customary greeting. As he called out the greeting, he raised his chin to look about him. The cave appeared to be empty. Then from the far corner a Bushman voice replied and hard on the voice Xhabbo appeared, limping out of the shadows to stand in the centre of the cave, caught in a shaft of slanted sunlight. There he paused for a moment, the bow with an arrow already fixed in it in his left hand, the spear used as a crutch in his right.

François immediately leapt up and ran forward to meet him. But Hintza beat him to it. Recognizing Xhabbo instantly he gave a great bound forward, sat down on his haunches in front of Xhabbo and held out a paw in greeting. Xhabbo immediately dropped his bow and arrow, took Hintza's paw in his hand, while a wide smile broke over his Mongolian face and illuminated his delicate features. That shaft of the sun was enough to show François a face restored fully to its bright, natural apricot colour and a great surge of reassurance went through him. He went forward to put a hand of welcome on Xhabbo's shoulder and found that the skin he touched was as dry and cool as his own.

'You come again as you did yesterday, Foot of the Day,' Xhabbo greeted him.

'Foot of the Day?' François repeated, puzzled by the phrase.

'Yes, indeed,' Xhabbo answered, his voice now solemn and grave with emotion. 'All the morning Xhabbo has been feeling utterly that when he was caught between the teeth of the monster in the bush the night before and was lying and struggling in the darkness, feeling that there was no escape or end to the night for him, you came, like Foot of the Day, carrying the morning to him. Therefore you are for Xhabbo utterly also "Foot of the Day".'

Xhabbo was speaking slowly and deliberately, seeking his meaning like a hunter following a difficult spoor and giving François time to understand what he was saying.

François remembered how old Koba had taught him that there were two great stars in the sky, both legendary hunters. The two were called, in order of importance, Dawn's Heart and Foot of the Day. Dawn's Heart and Foot of the Day took turns in being morning and evening stars. When Dawn's Heart, as its name implies, was morning star, Foot of the Day was the evening star and was then known as Heel of the Night. When Foot of the Day was morning star, the Dawn's Heart became the Eye of the Evening. It came to him then in a rush that in calling him Foot of the Day, Xhabbo was bestowing upon him one of the greatest praise-names of which Bushmen were capable. He felt so unworthy of his promotion to stardom that he blushed and tried to explain to Xhabbo that at home, far from being so exalted a person, he was known to the Matabele and even old Koba as the smallest of little feathers.

But at the word Matabele, Xhabbo became quite angry. Those dark, wide, archaic eyes of his flashed with ancient light. He made a gesture as if that were just the sort of thing one could expect from people so unimaginative, overbearing and full of brute strength as the Matabele, and hastened to add at great length that as far as he and his people were concerned, François would be known from then on as Foot of the Day.

François thought it best to let the matter rest there, but remained secretly determined that no one around Hunter's Drift should ever know the exalted title which had just been bestowed upon him because if that happened he would never hear the end of it. The 'Little Feather', although sanctioned by long years – that is, long to him – of love and care was already smarting quite enough in a self closing in on its young manhood, for him to want any other name, however flattering. It would embarrass him with his elders and betters who, as one has seen, were only too prepared to tease and correct him.

So there and then he asked Xhabbo to sit down with him in the biggest shaft of the sun, because it was rather cool inside. He had noticed that Xhabbo's naked skin was like goose-flesh and he thought the sun there would warm him through. He immediately took the big thermos flask out of his haversack and poured out some of the hot, sweet coffee for Xhabbo to drink with a couple more of the pain killers he had brought. That done, he undid the dressings of the day before. He warned Xhabbo in the process that in unwinding the last of the bandages and particularly the field dressing which had become firmly stuck to the leg with congealed blood, he would hurt Xhabbo a great deal. Xhabbo, however, just laughed at the thought that he could regard what he was doing as inflicting pain, since he clearly had far higher standards of what constituted pain for a man than François had. Once the wound was exposed, François, although still horrified by the extent and depth of it, was delighted to see that it was quite clean.

He only wished that Lammie was there to help him put some stitches in the wound because the mouth of the gash seemed to him still to be yawning wide and dangerously. Lammie had become forced, by circumstance, to specialize in that sort of thing at Hunter's Drift. However, since that was out of the question, all he could do was to re-bandage the leg tighter so that the pressure would hold the two sides of the wound more closely together.

He was about to do this when Xhabbo asked, rather pleadingly, if he could not have some more of that powerful medicine François had poured into the wound the day before. He was obviously referring to the iodine, which he judged, by its power to inflict burning pain, to be powerful medicine. But François, knowing iodine should only be used sparingly, felt compelled to disappoint him. He dressed and bandaged the wound as quickly as he could. By the time he had finished the pain-killer had made Xhabbo wonderfully relaxed and he could sit down to enjoy the food which François now spread out in front of him.

To Xhabbo it appeared like a great treasure trove. He greeted the appearance of everything with sounds of great appreciation. The greatest explosion of wonder was for the biltong which had been packed at the bottom of the haversack. The Bushmen, too, François knew made a kind of biltong themselves and therefore had a standard of comparison for their own for the chunks of beef biltong produced at Hunter's Drift.

'That,' Xhabbo exclaimed, pointing at the biltong, 'will make Xhabbo utterly strong and well before the day is ended.'

Perhaps the remark had not to be taken literally. But it did suggest to François the danger that Xhabbo might be in too great a hurry to get away. Involuntarily he found himself protesting because he was afraid that unless his leg were properly healed, great harm could come to Xhabbo should he set out alone for his long desert journey back to his people.

But François also had an all-compelling reason of his own. He just could not bear the thought of parting so soon with the little Bushman. There was for him something magical about this unexpected appearance of a member of his beloved Koba's people. He had thought them vanished, with their child-man shapes and bows and arrows and paint-brushes, for ever from the world of Africa. He had many good and true friends at Hunter's Drift, but they were not of his own choosing. They seemed to have been provided for him by Ouwa, Lammie, 'Bamuthi and others. Whereas he felt deeply, beyond any words accessible to him, that Xhabbo had come to him and to him alone. At the very moment when he most needed someone of his own free choosing he – no, he and Hintza had discovered Xhabbo. With all the awe of coincidence which he fully shared with 'Bamuthi, Ousie-Johanna and the others, the coming of Xhabbo, just at the moment when he was separated from his parents, was by far the most important thing that had ever happened to him.

A happy confirmation of this lay in the fact that there appeared to be no lack of ease between Xhabbo and himself. They talked as if they had known each other all their lives. Nor did Xhabbo find it a breach of good manners at times to correct François's pronunciation. Koba's Bushman, which François spoke, came from another part of the country some thousands of miles away. The remarkable thing was not that it differed from Xhabbo's but that on the whole the differences were so slight.

It happened for instance, when François was telling Xhabbo about the klipspringer ram, standing so calmly and confidently on the roof of his dwelling. He referred to it as 'Mantis's own', that is, 'Kaggen's own', just as old Koba had always done.

Xhabbo looked perplexed for a moment. Then a smile of pure delight broke over his face and he exclaimed: 'Ah, you mean Koeggen-A's own creature.'

Xhabbo went straight on to elaborate how he agreed with François that they could not possibly have had a better omen. He explained that the cave in which he sat was also Mantis's Place. Indeed, it was the place of Mantis before it had been the place of Xhabbo's ancestors. He stopped eating and to François's alarm stood up and hobbled without the help of a spear, to the smooth, honey-coloured wall of the cave. There the reflection of the yellow shafts of sunlight lapped like the water at the painting of Mantis, his son-in-law, the rainbow, and his grandson, the mongoose, facing an enormous serpent. Xhabbo indicated it with the tip of his first finger folded back, so that he should not be guilty of the rudeness of pointing straight at so sacred an object. It was an illustration, he told François, of how Mantis had gone into battle against the great serpent at the beginning, destroying it in order to make the cave his own both for him and for the people of the early race.

Xhabbo then hobbled back, speaking with increased animation of how convinced he was too that the little antelope was a clear indication that Mantis still regarded the cave as 'his place and the place of his heart's own'. Xhabbo thought it proof that it was still under Koeggen-A's protection, and that there François and his coming together was not an accident but something which he, the Old Fire Thief (Mantis's greatest praise name) had engineered in his infinitely cunning way.

From then on Xhabbo, encouraged by François, talked a great deal about himself and his own people. He told François how his father had died some thirty-five days before. Since his grandfather was already dead, had 'gone the way of the hyena' as he put it, Xhabbo had become the head of the family. It was therefore immediately necessary for him to hasten and report the matter to the cave so that at once it would know the new person who was to be responsible for it. Xhabbo stressed that, although it was a time of crisis out there in the desert because of a great drought, a scarcity of game and practically the last of the desert melons used up, he had been forced to leave at once. The urgency of the matter had been stressed by an unmistakable sign.

This sign had been the appearance in the sky the very night his father died, of the biggest, longest, slowest and reddest shooting star they had ever seen. He had of course expected a shooting star. That is something that always came to announce the death of one Bushman to another. The stars saw and knew all. Shooting stars came, as Xhabbo put it, to show them that one of their members 'who had been upright until then, had utterly fallen down as that star was falling down and was about to lie utterly upon his side in the dark, until the Dawn's Heart came to show him the way'.

But no one, not even Xhabbo, had expected so red and great a shooting star to signify this event. Judging by its magnitude and colour, it could have been a grave portent of the shedding of blood. Everybody had agreed he should hurry to the cave as soon as possible; and then hasten back to his people.

He had, he admitted, set out perhaps not as well prepared as he should have been. The heavy nature of his mission and the possible consequences of his father's death were weighing too heavily on his heart so that his eyes 'were feeling themselves to

136

be full of the things within and were not empty and open enough to be filled with the things from without'. If not he would never have stumbled into the jaws of that beast which had caught him in the early hours of the morning. But perhaps that again was the wise and cunning Mantis's doing. Had not his misfortune brought him and Foot of the Day together? It was only this and nothing else, Xhabbo made clear, which reconciled him to his accident. Nevertheless, he explained with a certain melancholy to François, he must start on his journey back as soon as he could.

And how long did he think that would be? François asked him. Xhabbo did not answer at once. He stood up and tested his leg by walking round and round the cave. He did so much more easily than the day before. Part of this François knew was due to the pain-killers; part to the fact that Xhabbo had recovered from the profound sense of shock that the accident had inflicted on him and also to the sense of reassurance brought to him by François's friendship, and by the knowledge that he would not lack food and water. It seemed to François that twenty-four hours' rest and European medicine had set Xhabbo on the road to recovery much faster than he would have thought possible for himself or, for that matter, the toughest of Matabele boys. It was such striking evidence of the quality, resilience and spirit of the Bushman people, exceeding even the highest expectations raised in him by old Koba's reminiscences at her nostalgic best, that François warmed to Xhabbo all the more.

Even so, he went cold all over when Xhabbo, after a short round on his feet, sat down beside him again and said, 'Xhabbo feels that his leg will be able to walk properly beside its brother in three, if not two days' time. When that moment comes, would not Foot of the Day come too, for that would be utterly pleasant to Xhabbo and pleasant to his people in the desert as well.'

François took the invitation as a great compliment and was surprised how keenly the longing to be able to say yes flared up in him. It was almost as if the longing was presenting itself to him not for the first time but had been secretly at work in his imagination ever since Koba first spoke to him of her people and their ways.

Of course he knew that there could be no question of his

going. Quickly his dismay was increased by despair at the thought that Xhabbo might vanish in three, if not two days' time, perhaps for ever. So he immediately protested. He said that judging by the nature of the wound, it would take at least a week if not ten days before Xhabbo could think of undertaking such a journey on his own, since François could not come with him and help him on his way. He explained that his own parents were not dead, but had gone on a journey leaving him alone to take care of Hunter's Drift. He could not dream of going until they came back and gave him their permission and blessing for such a journey which he longed to do more than anything he could possibly imagine.

The thought that it might take his leg as long as a week, or ten days, to recover struck Xhabbo as so outrageous that he laughed and laughed as if he had never heard anything so funny before. François had never heard or seen such wonderful abandoned laughter. It was as if the whole of Xhabbo had been taken over by laughter. From outer skin to the inmost and most secret place of his body he seemed possessed by nothing but laughter of flame and had no room in him for anything else. Indeed, it was so wonderful a laugh that although François did not feel at all like laughing he was infected by it and a smile came to his face.

Even Hintza, lying there on the yellow sand beside him, looking attentively from François to Xhabbo and Xhabbo to François all the while they talked, with the electric consonants he knew so well travelling forth between the two of them like a do-it-yourself lightning, seemed to be gripped by a powerful desire to laugh himself. He was already grinning at François; the corners of his mouth quivering and his long pink tongue suddenly darting out to lick the quick trembling corners of his long black lips as if they had suddenly gone dry with emotion. But after a while he exhausted all his powers of grinning and there came a moment when his tongue disappeared, and a violent sneeze burst from him which François knew of old was Hintza's way of getting rid of an excess of inexpressible feeling in himself. When that happened, Hintza leapt up and started racing round Xhabbo and himself at top speed, until the shafts of sunlight were so dim with yellow dust that François had to call him to order and make him lie down once more beside him. He was reduced to grinning and baring his teeth rather clownishly as a substitute for that glitter of laughter which was flashing from Xhabbo.

All in all, the power and the beauty in Xhabbo's laugh, despite all the other complicated reactions of the moment, shone so brightly in François's imagination that he had time to know he was rather envious of it and to feel that there was almost nothing he would not give in exchange for being able to laugh like that himself.

When Xhabbo's laughter began to show signs of ending and he was able to pick himself up from the floor of the cave on to which he had fallen, helpless and wriggling, as if mortally wounded with laughing, so that he could sit upright again, and though still giggling from time to time, François was able to protest: 'Xhabbo, it is too serious a matter for laughing. You will not be ready to travel for many days.'

For a moment it looked as if Xhabbo would be provoked into a fresh outburst of laughter, but he contained himself, became serious at last and said, 'Foot of the Day, the wounds that fill the eyes of Bushmen are never difficult to cure. The wounds that Mantis has taught the Bushman to fear are the wounds that do not fill his eyes or those of his people.'

François however continued to argue and plead with him, until he got Xhabbo to agree that they would review the state of his leg each morning before deciding when precisely he would leave on his journey back to the desert. Above all, François made him promise that he would not suddenly decide the issue for himself and leave without seeing François first.

The other matter of immediate concern to François was to get Xhabbo to promise that he would not show himself at any time outside the cave. There was always a chance that a Matabele might catch a glimpse of him. No matter where one went in the bush, there was, as François stressed, always some eye fixed upon one. Had not Mopani Théron always warned him that such an eye, no matter whether animal or human, usually started a chain reaction in the natural life of the land, robbing it of its routine manifestations to proclaim to all and sundry that some abnormal ingredient had come to disturb the abiding rhythm of the bush? Once such a chain reaction started, Mopani had stressed, one could never know to what it might not lead.

All this made sense to Xhabbo and he readily gave his promise. By this time François was horrified to see, from the angle of the shafts of sunlight streaking into the cave that he had already been over-long on his visit. He felt compelled now to say a hurried goodbye to Xhabbo and to promise to return with more food and powerful medicine the following afternoon.

François had no watch of his own. He had been accustomed, like everybody else at Hunter's Drift, except his parents, to make the sun both watch and compass. As he emerged from the mellow cave he saw that it was already past his lunch hour and knew that he would have to face a grim Ousie-Johanna whose sense of authority, heightened by his parents' absence, would have been made sterner still by anxiety. For it was not at all like him to be late for food. Worse still, he had done nothing at all yet about the ostensible purpose of his excursion so early in the day into the bush. He had shot neither guinea nor gum bustard, which he had promised to Ousie-Johanna. He could not, therefore, hurry back to Hunter's Drift to lessen the crime of his unpunctuality. He would have to shoot something for the kitchen first.

Unfortunately, as everybody knew, those hours between noon and three in the afternoon were the dead hours of the day in the bush. All animals, birds and even serpents went into a deep dream of sleep at that inert time. It was as if the whole of life contracted out of the business of living, to such an extent that both Matabele and Bushmen spoke of the period as the hours of death, and implicitly took it to be the time when ghosts emerged from the graves to brush one pale shadow after another as with black crows' wings, on missions of vengeance and reproach.

Yet François had to do something to redeem his promise to old Johanna. At that moment, to his amazement, he heard the sound of some bustards calling to one another from the foot of the hill. This call happened to be one of his favourite sounds, because it was rare, round and full of a glowing passion, and the concern of all that is maternal in life. A bustard was soliciting the help of an aloof male to control the behaviour of their young.

140

Hintza too had heard the lovely call floating like an iridescent bubble on the graveyard silence of the day. He had to repress his musical self from responding in kind by reminding himself of the depressing socially realistic reasons for his presence there with François. So he merely drew François's attention to the sounds with his high-pitched whimper, while promptly aligning his tail, spine and nose like a compass needle on the sound. So unusual was this lovely sound of life at that hour that François, quite unbidden, had the most supernatural of promptings. The hair at the back of his head became absurdly sensitive. Fresh as he was from his meeting with Xhabbo and all this talk about Mantis and Mantis's proprietary right over hill and cave he had an acute feeling that the Bushman god himself might have come to help him in his predicament.

Quickly he cocked his muzzle-loader, knowing that the click of sound later would certainly disturb birds with such fine and alert senses as bustards.

He bent down and whispered in Bushman in Hintza's ear: 'Show me Hin, show me quick. But careful, this is our only chance.'

Hintza clearly understood. He led off at his most careful pace. Indeed he took such elaborate precautions not to brush against the bush or tread on any dead wood or leaves that he gave the appearance of a somnambulist stepping high over nightmare obstacles. François, who knew of old that it was far better for him to let Hintza be his eyes and ears and just follow with his own eyes concentrated for news on Hintza's movements and reactions, could not help smiling affectionately at the exaggerated lift of Hintza's legs. They had not gone far down the hill when the birds suddenly went silent. François immediately feared they must have overheard in spite of all the care they were taking, simply because he and Hintza, apart from their quarry, must be the only living things on the move just then.

But Hintza appeared untroubled by doubts of any kind. His whole attitude was one of the utmost certainty. A bare five minutes from setting out he came to a stop in the shade of an enormous red boulder, his tail straight out behind him, rigid and glowing like one of the Amanzim-tetse's finest yellow reeds, tip quivering like a tuning fork with vital apprehension and his shiny black silk nose wrinkled with the subtle impact of the scent of some living thing ahead.

François went forward slowly to join him, knelt down in the shade beside him, taking great care to see that his old muzzle-loader was out of the sun and not mirroring any of its light to signal a warning of their intent. Aligning his own vision on Hintza's quivering tail and nose, creasing and uncreasing with the excitement of this new smell, François looked through a screen of skeleton white thorn bush and long yellow grass, tied in tassels of burnished seed. For a moment he thought the earth in front of him was empty of life. But suddenly there came again that round, full call of proud concern of a bustard mother, and hard on the call the movement of a dark blue head and crest of bright feathers burning in the pallid shade not twenty yards away.

Taking great care to see that he remained well within the shadow thrown by the boulder, François slowly rose up to his full height. Down in a small clearing two large female bustards and one enormous plump bustard cock, feathers all glittering in the sun, swollen with pride and desire to shine in front of his women and children, were all three concentrating on teaching three little bustard chicks to set about the business of feeding themselves. It was a touching, innocent sight. François, in spite of Hintza's impatience would have given anything not to have to shoot. But he realized that this was probably his only chance of getting anything for Ousie-Johanna's pot, and that if he failed to do so, his behaviour could become fatally suspect at Hunter's Drift and thus jeopardize all his plans to help Xhabbo.

So, perhaps more reluctant than he had ever been, he brought the old muzzle-loader carefully to his shoulders, waited until the three grown-up birds were within the zone of the spread of his shot and pressed the trigger. As always, a blue cloud of gun-powder hid the result of his shooting from François; but he knew he could rely on Hintza to do whatever was necessary. Indeed, as the shot thundered out with unusual violence in that dead, hypnotic silence, Hintza leapt forward and vanished into the grass and the blue drift of smoke.

François, obedient to Mopani's training, stood there for a while longer, reloading his muzzle-loader, putting in an extra heavy charge of gunpowder and ramming a round ball of lead on top, in case something more dangerous than bustards lay ahead. Only then, with the gun fully primed and the hammer cocked, and stock at the ready in his elbow, did he follow Hintza. All three bustards were dead but to his amazement Hintza, with one baby bustard in his mouth, was prowling round and round two other chicks like a collie dog trying to pen in some recalcitrant sheep. He immediately went up to Hintza and, so sensitive was Hintza's use of his mouth that he released the little bustard chick completely uninjured into François's hand. The moment he had delivered it safely he went after the other two, caught another, brought it back also unhurt so he could whisk around and do the same for the last terrified little bird.

To François's delight Hintza seemed proud of this part of his work. However he had no time to waste in congratulations, for the presentiment of what awaited him in the kitchen at Hunter's Drift was growing more ominous by the second. So he made certain that the three little bustard chicks, whose agitated hearts were beating visibly in the soft down at their throats, were comfortably housed in a mass of dead leaf and dry grass in his ample and now empty haversack, before he started to gather up the three dead bustards.

To his dismay, they were so plump and heavy that he despaired for a moment of ever being able to carry all three home together. He was compelled to waste a quarter of an hour making them lighter by gutting them. He then tied their legs together and slung them over the end of the muzzle of his gun to carry them over his shoulder along the shortest way home.

Even so, the birds were so heavy that he reached the Matabele kraals breathless. Fortunately no one was visible outside the beehive huts and he was not delayed by having to answer awkward questions. He hurried on straight to the kitchen where the moment his steps resounded in the courtyard, Ousie-Johanna appeared. Her dark skin was pale yellow with anger and anxiety and she was clearly determined to give François a lashing with her active tongue.

However, the sight of three superb bustards suspended over François's shoulder had the most disarming effect on her. So

143

François had time to speak up first and say: 'I'm sorry, old Ousie, that I'm so late, but I've never known the bush so dead. I didn't want to come home without keeping my promise to you and it was only by sheer luck that I came across these birds just a short while ago. You do understand, please, don't you, dear little old Ousie?'

Ousie-Johanna, softened inwardly, still felt in duty bound to deliver some reprimand to him. However, just at that moment 'Bamuthi appeared from the direction of the barns where he usually had his own food in the heat of the afternoon. His experienced eyes immediately took in the high quality of the birds François had brought home and he immediately uttered a series of Matabele praises in such words as *'Auck! Yebo! Hakiso!'* and so on.

Anxious to have an ally to mollify the sorely tried Ousie-Johanna, François made the most of the opportunity and spoke again. 'I'm certain, little old Ousie, that one gum bustard will be enough for the two of us, and that you would like 'Bamuthi and his people to have the other two? Please choose one for us and let the old Father have the others. Besides, I have brought you something even better than food for the pot.'

Ousie-Johanna, who had been a widow for many years and who had come to regard 'Bamuthi as the main substitute for the authentic voice of male authority she lacked in her life when Ouwa was away, immediately complied in a characteristic manner by pretending to be indignant with François. 'You should know better than to teach me what is right in these matters François,' she told him severely, as the 'François' instead of the usual 'Little Feather' indicated. 'From the moment I saw what you had on your shoulder, I decided to give 'Bamuthi the pick of the birds. Choose, 'Bamuthi please. But what is this talk of something else that you have got for me?'

François had already unslung his haversack and was by now sitting, breathing hard from his long slog home, on the edge of the stoep on to which the main kitchen door gave. Ordering Hintza to watch, he took one bewildered little bustard chick after the other out of the bag until all three were standing on trembling legs on the stone stoep, their bright turquoise eyes after the gloom of the bag in which they had travelled blinking

144

and glittering in the platinum sun. The sight of the three helpless little birds overwhelmed Ousie-Johanna's great and under-employed maternal heart. Her whole being flared up into a white heat of protective emotion. She gathered up the little birds and carried them straight into the kitchen where François and 'Bamuthi heard her making her idea of bustard mother noises over them. Since Ousie-Johanna was in charge of the domestic chicken run at Hunter's Drift, François read the noises as pure proof that the three little birds would soon have a foster mother in the shape of a desolate hen whose eggs had failed to hatch and whose fate she had bemoaned to him only the day before.

François and 'Bamuthi looked at each other. Their eyes met and they started laughing silently together until 'Bamuthi brought the episode to a close by whispering to him: 'It would be well to remember, Little Feather, that only once in a lifetime will bustards come in the dead hours of the day to save you from a well-deserved lashing of a wise old lady's tongue. Remember that he who fetches water at the same place on the river bank too often, ends up in the crocodile.'

It really was not necessary to remind François that he had pushed his luck in the last two days as far as it could go. He had already showed his awareness of this by warning Xhabbo that he would be unable to come to him until the afternoon of the following day. None the less he took 'Bamuthi's admonishment fully to heart. He spent the rest of the afternoon helping Ousie-Johanna about her kitchen, and getting the bustard chicks legally adopted in the chicken run, which was not difficult. So eager was the bereaved hen for some living thing to care for that 'Bamuthi exclaimed, 'Auck! Old Mother, your bird is so hungry for children that she would have taken newly hatched crocodiles into her nest.' That done, François went to the milking sheds at the far end of the garden, making himself as useful as he could to 'Bamuthi and the others.

Yet the moment he was in bed and alone, he found he did not even have the mind for reading one of his favourite adventure stories. All he could do was to struggle dutifully through his nightly reading of the Bible, on which Lammie and Ouwa insisted as the one imperative preparation for the night. On this particular occasion he found by another coincidence that the piece prescribed for his reading by Lammie, who had drawn up a list of readings for him to last six weeks, was the twenty-third Psalm, 'The Lord is my Shepherd'.

So much was Xhabbo in his mind that he found himself amending the opening lines to read, 'The Lord is my Shepherd as Koeggen-A is Xhabbo's shepherd'. So complex a mixture had François become that he found nothing contradictory or even the least bit incongruous in joining the name of Christian overlord and pagan god in one and the same poetic prayer.

Once the reading of the Psalm was ended, he said goodnight to Hintza, who was lying, eyes tightly shut and making little whimpering noises, legs and muscles twitching, as if he were engaged in a dream hunt after a dream quarry. He was, after all, as much a dreamer as a dog of action, to François's unending satisfaction. At the sound of François's voice, Hintza opened one reluctant eye, gave a feeble wag of his tail in acknowledgement and then instantly was fast asleep again, whimpering and twitching as he eagerly took up his dream hunt where he had been compelled to leave it off.

But François lay there awake for an unusually long time. His imagination was entirely absorbed by the whole thought of Xhabbo warm inside him like a mug of Ousie-Johanna's best and hottest coffee on a cold winter's morning.

At the same time his increased sense of having to be careful not to give him away stayed with him all through his sleep, until Ousie-Johanna called him as she always did with a cup of coffee and a couple of home-made rusks at dawn the following morning. As a result it was not necessary for her to remind him, 'Now, my Little Feather, no wandering off into the bush after breakfast. I promised Lammie and Ouwa that you would do your school work for two hours every day, just as if they were here.'

Accordingly François sat dutifully at his school books after breakfast but it is doubtful whether he learned anything at all. His mind was still on Xhabbo in his cave and the long journey of at least thirty days' hard walking which lay ahead of the little Bushman. He hardly saw the lines in his books, but kept on wondering how best he could help. One thing stood out clearly. He must gather extra provisions so that Xhabbo, whose wounded leg would handicap him sorely on his long march home, would not have to be strained in any arduous stalking of game for food. Happily that was the least of François's problems. There was the vast store of biltong to which he could safely turn. He knew he could extract enough of it to last Xhabbo a month without anybody really noticing that any was missing. Also he could secrete enough dried peaches, apricots, raisins and figs, all light and nourishing substances, to add to the biltong. No, his real problem was how to give Xhabbo useful presents that would not just clutter up his person with unnecessary weight, making his march more complicated.

Here he was appalled by the narrowness of the choice which confronted him. Most of the material things in the world of Hunter's Drift were far too cumbersome and complex to be of help to a Bushman, whose life was one of constant movement. Old Koba had always told him that Bushmen could never own more than they could carry easily on their persons.

He gave the problem all his thought and imagination which was as quick as only that of a young person compelled to spend much of his time alone, could be. Towards the end of his two hours he seemed to have come to some solution. He would give Xhabbo the best and sharpest of his own hunting knives, since Xhabbo carried none with him. Then he would add the lightest and biggest field flask which they had in the large store of army surplus supplies which they kept in the attic. He knew that Xhabbo had done the thirty days' march out of the desert with only such water as he could carry in three ostrich egg shells which he had buried near the river, ready for filling for the return journey. So their largest flask would not only hold more than half a dozen ostrich egg shells of water but would also be unbreakable and far less of an encumbrance, slung across Xhabbo's shoulder.

But perhaps his one real inspiration was remembering they had in their stores some old-fashioned flints with yards of inflammable flex for making fire, as his mother's ancestors had made fire on their trek into the interior of Africa. He could easily show Xhabbo how to make fire with these flints and Xhabbo would then be certain of fire even on the windiest and stormiest of days, when the classical Bushman method of laboriously twirling a round stick on a hole made in another piece of wood, would be most difficult, if not impossible.

Although his mind was full of other precious possessions that he would have liked to heap on Xhabbo, who seemed so vulnerable, defenceless and deprived that it brought tears to François's eyes, he sadly accepted that anything more would not help but just burden the wounded man to the point of dangerously slowing him down.

Immediately his two hours were over he sought out 'Bamuthi and handed over to him his three favourite hunting knives complete with leather sheaths. He explained to 'Bamuthi that they were dull and begged him as a great favour to sharpen the knives for him, declaring, undeniably flattering as it was to 'Bamuthi because it was also true, that no one in the world could sharpen knives so expertly.

'All three knives at once, Little Feather?' 'Bamuthi exclaimed, giving him so shrewd and questioning a look that François felt uncomfortable. Was 'Bamuthi, somewhere inside his observant self beginning to suspect that since the shooting of the leopard, something new and strange had entered François's life? Suddenly afraid, he knew that even with the utmost care and forethought, he would be very lucky if this wise, experienced and extremely imaginative old Matabele gentleman who knew him perhaps even better than Ouwa did, were not to find out what he was contriving.

Almost like a stranger he heard himself covering up and saying, 'One will do, Old Father, if you're busy. I only thought that in the long run it might be less trouble to do the lot while you were at it.'

As he said it, François secretly was deeply appalled that he could suddenly be so cunning. He blushed with shame, remembering all the warnings that 'Bamuthi had given him in the past against having secrets. But the shame dispersed at the thought that it was all in a good cause. Had not 'Bamuthi himself on that memorable evening of punishment and redemption some years ago, observed that one could deceive for the good of one's own people? What more was he doing than just being secretive to save Xhabbo from enemies?

Happily, 'Bamuthi grunted as if he felt himself ungracious

and declared that three indeed were hardly more trouble than one. So he took François to the great grindstone in the barn where all the sickles, knives and assegai blades were brought for sharpening. While 'Bamuthi sharpened the knives, his grey head bent over the stone with that air of dedication which comes to primitive people whenever they do something that has its origins in the long forgotten millenniums of their beginnings, François turned the wheel for him and from time to time when 'Bamuthi asked, poured a little water on the stone, where the blades of his knives soon shone like the most precious of metals and flashed in the shadows. At last 'Bamuthi was able to test them by using them as razors on the side of his cheek.

Then, holding them triumphantly out to François, he said, 'Look, Little Feather, how easily it removes the hair from my cheek. You will have no trouble in skinning a hippopotamus or even an elephant now with any one of these.'

François thanked him profusely and ran back into the house to collect the rest of his presents for Xhabbo. Even so he had to wait for another couple of hours before Ousie-Johanna called him in to lunch with her in the kitchen. By that time he was so tormented by his desire to join Xhabbo, that his appetite had completely gone. Yet this new cunning self forced him to eat as big a meal as he had ever done, lest his loss of appetite was noticed.

Even with a meal eaten, he did not feel it safe to rush off at once into the bush at that dead hour of the day. Ousie-Johanna, he was certain, would have found this so unusual that she might even have tried to restrain him. The last thing he wanted was an argument, because he was no match for her. All he could do was to think of something to distract Ousie-Johanna's attention.

Something prompted him immediately to think of the gramophone. He suggested to Ousie-Johanna that as she had been up so early and had had so many anxieties recently she should go and have a rest in her room while he fetched the gramophone and her favourite records, which were all hymns. They were not the happy, rousing, militant, uplifting tunes of the church which François himself liked, but the most solemn, grave, slow, ponderous and lugubrious dirges of which religious composers over the centuries had been capable. They were moreover interpreted by old-fashioned singers at their most fatal, grim best. It is true that Ousie-Johanna had managed to make 'Abide with Me' into the liveliest one of the lot. But the rest of her repertoire seemed to specialize in nothing but ultimate gloom. Even 'Lead kindly light' seemed to be sung by her not for the sake of the 'leading light' but because of her love and enjoyment of the gloom which encircled it.

Ousie-Johanna's eyes softened at such forethought for her pleasure from François and she consented immediately, with relish. In a few minutes she was in her room where François came to put the gramophone on the table beside her brass bedstead. The brass was always so polished and shining that it gleamed like gold. He placed the records beside it and had not forgotten 'Work because the night will surely fall' because it was also a favourite with Ousie-Johanna, who always saw herself as working as if the night were about to fall like a mountain top upon her. Also 'Rough storms may rage, around me all is night?', 'For those in peril on the sea', 'Lord how does the light fade towards the sea', 'Be thou also a Daniel', 'God be with you until we meet again' and so on and on until the summit of transfiguration for her, 'Nearer my God to Thee'.

As she stretched herself out on her bed, her face shining with anticipation at this great musical treat ahead of her, François wound up the gramophone and said, 'Now, Ousie-Johanna, you know what you like best and what to do. Don't worry about me. I'll make myself a flask of tea and take Hintza for a run into the bush.' Knowing himself safe at last he went out.

Gathering up his presents, another flask of coffee, a loaf of bread, a bag of rusks, more biltong, a field flask full of water, more medicines and his own ·22 rifle, as he had made no promises to do any shooting today, he set off in a new, roundabout way for the hill.

In the courtyard he could hear in that still, trembling afternoon air the sound of Dame Clara Butt at the top of her volcanic voice emerging with a realistic crackling from an eroded old record, thundering so that the day all around him, and Hintza, vibrated with 'Nearer my God to Thee'.

Hintza stopped for a moment, looked up at François and whimpered as if he too wished to join in being nearer to God but François had no such reaction. He gave Hintza a robust order to be his full hunting self, admonishing him smilingly, 'Nearer to Xhabbo but not to God just yet we hope, touch wood!'

Hintza, knowing the order well, obediently placed a paw on the stock of the rifle François held out in front of him, and then led off into the bush.

Within half an hour François was back in the cave with Xhabbo. He had progressed so much in the twenty-eight hours since François had seen him last that, much as François wished him to be altogether well, he could not help being a little sad that Xhabbo's recovery had not been somewhat slower. Progress at such a rate meant that the little Bushman's stay in the cave was going to be even shorter than he had anticipated. The first thing that François noticed, after greeting Xhabbo, was a deep circular track in the yellow sand on the floor of the cave where he obviously had been walking round and round the fringes of his wide shelter in order to prepare his leg for the journey home. Even more ominous was the trend of their conversation once François had seen to the wounded leg and fed Xhabbo with fresh food.

Glad as Xhabbo was to see him, François noticed that he was restless and uneasy. He had a clouded and troubled look in his slanted, dark eyes.

Asked what the matter was, Xhabbo replied that he had been awake a great deal in the night because of a 'tapping' inside himself.

'A tapping?' François asked. 'I don't understand.'

Xhabbo explained with animation and at great length. He said that all Bushmen from time to time had a kind of tapping thing that suddenly started up inside their chests.

'You mean,' François interrupted, 'that your heart starts beating faster?'

'No, Foot of the Day!' Xhabbo answered, shaking his head emphatically. 'It is not the beating of the heart. It is utterly different. It is like a finger tapping against the skin of the chest, like a finger on a drum, telling the ear to listen and hear talk of things from a far-off place. All we Bushmen are taught from the time we are young that we have to expect this tapping inside

151

ourselves in order to know things that the eyes cannot see, the ears cannot hear and the nose, even the nose of a porcupine woman cannot smell.' The porcupine, according to the Bushman, had the finest sense of smell of any living thing.

He went on to explain that all Bushmen were taught to go and sit apart when this tapping started in them, and listen carefully until they knew what it was saying. 'Only fools,' he said, 'would not obey the law of the tapping.'

Many evil things had come to Bushmen in the past because they had not listened to what the tapping was trying to tell them. This tapping was always of two kinds. There was tapping which told things of the world without; this would come to the best of hunters and told them in which direction they had to go to find game. But there was another, more important tapping that would tell of things many seasons before they were to come. Many a calamity had come to Bushmen who had not listened to this kind of tapping, as it was the most difficult of all to believe. Perhaps only one in a lifetime among the Bushmen could hear and know what this kind of tapping meant. And he was afraid that he, Xhabbo, felt 'not a little' that he was one of those.

'Afraid?' François asked.

Xhabbo nodded his head vigorously and replied, 'Yes, Foot of the Day, afraid, because the tapping I hear is not pleasant to me. It tells me that every day as the sun goes up and down, ringing in the sky, the things approaching Xhabbo and his people are not pleasant. Utterly I must tell you that this tapping is not pleasant and makes Xhabbo utterly afraid.'

Xhabbo went on to explain that when he was lying down with sleep like a cloud of thunder in his head, the tapping started against his chest and became so fast and loud that the cloud of sleep left him. He was forced to sit up and let his ears become full of the sound of the tapping. It was, he realized, tapping that came from a great distance, come to summon him back to the desert and warning him that he must not delay because his people had to leave the place where he had left them as soon as possible. When he had tapped with his hands on his chest, to show that he had heard and would obey, the tapping had stopped and he was allowed to sleep.

But in the middle of the night the tapping had come back with the same message, more urgent than ever, and again he had answered. Yet that had not been enough. Just before dawn the tapping started again.

'Tapping once, Foot of the Day,' Xhabbo observed, almost fearfully, 'can be heard and discussed before believing. Tapping twice is grave and must be heeded after talking. But tapping thrice, is from Koeggen-A himself and must be obeyed at once. So I stood up and all day have walked round and round this cave to make certain that I had two legs and not one for the journey. Therefore, I feel utterly that now Xhabbo must turn round on his heels and go to the place of his people.'

François, desperate, immediately pleaded with Xhabbo to wait at least one more day. He told him of all the preparations he had in mind to bring him more food and supplies for the journey. He argued, in a voice shrill with emotion, that he could give him so much more food, that he would have some biltong to spare for his people when he arrived. Besides, another day or two of rest would enable him to go faster than if he left at once.

He put this to Xhabbo all the more persuasively because he really believed in his reasons. But he was only partially successful. In the end Xhabbo agreed with great reluctance to wait only until the evening of the next day. Then as soon as it was properly dark, he said not without sadness, that he would have to set out on his journey.

That done, François produced his gifts. Inadequate as they seemed to him, to Xhabbo they appeared miraculous. Regarding the flint and its fire-flex he was overcome with joy. He tried the flint again and again, with the air of a magician, and in the end François had to ask him to stop, saying the flex was too precious to be used unnecessarily.

All these things, the talk of the future and preparations for the journey, again made the time pass so quickly that when François emerged from the cave, he was amazed to see that the sun was already low. He would have time enough, provided he hurried, to get to the milking sheds before dark and go through another round of deceptive appearances of having come there from the simple desire to help 'Bamuthi and his fellow herdsmen.

So, going back the straightest way at the fastest pace that he and Hintza could manage, he arrived in time to help carry the last pails of sea-foam milk and empty them into the great metal churns in which the milk was to be conveyed to Hunter's Drift Siding and so by train to the mining city beyond. Even then, he was not soon enough to prevent 'Bamuthi from looking in his direction from time to time, as if he were making a special effort to suppress a strong intention of having to reappraise François's behaviour. Whenever François caught that look he had to admit to himself, however much it went against his emotional grain, that Xhabbo might be leaving the cave just in time to prevent 'Bamuthi from discovering what the two of them had been doing.

The rest of the evening, and the night, followed the same pattern as those of the day before, except that now it was François's turn not to sleep well. He got up early, sad and worried. He never knew how he got through the dutiful pattern of the day because the prospect of losing his new friend made him more and more reckless even as the sun rose higher in the sky. In the end he did not care whether he made Ousie-Johanna and the others suspicious or not. He just went into the kitchen and wheedled and implored her until she agreed to give him an early lunch. That done he purloined a pair of leggings made of webbing, the largest haversack in their store, stuffed it full of more biltong and dried fruit without any attempt at explanation and walked out of the door at the far end of the homestead while Ousie-Johanna was still washing up the dishes. He started off into the bush in a completely new direction and as a result was in the cave two hours earlier than the day before.

As he and Hintza crawled through the narrow entrance they saw Xhabbo quite near, standing facing them and indicating with his finger to his lips that he did not want François to speak. Then he beckoned François to come closer and whispered in his ear to be as quiet as possible. On the tips of their toes they went slowly to the farthest recess of the cave. There Xhabbo stopped to point with his finger folded back in reverence, at a trembling circle of sunlight aglow on the fine yellow sand.

For a moment François, whose eyes were not yet accustomed to the light of the cave, saw nothing. Then, suddenly, the whole meaning of Xhabbo's attitude became clear to him for there, almost as transparent as amber in the sun, was a large praying mantis.

François, of course, had often seen praying mantises around Hunter's Drift. But never before had he seen one in the awesome surroundings of what Xhabbo had taught him to regard as the natural temple of his god. Moreover the timing of it all seemed deliberate as if meaning to crown the climax of all that had happened between him and Xhabbo. Again, he had that odd, prickling sensation in the hair at the back of his head.

Xhabbo, who apparently already had come to terms with this visitation of the living image of his god, whispered to François in a tone full of hope that at last François would be able to understand all. 'You see, Foot of the Day, Mantis himself has come to call me. When Xhabbo woke this morning, and the sun came through this hole in the cave, Mantis himself was sitting there, looking with eyes of fire at Xhabbo. Ask Mantis yourself, please, why has he come?'

François was afraid that at the sound of his voice the praying mantis would fly away instantly. Also, he was convinced that he would not know how to do it properly. Ridiculous as it may seem to sophisticated persons, he was suddenly terrified of giving offence to what most people in the world regarded as a common insect. Xhabbo assured him in vain that if he went down on his knees and spoke politely with the proper voice of reverence, Mantis would most certainly not fly away, but answer him.

'But what shall I ask him Xhabbo?' François implored him, certain he would make a mess of it. 'No, Xhabbo, no. Forgive me but I fear not a little that I will utterly fail. Could you please ask him for me?'

Accordingly, Xhabbo knelt down and as he did so François was amazed to see Hintza going down on his stomach too, and even wriggle into a position where he was close to the little insect and began regarding it in the most extraordinary way, as if he were seeing a dog's idea of a ghost. Ashamed that he had not thought of it sooner, François sank on his knees beside Hintza.

As he did so he heard Xhabbo in a voice as soft and tender

as a Bushman mother chanting a lullaby, addressing the mantis. 'O Snatcher of Fire, Dweller in the Rainbow, Giver of names to the flowers and animals and all things of the earth, Fixer of colour not a little pleasant to all animals with honey; Person of the early race who hears sounds that come from far away places and whose ears listen to the wind from the other side of the desert and the tapping of stars talking of the hunt in the desert of the night, please, oh please tell me, are you come to call Xhabbo to the place of his people?'

At the first whisper from Xhabbo that strange head of the mantis, so oddly Mongolian, if not Bushman, in its shape, was turned slowly about. Its large brilliant eyes looked sideways at Xhabbo. The eyes seemed to flash like jewels in the shaft of sun and to François's amazement, the mantis's front legs were raised slowly up into the air and then slowly brought down again.

'You see,' Xhabbo exclaimed in a taut whisper. 'You see, Mantis answers yes.'

But that was not enough for François. 'Ask him please, will all be well with Xhabbo on the journey?' he whispered.

Mantis's eyes flashed fiercely, as if the question implied doubt in his power to speak and know there, in a place which the questioner must know was peculiarly Mantis's own. All the same the legs went up and down again, not once but three times, for emphasis.

François had many other questions he would have liked Xhabbo to ask but something about the mantis's attitude, above all the last look of fire in his eyes, warned him that he had already presumed enough. Xhabbo obviously had come to the same conclusion because he took François by the arm, gently pulled him up and silently led him well away to the centre of the cave. The mantis, meanwhile, went on sitting there motionless, in the most contemplative of attitudes, his head turned sideways as if the faint sound of the afternoon breeze coming through the holes in the cave, to murmur as the memory of the sea murmurs low in a mother-of-pearl shell at one's ear, was bringing him news of a future beyond sun and stars.

François had spent a great deal of the night thinking about Xhabbo's best way back to the desert. He was also concerned about all those lion traps set in the game tracks around Hunter's

Drift. He had made a point of finding out from 'Bamuthi exactly where they were all to be concealed in the night to come. So straight away he started by describing at great length to Xhabbo exactly where the traps were to be located.

That done, he helped Xhabbo to pack the haversack with the supplies he had brought, lifted it and adjusted the straps to Xhabbo's shoulders, made him walk with it around the cave for some minutes until he was quite certain Xhabbo would be able to carry it in such a way that the tough webbing equipment would not rub and blister his shoulders. Xhabbo seemed delighted with the haversack. But what pleased him most, just then, were the leggings which François, after a final dressing of the wounded leg, strapped round both his calves. With those on, François explained, Xhabbo could go through thorn and scrub without fear of reopening the wound. So indifferent had Xhabbo shown himself to be to physical pain that François could not be certain whether he appreciated the leggings more for decorative than protective reasons. However, in the end, François was happy to feel that no Bushman had ever been better equipped for a long journey into the desert than Xhabbo. All the omens, despite all his own personal fears, seemed to indicate that Xhabbo would accomplish his journey safely. But by the minute he was becoming more and more aware of another and greater concern. Were he and Xhabbo ever to meet again?

Of such overwhelming importance was the question to him that he was almost afraid to ask it, and when the last practical details between them had been arranged there came a period of awkward silence so that they were both sitting, staring at each other as if hypnotized into speechlessness.

Suddenly Xhabbo broke the silence. 'Xhabbo's eyes are so full of Foot of the Day that Xhabbo does not know whether Foot of the Day is not utterly inside him rather than outside as he appears to be.'

François, strangely enough, had been experiencing something of the same feeling. Indeed he had the strange notion that there had never been a moment in his life when he had not known Xhabbo. He said, therefore, something to this effect to Xhabbo.

Xhabbo nodded his head and replied with the utmost seriousness, 'Perhaps there was a time when Xhabbo and Foot of the

157

Day were clouds together as they will be clouds together when the wind comes to remove the last prints of Foot of the Day, and Heel of the Night, and Xhabbo the hunter from the sand.'

Again old Koba's teaching came to François's rescue. She had always taught him that clouds and the spirit of human beings were interchangeable and went into one another's making, before birth, during life and after death.

With this reassurance he felt free to ask the dread question, 'Xhabbo, you will come back again one day, won't you? You are not going for ever?'

Xhabbo answered emphatically: 'Foot of the Day, Xhabbo will come back always to see you. It is not possible for Xhabbo to say how many moons will grow and die, how many leaves will fall and how much grass will grow green and utterly fade away again before he comes. But he knows from another tapping that came to him in the night, that he will come back to see you in this place of Mantis again.'

'But Xhabbo!' François exclaimed, as a new anxiety gripped him. 'You'll remember always about the danger of the traps, won't you? And there'll always be Matabele and others here, who won't find your coming pleasant. You'll have to come with such care that even I won't know you have come unless you give me a sign. How can you give me a sign that the others won't know, but that I'll recognize at once?'

'The tapping in the night told me of such a sign,' said Xhabbo instantly. 'The tapping, now that you have met it, will tell you of Xhabbo's coming. But also with the tapping Xhabbo will give you another sign. By day it will be the sign of the night plover calling. And to make certain that it is Xhabbo who is calling and not a real plover, he will call long and clearly, three times. But if it is night, Xhabbo will call once like a night plover, and then immediately bark like a jackal. Then he will call like a night plover again and bark like a jackal immediately afterwards, and do the same thing three times. By these sounds you will know that Xhabbo is on his way to Mantis's place to wait for you.'

For once Xhabbo refused to stay behind when François was leaving and insisted on going out of the cave with him. François, who had never experienced such a tumult of emotion in his life before could not find it in his heart to say no. All the more so as, in that mood of recklessness with which he had started the day he had stayed in the cave until the last traces of sunlight had vanished from it and he knew that the light outside would be so dim that the chances of their being seen were slim. Indeed, they emerged from the cave to look west at a light of brilliant ruby, sparkling against the tall upstanding Brahmin dusk, the sunset like a sign of its high priestly caste, upon a darkening brow.

For François it was as if even the sunset was conspiring to make the parting as awful as it could be for him by producing one of its most beautiful valedictory images. Full to overflowing with emotion he gave Xhabbo the farewell that Koba had taught him, 'Go in peace Xhabbo, go in peace.'

'Stay in peace, Foot of the Day,' Xhabbo answered, raising his hand, palm wide open to his shoulder, and added, trying to make both himself and François lighter at heart: 'Stay in peace, while Xhabbo starts on the road back this night until our meeting here again in Mantis's place.'

François quickly turned to go down the hill as fast as he could. But it was not fast enough to prevent him from realizing that he was not followed by Hintza, who, at that moment of bereavement so intense that it felt like an amputation, was more precious to him than ever. He looked back. Hintza, who must have recognized the meaning of François's Bushman goodbye, was sitting down of his own accord in front of Xhabbo, holding out his paw and Xhabbo was taking it in both his hands and fondling it. Although the light was fading rapidly and François could not be certain that he was seeing accurately, he believed that Xhabbo, in the manner of all Bushmen who are perhaps the most natural people the world has ever seen, and so without inhibitions of any kind, was near to tears himself.

Too upset by the sight, François looked away and saw, right on the top of the cave, rigid as a glowing bronze statue of itself, the little klipspringer. It was taking no notice of any of them but was just looking steadily with infinite calm into the heart of the dying day. At that very moment, from the bush on the other side of the river, the great titian-haired old lion who ruled over a valley of its own over there, let out one of its most imperative roars, just to show the night his contempt of it. Yet the little klipspringer took no notice of the sound, as if it wanted to indicate to François by his pose that he knew that all possible manner of things, no matter how dark the coming night, would be well for them all. And that, François somehow knew, was sign enough and that he no longer had cause to delay his going.

Fast as they went, it was quite dark when he arrived at the kitchen door. He found Ousie-Johanna, 'Bamuthi and five of the herdsmen armed with shields and assegai, consulting whether they should set out to look for him. Indeed, 'Bamuthi must have been just about as worried as he had ever been because seldom had he spoken to François with such anger. 'Little Feather,' he observed with dignified scorn, 'for days now your friends on the river bank have called you to join in the washing of the horns with them as you have always done. You have not come. For days now, it has come to this that we have had to leave undone the things that we should have been doing in order to be ready to go out into the dark and look for you. It is not right. You are not a dog of the wind [the Sindabele way of describing someone who is homeless]. You are not . . .'

He got no further. Suddenly it was all too much for François and despite all his desire to hold himself like a grown-up and not appear weak in front of people who admire stoicism as much as these people did, he could only murmur, 'How do you expect me not to feel a dog of the wind when my father and mother have left me?'

He knew that the answer was prompted in part by his new, cunning self born out of the need to deceive. Yet there was enough truth in it to make him sit down there and then on the edge of the kitchen step and burst into tears.

'Bamuthi and the others, like all Matabele, had a horror of making young people cry. Indeed they felt guilty even if they saw a small child in tears and had accordingly developed care of children to such a fine art that François had hardly ever heard a Matabele baby cry. He at once felt guilty of having failed in a fundamental of the traditions which he, 'Bamuthi, was especially charged to uphold as the head of his people at Hunter's Drift.

Distressed and contrite, he immediately went up to François

160

and took his hand in his own. In a voice unusually moved, because it was deep and heavy and sure with tenderness, not light and trembling and soft as a woman's would have been in the same predicament, he said, 'Little Feather, I spoke as I did only because I feared for you and because I have been left to be a father to you. Look, come back with me to my kraal and eat with me and play games with your brothers who have been calling for you in vain all these long days.'

Ousie-Johanna, whose tender heart was as upset as 'Bamuthi's and from which all desire to scold had vanished at the first sign of François's tears, was about to protest because she had already cooked François one of her best meals, but the quick, observant 'Bamuthi forestalled her to plead, 'And you, Old Mother, will you not please come as well and tell the children some of those stories that only you can tell and that they have hungered for all these months?'

François warmed to the prospect, again with that odd sort of duplicity which the secret and special needs of Xhabbo had inflicted on him, since he knew that not only would a meal and conversation at the Matabele kraals help him as much as anything to enjoy himself on such a sad night; but also that the celebration would ensure that nobody in the kraals would be prowling in the night to notice any signs that might betray Xhabbo's departure from the cave and his movements through the bush.

As a result François spent a less distressing evening than he would have thought possible during the day, particularly as besides the story-telling, at which Ousie-Johanna excelled, they played a game of riddle-di-mee that forced François's mind out of itself. It mattered less than ever to him that the Matabele boys and girls of his own age were far better at the game than he was. All he cared about was that they should go on playing and make so much noise that no one could hear the sounds of the night outside.

In fact the whole evening was so important to him that he never forgot the riddles put to them all that night. There was, for instance, 'Bamuthi's: 'What is it that always stands and never sits down?'

François could not think for the life of him what 'Bamuthi

was after but one of 'Bamuthi's smallest young daughters immediately screamed in a voice of silver: 'Old Father, what a stupid riddle! Of course it's a tree!'

And 'Bamuthi had to join in the laughter raised by the whole hut against him, since he was old enough after all to have known of something more intelligent. Now a far more difficult one followed immediately from his eldest son whose voice was just breaking, and who seemed to speak on two different levels of sound simultaneously, causing his sisters to snigger slyly behind their hands. 'Riddle-di, Riddle-di-mee, I give you a billy goat who grazes with a herd of white goats. Although the goats move about a great deal they manage to munch in the same place.'

That caused a long silence. By the light of the fire in the centre of the hut, François could see one pair of large, glittering black eyes look in vain to another for guidance and in the end 'Bamuthi had to supply the answer, restoring some of his lost honour by saying, 'Surely it can only be the tongue and the teeth.'

Another riddle which caused a great deal of mind searching was, 'There are things in the world that fall from the tops of mountains without breaking themselves. What can they be?'

The answer, of course, was waterfalls, as they all should have known, since they lived so near to the greatest waterfall on earth, The Smoke that Thunders.

One that François liked best came from 'Bamuthi's eldest daughter, who asked shyly, 'What is it that no one can see but goes in and out, round and about, hither and thither, all over the earth, making the dead alive and the living awake?' The answer, of course, was the wind.

Even Ousie-Johanna was to show a surprising inventiveness and produce a riddle which certainly could not have come out of any Bantu tradition and was as *avant-garde* as any riddle in the bush could be. 'Can any of you tell me who is that quiet, patient, lovable little fellow who dresses so warmly during the day but is left bare during the coldest of nights?'

No one, not even 'Bamuthi, could supply the answer, and a triumphant Ousie-Johanna, her round face glowing like a full

162

moon, was declared to be the great princess of riddles when she answered, once the noise of clapping which the people of Osebeni used to show approval, had ended, 'A clothes peg'.

There was only one riddle which for a moment took François out of that warm, friendly atmosphere of the crowded hut. That was when one of the other Matabele herdsmen asked, 'Could any of you tell me the name of the longest snake in the world?'

When the answer came – a road – François found himself thinking, 'And the longest of the long snakes of the world is the track which Xhabbo is walking out there in the dark.'

When he was back safely in his room with Hintza, the light extinguished and, tired as he was, trying to sleep, this vision of a road, or rather one of those unending footpaths and tracks of the Dark Continent, wriggling westwards like a snake through the bush and out across the great desert, stayed vivid in his imagination, so much so that he found himself sitting up from time to time listening as carefully as he had ever listened before to the sounds of the night, to discover if they were out of tune with themselves, and whether the rhythm of the dark had not gone out of life outside. He even woke Hintza several times, much to Hintza's displeasure, since he obviously felt François ought to know by now that if there were anything wrong in the night he would be the first to know of it.

All the same, Hintza had sat up and gone through all the motions of sniffing the air, turning his head sideways, hither and thither and listening dutifully. The hippopotamuses were grunting down on the banks of the river where they were feeding on lush green grasses. A gallant bushbuck was barking to show its courage. Some auburn-haired baboon, now and then, whimpered with fear as, perhaps, a leopard prowled under the tree in which his family was sheltering. An elephant on the other side of the hill was stripping bark from a tree with such appetite and force that the sound snapped out in the night like a pistol shot. The bull-frogs were ogling the starlight in the pools of muddy water in that wide, shallow tributary of the Amanzim-tetse near the homestead. Night-plovers, too, were calling and re-calling to one another with flute-like voices, and the great old ghost owls were making philosophical noises at one another in order to answer that perpetual: 'Why, what, how and who?' that the

Matabele attribute to them. But there was nothing, absolutely nothing, unusual happening. So Hintza instantly fell asleep again.

Yet François could not do so because the meaning of all the immense variety of night sounds had become different. His feelings recognized the harmony. But it was harmony implicit with a kind of terror of its own. François had seen enough of life in the bush to know (though of course he could not put it in that way to himself) that it was a counterpoint of great and terrible opposites, always at one another's throats: like life and death, and light and dark. All were forces of perpetual threat and fear which demanded constant vigilance and courage from all living things, animals as well as human, to combat them.

How often indeed had not both Ouwa and 'Bamuthi exhorted him to know that in the end only courage made a person free. As he thought of courage, he remembered all that Xhabbo and Koba had told him of the great star hunters up there in the sky, hunting bravely in the terrible forests of the night, fighting for light against the Antarctic darkness above, with their bows, arrows and spears so that even in his bed the distant star din vibrated at his ears. A new reassurance resulted from it, forming the one clear thought that Xhabbo, making his way so gallantly through the danger of night and bush, was not alone but was travelling in the company of embattled and belted constellations. Only then, utterly exhausted, he fell into a deep sleep from which Ousie-Johanna woke him with great difficulty the next morning.

One need not emphasize how pointless the day ahead appeared to François; how he wondered if he could ever again get through the routine of a normal day. He had no doubt that he would try because all the examples of the people around him, no matter of what race or colour had so profoundly influenced his behaviour that it would not have occurred to him that there was any alternative to trying and trying, however helpless and pointless all might seem. All the same, before slipping back into the uniform of everyday behaviour there was one imperative; he had to be absolutely certain that Xhabbo had indeed left and had not been prevented at the last moment from going by something awful. So between lunch and reluctantly joining his friends

164

where they came down to water the cattle in the afternoon by the river, he allowed himself half an hour to look in at the cave.

Yes, Xhabbo had gone. Moreover he had left the cave as clean and tidy as if no one had ever been inside it, except that right in the centre, where the strongest shaft of sunlight fell on the yellow sand, he found that the surface had been smoothed over, levelled out and damped down with water, and right in its centre there was a clear imprint of Xhabbo's spread-out hand and arm. Beside the hand and arm, drawn with Xhabbo's finger, there was a large, symmetrical cross.

The cross, as he knew from Koba and Xhabbo, was not only a magic sign of healing for the Bushman but was also used a great deal in desert and bush, to show the place where two vital tracks met. He had no doubt that the hand imprinted in the sand in that gesture of greeting and the cross drawn beside it was to confirm Xhabbo's promise and belief that they would meet again one day in the cave, and that between now and that unknown moment, all would be well.

5 • Mopani

For a week after Xhabbo's going, François tried to behave as if
nothing unusual had happened to him but it seemed a hard, if
not impossible task. Even his appetite went, to such an extent
that Ousie-Johanna was seriously worried and thought he might
be sickening for something. He did his best but the taste of food
seemed to have gone from his tongue, 'utterly' as Xhabbo, who
was perpetually in his mind, would have had it. Everything
tasted alike. Suddenly he was aware of how insupportable life
was when a person could no longer feel hunger. Up to then he
had always taken it for granted that hunger was the great terror
of a young person's life. Now he found as the slow, long days
went by that the absence of hunger was a far, far greater one.
He was too young, of course, to wonder whether all this might
not be because a greater hunger that had nothing to do with
food had possessed him, particularly since for the first time even
the taste for things like playing with his friends on the river bank
and going through the tangled fringes of the whispering bush
with Hintza and one of his guns to hunt for his and Ousie-
Johanna's pot, had vanished. By the end of the third day after
Xhabbo's going he just had to give up all pretence of wanting to
play with his friends.

More significant still, instead of helping with the milking,
slaughtering, loading up the mule wagons with fresh meat,
vegetables, fruit and milk for the great mining city whose needs
were making Hunter's Drift so prosperous, all things he had
done spasmodically in the past, his inclination now was to help
in the irrigation of the immense vegetable garden and orchards
which were perhaps the greatest glory of the ranch. In the past
he had regarded all this as the dullest work because it meant he
had to stand patiently by the irrigation furrows at the loveliest
time of the evening, letting water slowly into one great vegetable

166

bed after the other, waiting for the beds to fill gradually with water, then shutting off the sluices, opening others and allowing water into the next bed, and so on and on until the bat-black end of day.

He did what he did instinctively. Yet responsibility for an accurate report on his life forces one to ask oneself something about the nature of this instinct. One wonders whether it was not the process of growth, produced by the urgent feeling for life within himself, hastening to the rescue of an inexperienced and vulnerable nature, in danger of having its evolution arrested, compelling him to concentrate on the growth of things in the world without so that their example would set in motion again growth within himself. World without and world within, after all, whether one knows it or not are expressions of one another; interdependent and ceaselessly in communication, serving something greater than the sum of themselves. They are, however stern and exacting, allies of a questing spirit, particularly a young spirit, charged to join them both in a little garden allotment of space and time. Happy for François, therefore, despite the miseries of the moment, that he was free of the mistrust of instinct and intuition wherein contemporary Europe tends to imprison human imagination, and that the pagan influences of his environment encouraged an unquestioning acceptance of this impulse which came to him.

So for some days, he kept to watering the garden so diligently that 'Bamuthi praised him for it in public. Yet it had so little apparent effect on François's state of being that one might have thought this reflection irrelevant to the story. Then a week after Xhabbo's going something, slight as it was, did happen to François in the garden which suggested that time once more had started to move on for him.

With a thoroughly disgruntled Hintza at his side, because Hintza made no secret of the fact that he regarded irrigation as utterly below the dignity of a self-respecting hunting dog, François was turning the water into the broad beds of tomato plants. The plants were tall and strong, covered with fruit in all stages of their growth from white flowers open to the sun, to tiny shrill-green berries, bigger yellow ones and so on to tomatoes of an explosive Oriental red, a colour imparted to them by the

167

passionate, sun-inflamed earth of Hunter's Drift. The moment the water reached the plants it began gurgling as the parched dried earth at their feet greedily sucked it in.

Such was the intensity of the scent from the tomato bushes and so evocative the yellowing air, the rays of sun vibrating like the strings of a great harp between the emerald garden and the proud west, that François was provoked into plucking one of the biggest tomatoes. He bent over and rinsed it quickly in the water in the furrow. As he did so, he saw the head of an enormous thunder-cloud which was building up in the Madonna blue above him now reflected, like a giant cauliflower, in the shadowy water: quivering in the moving water his own face stared up at him like that of a stranger. The sight seemed to touch an odd feeling of guilt, as if he were suddenly confronted with the face of a friend shamefully neglected. Quickly to dispel the feeling he bit deeply into the tomato. To his amazement, he felt the taste for food ready to welcome it on his tongue. The tomato was cool. It had a sharp, wild, barbaric tang.

A feeling of excitement, quite disproportionate to the stimulus, possessed him. A lost savour was back in his being. Excited and delighted, he plucked another tomato and offered it to Hintza, who gulped the tomato down.

Hintza was still licking his long black lips with relish when there came another of those meaningful coincidences which appeared to be such a speciality of their life in the bush. Something new assailed Hintza's acute senses. His tongue vanished, his mouth shut so violently and quickly that the air unexpectedly trapped inside made him sneeze and shake his head. That done, he started leaping up and down in excitement, finally posing himself in front of François, looking intently into his eyes and uttering that high-pitched code of his to indicate that a new element was entering the circumstance of their day.

François, of course, took immediate notice but he could not tell for all his trying what was the cause of Hintza's sudden emergence from sullen indifference to active interest in the measured life of that placid, platinum afternoon. Indeed he appeared so slow in the uptake that Hintza started again to bounce up and down as if he wanted both of them to make for the homestead as fast as they could.

François was still hesitating when the noise of all the mongrel dogs around the homestead barking out wildly reached him, to prove that Hintza was right and immediate action was needed. Sticking his spade into the wet earth beside him, he set off at the double for the homestead. He was not fast enough for Hintza who, without waiting for orders, was running on ahead as if entering a race for his life.

Hintza vanished beyond the fig trees before François was half-way there. When he finally reached their far side, from where he could see the approach to the front of the homestead, he observed Hintza and two other dogs almost exactly like him going through all the choreographics of greeting for which dogs of their kind have so great and gracious a gift. Just beyond the dogs he saw the tall, lean, ascetic figure of Mopani Théron getting down from his favourite, though obviously tired, horse.

The dogs, of course, were Nandi and 'Swayo, Hintza's mother and father. François could not help smiling because it was obvious as he came nearer that neither Nandi nor 'Swayo felt that they were getting all the respect from Hintza to which their senior status entitled them. Though Hintza could not have been more pleased to see them, he was pleased only on his own terms, there on his home ground. He clearly had long since lost all respect for any ridge-back establishment that there might have been in the life of the bush, if he ever had had any. The moment Nandi and 'Swayo started to look down at him along their aristocratic noses to avoid his exuberant advances, he showed them what he thought of such stuffiness by turning his back on them disdainfully. He calmly trotted away to join François as if they did not exist, pushed his way through the homely mongrels, ignored their own disproportionate display of greeting, and gave Mopani an almost suburban paw, wishing a refined 'How do you do?'

Nandi and 'Swayo, thus rebuked, had to make the first advance back into Hintza's favour, an advance he accepted as some sort of apology. With an air of exaggerated authority he led them round to the kitchen because he knew it was just about the moment when Johanna would be extracting some of those delicious marrow bones from the vast cauldron in which she prepared the stock for the soups at which she excelled. He was not disappointed and as a result of having had scientific proof, as it were, of superior knowledge, it was most noticeable from then on how both Nandi and 'Swayo respectfully allowed him to lead and set the tone in all things during their stay at Hunter's Drift.

Mopani, from François's point of view, could not have come at a better moment. Apart from his sadness over Xhabbo's going, he was feeling neglected and anxious because he had as yet received no letters from Lammie and Ouwa, although it was perfectly possible for letters to have reached him at Hunter's Drift Siding at least three, if not four days before. His delight at seeing Mopani, therefore, could not have been greater. That part of Africa in which he lived, as Ouwa was so fond of saying, was truly 'Old Testament country'. Both men and women tended to behave in Old Testament ways and it was the custom even for men when meeting after a long time to embrace and kiss each other in a truly Biblical manner. François's embrace on this occasion was long and rather desperate. Indeed it is doubtful whether François had ever realized until that moment just how devoted he was to this singular, lonely and great old hunter.

His embrace ended, he took Mopani by the hand, begged one of the Matabele on duty at the house to see to his horse, and led Mopani to the most comfortable chair on the stoep before rushing to ask Ousie-Johanna to bring them a pot of her hottest coffee and a large plate of rusks and cake. This she gladly did, but not without adding to her greeting an implied rebuke that a visit from him was overdue, even remarking, 'Has there been then an outbreak of horse-sickness in your camp to prevent you from coming sooner to a place that has always been home to you?'

Not so François. Seizing one of Mopani's brown, long-fingered sensitive hands between his own, he just said: 'Oh Uncle, I'm so glad you've come! Are you on your way after more poachers, or have you come just to see us? You know of course that Lammie and Ouwa have gone to the capital?'

As he said this, François felt quite angry because suddenly he was rather sorry for himself and stupidly on the verge of tears. Happily Mopani was not looking at him, as he answered understandingly, 'No, Little Cousin, I'm not after poachers this time and of course I know that Ouwa and Lammie have gone. I have come entirely because I wanted to see how you and that dog of yours are getting on, though it is true I also have a message for you.' He did not add that he had already promised Lammie whom he loved, that he would keep regularly in touch with François.

'A message, Uncle?' François was puzzled, because who could there be in that vast game park of which Mopani was warden who knew him well enough to want to send him a message?

Mopani immediately explained: 'You know of course that I have a telephone line to the capital at my main camp. I spoke to Lammie last night and she gave me a message for you. She asked me to explain that neither she nor Ouwa have had a moment to write to you. She asked me if I would come and tell you all her news. And as in any case I was coming to see you the next day, of course, I said "yes".'

He did not even then hint at the fact that Lammie had expressed great anxiety as to how François, on his own for the first time, might be getting on at Hunter's Drift. He thought that even a hint of such an anxiety might hurt François's self-respect. So knowing how hungry François might be for reassurance at that moment he repeated, 'No, Little old Cousin, I was indeed about to visit you. It is far too long since you and I have had a talk together.'

The wise old hunter could not have chosen words to please François more. Yet the fact that he had by-passed Lammie's message made François uneasy.

'I'm so glad to have you here, Uncle,' he said, 'but what did Lammie say? What did the doctors say? When are they coming back? How is Ouwa?'

These and a dozen or more related questions fell from him so fast that Mopani, smiling one of his rare smiles said, 'Little Cousin, slowly please! Slowly over the stones, as the old pioneers said. Besides, you know the Sindabele saying, one anxious person can ask more questions in half a minute than seven *Indunas* can answer in a year. Be patient, please, and I'll tell you all.'

Mopani spoke very slowly in that deliberate voice so characteristic of him. It was as if thinking and searching for the right word to express a thought were another form of hunting; the human mind following the track of meaning like a hunter the faint and enigmatic spoor of the most elusive of animals through a tightly tangled bush. He started wisely by giving François all the messages of love which Ouwa and Lammie had sent him, elaborate apologies and explanations for their not writing and reminders of things they wished François to do at Hunter's Drift in their absence. Only then did he get to the heart of the matter. Ouwa had already seen two of the foremost specialists in the capital. Both had declared that they could find nothing organically, or indeed seriously wrong with Ouwa. They thought it possible that he had been too long without a break in the hot climate of Hunter's Drift and was suffering only from a prolonged kind of climatic exhaustion for which they had a long, strange word which Mopani could not remember. It was not important however because, in essence, in their view all that Ouwa needed was a change. They urged Lammie to take him at once far down south to the sea at the Cape of Good Hope, not only to recuperate there as they had every belief he would, but also to have confirmation from more specialists, whom they regarded as the greatest of their kind in the whole of Africa, if not in the entire world.

Mopani did all he could to exclude the tone of discouragement with which Lammie had told him this, also her deep disappointment and increased concern that such eminent people could only repeat themselves as before in general terms, without a specific diagnosis of Ouwa and exact prescription of a remedy. In fact Mopani himself, in that quick, intuitive way all great hunters have, had put the telephone down feeling far more uneasy about his friend than he had ever felt before.

Some of this uneasiness of his got through to François from the way he told the story. When he had ended, François sat for some moments in silence, becoming so uneasy himself that the taste he had rediscovered only half an hour before vanished and he could not face his coffee. He just watched Mopani, not unnaturally after that long ride in the heat of the day, enjoying coffee, rusks and cake, as if he had not eaten for days. Watching him, François felt this uneasiness build up inside him like

172

electricity in a thunder-cloud, until finally, before he could even think a clear thought, a question was suddenly completed in his mind and darted like lightning out of him. Yet it was not fast enough for him not to feel so frightened by its nature that he again took Mopani's hand as he asked it. 'Is Ouwa going to die?'

Mopani was so startled that his steady hand trembled and some coffee spilt over the edge of his cup. He was by nature as truthful a man as there has perhaps ever been. Truth, or accuracy as he, in that quiet, unassuming way of his, would have preferred to put it, was perhaps the greatest of life's commandments for him. If it were not for the fact that he put truth and accuracy before anything else, he could not have been so accurate, or should one say so true a shot and hunter. It was precisely because there was nothing false anywhere in his person that there could be nothing false in either his hunting and his shooting. And, out of this love of accuracy of his, it had become an axiom of behaviour to him that any human being, no matter how small, was entitled to a precise answer to any question which he could form. He believed that when a person could form a question, it was a sign from life that the person was ready for a truthful answer.

After a long hesitation he put his arm round François's shoulder and said, 'Coiske [not Little Cousin as in the past], look at me. I have told you what the doctors have said. They know far more about these things than I or you do. And it would be wrong to ignore the importance of what they have said. But I myself have to tell you in reply to your question that my own feeling is that Ouwa is about to die.'

François's reaction was the most moving vindication of Mopani's belief in the truth which he had ever experienced. All traces of the tendency to self-pity which had assailed François a moment before had vanished. On the contrary, there was that odd look of relief which comes when pretence and unreality are at last defied and banished from the imagination.

Knowing that he had finally found honest companionship on a fearful road he had previously walked alone, François exclaimed, 'D'you really think so? You know, I've feared this ever since the day Ouwa brought Hintza home as a puppy from your camp. It's so good of you Uncle, to tell me what you really think. I can't thank you enough.'

At this unexpected reaction from François, it was the old hunter's turn to look away, his eyes blinking for the first time in many years.

Mopani, of course, was right. No imagination has yet been great enough to invent improvements to the truth. Truth, however terrible, carried within itself its own strange comfort for the misery it is so often compelled to inflict on behalf of life. Sooner or later it is not pretence but the truth which gives back with both hands what it has taken away with one. Indeed, unaided and alone it will pick up the fragments of the reality it has shattered and piece them together again in the shape of more immediate meaning than the one in which they had been previously contained. Yet one must hasten to admit that even that was not the whole of the matter.

Like Mopani, François had the natural life of the bush to aid him in this moment of truth. Young as he was, death was no stranger to him. He could hardly remember, had he found it necessary to give so routine a matter a thought, a single day in his life in which he had not witnessed the death of some living thing. For instance, he had seen animals he had known personally as it were at Hunter's Drift, killed daily for food. He had learned to make his peace with the fact because it was death inflicted in a cause of life. He had been encouraged in this acceptance of this aspect of reality by seeing the same law at work in the life of animals, birds, insects and even plants. Moreover, he himself had been forced to be an instrument of death, by helping to shoot from an early age for food. He had also on several occasions seen people dying what men call a natural death. Lammie and Ouwa both insisted, when any of their friends or servants were dying, that they all should rally to their side and stand around them so that they should know that they were not left to face that great departure alone in their little beehive huts. It was utterly impossible, therefore, young as he was, for him to think of death as the outrage which it is increasingly becoming in the view of metropolitan man, who keeps himself and his young as far as he can from witnessing death of any kind and·so allows all the natural aids life has built into man for facing death to crumble by neglect and default. Death was as much part of the natural landscape of the spirit for François as that of the physical world. It was always near. One crossed the Amanzim-tetse river at one's peril from crocodiles and hippopotami. One entered daily the great bush so full of danger that from time to time men vanished into it, never to return. Nature, one's instinct informed one, was the example one neglected at peril to one's progress through life, was perhaps the world of the spirit made manifest without so that one could recognize it from within.

All this did not mean that one was tamely fatalistic about death. As François had learned, there was in the bush a vast difference between killing for survival and giving into death oneself before absolutely forced to do so. Even the mortally wounded animal fought death, as if a point of ultimate honour, until, it seemed to men like Mopani, it achieved at the final transition a transfiguration of anguish into utter peace of spirit which was clearly recognizable in the expression as one looked down at the face of the body lying dead at one's feet. Of course there came a point when death was inevitable and natural. Then the reward appeared even greater because no one, not even a child, could have stood beside a deathbed in one of those bee-hive huts without being deeply impressed by the majesty, the impartial authority, the tenderness and reverence with which it did its final work.

'Death,' the Matabele said, 'knows no kings, it is its own king.' But until that moment came, as Mopani knew even better than François, to whom he had been the great example and teacher in the ways of nature, both animal and man were charged by life to do everything in their power to defeat death, if only to make certain that when it ultimately came it was the right kind of death.

Once again one has been compelled to draw attention to concepts which a person so young as François could not have articulated because without them one cannot map, as one is in duty bound to do in the interests of his story, the great new area into which his urgent feelings were carrying him with an unutterable logic of their own to the next natural stage in his reaction to Mopani's tragic evaluation of Ouwa's condition.

Mopani's face was still averted, his eyes still blinking at the west, when François's voice, unexpectedly loud, determined, perhaps even angry, since he was prodded by a notion that if only Ouwa and Lammie had been franker with him earlier, he would not have hesitated so long, asked, 'May I tell you something, uncle?' The question was purely rhétorical, because François, his voice louder and more intense, did not wait for an answer. 'I'm not going to let Ouwa die.'

Mopani was so startled by this outright declaration, as it were, of war on fate that all his pity and compassion for François vanished. He turned his head sharply to face François, the sun-wrinkles at the corner of his eyes vanishing as his keen, long-distance look focused on the determined young face turned up to him. One might have thought a gun shot had just gone off in his ear, so abrupt was his movement.

'You will not let it happen, Little Cousin?' he exclaimed with unbelief. 'Like you I would do anything to prevent it from happening, but what could you and I do, when the greatest doctors in the land can do nothing, except perhaps to pray for him, as I have done now for more than a year.'

'Never you mind, Uncle,' François replied, his odd new resolve stimulated by the discovery in himself of a greater confidence which in fact was the result of the growing realization that perhaps he had handled without outside help of any kind, the whole of the difficult Xhabbo affair in a way not without credit to him. He already had his suspicion that what people called growing up was, in a measure, one of being educated out of reality, above all the great invisible realities which matter so much more to a young person than the physical ones by which men set by far a greater store as they grow older. So many evasions and unrealities, so much wishful thinking seemed to have been inflicted on him, young as he was, that the time seemed to have come when he should take counsel only with himself more often. The less that other minds, even a mind so experienced and close to his own as Mopani's, interfered with his own, the better it would be for the plan forming inside him.

Even more emphatically, he repeated, 'Never you mind, Uncle. I think I know what to do to stop Ouwa from dying. I shall give those doctors in the cities one more chance. If they can still give no name to Ouwa's illness when both you and I sitting here know he is dying, I shall think of something to do myself.'

'But what on earth can you do, Little Cousin? Tell me and I'll do what I can to help.' Old Mopani was touched by what he took as a resolve doomed to failure.

'Please, Uncle. Just let's wait and see what the new doctors say,' François countered evasively. 'I promise I'll come to you when I feel I need help.'

Mopani was far too wise and too fond of François to force an answer out of him when he was so obviously reluctant to give him one. So he wisely left it at that, thinking of one of his own favourite hunting maxims, 'Never try to go ahead of your spoor. Many a man has died because he has not observed the discipline of the spoor to the end.'

It was, perhaps, just as well that he did so, because had he continued to press François, he would have been unable to resist telling him. Firstly, he was aware that his response to Mopani's question was prompted partly by his new secretive self, born on the day of Xhabbo's strange coming into his life. Secondly, he knew that if any European could understand what prompted his reticence, Mopani surely was that person.

In fact, during all the three days Mopani stayed at Hunter's Drift François was harassed by a sense of guilt over his refusal to take Mopani into his confidence. There were times when he was on the verge of discussing with Mopani the plan forming in his imagination, but always the pagan Matabele and Bushman aspects of his character rose up to throw a shadow of warning over the impulse and he would think over and over again of the Sindabele saying, 'The partridge hatches the egg in secret alone.'

The most difficult moments of all came at night, after dinner, when Mopani, sitting in Ouwa's chair at the head of the table, would produce the large leather-bound family Bible, its great brass clasps flashing, and just inside the cover that sprawling illustration of a green and yellow family tree. There, before the Genesis of man was inscribed the Genesis of the Joubert family in Africa, with all the names of the descendants of the original Pierre-Paul Joubert, who had fled with his family some three hundred years before from La Rochelle.

Mopani always read as he spoke, slowly and deliberately, since he was barely literate. He seemed to follow the words in François's observant senses as he followed the spoor of an animal through the bush, with the result that there was little rhythm but great certainty in his reading.

For some reason, Mopani's favourite parts of the Bible were the books of the prophecies, particularly the Book of Daniel. Indeed the very first night he was there, he insisted on reading from beginning to end, almost more François felt for his own benefit than François's, Daniel's account of his ordeal in the Babylonian lions' den. With the sound of lions roaring beyond the river just then, it was remarkable how immediate that ancient story became. It was at moments like that, to the sound of sacred words read by a man so without falseness, that François's conscience worried him most. There was something so utterly humble, simple and innocent about Mopani then that keeping anything from him, however good the reasons, seemed utterly wrong. All the many dear associations he had with Mopani would pour into his imagination like troops going into battle, to try and break down the entrenched resistance of his instincts against revealing himself there and then.

He would think, for instance, how patiently Mopani had taught him to read what no man could read in books; the hieroglyphic spoor, the writing in the Bible of nature as Mopani called it, of all the animals of the great bushveld into which Hunter's Drift was carved. He remembered how first thing every morning after a night in camp with Mopani, the hunter would take him by the hand and they would walk all round the camp to see exactly what animals had been near them at night; how here, for example, a hyena had come limping along to try and steal some of their meat; how there a lion had crouched low, only some seven yards away behind a bush, observing the camp to see what they were about; or how a leopard had advanced and retreated, gone round to another flank of the bush, advanced and retreated again as it sought in vain for an opening through which it could pounce to snatch first Nandi or 'Swayo and later Hintza as well. In this way at first light, as if he were a teacher in the kindergarten, Mopani had patiently taught François all the marks that animals could possibly make on the earth; more, the significance of their timing, the meaning of their spoor and on many occasions the warning implicit in them of danger in the day ahead.

He remembered Mopani teaching him how to shoot and telling him that shooting was not a matter of the will but a kind of two-way traffic between target and rifleman and that if one wanted to shoot accurately without hurt or unnecessary pain to animals, one must never force one's shot by pulling at the trigger with one's finger. Instead one had to keep the gun aimed truly on the target, until the target filled not only all one's eyes but activated one's imagination, until one's finger gradually tight-ened on the trigger, releasing the shot only when target and rifleman were one. Mopani would talk almost as if shooting for him were allegorical, and the rifle the contemporary version of the symbol the sword once was in the mind of medieval man; the image of the spirit in its everlasting battle against falseness and unreality in life.

'Remember, Little Cousin,' he had often said, 'a good hunter does not force so much as grow his shots.'

All this was sanctified for François in recollection of Mopani's intense dislike of unnecessary killing and the scorn with which he spoke of the people from the cities who used their money to buy the right to shoot animals out of that strange, secretive lust for killing in civilized man which he once described as the 'eighth deadly sin'. That, Mopani had often emphasized to him, was the reason why he himself had turned to preserving the life of the wild and to creating his immense sanctuary for game and plants in the bush.

It is not difficult, therefore, to imagine how uneasy François felt in such a presence which in many ways meant as much to him as Ouwa or Lammie. On top of it all he was bothered that he, who knew so much less about life than Mopani, should feel just a little superior when he heard him reading from the Bible, because he himself could have done it very much more easily and fluently.

He remembered, in particular, an occasion when Ouwa and Lammie had taken advantage of one of Mopani's visits to ask him if he would witness their signatures to some legal document. Mopani had taken up Ouwa's pen as if it were some highly complex and advanced technological instrument, dipped it with a kind of fearful care into the inkwell, cleared his throat nervously several times as he aimed the pen almost like a spear about to give some wounded animal a *coup de grâce* and, even after that, hesitated so much that Lammie had whispered to François, who was starting to fidget and, in the irreverent way of the very young boy he was at the time, finding it all so comical that he was in danger of sniggering, 'Quiet Coiske, quiet. Can't you see that Uncle Mopani is about to sign his name?'

François, abashed, of course obeyed and in a silence so great that one could hear the pen scratching the paper as if the nib were tearing holes in it, Mopani signed himself, 'H. H. Théron'.

There then was the moment, still illuminated in his memory as by the light of the great oil lamp of the dining-room, when François first realized that Mopani was not the old hunter's only name. He had others. And what could they be?

Even Lammie was unaware of what they were because when Mopani left the house, as he always did every night of his life whether in his own main camp, in a tent out in the blue or at Hunter's Drift, to have a walk around in the dark to look at the sky and the night as if he knew that the whole of the world out there would want him to wish it goodnight, as it obviously would bid him one in return, he heard Lammie whispering to Ouwa, 'Look, he's signed himself "H. H. Théron". What on earth does the H. H. stand for?'

Ouwa had looked round at first to make certain that no one was listening. Luckily François knew from experience how quickly grownups could go silent on children. Everybody, including 'Bamuthi and Ousie-Johanna was only too often reminding one another in his hearing that 'little pitchers have big ears', which in his view was one of the most humiliating proverbs ever invented by insensitive adults. So he had instinctively looked away with an expression of almost histrionic indifference, but with his ears bigger than they had ever been.

Listening obliquely but intently, he heard Ouwa say, 'I will tell you but you must promise never to speak of it to a living soul. I only discovered it in the war in Ethiopia when as you know I was one of the scouts under his command. We'd been lying in our shelters for some days. We couldn't move because the rain was pouring down on us so heavily and the misery and inaction of it all had thrown us all back deep into ourselves. Mopani was lying beside me and we were sharing our blankets because it was so cold at that height in the middle of the night, and he suddenly said to me, "Pierre-Paul, you are an educated man. I wonder if you can help me if I ask you something that has bothered me for years. Only you must promise you will never tell a soul what I am about to ask. I have two names. They are names that have always been given to the eldest sons of my family. I have some idea what the first name is about but the second one has always puzzled me. I have no idea where it comes from, I have always been happy to let people call me nothing but Mopani. I should be happy to die as Mopani but you know, those two damned names nibble like field mice at my mind in the night, and perhaps you can help me get rid of the nuisance for good." Of course I promised, and I give you two guesses as to what the names are.'

Lammie had thought and thought and guessed and guessed, her large brown eyes lovelier than ever with wonder and curiosity, and her abundant hair shining like strands of the soft light itself of that old oil lamp hanging from the ceiling. She had tried all sorts of combinations of names but in the end had had to admit defeat.

'Well,' Ouwa had said, 'believe it or not, but he was christened Hercules Hyppolyte Théron. The Hercules, Mopani admitted to me, he might just be able to take but when I told him who and what the original Hyppolyte was in Greek legends, he groaned with embarrassment. In the end he told me with a fierceness you wouldn't have thought him capable of, "Much as I like you Pierre-Paul, I warn you I'll murder you if ever you tell a soul I've been called after such a fellow, or my name is not Mopani." And several times before falling asleep I heard him muttering to himself, "What a terrible thing to do to a defence-less child, giving it names like those. Thank God for Mopani!"'

François, sensitive as he himself was on the subject of names as one has observed, felt immediate sympathy for Mopani, but not so Lammie and Ouwa. They had not laughed outright, it is true, because they were far too fond of the old hunter but they had stood there silent, a kind of Mona Lisa smile on their faces – the sort of all-knowing, all-foreseeing expression which came to them when they shared not just a secret source of amusement but were at one in the esotericism of an entire age. It was something François found rather maddening because it shut him out so subtly from the inner world of his parents.

Yet even that was not the end of the matter for Lammie. She soon asked the inevitable, 'But how come the "Mopani"?'

Ouwa had given the appropriate explanation by telling Lammie at some length the story of Mopani's father, the prototype of the great hunter who figures so largely in the stories of John Buchan. Mopani's father had earned his name up and down the length of the great Hunter's Road and along its many branches right into the heart of Africa. Apparently he was called Mopani because, for all Africans, the mopani tree stood for all that was indestructible if not immortal in life. Once the mopani tree was fully grown it seemed never to grow older. Above all it was always green. Ouwa emphasized, that in all the many droughts he had lived through, he had never seen the butterfly-shaped leaves of the mopani tree wither or die.

He himself remembered the most terrible of all droughts when the earth had gone bald and black because all the grass and shrub appeared to have been burnt up by the sun. At midday, for months, one had seen under a sky of the most ruthless blue and completely without compassion of cloud, nothing but wave upon wave of the flames of heat breaking over it like the swell of some Ancient Mariner's quick-silver sea. Yet even then Ouwa could remember arriving on the edge of some bush and seeing, as something reflected in a distorting mirror, the mopani trees standing and holding their parasols of trembling green leaves on barley-sugar stems over the parched and dying earth. It was not surprising therefore that in the imagination of Africans the mopani tree was a striking testimony of the invincibility of the processes of growth in nature. Mopani's father was so called because he personified all these things, for Africans everywhere.

Ouwa had known him as a little boy. He clearly recollected how when he died he seemed no older than when he had first appeared in Ouwa's life. He still remembered the unbelief everywhere in Africa when the news of the first Mopani's death started being whispered around in the bush. By that time he was known as Great Mopani because on the death of his wife way down south, he had reappeared in the interior with a son aged only fourteen. The son already showed so many qualities of the father that he had immediately become Little Mopani. When Great Mopani died the 'little' was dropped from the son's name and he become just Mopani, which Ouwa thought implied an even greater stature than that of the father, as if he were the only one of his kind left in the world. As Lammie had probably noticed, Mopani had the same striking capacity of his father for looking ageless, so that no one knew exactly how old he was.

Lammie, in the way of women who seem to attach a greater importance to age than men, immediately asked, 'But surely *you* must know exactly how old he is?'

Ouwa shook his head emphatically. During the war he had indeed dared to ask Mopani his age. Mopani had looked at him in amazement. Somewhat bewildered, he had dismissed the question as if utterly irrelevant, 'You know, Pierre-Paul,' he said quietly, 'that is something to which I have never given a thought.'

'But surely, Mopani,' Ouwa who could not resist the schoolmaster in himself and was compelled to approach life by way of questions and answers had persisted, 'it isn't a matter for thought? Surely it's a very simple one of knowledge. You must have been asked the question for official reasons often enough to know the answer.'

'If I have,' Mopani replied in his normal, deliberate voice, 'I have forgotten. I've never thought of myself or my friends or anybody at all in terms of age, I'm only interested in what people are, and not in how long they have been what they happen to be. Age is a matter between man and nature, it's enough that the sun and the moon and the seasons keep an account of the span on earth of us all.'

Ouwa was about to go on but Lammie, whose eyes seemed to François to have widened and to glow more than ever at this reply, exclaimed, impressed, 'He talked like that to you? It sounds more like the talk of a poet than a hunter.'

'You'd be surprised,' Ouwa had commented. 'He has a great

deal of the poet in him, just as all Africans, Hottentots, Bushmen and all the other natural people you and I have known are poets at heart. You have only to listen, for instance, to old 'Bamuthi to know that he could give the average Poet Laureate a few lessons. Only Mopani is not even as articulate as they are. You have to watch how he behaves as man and hunter to see really that he is an artist in fact and deed rather than words.'

He had then gone on to elaborate on the incident, which obviously had made a great impression on him, perhaps because, as François for all his love of Ouwa was to realize later rather sadly, he was a person essentially of an analytical and inquiring mind and could have envied the accepting and trusting spirit so necessary for the 'Bamuthi or Mopani approach to life. He described how he and Mopani had sat there on a boulder looking at a great spread of baroque mountains and how, speaking thus, Mopani had waved an almost proprietary hand at the immense landscape suspended there so high in the blue and said, 'There is my calendar on the wall.' Then, pointing up at the sun he had added, 'And there is my time-piece. Between them, they know when I was born and when I will have to die. That is enough for me, even if it isn't enough for fellows like you.'

This part of the conversation was perhaps most important for François, who was all the time listening to his parents who were by now so absorbed in what they were saying to each other that they seemed unaware of his presence. François, as one has indicated often enough, had his own instinctive measure of time. He was, as he put it to himself, 'sick and tired' of having matters of which he could and could not do, or be told, or what he could and could not read, and a whole series of other choices, determined entirely in terms of what his age happened to be at a particular moment. His heart warmed even more, if that were possible, to Mopani for apparently sharing, even if not for precisely the same reasons, an equally dim view of the conventional approach to time and age. It struck him suddenly that Mopani had never really treated him like a child except in so far as his physical capacities were involved, never in matters of inner concern. It was as if Mopani's attitude always implied that he regarded François as an equal. Many tiny examples of this sparkled suddenly on the surface of his mind like flakes of a full moon on a midnight sea. The largest and greatest flake of them all, of course, was the way in which Mopani had unhesitatingly told François that he was convinced that Ouwa was going to die.

These and many other recollections assailed him as he watched Mopani sitting in Ouwa's place at the head of the table, reading from the Bible which was perhaps the only book he had ever completely read. The most wonderful feeling of being in partnership with the old hunter warmed him with reassurance and confidence. He had no intimation then that he was on the point of another demonstration of how much a partner Mopani was to make him feel.

Mopani had the habit of getting up not even at dawn but with the morning star, which at that time happened to be old Koba's Dawn's Heart. François knew this habit and, determined not to waste a minute of his time with Mopani, did not wait for Ousie-Johanna to call him in the mornings. He saw to it that he was up first, washed, dressed and waiting for Mopani in the breakfast room. He would be followed almost immediately by Ousie-Johanna, grumbling and muttering that it was just like men to expect women to be up at all hours of the day and night to serve them, since she too had to be up earlier than usual, but both Mopani and François knew she was secretly rather pleased to have such proof of how indispensable she was in the life of the men at Hunter's Drift. After all, what can be worse for natural human beings, particularly women, than not being needed or wanted?

On the third morning after Mopani's arrival, they had barely finished their coffee and rusks and were watching a classical pink dawn, unbelievably delicate and tender for so giant and rough a land, staining the glass of the windows.

Suddenly Hintza who, as usual, was sitting expectantly by François's side waiting for his share of a sweet rusk dunked in sweeter coffee, lost all interest in food and whirled about to stare at the window, his nose as high in the air as possible, ears erect and alert, causing François to break off talking to Mopani so that he could focus all his attention on Hintza's reactions. He was not absolutely certain, but he thought he could just hear a strange kind of sound vibrating against the windows, firmly shut

185

against the cool of the early morning. At that moment, 'Bamuthi burst through the door.

He wasted no time on formal greetings but addressed himself straight away to Mopani, asking him to get his gun and come at once because an enormous elephant had suddenly emerged from the bush, apparently in a great rage, and was already trampling the modest gardens beyond the Matabele kraals. Faint as the light was, 'Bamuthi was certain it was that great old rogue of an elephant which had threatened them some years before and whom they had succeeded in driving off. This old elephant was a legendary creature with a formidable reputation.

If all the stories told about it were to be believed, it was larger than the greatest elephant bull ever seen at Hunter's Drift. Always alone, it was one of the most eccentric personalities of the bush; an *éminence grise* of nature, turned destructive and known everywhere by the name 'Uprooter of Great Trees'. The only reason it hadn't been hunted down and killed by the people of the bush was that it was thought to be mad. Madness gave it some sort of taboo. There was a universal feeling that madness was caused by the presence within the body of the spirit of a great magician who would be made even more angry and more malicious if the home that it had made for himself in the body of the elephant, were destroyed and the spirit forced to emigrate.

On this occasion 'Bamuthi thought that this Uprooter of Great Trees was not only mad but drunk. The drunkenness surprised neither François nor Mopani because it happened to be the season when the delicious fruits of the marula tree were in such abundance that neither man, bird nor beast could consume them. Consequently the fruit was lying everywhere spread out on the earth, fermenting within their skins and becoming more and more charged with alcohol. Elephants who are perhaps the greatest gourmets of the bush, loved the fruit of the marula in all its forms but none so much as in an advanced alcoholic state. They would come from far and wide in the proper season to dine and wine on the fruit of the marula. As a rule, being decent citizens of the bush, they would take to their marula cups like honest gentlemen, just getting pleasantly drunk so that they swayed around full of an almost Teutonic *gemütlichkeit*; making noises that were their equivalent of hiccups; rubbing

186

shoulders again and again, and patting one another affection-ately on the back with unusually limp trunks.

When Hunter's Drift was first established, the problem of preserving its gardens and fruit against such creatures as ele-phants had at once to be resolutely faced. Pierre-Paul and his Matabele helpers had been forced to deal severely with the elephant invaders of their cultivated terrain, killing many of their leaders in the process. Being the intelligent, sagacious creatures that they were, the point of the lesson soon went home and was so well preserved in their fantastic memories that from then on they had left Hunter's Drift alone. But there was always from time to time the odd, eccentric elephant, made odder by separation from his community. Thinking himself the one valid exception to the rules of the elephant world, he would break out and try to plunder the succulent gardens of Hunter's Drift.

Uprooter of Great Trees was the greatest example of them all. Pierre-Paul would have shot him long since if it had not been out of respect for 'Bamuthi and his kinsmen who always pleaded that he should be given one more chance. The elephant had allowed himself to be scared away in the past, but 'Bamuthi made it clear this morning, that although all the Matabele women and children had immediately assembled and done all they could by shouting, screaming, beating their iron domestic utensils as loudly as they could, the elephant just refused to move. On the contrary it seemed to be getting madder by the moment, so that 'Bamuthi feared that not just the gardens but the lives of his own people were in great danger.

Mopani, who always gave the appearance of being his most leisurely when there was need for speed and action, looked steadily at 'Bamuthi over his steaming cup of coffee, and ob-served: 'Elephants, like men, should know that it is the begin-ning of the end, when they start drinking before breakfast in the morning.' He paused for a moment and then remarked: 'Well, cousin [endearingly dropping the "little"], I expect our coffee can wait for once and we had better see what we can do about this old Uprooter of Great Trees.'

Moreover, he gave François no advice, as Ouwa probably would have done, as to what gun he should choose for himself. Mopani left it entirely to François. He put his cup down, got up without another word and went out of the breakfast room to come back almost at once with his own favourite 9·9 mm. Mauser on his arm, just as François returned with Pierre-Paul's own elephant gun in his hands.

They left the house and the moment they were out on the stoep, they could hear the barking of the dogs, the shouts and cries of men, women, girls and boys, the clamour of cooking pot lids and empty paraffin tins being beaten, beyond the Matabele kraals. The din, though remote, was intense and obviously desperate.

Hintza wanted to be off at full speed. François's inclination was not altogether different but one look at Mopani clearly showed him that such an approach would not do, because although he was walking fast, Mopani was taking care not to move too fast and arrive on the scene short of breath, depriving his shooting of the accuracy which the occasion was obviously going to demand. That was another of his maxims François remembered; no hunter worth the name ever walked at a pace which forced him to breathe through his mouth.

So François restrained both himself and Hintza, adjusting their pace to Mopani's. But not 'Bamuthi. He quickly vanished into the garden, where by now the dawn had exploded beyond the fir trees and was fanning up and out like a bush fire.

When they arrived, there, in front of Mopani and François, right in the centre of the vast magic lantern slide which the dawn had made of the sky, soared the black shape of Uprooter of Great Trees looking like a giant apparition which had come bursting through barriers of unrecorded history and forgotten myth. He was surrounded in a wide circle by about forty screaming human beings who were pelting him as fast as they could with stones, burning faggots of wood that sped like swarms of fireflies through the air, long dark assegais, outsize knobkerries and anything else they could lay their hands on. But as 'Bamuthi had warned them, the elephant was refusing to be scared. At the same time Uprooter of Great Trees did not know exactly what to do.

Elephants are notoriously short-sighted, though they have the most remarkable senses of smell and hearing, but neither smell nor hearing could give this elephant a bearing on his enemies in his present plight since, totally surrounded as he was, his senses were assailed equally from all directions. The result was that at one moment he would throw up his trunk, trumpet a sort of cavalry call to battle, promptly roll up the sensitive trunk tucking it away for safety under his chin, and charge in one direction, only to find his enemies vanish out of range of his limited sight. So the next moment he would whirl about with fantastic nimbleness, charging the opposite way with the same vain result, except that with every charge more and more of the gardens were being trampled. Also, being faster than his enemies, each charge carried him inexorably closer to the frail circle of the Matabele kraal.

The moment Mopani and François arrived the Matabele men, women and children became silent with relief. They were obviously exhausted and worse still, near to losing their courage. The silence was more frightening to François than all the clamour had been. In the sudden silence, the morning air which always preceded sunrise made the leaves of the bush rustle like the sound of a remote sea, and the leaves in that light shone like scales of bronze. Soon their whispering was lost as birds, baboons, and a couple of lions sent up their own Hosanna to the day. When this was over, François heard plainly the stomach of Uprooter of Great Trees boiling like a witch's cauldron with spirit, rage and exertion. For a moment the vast marble elephant looked as overawed by the silence of its enemies as was François. It was standing still itself, its long trunk between the longest pair of ivory tusks that François had ever seen, stretched out searching for scent. A pair of enormous black ears fanned the speckled space between them for sound, like the fins of a giant fish keeping station at the bottom of some unfathomed ocean. He had time only to observe so much and no more. Mopani out of his immense experience knew such a moment could not last. Soon this strange, enraged, crazy and rather drunk elephant would be encouraged by the silence and resume his campaign of destruction.

Calmly, as if it were the most natural thing in the world, he looked down at François and said in his deliberate even voice: 'You take him, cousin.'

François could never tell how it happened that he, too,

responded as if the occasion were the most natural and ordinary thing in the world for him. He had no time for thought, fear, emotion or reflection that he had never before shot at an elephant. He seemed suddenly to have become an entirely objective instrument. His father's gun came to his shoulder. His eyes filled with the image of the head of Uprooter of Great Trees, focused on the one place in the bone of the massive brow where there was a small opening to the brain. He held the sights of his rifle on this central spot in the head of the elephant until his eyes and target were completely at one. Then pressure of his finger on the trigger tightened naturally, without a tremor, to release a flower of flame at the end of his rifle. A shot rang out, sounding oddly remote to him as though it had come from the rifle of someone else at his side. Instantly, unbelievably, the vast old elephant sank on to his knees, shook his head for a moment, shuddered like a torpedoed ship and rolled slowly on his side to vanish among the tall mealies and the long millet like a gallant destroyer going down into the incorruptible green of the high sea of morning.

Mopani, although it took François a long time to appreciate it, paid him the greatest of all compliments by not praising his shot. He just remained standing silently by François's side. But had François looked up into the eyes of the old hunter just then, he would have been surprised at the complex emotions showing in them.

François, however, was busy reloading his gun and then he had the duty of walking slowly forward with the gun at the ready towards the elephant in case the animal was just stunned. Yet it needed only one look at the elephant to know that it was dead. And then the strangest of feelings overcame François. It seemed to one part of himself that he had just made an immense black hole in his life. At one moment there had been so much life in the shape of the gigantic and embattled old elephant filling all the dew-fresh world. Now there was nothing, nothing at all. François had no feelings of triumph, or of personal achievement. All that had happened seemed to have had nothing to do with him. He was conscious only of this odd sort of melancholy.

Then he noticed that Mopani had come to stand beside him.

190

Looking down at the elephant, he exclaimed, '*Ja-nee*, he was *darem* a monument of his kind.'

Both *ja-nee* and *darem* used in Mopani's observation at this solemn moment needed no explanation to François. Both were fundamentals in the authentic vocabulary of this singular old hunter, as well as idioms of a vanished generation of pioneers in Africa. *Ja-nee* literally means 'yes-no', and Mopani always used it when he was confronted with an aspect of reality which to him went far beyond mere question and answer, positive and negative, or opposites of any kind. It was for him an expression in the here and now of the mysterious, inexpressible and abiding paradox that is at the heart of all inanimate and living matter, but most especially at the heart of man on his brief, zigzag trajectory through space and time. The way Mopani uttered the phrase, the 'yes' was perhaps some kind of entrance for the spirit, the 'no' an exit of a great cosmic paradox stretched in between the two extremes like a dark, unexplored bush.

Darem is even more difficult to explain, suggesting an apprehension of reality independent of all possible qualification of adjective or adverb, a word for which one has encountered no equivalent in any other language. If one were forced to translate it one would be compelled to use a combination of many terms as, for instance, in Mopani's exclamation beside the body of Uprooter of Great Trees. It would mean something to the effect that 'in the meantime, notwithstanding, however, Uprooter of Great Trees was a monument of his kind', implying that no matter what arguments, exceptions and objections the world could bring against this specific observation it would still remain permanently and indisputably true. It is not difficult to see, therefore, how well the *darem* also served the sense of the ultimate paradox of the 'yes-no' embedded in the foundation of Mopani's character.

That too is why one has been compelled to elaborate on these two favourite expressions of Mopani's, not only because they are part of the code of his character but also so that when the need arises to use them again, one will know not just their literal meaning but all they intimate of Mopani's wordless philosophy and of his awareness of the ultimate that was present in a specific occasion in François's life.

Perhaps as significant an indication of the transcendental emotions evoked by the killing of Uprooter of Great Trees, so strangely timed by life for first light, was the fact that 'Bamuthi reacted not in precisely the same way but on parallel lines, which, as François knew from his school books, met only in infinity. And who can dispute that infinity was not present there at that moment?

'Bamuthi, taller than the tallest among his clan, had come to stand also in silence beside them. The clan had followed close behind and was crowding around because they wanted the re-assurance of their own eyes that the unbelievable elephant was indeed stretched out dead on the earth in front of them.

After a while 'Bamuthi spoke with great solemnity. 'Uprooter of Great Trees was a great lord,' he said, 'and his trunk was his hand. He must forgive us for killing him but we could not help it.' Then he slowly turned his back on the elephant and com-manded his own people: 'See that you thank our lord the elephant for allowing himself to be killed so that we can live. See, there in his body we have food for many more days than the maize and millet which he trampled under his great feet could have given us.'

Obviously he was uttering what was in the hearts of all the men, women and children present. Immediately the women uttered the ululating sound that François had heard many times before. While this sound was still shimmering in the air as the sunlight was beginning to shimmer on the sea of the trembling leaves of the great bush, the men and the boys linked arms together and in a long line raised their legs high above their heads and brought them down simultaneously on the earth again and again, until the ground resounded like a drum, all in the manner which tradition prescribed for honouring a king.

That then was the end in the physical world of the affair of Uprooter of Great Trees. It was not the end, however, in the minds of 'Bamuthi and his people, who would go on talking about it with elaborations for generations. Nor, of course, was it the end for François whose memory of that morning would accompany him all his days. Far more important than these obvious considerations, was another consequence not so easily recognized, which would influence his own character profoundly in the months to come.

In this connection one faces the most subtle aspect of Mopani's role in the affair. He himself had hardly ever known any other schoolroom than the bush. Events such as the killing of Uprooter of Great Trees were examples of object lessons from which he himself had learned from his famous father. For them both the bush had been the blackboard of life.

From the moment 'Bamuthi first reported the appearance of Uprooter of Great Trees, Mopani's active imagination had seized on the possibility that this could be a unique opportunity to establish firmly in François a process of increasing self-reliance which he, Mopani, felt certain the boy was going to need much sooner than either he or his parents realized. He had seized the opportunity all the more eagerly because he knew that standing ready with his own gun at François's side there was really no danger in letting François shoot first. Yet he had had the imagination to do it with an appearance of such casualness that no one could have told that he also had been prepared to shoot if necessary.

François in his own inevitable review of what had happened, could not help suspecting something of the kind and in the frank manner customary between them, was prompted repeatedly to ask: 'But Uncle, could you really have thought that I'd kill Uprooter of Great Trees with my very first shot? Surely you were standing there ready all the time to finish him off if I failed?'

'Look, Coiske,' Mopani would reply patiently to each question, 'no hunter worth his salt would have faced such a moment with a companion, no matter how old or experienced, without being ready to come to his help. All sorts of things can always go wrong for the best of us as, indeed, they have for me. But I can honestly say, it never occurred to me that you would fail.'

With each patient answer Mopani's realization grew that the long-term strategy of his answers did not deprive them of a basic truth. His real contribution to the morning perhaps had been his inexorable perception that this could be an occasion, designed uniquely by life for François, and that no matter what the outcome he had to leave it to the boy to resolve.

Most important of all, he hoped, would be the fact that he had, indeed, never doubted the outcome of the occasion. He would, perhaps, have discussed these considerations with François but that would have needed a capacity for saying extremely complicated things in a simple way, which Mopani did not think he possessed. He thought he was capable, at the most, of saying simple things in complicated ways.

All he could get himself to do, therefore, was to talk at some length of the unfailing knack life seemed to have of confronting a man at the most unexpected moments with problems as large and dangerous as had been old Uprooter of Great Trees. Human beings, he stressed, always knew more than they allowed themselves to know. One of the things they never knew clearly enough was the power they possessed of overcoming problems even if they were thrice the size of Uprooter of Great Trees. Provided men looked them straight in the face, stood fast and directed their imaginations truly to the centre (as François had done that morning), they would find their strength. Would his little Cousin, for instance, he asked, putting his hand on François's shoulder, have known the day before that he had it in him to stop one of the greatest of rogue elephants from destroying the gardens, kraals and, perhaps, the lives of some of his Matabele friends as well? Surely if asked such a question the night before his little Cousin's answer would have been 'No'. Yet how wrong he would have been.

That part of it all was not over-difficult to express. Life for Mopani was, in essence, allegorical. The fact that almost the only books he had read had been the Bible and *The Pilgrim's Progress* had not only helped him to see but also to speak of all experience in an allegorical manner. What defeated him was how to tell François with words to match all his tenderness for the boy, that at the centre of all his generalizations was the immediate and specific concern of preparing him for Ouwa's death which was much nearer, he was convinced, than anyone else, except perhaps Ouwa, realized.

He was convinced that François's need for this kind of awareness was all the more urgent because François appeared to have an illusion that somehow he could prevent the inevitable for Ouwa. He feared the consequence of such an illusion for Fran-

194

çois, as much as he did Ouwa's death, because it would inflict on the boy when at his most vulnerable, two blows in place of one: the loss of Ouwa plus a sense of personal failure.

Mopani knew from his own experience that this sense of personal failure was the greatest Uprooter of Great Trees a man could be asked to overcome. His experience had taught him that the only answer in those circumstances lay in the way one stood up to the occasion. In the end neither success nor failure mattered as much as the manner of meeting the challenge. He would not, therefore, have suggested anything which might weaken François's resolve to challenge the inevitable. All he wanted to ensure was that the encounter of the morning somehow confirmed in François his overall capacity to deal with the future no matter what it might hold in store.

Whether his motives were suspected by François or not, Mopani could not know for certain. His relationship over the years with François had created such a quick system of communication between the two of them that François understood the inexpressible as well as he did the expressible in their conversation. More words could have blurred the meaning of all that had happened between them on that day. So when Mopani announced at the end of the meal that he thought he would have to get back to his own duties early the next morning, François was not surprised. He just accepted instinctively that it was the natural moment for Mopani to go.

Mopani's reason was simply that his departure on such a triumphant note, far from harming it, could help it to grow in the additional isolation that his going would impose on François. Yet he felt it necessary to accompany the announcement with the qualification that, quite apart from the call of his duties, he wanted to be at the end of the telephone in case he had more messages to bring from Lammie and Ouwa. Besides, he promised, that whether there were any messages or not, he would be back again soon to see François. Perhaps, the next time, he could take him away from his lessons for a few days on one of his shorter patrols into the bush?

So at sunrise the next day François found himself faced with another goodbye. It was extraordinary to him how the pattern of life at Hunter's Drift determined that most of the 'goodbyes' had to be said at dawn and most of the welcomings at sunset. All the same, having to separate from Mopani so soon after the going of Xhabbo, even in these most favourable circumstances made him miserable. Therefore as a pretext for putting off the moment of parting for as long as possible, he joined Ousie-Johanna in preventing Mopani from setting out on his journey on a first-light diet of rusks and coffee, as he obviously wanted to do, by insisting on his staying until he had eaten an unusually large breakfast.

In honour as well as in appetite bound, he set Mopani an example of how one should deal with such a breakfast. Hintza was as exemplary as his master, because when François gave the three dogs three large fresh raw lumps of meat, Hintza had done with his share long before Nandi and 'Swayo, who needed it far more than he did; after all, they had a long journey through the bush ahead of them.

Mopani's appearance, as he sat at the breakfast table, was typical. He was meticulously dressed. One would have thought that he was going not on a long journey through the great bush, but to a wedding in some community of pioneers. Ousie-Johanna had seen to it that one of her helpers had washed and ironed his green whip-cord uniform so that the cloth was un-crumpled and the trousers properly creased. His long bush jacket, with its ample pockets, fitted his tall shape as if made to measure. The wide-brimmed khaki-green bush hat had been brushed and dusted and the band of lion skin around the crown smouldered like gold. In the centre of the band shone a small cluster of blue down from one of his favourite birds, the swift Abyssinian roller that censors the indiscreet shadows of the bush with the long, decisive, blue pencil strokes of its quick flight. The sleeves of the shirt, always turned down against mosquitoes at night, were now neatly rolled back above the elbows in a manner which François always envied for, try as he might, he could never manage his own half as well. The ankle boots of calf's skin, which Mopani made for himself, were brushed and cleaned until they harmonized with the lion skin band around his hat and his pointed, Louis-Napoleon beard was freshly trimmed. Every detail of his appearance demonstrated a fastidiousness that had nothing to do with conforming to the world without but was the product solely of the abiding fashion of his exacting spirit.

As François carried the deep saddle-bags from the guest-room to dump them on the stoep outside, he found Mopani checking his 9·9 mm. Mauser, working the bolt backwards and forwards firmly but rhythmically, ensuring that its action was unimpeded. He even extracted the bolt, unplugged the barrel and held the rifle up to the sky to be quite certain that no dust had infiltrated it in the night – all precautions one might have thought super-fluous since Mopani never went to bed without cleaning his gun.

Striking a match, he held the front sight of the barrel in the flame for a moment, so that the wood smoke could remove some hint of a shine on the metal which even François had not detected.

At the same time Mopani could not resist reiterating lessons he had given François in the past, wisely speaking to himself as if for his own and not for François's benefit. For instance, re-blacking the sight of the gun with the match, he would say, 'Yes-no, you look innocent enough but I have seen that pin-point of a glint on the tip of your small nose make many a man miss because once the sun finds you, you make him take too large an aim and overshoot his target. So there, my little one!'

Finally he made certain once more that the magazine of the rifle was full of bullets and had one last look into the breech to be certain that no bullet had escaped into the barrel, saying, 'Mopani is too old and has seen too much ever to believe that there is such a thing as an empty gun. The Devil likes nothing more than slipping bullets up the spout of empty guns when an old hunter's back is turned.' He said this again as if he were quoting from his own private and personal Bible. François could not help wondering how many times he had been re-minded of that text from the moment far back in his own beginning when Mopani, finding him pointing an air-gun at a chicken, had immediately rebuked him with those very words. François had tried to excuse himself, 'But there is no pellet in the gun, uncle!'

Mopani had answered with something akin to anger, threaten-ing in that slow, patient but somehow irrefutable voice of his, 'A man, Little Cousin, never, never points a gun at anything or

197

anybody except in need, unless he is at target practice. Don't let me ever see you do that again.'

Close beside that recollection was the memory of how angry Mopani had been with him also long ago when he found him at the end of their garden without his first gun and scolded him severely: 'A man's gun in this world, Little Cousin, is always within reach of his hand.'

Then, although Mopani had done his own packing, he unstrapped his saddle bags and checked through every detail to see that nothing had been forgotten. That done, he and François went to the stables to fetch his horse. Although there were stable-hands to spare, Mopani insisted as always on caring for his horse himself. The horse, or perhaps one should say pony, as those small, hardy, inexhaustible little horses bred in the mountains of Basutoland in the far south, are called, was one of seven kept at Mopani's base. He set extraordinarily high store by them because they were all 'salted', the adjective used for horses who had survived the mysterious and almost fatal mosquito-borne disease of horse-sickness. There were artificial vaccinations available to protect the few horses about so far north in the interior, but Mopani had no faith in those. He believed only in horses which had acquired immunity against the mysterious disease by having conquered it with their own hardy constitutions.

No money could have bought the least among his little horse herd. Not only were they salted but they had come to know both the life of the bush and Mopani's voice and mind, and were a kind of radar to him. Often at night, in black storms or mist, they gave him his direction and brought him intelligence of things far beyond the range of his own senses. François knew many exciting examples of how these horses had come to Mopani's rescue in moments of crisis, how often in unknown country in the dark Mopani had just dropped the reins of his bridle on the saddle and allowed his horses to lead him safely home to his camp. So much was this known that these horses' reputation among the Matabele was formidable. 'Bamuthi himself had assured François they possessed second sight and that if one looked between their ears ahead in the dark, one could often see ghosts.

The horse at Hunter's Drift on this particular morning was Mopani's favourite. It had suitably been called Dapper. It was significant that, when François and Mopani were half-way across the courtyard which separated the homestead from the stables, Dapper recognized Mopani's long, measured tread and immediately greeted him with a silver chain of nickering.

Mopani immediately answered, 'Good morning Dapper boy, I hope you've had as good a night as I've had, for we've a long, hard way to go today.'

In the stable, they found Dapper's head already turned round at the door to greet Mopani. He rubbed his head with pleasure against Mopani's shoulder. From that moment on while Mopani quickly brushed him down and combed out his beautiful long black tail, Dapper, pleased that his lonely stand at the stable was over, responded accordingly. When led out into the courtyard to be saddled he was so clean and tidy that his black mane and dark brown coat shone like Oriental silk in the sun. The fringe of black hair, which he wore over his forehead between his quickly pointed ears was more like a medieval twist than just the hair of an hardy African animal.

Although Mopani must have saddled up horses numberless times in his life he put the saffron saddle-cloth on Dapper as if he were doing it for the first time. That was another of his favourite texts: 'No matter how great one's experience, always do everything as if for the first time.' So he adjusted and re-adjusted the saddle-cloth before he finally put the saddle on top of it, commenting that he had never caused a horse to blister yet and was not going to do so now. The saddle's position too was examined and re-examined until Mopani was satisfied he had found just the place where it would cause no discomfort to Dapper. He did all this as if he had all the time in the world, knowing it to be quicker than riding a quarter of a mile or so and then having to dismount and make readjustments to girth and saddle. There was, Mopani always emphasized, nothing more tiring, nor more likely to spoil the rhythm so necessary between a horseman and his horse than interruptions and re-adaptations on the way.

While all this was going on Nandi and 'Swayo were present to watch the final preparations for the journey with growing

199

excitement. They too had hurried out to greet Dapper, who appeared as pleased to see them as they were to see him. They leapt up to his head to salute him at the peak of their jump, and then sat down on their haunches in front of Dapper, their eyes going constantly from his face to Mopani, who was there, tall and devout as a priest, in his preparations at Dapper's side.

So absorbed were they in all this that Hintza was quite resentful at being left out of their reckoning. At one moment he felt his exclusion so keenly that he tried to ingratiate himself with Dapper in the way that Nandi and 'Swayo had done, but he was pushed aside with a brusque movement of Dapper's head. Being the sensitive dog he was, he took the hint and returned to François's side, looking as proudly forlorn and abandoned as François himself was beginning to feel, the nearer the moment for Mopani's departure came.

Leaving the reins of the bridle hanging down in front of Dapper, who had been trained to take that as a sign that he was to stand in that position until his master returned to him, no matter how desperate the noise or other commotion around him, Mopani slung an old-fashioned bandolier full of ammunition across one shoulder and his rifle over the other. He then went up to François, embraced him and said only, 'God willing, Little Cousin, I shall be seeing you again soon.'

That was another of the many things François loved about Mopani, he never patronized him with any sort of proverbial admonition to be good, or to take care. He always concentrated on a straight-forward goodbye that did more for François's morale than any proprietary advice could have done. He then turned about as lightly as an agile boy, gave Nandi and 'Swayo a warm, authoritative look out of his own blue eyes, and ordered, 'Nandi, front! 'Swayo heel!' At once Nandi took up position in front of Dapper and 'Swayo did the same behind. This arrangement, François knew, was the result of another conviction Mopani had derived from his own experience. Had he not told François often enough, 'Animal or human, it makes no difference: the female is far better at telling the unseen ahead, the male, despite Lot's wife, is better at looking over his shoulder and spotting the danger from behind.' And when François at first had asked why, Mopani had given him one of his rare smiles and said wryly, half in jest, half in earnest, 'Because all males always have a bad conscience.'

Without looking back, Mopani then swung easily into the saddle, his long legs, in that long, natural stirrup he used for long-distance riding, almost reaching to the ground. He did not tug unnecessarily at the bit in Dapper's mouth. He just spoke a quiet, 'Off we go, Dapper boy' and at once the little convoy was on its way to the footpath which, as the Matabele riddle would have it, wriggled like a long snake through the bush, on this occasion, in François's imagination like a gigantic version of the copper cobras so common at Hunter's Drift.

François and Hintza watched them until they disappeared into the bush. Though Mopani did not once look back he must have known in his intuitive way that François and Hintza were there, because just before he vanished from sight he raised his hand high above his head, as a final salute.

François may have liked to pretend to himself that this separation from Mopani, which after all was only another in a long series of important separations, was no worse than any of its predecessors. Yet he had an uneasy feeling in his heart that a great storm was on its way and that this separation was unique, marking perhaps not the end of an era for him so much as the end of the beginning of another. Considering that he had lost Xhabbo, Lammie, Ouwa and Mopani in the matter of only a few days, it would perhaps have been too much for him to accept, had he not remembered that, painful as the separations were, they did possess this one great advantage; they made him free now to set about preventing Ouwa from dying.

So the moment Mopani and his escort vanished from sight, he went round to the kitchen. Ousie-Johanna rebuked him for rushing in so abruptly, telling him that he was making such a commotion that the bread, which was rising under its blanket beside the great kitchen range, would collapse and be utterly spoilt if he behaved in that inconsiderate manner. But for once he took no notice. He just drew out a chair very gently, quietly sat down by the table, rested his chin on his hands, gave her a keen look out of his wide, blue eyes, dark with concern, and said pleadingly, 'Ousie-Johanna, I need your help and advice. The time has come when we must do something about Ouwa or it will be much too late.'

At this, Ousie-Johanna forgot all about her cherished bread and waddled towards François with such energy that the broad wooden kitchen boards shook under her massive steps, endangering the bread far more than François's abrupt entry had done, all because the look on his face and his announcement had made her anxious to the point of anger.

'I might have known that wily old Mopani didn't come all this way to see us,' she declared vehemently. 'A proper skelm he is, that one. The older they get, the more cunning they become.' *They*, for her, of course, were always the breed of men. 'I should have known only bad news could have brought him here although I would have thought you would have told me before now. It was not right to keep a poor old woman who is thinking about all of you all the time, so much in the dark here alone in her kitchen.'

Knowing from personal experience what a formidable combination anxiety, a feeling of having been slighted and a tendency to be sorry for herself could be in that grand old lady, François immediately set about mollifying her. He explained at length how impossible it had been for him to do anything until Mopani had gone, since he was not at all certain that Mopani would have approved of what he had in mind. Even if Mopani had approved, he might have wanted to take part. That, François thought, would have been risky since 'Bamuthi had warned him often enough that the sort of plan they had in mind could only work if everyone concerned believed in it completely. And he was not certain to what extent Mopani could have believed as they did, though he would not have stopped them.

François had a great deal more to say, but Ousie-Johanna interrupted. It was almost as if there and then she was going to give him proof of Mopani's distinction between male and female minds and already knew what the future had in store for them. Her expression brightened, her eyes shone with the delicate quality induced by the sweetest of smiles, and she exclaimed, 'Ah! You cannot fool this child of a baptized 'Xhosa father. You are going to uLangalibalela at last as you should have gone months ago, had you and that Lammie of yours listened to poor old Johanna instead of thinking that she is good only for cooking and nothing else at all. But what has that Mopani man told you to bring you to your senses?'

François then described how Lammie had telephoned to Mopani to say that the doctors in the capital had once more failed them, and that they were, at that very moment, in the train on a journey of four days and four nights to consult more doctors in the far south.

At this last piece of intelligence Ousie-Johanna snorted and exclaimed: 'A thin lot of good that will do!' Ousie-Johanna, like 'Bamuthi and all the other Africans regarded fat in any form as a singular blessing, and thinness as a manifestation of misfortune, a belief to which her monumental appearance testified. She then went on immediately to say: 'We must catch that slim Matabele [her favourite name for 'Bamuthi] this very lunch-time and make a plan.'

Once the midday meal was over, 'Bamuthi was duly summoned to the kitchen and listened to François and the immense elaboration of Ousie-Johanna's fears and ideas on the situation with his characteristic patience. He agreed that the time for making a plan had come but he had great reservations about doing anything immediately. Ousie-Johanna, inclined to be militant at the slightest hint of what she regarded as the male's universal compulsion to be obstinate and already driven to remorselessness by anxiety, upbraided 'Bamuthi long and unfairly.

When he did get a chance to get a word in, he was able to explain that his reluctance was due entirely to the fact that after all, he had been left in charge of Hunter's Drift and felt he would be betraying the trust Ouwa had put in him if he left it, as he would have to do if they were to consult uLangalibalela properly, for was not that what they all had in mind?

Ousie-Johanna's anger vanished at once and she tried to reassure 'Bamuthi, asking rhetorically what it would matter if some cows were not for once milked as well as normally for a few days or indeed if a week's supply of vegetables and fruit rotted, if it meant that Ouwa's life could be saved thereby? Had they not all agreed that those silly white doctors with spectacles on their noses were no good when a man was bewitched? And had 'Bamuthi overlooked the fact that Hunter's Drift would not be left all that much uncared for in his absence, since he had enough experienced helpers? And did he not know after all these years that there would be old Johanna to keep an eye on them all for him whom no one had yet fooled? Let just one of them slacken and they would have her to reckon with.

The thought of Ousie-Johanna trying to discipline the male Matabele staff seemed to appal 'Bamuthi even more than his fear of betraying Ouwa's trust. Taking orders from a woman, no matter how wise and revered, went against all the deepest instincts and traditions of Matabele man. Even François, young as he was, knew this only too well and did his best to erase immediately Ousie-Johanna's tactlessness by creating a diversion and saying to 'Bamuthi, 'It is true, is it not old Father, that the farther away Ouwa goes from uLangalibalela, the less powerful the medicine against the spell on him will become?' 'Bamuthi answered with a sombre 'Yes', admitting that the danger to Ouwa had already been gravely increased by this long journey to the south.

Encouraged by the effect of this revelation on 'Bamuthi, François pressed on. 'And will you please consider, old Father, that should the doctors in this great city by the sea also find that they cannot put a name to Ouwa's illness and cannot produce the right medicine for him, they might decide to send him even farther away?'

'Bamuthi and Ousie-Johanna, as mystified as they were alarmed by this thought, exclaimed together, 'But how can they send him farther away than the great water?' their name for the sea.

'They can put him in a ship and send him to Britain where the greatest white doctors of all live in a world which knows even less of magic than the doctors here. What good will uLangalibalela's medicine be then if they too fail, as we all know they must?'

'Do you really think they will do this to our Great White Bird, Little Feather?' 'Bamuthi asked, appalled at the prospect.

'I do indeed, old Father,' François answered, sincerely. He too was as afraid of the prospect because he knew there were no lengths to which Lammie would not go to get Ouwa cured except the length of entering into the world of magic in which the three of them there so firmly believed.

'And then the fat will be in the fire for all of us,' 'Bamuthi commented in a voice of doom, 'because it is known, even to children, that the most powerful medicine in the world grows weaker the longer it crosses water.'

Both François and Ousie-Johanna seized on this admission with such effect that the last of 'Bamuthi's hesitations were overcome. Characteristically he showed this by rising quickly from his place at the table to announce that the sooner they started on their way to uLangalibalela, the better. He himself would go immediately to the kraals, to give the proper orders to his people and prepare for their going. They had better leave early the following morning, he said, as it would take them at least two days and a night on the journey there and a day and a night back. So would Ousie-Johanna please see to it that they had food enough for at least a week, for so busy and important a seer as uLangalibalela might well not see them at once.

François wanted to know why the journey back would take a day less than the journey out.

'Because, Little Feather,' 'Bamuthi replied, 'one cannot go to uLangalibalela without gifts, and in so important a matter they will have to be animals that we will have to lead along slowly so as not to make them lose weight. And they will have to be animals you value yourself because it is a law of the greatest doctors that in matters as urgent as these, they cannot help unless the persons to be helped are prepared to give up, for their cause, something of the greatest value to themselves.'

'And what do you suggest, Old Father, is the thing I value that I should take along as a gift?' François answered, suddenly sick at heart because just for a second it flashed through his mind that 'Bamuthi could be thinking of Hintza, since there was obviously nothing in the animal world that he valued as much as Hintza.

Whether 'Bamuthi knew what had passed through François's mind or not it was significant that he answered François obliquely by saying: 'Before we go into the matter of gifts, Little Feather, I must tell you that if you value the life of Hintza we had better leave him at home. The track to uLangibalela's kraal is narrow and crooked and leads through the wildest parts of a bush full of great leopards that will like nothing more than to kill Hintza for food.'

François's relief was greater than his fear for the life of Hintza. He had never been separated from Hintza for a moment and was not prepared to contemplate leaving him at home now. He said immediately: 'I shall do nothing of the sort. Where I go, Hintza goes.'

He looked so outraged and determined that 'Bamuthi, far

from being aggrieved, was touched. He merely shrugged his broad shoulders as if in uttering the warning he had done all that could be expected of him. Then he went on to say, 'As for the gift, I must ask you, Little Feather, to search your own heart for what thing of greatest value to you will help uLanga-libalela's medicine most.'

Both François and 'Bamuthi would have liked to leave the matter at that but not Ousie-Johanna. She seized on the opportunity to go on talking to them, advising them in all sorts of ways and bombarding them with a bewildering series of suggestions. Although they both recognized that the outpouring was the result of long, pent-up anxieties and proceeded from her desire to help, it became frustrating and wearying, considering that they still had much to do before starting on their journey. It was not surprising, therefore, that afterwards 'Bamuthi made the only criticism of Ousie-Johanna François had ever heard. Even then he did it not in anger so much as with a certain resigned compassion. Shaking his head before looking around to make certain he was out of hearing of the kitchen, he remarked to François in a deep whisper, '*Auck!* The princess of the pots, Little Feather, reminds me that water is never tired of running.'

François could not help smiling at this because he recognized the observation as a cry straight from 'Bamuthi's heart, who as head of his clan almost daily had to face numbers of Matabele ladies who brought their troubles to him.

François's amusement, however, was brief for he had left the kitchen with his imagination uneasy about what to give to uLangalibalela. When 'Bamuthi had stressed how the gift had to be something of great value to him and, once reassured that the something was not Hintza, it was as if a suggestion of what the gift had to be was already darkening his mind. Now back in his room with Hintza to sort out the few things he needed for the journey, and in the midst of deciding that he would have to take with him both his ·22 rifle and his octagonal muzzle-loader, he was aware of an increasing undercurrent of uncase in his mind. He tried his hardest to bring it to the surface but the more he tried, the more intangible this sense of foreboding appeared. In the end he completely renounced the idea of arriving at a solution by himself and resolved to go out and consult 'Bamuthi once again.

Oddly however, the moment he renounced the idea, the knowledge of what the gift had to be came to the surface of his mind like a cork released from the bottom of an ocean. Dear Heaven, how could he have been so dense? There was only one thing it could be. The realization saddened him extremely. Of all the many animals he loved at Hunter's Drift there was no animal after Hintza so dear to him as Night and Day. He knew now that 'Bamuthi himself must have had Night and Day in mind although his natural delicacy of manners had prevented him from telling François so outright. Night and Day was a year-old heifer. She was called Night and Day because she was a black and white roan; a combination of colour to which all the Matabele attached an almost mystical importance. François could still remember the great cry of happiness and wonder that had gone up in the cattle kraal at the end of the garden when it was announced that a calf of this miraculous combination of black and white had just been born in the shape of Night and Day.

It happened significantly on the morning of François's eleventh birthday. Ouwa had made it a custom to present François on his birthday with a heifer calf. He did this so that in time François would have a herd of cattle of his own and in fact François now was the proud owner of a little herd of his own cattle. But for him, too, Night and Day was special. It had come to know him and his voice too, and from early on would even go for walks around the farm with him and Hintza. It sparred and played with Hintza and answered to its own name, coming when called. Indeed on one occasion it had annoyed Ousie-Johanna considerably by calmly walking into her kitchen to find out why François who, for once in his life had overslept, had not yet appeared outside to say good morning.

The more he thought about it the sadder François became, for it seemed that in giving Night and Day to uLangalibalela, he would be betraying a friend. Then the thought of how 'Bamuthi had been forced to overcome his own feeling of betraying his trust as guard of Hunter's Drift in Ouwa's absence, came to his rescue. He realized, as 'Bamuthi had done, that of course there was nothing they could possibly value more than Ouwa's life.

So, quickly, before any more thought could weaken his resolution, he went straight to 'Bamuthi's kraal. He found 'Bamuthi busy with a couple of cow-hands separating his own calves from the part of the herd he was allowed to keep at Hunter's Drift. He was in the process of putting a leather band round the neck of a beautiful shining black heifer, also about a year old, and one which François knew was a special favourite of his. She was called Little Finger, the first calf of a noble heifer and great new bull of whom 'Bamuthi and all his clan were certain a new chosen race of cattle would spring, and from it more children would be born than could be counted on the fingers of two whole hands. Therefore, 'Bamuthi had asked one and all when they watched the small black calf which had just been dropped, a silk-like sheen upon its skin, as it struggled on trembling legs to its feet, what name could be better than one beginning the great count to follow, with the little finger of the hand? However, the significance of this did not strike François at once. He was too absorbed in his own agonized feelings and, rushing up to 'Bamuthi, he announced at once, almost with tears in his eyes, 'It has to be Night and Day, has it not, Old Father?'

'Bamuthi put his hand affectionately on François's shoulder and said in a voice as if he were born to be the father to all living things in that world of the bush, 'No *Induna*, Little Feather, could have chosen half so well.'

Then, in order to comfort François, he drew his attention to Little Finger, which he now had firmly roped in hand. 'Look, Little Feather, look. Night and Day will have the company of a friend in her new home, because this child of a bull of the night is my gift of value to uLangalibalela.'

There and then all self-pity left François. He grabbed 'Bamuthi's hand in both his own, pressed it as hard as he could, incapable of words. Young as he was he knew how much cattle meant to people like 'Bamuthi, carrying as they did within them the spirit of the ancestors and how great a proof it was of 'Bamuthi's love for Ouwa, Lammie and himself that he was joining, perhaps even unnecessarily, in making this sacrifice for them, for surely an animal as fine as Night and Day might well

have been incentive enough even for so illustrious a doctor as
The Right Honourable Sun-Is-Hot.

Comforted, François was about to go back home when
'Bamuthi took him by the arm and whispered in his ear, 'You
have not forgotten that we have to take with us something of
your Ouwa's person.'

François happily could reassure him. Ever since the possibility
of going to uLangalibalela had first been raised, he had made a
habit of slipping into his parents' room every day and gathering
some hair from Ouwa's brush. He had by now a small strand of
hair wrapped in tissue paper and hidden underneath his clothes
at the bottom of a drawer in his room. He had in fact become
extraordinarily aware of some magnetic quality about this
secret possession. Lammie and Ouwa, of course, would have
dismissed it as sheer superstition but for François it was an
acute reality. It had reached the point where he did not
even like touching the paper in which the hair was wrapped
because he felt it an intrusion into a forbidden zone of Ouwa's
personality.

The first thing he did when back in his room was to wrap the
tissue in a sheet of brown paper and tie it up with string.
Although he would never know what prompted him to do so, he
took the little parcel to Ouwa's study, extracted a stick of red
sealing wax from his drawer, lit the wick and dropped a large
red blob of melted wax on the knot of the string and then sealed
it down with Ouwa's private seal, which he had used in the days
when he had been the head of a department of state. For some
odd reason, he felt better after that, leaving Ouwa's study so like
someone coming out of the side-door of a church that one is
compelled to explain his behaviour in a way which he could
not do, but which was familiar to the pagan world about him.
The nearer one comes to the great imponderable forces of
nature and the more one moves in the presence of the unknown
gods of the bush to seek their help, the more urgent it is to have
a formal, precise and respectful ritual for one's advances. Thus
the pagan in François which one has observed before, came by
instinct to his rescue where the reason of Lammie and Ouwa
would have failed him, and provided him with the only possible
way to the appropriate state of grace before the Lords of the

210

bush, whom The Right Honourable Sun-Is-Hot was only one of many servants.

François was up and about ready for the journey just as Dawn's Heart showed above the dark line of the fig trees at the bottom of the garden. Ousie-Johanna was already there in the kitchen, not only with his breakfast and supplies ready but with a large tin of condensed milk and an even bigger bottle of castor oil, which she wanted François to take as her gift for The Right Honourable Sun-Is-Hot. François thought the sweet milk made sense but he had such strong feelings himself on the subject of castor oil that he feared nothing could be more likely to antagonize uLangalibalela. At the moment of his greatest doubt, however, 'Bamuthi appeared to fetch him. Seeing the large bottle of castor oil on the table, he congratulated Ousie-Johanna so profusely on such an imaginative contribution to their gifts that François realized he had nearly made a grave tactical error.

Leaving Ousie-Johanna in tears as well as in doubts that she had perhaps induced François to take on more than was fair for a person so young, and exhorting 'Bamuthi, therefore, at great and unnecessary length exactly how he should take care of him, the two of them left for the Matabele kraals. 'Bamuthi carried the muzzle-loader, already loaded, in case of immediate need, powder-horn and lead bullet-wallet as well as a large haversack full of provisions on his shoulders. François carried another haversack also full of provisions with that sealed little brown paper parcel underneath them. He also, for once, had his best bush hat on his head. He had been in two minds whether to take a hat with him or not, until 'Bamuthi had insisted on it, finally settling the matter by saying: 'So that you will have it on to take off at the proper moment, Little Feather.'

With Hintza alert and excited at his heels they made their way to the kraals where Night and Day and Little Finger were being held ready for them. Loaded as he was, 'Bamuthi insisted on adding to his armoury his finest hunting spear, *U-Simsela-Banta-Bami* [He-Digs-Up-For-My-Children] and the great club *Igumgehle* [The-Greedy-One], commenting as he did so that, on this narrow zigzag track on which they were going, a man could not be too well prepared.

François somehow had assumed that he and Hintza would go

at the head of the line, but 'Bamuthi had other ideas. He made it clear from the start that he alone was in charge. He told François that he would go ahead leading Little Finger; then Night and Day would follow, and François and Hintza would come last. All he begged François to do was on no account to lag behind but to keep in a close, compact formation.

If he, 'Bamuthi, became aware of any danger in front he would stand still at once and raise his hand high above his head. No, not the hand with the spear because the blade might catch a flash of light and betray them. He would raise the hand which held the black heifer's lead. It would be a sign for François to come up as quietly as he could to hear and see what it was that 'Bamuthi feared. He himself would be watching constantly over his shoulder. But should anything disturb François when he was not looking, François was to make a small noise like a baby fever bird and 'Bamuthi would come immediately to his side. Above all Hintza had to keep close to François.

So there and then, before sunrise, the little procession vanished into the bush on a track which after the first ten miles or so was completely new to François. It was astonishing to the people at the kraal, used as they were to these sights, how quickly and completely the awakening bush swallowed them up. They, of course, had never seen the Great Water but, had they seen it, they would have known that the bush was for them what the sea was to fishermen and sailors, and Hunter's Drift a safe and welcome harbour. Men would suddenly come out of the bush, like ships over the horizon of the sea, to dock for a night or two at Hunter's Drift and on leaving they would vanish as François, 'Bamuthi, Night and Day, Little Finger and Hintza vanished into the copper-roofed forest of the burnished morning, with only one great difference. Whereas the arrival and departure of strangers might occasion surprise and interest, the departure and disappearance of one's own struck at the hearts of those left behind, because that bush, full of as many voices as the five oceans, and so full of hidden forces, made them as uncertain of the travellers' return as those who once watched the black ships at the beginning of man's Odyssey disappearing over the rim of a wine-dark sea.

For the first mile or so 'Bamuthi kept up a conversation with

François without bothering to turn his head while doing so, in the manner of a people so accustomed to journeying through life in single file along winding footpaths. When he did look back it was only to make certain that his little convoy was keeping proper formation. But so soon did they all fall into the routine he wanted that even the occasional backward glance became unnecessary.

Once they had crossed the unmarked boundary where the track entered the unknown, 'Bamuthi signalled to him that it would be as well from now on to keep silent so that they could concentrate. It was always extraordinary to François that a bush which reverberated so much with the sound of bird, insect and animal life when observed from the great clearing around his home, could be so silent, grave and sombre when one was deep within it. He had questioned Mopani once about this strange phenomenon. Mopani had told him that it was because the trunks of the trees were so tightly interlaced with thorn bushes, shrubs and creepers of all kinds, the rare spaces of unclaimed ground were so thickly overgrown with tall grasses, as well as padded with the dense multitudes of leaves, that any sound except their own stifled before it was born.

It was indeed remarkable that although 'Bamuthi and the two heifers were only a few yards ahead, François could not hear the sound of their movements. What was stranger still were the great bush apes, swinging like acrobats in a circus, from tree to tree at the end of the long creepers that the Matabele called monkey-rope. As they passed over the track and saw this little procession close underneath them, they would utter cries of alarm and warning to the rest of their family still hidden nearby in the trees. François could see their long lips draw wide apart, their pink gums glistening, their white teeth bared and mouths wide open, as they did so, yet no sound at all reached his ears.

There was only one exception and that came at about ten in the morning when it was really hot and all the billions of mopani beetles, hidden behind the butterfly leaves of the trees, began to sing their Messiah to the day. The hotter and brighter the day, the louder they sang, until it sounded as if all the insect minstrels of Africa had come together to celebrate. By two o'clock in the afternoon the silver sound was deafening. It was also so hot that

213

the collar of François's bush shirt seemed to burn the skin at the back of his neck whenever they came in contact. He knew from his own experience and from Mopani and 'Bamuthi that all animals in the bush, even the black mamba with its heart of ice, would now be fast asleep. Yet these dedicated beetles just went on and on with their singing, louder than ever. François did not object to this at all. To him there was something fantastically exhilarating about their singing. When the transport of sound was at its highest, 'Bamuthi halted them for the first time and all together they rested for an hour in the shade of the densest tree they could find. But so strong was the sun that even there the shade was only a paler form of sunlight.

François had thought that having walked so far without rest they had done rather well. Not so 'Bamuthi, who had done the journey many times before. He said he was sorry he had had to force the pace, but they were about to enter a depression where the bush was at its thickest and would end in a long savannah full of antelope of all kinds; and therefore also full of lion and leopard. Considering how great a temptation two fat heifers, not to mention Hintza, would be to animals of prey, he wanted to get to a particular place well before dark, where he hoped they could spend the night in comparative safety.

He was interrupted by a startling demonstration of how far from empty already the bush had become. Hintza, who had been lying close to François with Night and Day bedded down next to him, her eyes shut for an obviously welcome siesta, was suddenly on his feet. The change from sleeping to being fully awake was swift and complete. Already the magnetic pattern of hair on the ridge of his back was erect and his nose and tail were pointing in the direction from which some warning had reached his acute senses. He had hardly posed himself for pointing when, dense as the bush and loud as the insect hosannahs were, a noise of wood, crackling as if on fire, crashed through the sound.

The mopani beetles stopped their singing. 'Bamuthi leapt to his feet, seized his own heifer by the halter and whispered imperatively to François, 'Quick, Little Feather, quick!' and led off the track sideways into the bush.

Night and Day, however, was enjoying her siesta so much that her only response was to open her purple-black eyes reluctantly and look reproachfully at François from underneath her Hollywood eyelashes. François had to order Hintza in his fiercest Bushman to remind Night and Day that she was not there just for fun but on active service. Hintza responded by giving the tip of her tail a sharp nip with his teeth. It was something Night and Day had experienced before in longer and sharper measures in her kindergarten days with François and, coming to her feet, she trotted off smartly after her black companion.

Fortunately they did not have far to go. 'Bamuthi had come to a halt behind a clump of enormous assegai trees where he signalled to François to join him. There they stood, partially hidden, while the crackling became louder and louder until at last they saw on the track which they had just abandoned an enormous old bull elephant come striding past with all the pomp of Admiralty, swaying sailor-wise in his walk.

The bull was followed by a procession of cows and their young, completely at ease. Because of their poor eyesight, and the fact that the total absence of any movement of air in that dead hour of the day made their fine sense of smell useless, they were unaware of the presence of strangers in their vicinity. They gave themselves time to stop and pluck some of the more subtle delicacies of the bush for the young calves who were with them. After stripping a wild raisin bush of all its brown, succulent berries, they would stand still with expressions of intense gratification on their wise, wrinkled old faces, watching the joy which the unexpected sweetness gave the calves. They had time, too, for stopping to fondle and encourage the smallest of these who showed signs of flagging in the heat. Sometimes they would urge them along gently with a nudge of their granite heads when affectionate persuasion failed to make them move.

With all their obvious depth of feeling, they seemed to have an almost human awareness of the need of discipline. A young bull calf, who already had more than his fair share of berries and was trying to snatch away the ration of one of his weaker companions, was immediately set upon by irate elephant mothers who walloped him so smartly with their trunks on his behind that he blew a toy-trumpet scream of pain before promptly giving way.

Then there came what proved to be the climax of this

'happening' in the bush. Just beyond the point where 'Bamuthi had left the track, two large assegai trees, no doubt undermined by the formidable armies of white ants who constantly marauded the bush, had collapsed and thrown a barricade across the track. The elderly elephants and the adolescent calves had no difficulty in stepping over the barricade. But there was one little calf who found it impossible. So two elephants who apparently were responsible for conveying the rear of their procession, turned back, stepped back over the barricade and took up position on either side of the little calf, who was beginning to whimper pitifully with dismay. They put their trunks underneath its stomach and carefully helped it scramble over the fallen tree-trunks. So delighted was the little calf at being restored to its family that it ran up and down the line, almost like a puppy, thanking the rest of the crowd by fondling them with its trunk. François then heard the strange rumbling sound of the stomachs of well-fed elephants, not boiling with rage like that Uprooter of Great Trees but gently, as though it were the elephant equivalent of purring. But no sooner had the grey, wrinkled behind of the last great old elephant (so like the baggy flannel trousers of an old country gentleman in danger of parting with a last button) vanished around the curve of the track than the rumbling vanished and once more the mopani beetles took to their devotions.

'Bamuthi's dark eyes were shining and his deep bass voice, although low, was round with contentment as he exclaimed, 'It is a good sign, Little Feather. You see what a great seer and doctor uLangalibalela is. Even the Lords of the forest are going his way.'

'But if so, Old Father,' François asked, not out of unbelief but merely out of wonder, 'why did you pull us off the track at such speed as if we were in great danger?'

'Because I mistook the first sound of the crackling,' 'Bamuthi replied. 'I thought it could be a rhinoceros coming straight at us and that would not only have been dangerous but the worst of all possible signs for our journey.'

More bemused than ever, François asked simply, 'Why?'

'Because like all things evil, the rhinoceros is always in a hurry and it always charges in straight lines, crashing over everything,

216

even the innocent. You must know that evil is hot in action and travels always in a straight line. Only the good and wise, such as our lord the elephant, go slowly in and out, round and about, making their way through the bush as the wise among men go through life, like a river seeking that Great Water which 'Bamuthi has never seen.'

He paused for a moment with a strange, nostalgic look on his face. Then exclaimed, 'But do not let us stand here gossiping like old women. We have a long way to go before night and we can do no better than follow closely behind the elephants who will clear the way ahead of evil for us.'

So in a moment the little procession was back on the track, following the elephant spoor. François expected that they would soon catch up with the elephants, so leisurely had the progress of the animals appeared to him to be. Of course, he did not realize as 'Bamuthi did that even at their most leisurely pace, elephants with their long strides travel at incredible speeds, walking at a pace that a man can hardly match even by running. They caught no glimpse of the elephant group again that afternoon although their satin foot-prints lay in the track. Then, just about an hour before sundown, 'Bamuthi announced that the place he had in mind for making camp for the night was only a mile or so ahead.

At that point they were amazed to notice that the elephant spoor had vanished from the track. 'Bamuthi did not like this at all. He stood there for a long time studying the signs before he whispered: 'The signs clearly show our elephants were frightened from going their chosen way and, when the Lords of the forest are frightened, it would be foolhardy for us not to take notice. We must not speak from now on but go as silently as we can because soon we shall reach the end of the bush and look down on the great open place of grass and water of which I have told you.'

François, though he tried not to show it, was perturbed by 'Bamuthi's words. He, too, knew that only something exceptional could have made a large, well-organized group of elephants swerve away so abruptly from a course they had obviously been following for days. Elephants normally were not impulsive creatures. Compared with other animals, they never did things without good reason, and what reason could have sent them off in such a hurry to seek shelter in the bush? The elephants feared no other animals, no matter how powerful or fierce. The answer, obviously, could only be man. But what sort of a man would not give way to a cavalcade of elephants and take good care not to offend or disturb them in any way?

'Bamuthi obviously had come to the same conclusion. He studied the track and bush around him carefully for any signs that might indicate the cause of the elephants' evasive action but found none. Finally the bush came to an end and right on its edge, 'Bamuthi stood still in its shadow, which was now dark and long from the sinking sun behind them, and raised his hand for François to join him.

Ordering Hintza to sit and watch the track, François hastened forward. He stood by 'Bamuthi's side and looked out on one of the most beautiful savannahs he had ever seen in his young life. The country in front of them was open and covered with long green-gold grass, all aglow in the evening sunlight and falling away steeply to a flashing river winding slowly in and out between banks covered with tall, copper bulrushes. The air above them was dark with a tornado of wings of weaver-birds, with a vortex of bee-eaters, starlings, finches, and Abyssinian rollers, seeking a home for the night among them. On the far side of the river, the grass slope again rose to meet the other arm of the forest some two miles from where they were standing. In between was a vast, glittering assembly of practically all the vivid animal life of the land, all that is except the elephants.

The scene was so beautiful that François speechless could have watched it for hours. The colour and freshness of it had all the quality of a dream. The animals themselves looked brilliant in the precise light of the African evening.

Then 'Bamuthi broke his silence with a forcible exclamation in Sindabele: *'Mawu!* Now we know why the elephants in their wisdom swerved away.'

As he spoke he pointed out what François, in his general absorption in the beauty of the scene, had not noticed: a steep mound of high rock between them and river. From the centre of the mound rose smoke, standing almost still in the air.

Why this sight should have disturbed 'Bamuthi mystified

François. Normally other people camping on the way were a welcome sight for tired European travellers, and there was no doubt that the whole of the group, not excluding Hintza, were exceedingly tired by the long march of some ten hours.

François questioned 'Bamuthi accordingly but he would not say much remarking in general that what induced fear in elephants, should induce even greater fear in humans. But without any doubt it was the smell of that palm of smoke and those who made it that had turned the elephants away. Until he, 'Bamuthi, knew more about it, he was not going to allow them nearer the place. All of which François thought a pity, since that steep, high mound was to have been their fortress against the night. Now they would have to hurry and find another since the night was hastening to fall.

François, partly because he was tired, partly because he thought that 'Bamuthi was giving way to the long inbred suspicion of strangers which Africans have had to cultivate over the turbulent, unpredictable and tragic millennia of their history, tried to argue against the decision. But 'Bamuthi was unusually abrupt with him, remarking with a cut to his voice, 'Two heads in charge of a party only provide food for lions and hyenas'. He there and then turned back into the bush for a quarter of a mile, leaving François with the two heifers and Hintza.

Some minutes later he was back, and ordered François to follow him. About two hundred yards from the track, he brought them to a small open space between the trees which even François, inclined as he was by now to be critical of 'Bamuthi out of sheer fatigue, had to admit was well chosen because, except for the one opening which had led into it, the space was surrounded by the most formidable thorn bushes of all the hundreds of militant thorns in that part of Africa. It was the thorn the Matabele call *Ipi-Hamba?*, literally the 'Where-are-you-going?' thorn. This thorn, tough as steel and hooked with a point as fine and sharp as a hypodermic needle, had an unfailing knack of catching in the skin and clothes of anyone who brushed against it, forcing him to stand still for quite a long time to disentangle himself. It was just as if the thorn were a tough Botanical immigration officer, officiously asking strangers, *'Ipi-Hamba?'*

No animal would attempt to break through this dense cover of hundreds of thorn bushes. Indeed, it was an established fact that antelope, when pursued by the wild dogs of which there were hundreds in the bush, would seek out just such a bush of thorn, retreat with their backs against it (so that no attack from behind was possible), and then would lower their horns to fight back on one front only. François recognized that 'Bamuthi had found a place where they ought to be nearly as safe from attack by lion and leopard as they would have been in any of the kraals at home.

He was not left any time, however, to admire the site of their camp. 'Bamuthi immediately ordered him to get busy collecting dry wood for the fire that they would need as an additional protection that night. It took both François and 'Bamuthi until sunset before 'Bamuthi was satisfied that they had enough wood. He had barely come to this conclusion when from the direction of the mound of rock where they had seen the smoke there came the shattering, stuttering sound of gunfire.

François could tell at once that there were not only a number of men shooting, but that it was the wild, uncontrolled shooting of inexperienced men. In fact so sustained and savage was the sound of shooting that it sounded as if a war had broken out down there in that beautiful and peaceful savannah.

'Bamuthi looked as if he had fore-suffered it all. He just straightened himself over the pile of wood he had laid for a fire, listened with his head turned in the direction of the shooting for a second or two, and exclaimed: 'Perhaps now you will know why this old 'Bamuthi did not want to join such men. I tell you, Little Feather, we shall have to know more about the kind of men they are before we go farther. Use what light there is left to get grass enough to keep Night and Day and Little Finger quiet for the night. Start the fire here, where I have laid it, because all its light and smoke will be lost in the leaves of the trees. I am going at once to look, before it is too dark, to find out what kind of men they can be. I fear that something tells me they are men whose hearts are black.'

François didn't like the prospect of 'Bamuthi venturing out alone on such a mission, in such country, at one of the most dangerous hours of the night, when lion and leopard do much

220

of their killing. He tried to persuade 'Bamuthi to leave it till the morning. But 'Bamuthi thought the morning, when they could easily be discovered by the first light of day, would be far more dangerous than the hour of falling darkness.

François's fears increased all the more when 'Bamuthi, with only his spear in his hand, said: 'If I am not back before morning you must not come looking for me. Go back straight home, leaving Night and Day and Little Finger behind so that you can travel fast. Then send a message to warn Chief Mopani. He will know the right thing to do.'

'Do you think then, Old Father, that they are poachers down there in the valley?'

'Bamuthi shook his head emphatically and said: 'Poachers usually go only where the elephant and rhinoceros go. All poachers here know that except for that one great rock on which we saw the smoke, this is a land of death for men. That is why it is uninhabited and all men, even hunters, hurry through it as fast as they can for each midnight a mist rises from the river bringing the sickness of death with it. Many a man has tried to make a home here since the first Matabele came to this land, but all have died or wasted away. For years, no one has tried it, since all men know that only the top of that rock is safe, and who can make a home on a pimple of stone? But look, the sun is going and I, too, must go.'

For the next hour or so, François kept himself as busy as he could, both because it was necessary, and also because it kept his mind off his acute anxiety about 'Bamuthi. He collected more than enough grass to see the heifers through the night; unpacked their provisions; extracted the biltong and a long chain of home-made sausages Ousie-Johanna had provided; prepared spits so that the moment 'Bamuthi returned, they could sit side by side grilling their meat by the fire he had started. He took out the coffee, sugar and powdered milk, in fact all that was necessary to make a perfect supper for tired and hungry travellers at the end of their long day. When all this had been done as effectively as he could, and when there was nothing more to fill in the time, he came to a pause. Still there was no sign of 'Bamuthi. François's anxiety became the most acute fear.

He checked quite needlessly to see that the old muzzle-loader was ready for use; looked at his ·22 rifle for the tenth time to make certain the magazine was full. He took up his station sitting well away in the shadows dancing on the rim of the fire at the entrance to their natural kraal, with both the muzzle-loader and rifle close at hand, listening for any change in the noise and rhythm of the night to show that 'Bamuthi might be on his way back.

The sound of shooting, of course, had long since died away. He heard nothing but the usual night sounds that he normally loved so much. There was nothing to fill the wide silence round about him except one fearful moment when he heard the peculiar quick snorting sound that lions make when they move in like lightning to strike down their quarry. It could not have come from more than fifty yards off their camp. When after three hours had passed with no sign of 'Bamuthi's return he was almost on the point of summoning Hintza, and, despite orders, setting out in the dark to look for him.

But, suddenly, there in the flickering light of the fire stood 'Bamuthi himself, a smile on his tired face as he said, with an almost boyish note of triumph in his voice: 'Old 'Bamuthi is not so old as 'Bamuthi thought when he can come so close to Little Feather without being heard.'

François was so overjoyed to see him that he immediately rushed to the fire, poured out a large enamel mug of coffee, long since ready, mixed it with milk, poured sugar into it in great quantities, knowing how great a treat sugar was to 'Bamuthi, and handed the steaming mug to him. Then he asked him what had happened.

'Bamuthi at once became very serious. He told François in great detail how, knowing the country of old so well, he had succeeded in crawling right to the top of the outcrop of rock and among the boulders without being detected. There he had looked long at one of the most extraordinary collection of men he had ever seen. There were about thirty of them, mostly African of many tribes, except that of the Matabele. They were all dressed in uniform, like soldiers, and all possessed guns like the police had used when he was a boy. But there were three men among them of a people he found difficult to describe. They were, he said, not black but yellow people. If it were not for the fact that their hair in the firelight appeared different, he could have thought they were Massarwa (Bushmen), dressed in the clothes of 'red strangers'.

'Massarwa!' François exclaimed, his heart beating faster. Immediately he thought of Xhabbo and wondered if, after all, some poor Bushmen had fallen into the hands of their traditional enemies and were being held as prisoners.

'Yes, they could be Massarwa, although I am not sure. But if they are Massarwa,' 'Bamuthi replied, 'they are strange Massarwa because they appeared to be in command of these men.'

'But who possibly could such men be, Old Father?'

'I fear, Little Feather, that they are "men of the spear",' 'Bamuthi answered sombrely.

'Men of the spear? Who are men of the spear, Old Father?'

'Bamuthi, normally so frank, was suddenly reluctant to go into this aspect of his mission. He merely answered rather apologetically that if François had not heard of the 'men of the spear', he had better wait until Chief Mopani or his Ouwa could come and tell him about them. They knew far more about these things than an ignorant old man of the bush did. All that it was necessary for François to know was that 'Bamuthi knew them to be the most dangerous of men.

'But what could such men be doing in such a place at such a time?' François pressed.

'Bamuthi answered that the men certainly were not there in order to go to uLangalibalela. He explained that close by that outcrop of rock, another historical track crossed the one along which they were travelling. It was the track which led from the Great Water to the far-away junction of the Chobe and Zambezi rivers, where there was a secret ford into a country called Caprivi. Across Caprivi lay the great hinterland of Angola where, as everyone in the bush knew, fighting had begun between black and the 'red strangers'.

Beyond that 'Bamuthi refused to go, and soon the relief of having him safely back and sitting, tired and hungry, grilling Ousie-Johanna's delicious sausages directly on the flames of their fire drove all sense of danger and curiosity from François's mind.

While he had been waiting, a great full moon had slowly

223

climbed into the sky and although it had not cancelled any of the bright, urgent stars of the African sky, it provided them with an immense phosphorescent foreground for their light to dance upon, that was as exciting as it was beautiful. It was indeed so provocative a moon that François felt rather sad that for Hintza's sake he had no music to go with it, for tired as he was Hintza obviously endured a severe temptation to serenade the moon. From time to time he made little moaning noises, as if in protest to his musical self, and he would press against François's side, so that François had to stroke him constantly to comfort him. Even the two heifers appeared similarly afflicted because they too suddenly stopped eating and came to lie down immediately behind 'Bamuthi and François, all of which in the end was very reassuring to François, for it gave him a warm feeling that the barriers between man and animal were downed by the moon and that they were all a single unit of life made one with the mystery of the bush full upon them. The animals came even closer when, from all around them, lion after lion started roaring.

Remarking, 'The lion who roars is never the lion that kills' (the Sindabele dismissal of men who boast), 'Bamuthi told François that he was certain that that night they should fear nothing from either lion or leopard. On his way to the mound of rock he had seen the carcases of so many dead animals killed in the outburst of shooting before sundown, that he was convinced that there were no lions, leopards, jackals, or hyenas that would need to hunt for food that night.

Then something of 'Bamuthi's reassurance seemed to communicate itself to the animals. The signs of alarm they had first shown when the great chorus of lions, joined subsequently by the coughing of leopards and the snorting of hippopotami who had emerged from the river to come grazing right up to the edge of the bush, soon vanished; all the fierce night sounds seemed to become a lullaby for sending the tired little group of humans and animals to sleep.

Nevertheless, some unease must have gone on working in the depths of François's mind while he slept because many hours later he woke and instantly sat up, his mind alert. He stretched out his hand to feel if Hintza, too, was similarly uneasy but, apart from a contented little whimper at his touch, Hintza went on sleeping. Then François knew that the cause of anxiety was not in the bush around them but in himself; and suddenly it came to him. It was the word 'Massarwa' (Bushman) which 'Bamuthi had used to describe the men held in charge by that group on the rock. The thought of Xhabbo, of Koba, and his love for the Bushmen, together with a child-like desire to make amends for their pitiful fate, all combined to make him feel that he had no choice but to go to the rock and discover what terrible cause had driven them to keep the dangerous company that 'Bamuthi had described.

He looked at 'Bamuthi lying fast asleep on the other side of Night and Day, just next to Little Finger. There was no indication that 'Bamuthi was troubled. Yet François knew that if 'Bamuthi had an inkling of what was going on in his own mind just then, he would be instantly awake and making sure that François had no chance of following his overwhelming impulse.

Getting up quietly, he took some wood and put it on the fire which had sunk low on to its coals. This was a task he normally shared with 'Bamuthi throughout the night. The fire flared up high and showed up their little group clearly. Neither the light nor the noise he had made had disturbed 'Bamuthi's sleep.

That strange, new cunning self of François one has mentioned before, suddenly took command of him again. He went quietly to collect 'Bamuthi's and his own haversack; the old muzzle-loader and veld ankle boots. He arranged them underneath his one blanket, his bush hat at the head, to make it all look to any casual glance that he lay there inert with sleep. He woke Hintza and whispered in his ear repeatedly in Bushman, 'Stay and watch until my return.'

Then, taking up his own ·22 rifle in hand, his heart beating faster with fear but driven on by something more powerful that was utterly beyond his comprehension, he made his way silently to their track and proceeded barefoot along it until he came once more to the edge of the bush.

There he was startled to see that the moon was rapidly expanding and becoming a deeper orange the nearer it dropped to the horizon. Soon it would set altogether, Dawn's Heart must be close to rising, and the day near, so that he did not have much time to do what he felt he had to do. The whole depression before him, moreover, was covered with a thick, ghost mist, no doubt the 'mist of death' of which 'Bamuthi had spoken. It was an awesome sight. Yet François, in spite of the fear of the mist and its consequences that 'Bamuthi had impressed upon him, did not find it as unwelcome as might have been expected, because there could have been no better cover for him. He walked swiftly and silently, straight into it. He was surprised and relieved that, thick as the mist was, he could see through it some of the brightest stars to take his bearings should the unknown track ahead fail him. It was an alarming walk because all round him were the sounds of lions, leopards, hyenas and jackals quarrelling for their food over some dead animal, and he drew heavily on 'Bamuthi's assurance that the shooting of the evening before had left more than enough meat for the carnivorous·animals of that world to swing the balance of his spirit away from fear in favour of courage. Happily, in spite of the heaviness of the mist, the track was so clearly defined to the feel of his bare feet that he managed to go silently much faster than he would have thought possible. Within twenty minutes he was at the foot of the mound of rock.

He stopped there for several minutes, listening carefully for any sound that might indicate whether the men above had left a guard on watch. When he heard nothing, as if stalking game, he crawled on his stomach right up to the top. He had hardly got into position among the boulders, in a place clear of the mist where, at last, he could see the coals of an almost dead fire, when all sorts of dark shapes rose up from the earth round about it. People started stretching, yawning loudly, and then to chatter curiously enough not in a Bantu tongue but in a broken sort of English that he could not follow. They did all this very loudly as if they were convinced they were the only people in the land. Somebody must have been seeing to the fire for soon an immense spire of flame soared up into the sky showing François every detail of the scene. He saw the men themselves and, as they crowded round the fire, every line of the expressions of bitter, determined, unhappy if not utterly tragic faces of men of many different tribes.

Yet it was not the faces of the Africans which caught François's attention but that of one man squatting calmly and serenely in an Oriental fashion beside the fire. There was something reminiscent of the Bushman about the colour, high cheek bones and slanted eyes of this face. But the long, sleek black hair, neatly brushed back, showed it to be the face of a man infinitely more sophisticated, and in the circumstances more sinister than that of any Bushman of Africa could have been. There was no mistake about it, François knew that he was looking at a Chinese, moreover a man who, compared with the desperate, uncared-for look of his companions, appeared centred, assured, fastidious, self-respecting, and inwardly at home, though he was there some ten thousand miles at least from his native land.

The moment François had established this, relieved and at the same time bewildered, he quickly crawled backwards into the mist, made his way as fast as he could down the rocky mound and hurried along the track to the camp. He was barely half-way there when he collided with a tall figure looming abruptly out of the mist. It was 'Bamuthi, and he narrowly escaped being severely man-handled since 'Bamuthi's first thought not unnaturally, was that he had collided with one of the desperate men from the rocky mound below.

'Bamuthi's relief was greater than the anger originally inspired by his anxiety when he had discovered François's deception and absence. All he did was to say rather sorrowfully. 'How much longer, Little Feather, will you go on wandering with folly as a companion? You are old enough to know by now that he who refuses to listen, will not hear in time of trouble.'

François made the most of this windfall of leniency and hurried into a brief explanation of why he had felt compelled to find out exactly what sort of men 'Bamuthi's Massarwa had been. He was certain, he said, that on their return it would be one of the things Mopani would need to know, seeing how close to his own game sanctuary that unnecessary massacre of animals had taken place. All this took time and a great deal of explanation, mainly because 'Bamuthi had never heard of China or Chinese before. However he was so happy at having François safely back that there were no further reproaches. Besides, he had another important consideration on his mind.

When they reached the edge of the bush, he stopped, turned about and, pointing at the east said urgently, 'Little Feather, *Ku' Mpondo Zankomo.*'

One gives this expression here in its original because François found that his own mother tongue, although influenced by three centuries of history in southern Africa, still could not match its native languages for describing natural phenomena of the land. The expression 'Bamuthi had just used was one of his favourite both for its sound and for its associations. Its literal meaning is, 'It is the horns of a bullock', but it implied the most evocative image of the very first light of day, the moment when the horns of the beloved Matabele cattle just became visible against the glow of day in the east – a far more manly description of dawn for François than the famous Greek cliché for the break of day which, for all his love of Homer instilled in him by Ouwa, sounded incredibly effeminate and feeble. He was thinking of Homer's tiresome and oft-repeated, '... came the rose-fingered dawn'.

There was in fact nothing at all 'rose-fingered' about that explosion of violent light which followed 'Bamuthi's observation and nothing at all effeminate about the speed and vigour with which the sun strode upwards and soon was well above the bush on the far side of the open depression, sending the great midnight mist like an immense flight of the sacred white ibis scattering before it.

When that happened 'Bamuthi and François were lying down under cover just inside the edge of the bush, watching the rocky mound below clearly emerge into view in its entirety. Another tall palm of smoke was revealed standing on the crown of rock for about an hour or so. Then a line of men, heavily laden and bowed with the weight of equipment on their backs, could be seen coming slowly down the winding track to set out, as 'Bamuthi had surmised, westwards in the direction of the far-off and, to them both, fabled land of Angola.

They went on lying there under cover just long enough to make certain that all the men had gone from the rock. Then 'Bamuthi leapt to his feet, calling on François to hurry and saying it was more important than ever to get to uLangalibalela as soon as possible. They had one good omen, that of the elephants, he said, which had made him very happy because it confirmed that he and François had chosen the right way. But the way now had been crossed by another, and the black omen of the men they had just seen vanishing to the west, darkened the first. He told François to look at that great depression below them to see just how bad the new omen was.

François looked and knew at once what 'Bamuthi meant. He counted forty different groups of large vultures hopping awkwardly up and down in the lovely grass, staining its morning sheen with the flapping of dust-brown wings as they tried in vain to get airborne, so filled were they with food.

'You see,' 'Bamuthi remarked, 'half of one of those dead animals under the vultures would have been enough to feed these men. Clearly they killed because they have death in their hearts and have come to like only killing. And that is a sign not good for us or for the time left to your Ouwa, our Great White Bird, or indeed any of us.'

On this sombre note they arrived back in their camp, ate a quick breakfast, packed up, arranged their little convoy in the same order as the day before, and soon were moving along the track, out into the open and down into the valley as fast as they could go. They found an ancient ford of stones in the flashing river and within an hour were home, as it felt to François, in the bush on the far side of the depression.

'Bamuthi found great satisfaction in this. He told François paradoxically: 'We must still travel as fast as we can but now we can let our bodies be long'; a Sindabele way of indicating that 'Bamuthi thought they could now relax.

His reason was that the country through which they would be travelling henceforth was healthier and less dangerous because it was on higher and steadily rising ground. Soon they would be in the untroubled world of friendly Matabele people. The dangers from the bush and ruthless men were ended. Indeed 'Bamuthi promptly practised what he preached. He started telling François all sorts of fascinating things about the people among whom they would soon find themselves; their history, and the nature of the land. They were men of uLangalibalela's own clan, the Amasomi; People of the Red-Winged Starlings.

Time, as a result, passed quickly for François and he was

surprised when they found themselves in a cleared area in the bush and among friendly Matabele kraals, where they were made most welcome. Was it not after all one of the greatest of Sindabele commandments that 'The road is king' meaning all travellers of goodwill should be received and helped like royalty? That night they slept safely in another Matabele kraal only a few miles from the hill on which the great uLangalibalela himself lived. At dawn the next day they were on their way again though they were beginning to tire, because as 'Bamuthi explained, he had come out of his sleep with a heart urging him that they had less time than ever to lose if they cared for a successful outcome of their mission.

This last lap of the journey was made memorable for François by the way 'Bamuthi prepared him for their reception at uLangalibalela's kraal. He started by telling François something of the history and standing of uLangalibalela. He did so without turning his head but with his eyes fixed and observant as always on the bush around him. He then carried on the conversation in as natural and clear a voice as if he and François were sitting face to face in his own hut.

Although he had never protested to anyone before, he told François, it was very wrong to think of uLangalibalela just as a witch-doctor. He was, of course, a doctor yet he was different from any European doctor 'Bamuthi had ever seen. 'Bamuthi knew that European doctors were great men who made powerful medicines for curing those sick in body. uLangalibalela did this but he also healed those who were 'thin' in heart and mind. He knew Europeans went for this kind of sickness to churches and consulted those men always dressed in clothes like the white-breasted crows of the land: the men they called in Sindabele, 'Heaven-Herds'. uLangalibalela was so great a man precisely because he, as one man, did all those things for which Europeans needed at least two men, since he was both a doctor of the body and healer of fading shadows.

François, he was sure, immediately would recognize the difference on seeing uLangalibalela. Men who were only doctors of the body, or men who were just sorcerers in his experience were always sleek, fat, fond of food and snoring away without dreams. Did they not have the saying, 'The inyanga Heaven-heard and Doctor who fasts not will see the back of Heaven turned on him', (that is, conquered by fate). But uLangalibalela, ever since he had been a little boy, had been a 'house of dreams'. He hardly slept at all, fasted a great deal and ate apparently only things which would make his dreams 'white' (Sindabele for clear) and 'strengthen his power of seeing things that were still to come over the rim of the years'.

'Bamuthi could go on for days telling François about uLangalibalela's upbringing and show him the pool where a voice had first spoken to him out of a whirlwind and where the birds had come to share his food. He knew the sheer purple cliff from which he had been commanded to dive far below into a narrow stream full of boulders to prove he was worthy of the voice of the wind. And he told François how, in spite of all discouragement from his family and people uLangalibalela, from there on, insisted on following voices other people could not hear. But the immediate matter now was that in moving into uLangalibalela's presence, they should do so in the right way.

For instance, when they arrived near his kraal, they must not go straight up to it but sit down just near enough to be in view of the people around the prophet. Hard as it might be, they would then have to wait until someone came to fetch them, because anything else would be a sign of great disrespect and forwardness. Ultimately, when someone did come to bring them into the presence of uLangalibalela, how, for instance, would François address so great a man?

François thought that was easy because he knew the polite Sindabele greetings too well, 'Why, Old Father, I'm not all that ignorant! I will raise my right hand as high as I can above my head with the palm open and say "I see you, indeed I see you".'

François as always uttered this greeting with enthusiasm because he much preferred it to the stiff 'How do you do?' There was always something extremely comforting and human to him about the Sindabele greeting, being a sign that he had been recognized and accepted for himself, whereas he had had so many 'How do you do's?' from people of his own kind who really could not have cared less how he did. In any case, when uttering the perfunctory greeting most Europeans had just looked at him uneasily, as if all their eyes could be expected to do was to condescend to recognize he was a child or boy, as he now would have preferred, and then were relieved of so petty a duty and free immediately to look away. No, to see and to be seen for what one was and felt to be, was for him a real greeting, almost as good as Mopani's embrace. He felt certain that with all the urgent hope he had of their mission, combined with the faith he already had in The Right Honourable Sun-Is-Hot, he would be able to utter the traditional greeting in a manner which would infallibly carry conviction.

But to his amazement 'Bamuthi gave him a pitying 'I might have known it' sort of look before saying severely, 'No, Little Feather. That will not do at all. Of course you must begin, "I see you, indeed I see you" but then you must immediately go on to say also, "But you will be here tomorrow when I have gone and can no longer see you, to see me and things that I cannot see for myself".'

'Is that all, Old Father?' François asked, not ungratefully but none the less sufficiently embarrassed by his ignorance on such an important subject to be unable to keep the merest tinge of a defensive sarcasm from coming into his voice.

'No,' 'Bamuthi replied firmly. 'You will then take your hat from your head and stand there silent until uLangalibalela speaks to you. He may not speak for a long time and when he speaks he may say: "I do not see you." In that case, I will ask his permission to send you back to the place where we have been waiting to fetch Night and Day, Little Finger, the tin and bottle from the Princess of the Pots, saying. "We have brought things with us to open your eyes" . . . It is also possible that he may say: "Yes, I see you" and, though the eye will cross the river before the body [a Sindabele way of warning François not to count his chickens before they are hatched], he could even go as far as to say: "I see you as I have seen you since you left your kraals by the Amanzin-tetse three daybreaks ago." That, of course, would be the best sign of all, because it would mean that his mind is already at the heart of our matter . . . But whatever his answers may be, you will have to be ready to bring him the gifts we have brought with us.'

Thus thoroughly initiated, François arrived within sight of their destination.

232

Even the earth and nature, or so François felt, looked as if they had recognized the special nature of uLangalibalela's being and calling. His kraal and the numbers of kraals of devoted followers who had attached themselves to him, were situated on a broad hill in the middle of a rich valley. The hill had been cleared of all brush and wood, except for some wild fig and marula trees to provide it with places of dark and cool shade. Up to this moment the land they had crossed on their journey had either been of black, brown or yellow earth. But the earth of uLangalibalela's hill was a rich, magenta colour, vibrating with quick electric intensity under the hot sun. It was all the more brilliant because until they arrived at the stream which ran at the foot of the hill they had been travelling in deep shade, and it was only as they came out of it, by the ford of bright water that the ample hill rose before their eyes with a blinding brilliance.

At the same time, they heard from everywhere on the hill above them, the lovely clear voices of women singing as they went about their work of tilling such obviously fruitful earth:

> *This is the earth of uLangalibalela,*
> *It is not for you baboon.*
> *These are the roots of the earth of uLangalibalela,*
> *It is not for you swine of the bush.*
> *This is the fruit of the earth of uLangalibalela,*
> *Who knows the tongue of birds,*
> *Keep away, all keep away.*
> *And there is the end of the matter!*

They would go on singing this over and over again. As they sang and François's eyes became adjusted to the brilliant light, he was amazed to notice rows of beautiful, massive young black women stripped to the waist, advancing step by step in long lines, lifting up the long-handled Matabele hoes to the rhythm of their singing and bringing them down all together as if with one instead of twenty hands. Each time the hoes struck the earth, they would follow up the 'baboon', 'swine', 'bird' or 'animal' (for the song was a syncopated catalogue of all the parasites that threatened the cultivator in the bush) with: 'And there is the end of the matter!'

'Bamuthi noticed François's amazement and remarked: 'You can tell the greatness of a prophet by the number of women who gather round him.'

This seemed so mysterious an observation to François that he immediately asked 'Bamuthi for an explanation.

It was quite simple, 'Bamuthi replied, because it was well known among the Matabele that their women flocked to the man who could make 'white' for them the things that they saw in the darkness of their own hearts but, in the manner of all women, could not utter for themselves.

Speaking, they climbed the hill and, though it was obvious that the scores of women singing and working in their fields had seen them, they behaved as if they had not noticed the strangers at all. When they were some two hundred yards from the largest kraal on the hill which they took to be uLangalibalela's own, 'Bamuthi stopped and made them both sit in the sun on the edge of the shadow of a great wild fig tree.

By this time it was exceedingly hot and François thought it ridiculous not to sit in the cool shade of the tree but 'Bamuthi rebuked him, saying that apart from being rude to treat the shade of uLangalibalela's trees as if it were their own, how were the watchers at uLangalibalela's kraal to tell what sort of men they were if they made themselves dim with shadow?

Fortunately they had hardly sat down, when François noticed a young boy coming running towards them from uLangali-balela's kraal. 'Bamuthi saw him too and was obviously extremely astonished and pleased by the sight. The young boy arrived at such a pace that he was out of breath. He panted out a polite reply to their greeting before hurrying on to say that they were to go at once to uLangalibalela's kraal.

Hintza, as always inclined to assume that he was an exception to every rule, started to follow François. But 'Bamuthi begged François to make him stay behind, saying that the invitation to come forward had only been for men and not for animals. Hintza was only a dog and like a dog would have to stay with Night and Day and Little Finger until properly invited.

François and 'Bamuthi, therefore, arrived at the entrance to the kraal alone. The kraal had in its compound another large fig tree which threw an opaque purple shade over the centre.

Coming out of the blinding sun under such a mantle of Roman shadow, the kraal looked empty to them both. They stood at the entrance hesitating and wondering what to do.

At that moment from somewhere within the imperial folds of the shadow, there came a clear, firm, authoritative and resonant voice, uttering in ringing Sindabele the words: 'Yes! Yes! Yes!'

'Bamuthi was so overwhelmed and put out by the voice that, had the matter not been so serious, François would have been unable to prevent himself from laughing.

However, 'Bamuthi managed to gather his senses together and to whisper hoarsely in François's ear. 'Not a word of greeting, Little Feather. All the greetings have been abolished, for all those "Yes's" mean he has already heard the greetings that were ready in us to be uttered and that he has already seen us.'

'But what do we do next?' François in his turn was over-awed by the bounty of uLangalibalela's welcome for there was no doubt from the tone and texture of the voice that it could only have been that of the prophet.

'We just stand and wait,' 'Bamuthi replied.

But they did not have to wait because uLangalibalela immediately spoke again, giving another demonstration of how foolish it is for men to plan in advance for a future that they do not know.

'Who is absent then?' the same voice demanded.

This greatly impressed 'Bamuthi. He took a deep breath and whispered: 'You see what a great seer he is, Little Feather: he answers with questions. His question says that all the persons necessary for the *Indaba* [consultation] are assembled and that we are to come forward at once.'

They started forward in such a hurry that François did not see in the shadow ahead of him a ridge of grey stone sticking up above the ground, and promptly he stumbled over it. He felt very foolish and could not imagine a less propitious and more undignified way of coming into the presence of the great man. But he was to discover later that fate had led him to introduce himself in the best possible manner to uLangalibalela. That ridge, he was to find, was made of stone from the river at the bottom of the hill. This stone was held to have derived from the river-water the property of coolness. Since uLangalibalela and his followers held that heat was a great source of evil, they had put a ridge of stone in all their kraals so that all strangers coming to visit them would stumble over it, and in the process have the heat extracted from them.

As François pulled himself upright, embarrassed, for he had nearly fallen flat on his face, he happened to look sideways over his shoulder and he saw a pair of black and white oxen led by a young woman, dragging some branches of thorn across the entrance to the kraal. This, too, he was to learn was done by one of uLangalibalela's favourite daughters so that the bushes which possessed highly protective qualities could erase the tracks and mend the break that his and 'Bamuthi's feet had made in the magic circle when coming to uLangalibalela's kraal. Knowing none of this however, it was a red-faced François who came face to face with uLangalibalela at last.

Prepared as he was for something unusual, he was taken aback at the simplicity and unpretentiousness of the man he saw before him. Such sorcerers and witch-doctors as he had seen, as well as those he had heard of, were always dressed up in fantastic clothes with necklaces of lions' claws, leopards' teeth, crocodiles' skin, porcupines' quills and all manner of furs, animal tails and even discarded snake-skins wrapped around their bodies. But this man in front of him wore nothing except a loin-cloth of soft yellow klipspringer leather, a very beautiful black and white necklace of beads around his long neck, an ivory bangle on one slender wrist, a bracelet of elephant's hair on the other, and on his head a broad ring of brilliant copper which shone in the shadows like the halo around the head of a saint.

The man was tall and beautifully made. There was no fat at all on his body and, although he was old, his skin was smooth and unwrinkled. The face was unusually long, the forehead broad, the nose exceptionally pronounced for a Matabele and the eyes, wide and large, were well spaced apart, set in what François thought was one of the most beautiful heads he had ever seen on a man. But what struck him most was the expression in the eyes. They looked as if they had seen not only all the things that had ever been but also all that could ever be. More, they appeared to be looking inwardly rather than outwardly, giving François the odd feeling that uLangalibalela saw 'Bamuthi and him not directly but their reflection in a mirror deep within himself.

François was still staring at him, almost in a trance, when uLangalibalela pointed with a hand, palm outward, unusually white in contrast with the dark skin of his wrist and the rest of his body, the fingers long and sensitive, saying, 'Sit'.

François noticed that a young girl had appeared silently behind them and was unrolling two mats for them to sit on, but before sitting down, 'Bamuthi began, saying, 'Eyes of the people [one of uLangalibalela's praise names], we have brought something to open . . .'

For the first time François, horrified with a conviction that 'Bamuthi was about to deliver himself of the customary description of a gift as something to 'open the eyes' which he thought unusually insensitive and tactless, seeing how wide open uLangalibalela's eyes had already proved to be, quickly interrupted, 'Father, with your permission I would like to go back and fetch a few small things we have brought for you.'

Without waiting for permission, he hurried out of the kraal, doubled back to the tree. Gathering up the condensed milk and castor oil and, leading Little Finger with Hintza and Night and Day following, he was soon back at the kraal. There he thought it best to order Hintza to wait by the entrance, and he led the two heifers into uLangalibalela's presence.

Although the mystic combination of the wonderful coat of Night and Day clearly pleased the great man, and the shape of Little Finger, so obviously that of a female born to be a mother of many, was also greatly to his liking, the unpredictable man of all wisdom surprised them by appearing to be most of all interested in the great, gleaming bottle full of Ousie-Johanna's castor oil. François noticed that, for once, the prophet's eyes seemed to be directly turned upon a thing in the world without. He stretched out both his hands, took the great glass bottle and held it up against the light blazing at the entrance. He seemed to recognize the contents at once but to make quite sure that it was indeed what he knew it to be, he removed the cork and smelt it. When the smell confirmed his impression there and then, he raised the bottle and took a little sip; rather as Ouwa's guests at table had sipped some of Ouwa's oldest brandy.

Throughout the rest of the consultation which followed, uLangalibalela every few minutes continued to sip this (to François) revolting liquid at regular intervals, timing the sips so that the bottle was emptied on the exact moment that the consultation ended.

This impressed 'Bamuthi because he remarked to François: 'Look how anxious he is to rid his body of even such little food as he eats and purge his spirit so that he can conquer all and make the sources of our trouble "white" to us.'

François himself would not have put it quite like that but, in essence, he was in agreement with 'Bamuthi since the way uLangalibalela swallowed the castor oil seemed to him the greatest triumph of mind over matter that he had ever witnessed. However, he had no chance of following this trend of thought.

uLangalibalela, unpredictable as ever, broke the silence again, saying to 'Bamuthi: 'Son of Osebeni, you have brought the Little Feather of the Great White Bird to see me because you are in grave trouble.'

François was not surprised that uLangalibalela should know all about 'Bamuthi. After all he had known 'Bamuthi and 'Bamuthi's father for years. What did strike him was that the prophet referred to 'Bamuthi as a Son of Osebeni, the kraal on the river bank where 'Bamuthi had been born. It was as if in doing so, he were demonstrating, right at the beginning, that his main concern was with the origin of things. More surprising was that he, François, who had never been to see uLangalibalela before, should be recognized instantly as the son of his father. Still, at a stretch, he could find a rational explanation for that. His father was well known to the Matabele. They were the only Europeans living within a hundred miles or so of uLangalibalela's kraal. Yet all was so confidently stated that François could not help feeling these opening remarks indicated a kind of knowledge which, at any moment, could go far beyond any rational limits.

So, overawed, François remained silent.

'Bamuthi, however, knowing the correct procedure in these

238

things, immediately responded with the loud remark: 'We smite the ground.'

As he spoke he looked hard at François to see why he was not joining in, since all it meant was an admission that what the prophet was saying was true and relevant. The remark had its origin in the ancient days when men of the Matabele, consulting a prophet would, in fact, smite the ground with their sticks, whenever he spoke words of truth to them.

'The trouble that is darkening your hearts,' uLangalibalela went on, his eyes still appearing to be focused within, 'is the trouble that the Great White Bird is outside his body.'

This time François, remembering 'Bamuthi's initial look, joined in with: 'We smite the ground.'

Saying it, François was impressed with the fact that the prophet appeared to have abandoned the technique of speaking through questions and was confronting them now with statements of fact, which presupposed a knowledge of information that they had assumed would have had to be extracted from them first. Yet even in this regard a rational explanation was possible since the knowledge of the decline of someone so prominent as Ouwa must have been discussed in many scores of beehive huts in the bush for many months.

'It is true that though the Great White Bird has taken the medicines of many white inyangas today he is farther from his body than in the beginning.'

Again the two of them had to indicate agreement by smiting the ground.

'It is true that the Great White Bird and his Little Lamb at this moment are on a journey to seek the help of more white inyangas?'

Here, smiting the ground metaphorically again, François felt the consultation was crossing the last limits of rational explanation. How else explain the prophet's certain knowledge of the journey on which his parents had set out not so very many days before?

'It is true that on this journey so far new inyangas have failed the Great White Bird and that is why you have come to uLangalibalela. You feel that Heaven has turned its back on the inyangas and the Great White Bird. It is true that you have come to uLangalibalela to put a name to the trouble and to strike down its cause.'

They agreed quickly in the traditional manner, expecting uLangalibalela would wish to hasten on with his authoritative pronouncements.

Instead the great unpredictable man paused to regard them steadily, filling them with acute discomfort, before saying: 'You have come to me late and allowed the Great White Bird to go far away where it is most difficult for uLangalibalela to help.'

'Bamuthi and François had of course to agree humbly that they had left it too late. They should have come long before. Still uLangalibalela did not respond except by looking as it were far beyond them.

'Bamuthi, thoroughly uneasy, nudged François and urged him in a whisper to apologize and explain why they had not come before.

François obeyed at once, starting in a nervous way but gathering confidence as he went on at length, giving uLangalibalela a full account of when he had first had a premonition of Ouwa's decline on the evening that Hintza came into his life, right up to that moment in uLangalibalela's kraal. He ended with an emphatic assertion that if the matter had been one for 'Bamuthi and himself alone they would have come to consult the prophet many months before. He stressed that his parents had considered it right to go to the inyangas of their own race first (something he thought, of which the prophet would approve). And what, he asked, would uLangalibalela have thought if the young son of a man of Ouwa's standing, presumed he knew better than his own father and had gone ahead of his wishes in the matter?

uLangalibalela could not help being impressed by François's question. The whole basis of Matabele order was recognition of parental authority.

'Bamuthi himself was moved to whisper: 'Well spoken, Little Feather.'

'We will not begin to herd the cattle after it has been killed by lions,' uLangalibalela announced magnanimously, indicating that he had no desire to close the stable doors after the horse had bolted. 'Let us go to the heart of the matter and open the gates of distance.'

At this, uLangalibalela turned about and from somewhere behind him produced a mass of fine, dried twigs which came, François was to discover later, from shrubs and bushes of great magic quality. With these twigs he laid meticulously in front of him two little bonfires. When they were both ready for lighting he commanded the daughter, to bring two coals from the fire within his own hut.

When they arrived on a metal scoop, to François's amazement, he picked up one between finger and thumb and then inserted it carefully into one of the two little fires. He bent down and blew on the coal steadily with his own breath. Suddenly the twigs burst into flame, and there stood a long, slender little pillar of fire between them and the prophet.

For a moment or two, uLangalibalela regarded the upright little flame, a look of the infinite in his eyes, before uttering the words: 'A straight, clear flame is he: clearly the flame of a man.'

He then did precisely the same with the other coal. Although François would have sworn there was no difference in either the shape or nature of the twigs used in the two identical fires, the second little bonfire mysteriously caught light in a totally different manner. Instead of catching at one point in the centre and soaring in one aspiring flame, it caught fire in several places at once and proceeded to spread out and about, emitting a darker smoke more inclined to linger and cling to the earth.

Yet uLangalibalela regarded this fire too with the same satisfaction as the first, exclaiming, 'A fire that tries to possess and cling, clearly a female fire is she.' By this François knew that one flame represented Ouwa and the other Lammie.

There followed a long and extremely strenuous silence for 'Bamuthi and François while uLangalibalela first studied the two fires in front of him and then went into some sort of trance, looking far beyond the flames as if at a multitude of presences invisible yet real enough, making 'Bamuthi and François feel as if hemmed in a crowd. Although it was morning and the day was bright, François trembled inwardly, finding the moment dark, and comparable only to those sessions he had had long ago with old Koba by the fireside in his home, when she had told him stories of sinister magic and supernatural phenomena.

As a result it seemed an age before he heard uLangalibalela grunt with approval and declare in a voice like a ventriloquist's that now he saw all. Straight away uLangalibalela began a long account of his father's condition, during which François and 'Bamuthi had to 'smite the ground' so often that their mouths went dry with the effort. At that very moment, uLangalibalela declared, Ouwa and Lammie had arrived by train in a great city. They had already been to see the great white inyangas. The result had been the same as before. Heaven was continuing to turn its back on them. François's father was farther away from his body than when he had left. Soon he would be out of reach of it for ever.

At this point, François and 'Bamuthi were horrified to note the tall upright fire which apparently represented Ouwa, was beginning to splutter, weaken and to give out almost more smoke than flame, though it still had many twigs to feed it.

On the other hand, the prophet stressed, the Little Lamb was more determined than ever to make Ouwa return to his body. She had succeeded in getting the greatest white inyanga of all to agree to make powerful medicines for him. Hearing this, François's heart warmed to Lammie's gallant, single-minded spirit. He was overjoyed to observe how Lammie's little fire gathered itself together as if in harmony with his own inner warmth and burnt up more brightly until there was hardly any smoke left in it at all.

Unhappily uLangalibalela quickly drove all the warmth away by declaring sombrely that even so determined a spirit as Lammie would find that Heaven would still have its back turned on them despite the greatest white inyanga. It would remain so since none of them would find a name for the cause of Ouwa's departure from his body. The reason for this was simple: the cause was in their own hearts and the hearts of their people.

And what was more difficult for a man to perceive than the fault within himself? Was there not an ancient saying that it was easier to put out the fire in the house of neighbours than to deal with the smoke in one's own? There was no inyanga so dangerous as the inyanga who was part of the cause he was called upon to strike down. The cause, of course, was first in the Government. He, uLangalibalela, the Son of Osebeni and all the other people around the Amanzin-tetse river knew the Government had become the Great White Bird's enemy. But it was even worse than that. Gravest of all aspects of the cause was 'the turning of backs' on the Great White Bird by all his own people. This 'turning of backs' of a whole people upon a single man in all uLangalibalela's experience, was the gravest and the most difficult of the troubles to strike down. And it now, of course, had been made all the more difficult by the Great White Bird going to a place where uLangalibalela's words could not reach him; a place moreover close by the Great Water where, as everyone knew, medicines tended to lose power.

Hearing the terrible phrase, 'turning of the backs of a whole people', François looked to 'Bamuthi for comfort, but found none. It was as if the phrase had gone into him too like the blade of an assegai. The shock and dismay on his face could not have been greater. Young as he was, François was not surprised, because he had heard the dreadful words before. For instance, Ousie-Johanna and 'Bamuthi had given him many examples of how Bantu tribes would punish persons whom they judged to have been guilty of crime. They would summon these persons to some public place, not for execution, but to witness their own people, men, women and children, not excluding chiefs from far away and their *Indunas*, turn their backs as one upon them. The multitude would then sit down on the ground in utter silence, never again turning to look at the condemned man or men. The condemned men would know then that they had been cast out of the tribe forever and, their spirit wrapped in a skin of darkness, they would sadly slink away.

This, 'Bamuthi and Ousie-Johanna had emphasized was far worse than outright execution. It meant that men thus condemned would find that not only the tribe but Heaven too had turned its back on them. From that day on, there was nothing they could do but watch their own shadows fade. They would slowly begin to leave their bodies, until the day came when the last of their shadow vanished and they were outside their bodies, never to return.

Listening to all this and rapidly losing heart, François recalled all the many hurtful encounters he had witnessed between

Ouwa and Lammie and their own people. Adding to his recollections all he had been told about his father's career both in the south and subsequently in the capital of the country in which they now lived, François was bound to admit to himself that he had never heard a more accurate description of his father's fate than that implied in the single phrase, 'the turning of backs'.

His dismay accordingly was so great that he became convinced that uLangalibalela would soon announce that Ouwa was beyond his help. Despite a capacity of restraint unusual in one so young, a kind of cry broke from him. He called to uLangalibalela, 'Oh Father, is there nothing then that we can do?'

The Right Honourable Sun-Is-Hot looked at him, that strange inner light in his eyes perhaps less indirect than before, and he replied in a voice for the first time not without personal emotion, commanding obliquely, 'Produce the body matter that you have brought.'

This additional proof of the prophet's powers of vision after so many others, since the question of body matter so far had not been raised, restored some of François's confidence. He immediately took out from his haversack the little brown parcel with the bright red seal and handed it reverently to uLangalibalela.

From the way he took it and the quickening of light in those dark, inverted eyes, François knew that he not only approved but also that his own imagination had been excited by the sight of the picturesque little parcel. Clearly in all his long experience, no body matter had ever reached him in quite that manner before. Indeed, the experience appeared so novel that he did not know how to get at the contents of the parcel, and François had to offer with great humility, 'Father, would you allow me please to show you what I have brought you?'

He was allowed to take back the parcel. Some instinct told him not to cut the string but to break the seal first and then carefully to gather the pieces of blood-red wax in the palm of his hand and offered it all to uLangalibalela, who then dropped it, piece by piece, into Ouwa's declining fire. The pieces landed on the little bed of coals within, and immediately went up with a splutter of flame which made uLangalibalela utter a profound exclamation of approval.

François also undid the knot of string most carefully, unwrapped the paper, handed both string and paper to the prophet who put them on the fire as well, watching the growth of flame with even greater satisfaction.

Only then did François unwrap the tissue paper and without touching the strand of Ouwa's hair, for he felt more in awe of it than ever, he handed it over to uLangalibalela.

It was, of course, impossible to say precisely what the prophet had expected. All one can say with certainty is that he regarded the offering of hair as of great value, since he did not throw it to the fire.

Instead he lowered the offering carefully on the ground on his left, before commanding again: 'And now for the rest?'

'Bamuthi and François, surprised as well as disturbed, looked questioningly at each other, then asked simultaneously: 'What then is absent, Father?'

uLangalibalela gave them a pitying look. Did they not know, he demanded, that important as the hair of Ouwa's body was, it was as important for him to have in his possession something vital belonging to the men who were the cause of Ouwa's illness? How was he to continue his work as a healer, if having divined the nature of the trouble, he did not have for instance, also a hair of the head of the Government? Was not the Government, after all, one of the main enemies to be struck down? More important still, had they not thought to bring something vital belonging to the person paramount to even so powerful a Government and indeed the only authority who could make the Government first turn round, open its eyes and see Ouwa again as he, uLangalibalela, was seeing him, and seeing him thus compel the peoples they governed also to turn about to see Ouwa as one of his tribe again? Indeed, if they had no more to give him, if they had not even thought of bringing so obvious a thing as a single hair of the head of the Little Lamb so that he could strengthen her, there would be nothing uLangalibalela could do. And that would be the end of the matter.

François's despair was at its blackest, blacker even than

'Bamuthi's for unlike 'Bamuthi and apparently uLangalibalela, he knew the Government was not a single person. There was no question of producing a single governmental strand of hair as uLangalibalela demanded or even any kind of Government body matter which uLangalibalela could use in his cure of Ouwa's illness. More disquieting still, what was this other mysterious authority over the Government to which uLangalibalela had referred and which he clearly regarded as their one great hope of producing power enough to lift the terrible curses of the 'turning of the backs' resting upon Ouwa?

As far as Lammie was concerned, François was certain he could find something belonging to her person at Hunter's Drift which he could get to the prophet within a few days. But clearly that was the least of the 'body matter' needed. Worse, even that little could arrive too late. Moreover, the look of utter helplessness on 'Bamuthi's face and the sense of shattering defeat implicit in his attitude, gave him no cause for hoping that his wise old Matabele friend had any notion left as to how they could solve the terrible problem with which uLangalibalela had suddenly confronted them.

He was near to tears with despair, when suddenly he thought of Ouwa's desk with masses of papers neatly arranged either upon it or within its many drawers. Among the papers he had often seen many letters which had passed between Ouwa and various Departments of State. He remembered vividly how some of these letters bore not only sprawling signatures but stamps and seals of office as well.

Instantly he heard himself saying: 'Father, I can let you have within a few days, a red seal of the Government such as the one I have only just broken, as well as a long paper with the Government's own mark in black ink upon it. Wouldn't such a piece of matter do for your purpose?'

A great sigh of relief broke like a gust of wind from 'Bamuthi. Even more encouraging was the look in uLangalibalela's eyes as he condescended with a nod of his old head, to indicate that such a piece of matter as François suggested might well serve his purpose.

However, there still remained this other mysterious being in higher office over the Government of whom uLangalibalela had spoken so portentously. François could not begin to think what he should do in that regard unless he knew more about who or what this authority was.

Again, he found himself saying: 'As for this other person higher and more powerful than the Government, my Father, please tell me who or what this is, so that Old Father 'Bamuthi and I can know what else we have to bring to you?'

uLangalibalela obviously thought it unperceptive of François and 'Bamuthi not to have realized immediately to whom he had been referring. He looked sternly at them both as he said: 'And have you then forgotten that there is a Queen who from the other side of the Great Water tells the Government what to do? Who else but such a Queen can have the power to order the Government to turn himself about and open wide his eyes and face the Great White Bird, seeing him again as all men of one tribe should see one another?'

Once more another recollection from his father's library came to François's rescue. He remembered that in one of the cupboards in the library there Lammie had carefully stored for his benefit a number of illustrated overseas magazines which had given him great delight with their pictures in vivid colour of the Queen's coronation. One picture, in particular, stood out in his mind: a colour portrait of the crowned Queen in full coronation robes. He at once described the picture to uLangalibalela in great detail before he asked with some confidence, since he knew how the older generation of Matabele still invested even so common-place a thing as the camera with great magic, if such a portrait would do.

The suggestion obviously impressed uLangalibalela for he immediately stood up to indicate that, as far as he was concerned, the consultation had been brought to as satisfactory a conclusion as it could for the moment.

François leapt to his feet at the first sign of movement from the prophet in order not to appear rude. He was more impressed than ever at how tall, beside him, and how beautifully made the prophet was. He stood there upright and clear-cut as a long, throwing assegai, more dignified than any robed and crowned authority of the wide world François had ever seen in

247

magazines and books, although he wore hardly any clothes or ornaments.

In that position, from what seemed a steep summit of spirit, François heard uLangalibalela command them like a voice issuing from some Sinai of the Matabele past: 'You, Son of Osebeni, and you, Little Feather, hasten to your kraals by the Amanzim-tetse. It is always later than men think. Now it is even later than I, uLangalibalela, would have thought. We have not a day to lose. Hasten! Hasten! See that you send me these things of which we have spoken as fast as you can. When they arrive and, in arriving, come in time, I, uLangalibalela, will seek through flame and fire to persuade Heaven to turn about so that the Queen beyond the water too can turn about in order to turn about the Government over here, so that the nation and tribe of the Great White Bird shall be seen again and being seen shall be called to return to his body and throw a fine dark shadow once more upon the earth. Water and distance will make the work of uLangalibalela difficult and long, so hasten. Meanwhile I will work with this hair you have brought me to make the sickness of the Great White Bird stand still until the Government is commanded to change. Beyond that all words are naught.'

With that the prophet, taking their reactions for granted, turned his back on them, bent down and vanished through the doorway of his own beehive hut.

That night, 'Bamuthi, François and Hintza, with no heifers to retard them, had hastened with such effect that they camped in the same place where they had slept on their first night out from Hunter's Drift. They had arrived at the hill in the bottom of the depression just before sunset.

François, exhausted, would have liked to camp on top of the rocky mound in the centre but in view of the fact that the men who had possessed it on their way out could easily be followed by others, 'Bamuthi thought it too dangerous and had insisted on hurrying on through the dark to the site of their old camp.

By the following afternoon some hours before sunset, they were back at Hunter's Drift. Before the sun had set a Matabele herdsman known as a great runner, was sent back to uLangalibalela's kraal, fully briefed by 'Bamuthi on the need for speed and the dangers that might await him in the depression. He was carrying a brown cardboard box, securely wrapped in paper, sealed and containing not one but two of Ouwa's letters with imposing seals of Government. Also there was that vivid coloured portrait of the Queen, together with a crumpled little handkerchief that François had found hidden in a corner of the shallow drawer in the dressing-table of Lammie's bedroom – an emanation of the subtle scent she used rising like an autumn mist to his senses. It touched him deeply because it seemed such an apt image of what Lammie might be feeling at that moment.

The only real consolation that François could draw from the situation was that the man carrying the vital parcel to uLangali-balela was called Mtunywa, Sindabele for Messenger. From what he knew of Messenger's reputation as a runner he fully believed 'Bamuthi was right in saying that Mtunywa would be at the prophet's kraal before another sun had set.

All this done, he and 'Bamuthi joined Ousie-Johanna for supper in her kitchen to give her with lighter hearts a full account of their visit to uLangalibalela. Afterwards François and Hintza slept a deep, exhausted sleep in their own room. Indeed they only woke when the sun was already up. Ousie-Johanna, for once, had not had the heart to call them.

As a result François arrived in the kitchen just as the men who had taken the daily load of vegetables and fresh meat to Hunter's Drift Siding late the night before, arrived with some mail. He thought it a good omen then that it brought him a letter from Lammie. The letter gave him a full account of what had happened since she and Ouwa had left Hunter's Drift, and set out at length Lammie's clear and undiminished hope that, despite the fact that Ouwa had been tired by the journey more than even she had expected, she was convinced they would find the right answer in the great city by the sea.

It was not surprising in the circumstances that the letter was dominated by Lammie's concern for Ouwa and that she manifested concern for François's well-being in a slightly per-functory way. All that was only to be expected and highly understandable. Also it was flattering to François's claim to greater maturity than commonly acknowledged, that his well-being should be taken affectionately for granted. And yet one wonders again whether somewhere, quite selfishly as he would have been the first to admit, deep down, something in François would not perhaps have liked her to display not just deliberate concern but also a trace, however small, of simple, straightforward and involuntary anxiety on his own account. Even more characteristic than Lammie's lively and highly articulate letter was a postscript in Ouwa's writing, a hand so clear and unambiguous that it always seemed to one to presuppose a schoolmaster's blackboard in a classroom full of beings uninitiated in schooling.

Ouwa wrote in that clear, larger than life script of his, 'What is this that we hear from Mopani? Have you really gone on from being the terror of leopards to terrorizing the elephants of our bush? Will you and that hound of yours please condescend to see to it that there are a few of the greater fauna, not to mention imperilled lesser, left alive for us to enjoy when we return from this tiresome and futile excursion to the sea? And, as far as possible for a person of your energies, zeal and ambitions, and a hound of Hintza's indefatigable capacities, may you stay in peace as much as possible in this unpacified world.'

That 'stay in peace' of the Matabele farewell, the inevitable piece of teasing with its faint trace of sarcasm in the postscript, and which moved François almost to tears, was Ouwa's gallant way of sending his love.

The time between the coming of the letter and Messenger's return, two and a half days later (because Messenger, after his extraordinary exertions in reaching uLangalibalela's kraal in twenty-four hours not unnaturally returned in a more leisurely fashion), seemed very long to François. When he did come at last he brought word that the prophet wanted 'Bamuthi and Little Feather to know that he would send them news within a few days of how he had not only been able to make Ouwa's sickness stand but to strike down its cause at the base.

Hopefully, François, 'Bamuthi and Ousie-Johanna waited for such a sign from uLangalibalela. If there was anything in life, apart from real tragedy more likely to slow down time than hope against fear, François would have been most interested to learn of its existence. He realized that uLangalibalela could not feel it necessary to send messages by as fast a person as Mtunywa and that everyone said 'no news is good news'. He accepted that it would be at least four days before they would hear from the prophet. Yet he hoped to the contrary and hope made the suspense almost unbearable.

But when they had no sign by the fourth day, not only he but both 'Bamuthi and Ousie-Johanna became profoundly worried. The fifth day, as the three of them confessed to each other, was one of the longest they had ever known. It was only at sunset of that day that a great noise of clapping and cries of 'We see you, yes, we see you!' coming from the direction of the kraals beyond the milking sheds where François and Hintza were with 'Bamuthi and the herdsmen for the evening's milking, intimated that uLangalibalela's message might have arrived.

'Bamuthi immediately signalled to François and led the way at the double to the kraals. They arrived at 'Bamuthi's own hut just in time to see two strange men leading Night and Day and Little Finger into the stockade of the kraal. 'Bamuthi, after greeting them, unusually perfunctorily for so courteous a person, asked bluntly what the meaning of it was. Had these great gifts not been enough to open the eyes of The Right Hand . . . . . . -Is-Hot? Did they come back for more? Yet even as 'Bamuthi spoke, François somehow knew that he would never have asked the questions so rudely and so vehemently if they were not asked in an effort to balance a terrible fear which had gripped him, as it had already seized François's own imagination.

The two men slowly and politely replied that they had not come for more. They had merely been ordered by uLangalibalela to bring back the heifers to 'Bamuthi and Little Feather, as well as a certain tin, which François recognized as Ousie-Johanna's tin of condensed milk in the hand one of the strangers held out to 'Bamuthi. They said that the prophet had commanded them to speak as follows: 'uLangalibalela had a vision in the night and in the vision he saw the Great White Bird come in from out of the open to his home and that, therefore, the gift of the heifers and tin had not been earned and should thus be returned forthwith to the givers.'

It did not need 'Bamuthi to explain to François that this was uLangalibalela's way of saying that he now knew they had come to him too late and that Ouwa was already dead.

No telegram delivery, with all the authority of the efficient postal services of the land, informing François of Ouwa's death could somehow have carried more conviction for them than uLangalibalela's message and the manner of it. The shock was so overwhelming that François was not allowed, by some profound dispensation of man's nature, to experience it all there and then. It was great not only because it was the death of a father but because it struck at his self-confidence that he should have been able, late as it was, to save his father by his own exertions.

He did not break down and cry in front of his Matabele friends, as some of them did, including 'Bamuthi, who in that quite unashamed and uninhibited way of Matabele men when moved, stood with great tears running down his cheeks, and his wife beside him wailing in the manner of the women of the tribe when a man of their own is lost. François just went slowly back to the kitchen to tell Ousie-Johanna. Even when she broke down, and took him in her arms, sobbing, he did not cry. H̶ went through all the superficial motions of a̶ ̶n̶o̶ forcing himself to eat his dinner, as he had a̶l̶ to do by Ouwa and Mopani, not failing in mome̶ no matter how great his distaste of eating happened to b̶e̶

It was only when he was alone with Hintza in the dark o̶ room that a very small recollection among all the many memories he had of Ouwa, came to break through his composure. He suddenly remembered the morning of Xhabbo's coming and how he had not left his room to fetch the gun he should have taken out with him into the dark from the hall, in case the broad floor-boards creaked and woke up Ouwa when he needed his sleep so much. He remembered Ouwa chiding him for not fetching the gun and how he had been unable to explain to Ouwa exactly why he had not done so but left him believing it was sheer thoughtlessness. All this came back to him vividly, and he thought, 'Now Ouwa will never know that I did it all because I cared so much about him, that I preferred to face the dark with the wrong gun rather than deprive him of a little sleep.' At that his restraint broke and he cried himself to

252

selves had been caught unawares in some of this mechanism of rejection of the natural man in Africa, despite all the great love they had devoted to him and his welfare.

François experienced this aspect of Ouwa's and Lammie's lives, of course, only in its effects on his own, and in no sense ideologically. The jargon of our time would have called it a form of over-compensation for their unawareness of some vital element in themselves. And one is forced to admit that their concern for educating the natural man of Africa was most unusual. It would not have been possible to maintain this against their people and the trend of a whole age in Africa, had it not possessed so powerful a compulsive character. Reviewed under the microscope of tragedy this concern appears not to have prevented them from presupposing a kind of universality and absolutism in European values of education, which implied that the natural children of Africa themselves had little of value to contribute. One suspects, therefore, that François was about to take the first step towards the full realization that Ouwa and Lammie, in assuming that their values were superior, had themselves unwittingly and, however lovingly, been participating in this widespread system of rejection of natural Africa. Thereby Ouwa himself unknowingly became an accessory to the act of his own undoing.

François could not imagine two people more truly concerned in giving what they held to be of the best in themselves and their culture to the people of Africa. That had been demonstrated beyond doubt by Ouwa's career and the shared enterprise he had created at Hunter's Drift. Its vindication had sustained until his death. Yet there remained a still, small voice on some remote horizon of François's mind whispering the questions, 'Had Ouwa and Lammie ever really matched their longing to give with an equal longing to receive? Did they ever allow the people of Africa to give them what they could give only in their own unique way?' The questions moved like an unseen magnet below the surface of his feelings, and conditioned in a single pattern hitherto unrelated fragments of experience. The pattern was all the more telling because had not he himself experienced the agony of always being at the receiving end and so rarely at the point where one was allowed to give something of oneself? This was perhaps one of the greatest burdens of being young; one was always expected to take, and so rarely thought to be in a position of ever wanting and needing, to give as well. And what one had to give, even when accepted, once measured in the scales of deliberate values of the grown-up world, appeared trivial.

Surely no coincidence had ever been more significant than the fact that Ouwa's and Lammie's favourite maxim in regard to Africans happened to be, 'They are just like children really and must be treated like children.' Was one not forced into the position a mature philosopher would have found hard to sustain; to give to persons like one's parents only by offering oneself to them as a living receptacle for receiving everything they thought desirable to give from a lofty grown-up height? François was fortunate that he had experienced this less than others of his age. Yet the fact remained that much of what passed for education in the European world of Africa was a painful process of being extracted like an impacted wisdom tooth from the immense world of antiquity to which the young naturally belong – an extraction so complete that finally all contact with one's aboriginal self was lost and the instincts through which it had been maintained were totally discredited.

As a result one came to adolescence stripped of one's natural armament, if not utterly naked and ashamed, as if to a second birth, a purely private and personal birth into the contemporary world. It was not through imparted knowledge, but through experience of this process that François's heart suspected how fatal for Ouwa had been the deprivation of the life-giving riches which might have come to his aid in the terrible moment of his rejection and decline, through his inability, however plausible its rationalizations, to let the indigenous world around him give to him as much as he himself had given it.

The question, of course, existed only through its pull on François's emotions. At his age he was too busy acting out the new meaning that life was bringing to him to recognize it consciously. All one can say with confidence is that the immediate fact of Ouwa's death was to attach François more firmly than ever to the African influences of his surroundings. He valued them more, and held on to them even as a tree, through its roots, has its being in the black earth which forms the sap that sends it hurtling green into the daylight. If contact with the roots in the dark deeps below are cut, the tree withers and dies, as Ouwa had died.

So, instinctively, François now turned, as some hurt young animal shies away from the lash of a whip, from the presumptions of all-knowingness in his native European culture. It was significant how once he had recovered from the shock that Ouwa's death had administered to his self-confidence, his self-respect was restored through the conviction that it was not his fault that he had not listened sooner to the instinctive voices of Ousie-Johanna and 'Bamuthi, as well as to his own. He had been overawed by Lammie and Ouwa's reasoning, based on an assumption of the supremacy of European medicines and science. Had he listened to his own instinctive self and gone to uLangalibalcla straight away, Ouwa might still be alive. It was a fact not of his contriving that now, whenever he thought about uLangalibalela, the seer stood out in his mind as a saintly example of man; the most truly devout person he had ever seen.

François, as one may have noticed, was not a person of a predominantly accepting nature. The immediate effect of this tragedy on his feelings was to start a change in his attitude of relative indifference to the European world of Africa into one of aggressive antagonism.

The first intimation of this change was the way he came out of the sleep which followed his second night of grieving. He woke, finding himself stroking Hintza, who as always was standing by his bed and wagging his tail. Hintza was already looking straight into his eyes, the moment François opened them, as if the dog had known the exact moment at which this miracle of François's waking would take place.

Stroking Hintza with greater tenderness than ever, he heard himself saying loudly, 'If this is what they can do to Ouwa by turning their backs on him, let's see what happens when *we* turn our backs on *them*. What do you say to that, Hin?' Hintza's tail smote the ground as François's mind had done before uLangalibalela.

He had hardly made this determined pronouncement when Xhabbo came to his mind. Xhabbo had recently lost his own father and had been on his way to the secret cave to acquaint it with this fact when he had been caught in the lion trap. It seemed unbelievable that although Xhabbo was still somewhere alone out there in the great western desert making his way back to his own people, whom he had said were some thirty days' walking away, all these momentous things had happened to François in less than a month. He recalled that when Xhabbo had first taken him to the cave it had felt more like a church to him than any European church he had known. All that one has said before about this new meaning, which demanded to be acted out in living behaviour, was demonstrated now by an overwhelming urge to report Ouwa's death to Xhabbo's cave as well. Had not Xhabbo told him, after all, that since François had come into his life he was no longer one but two? Did not the same need, therefore, apply to him?

He got out of bed at once and dressed quickly, took his rifle and, with Hintza, hurried to the breakfast room. But early as he was, Mopani was there before him. Mopani himself had spent a sleepless night, wondering how best he could help François, and had looked forward to their normal meeting over coffee and rusks, hoping it would give him a clearer idea of what to say to the boy who, understandably, had been silent at dinner the night before.

But for once François did not respond to his greeting in his usual spontaneous manner. Without knowing it, grief and his overwhelming urge to deal with it had made him give Mopani the most perfunctory greeting, adding abruptly, 'Excuse me, Uncle, but I just have to go off and be alone by myself for a while.'

Mopani showed neither his disappointment nor anxiety that François should have come out of the night still apparently as impervious as ever to his presence. He merely nodded and replied quietly, 'You do just that, Coiske, but I would try to be back for breakfast if I were you.'

Had François not been so obsessed with the thought of Xhabbo and the need to identify his sorrow with Xhabbo's, he may have thought Mopani's 'Coiske' at that time somewhat unusual. Except on rare occasions he had always been 'Little Cousin', 'Little old Cousin' or, in moments of stress when

Mopani was instinctively appealing to his most mature young self, just 'Cousin'. Nor did he notice that the Coiske on this occasion was uttered in a new tone and could not know, as perhaps even Mopani did not just then, that all his old ways of addressing François had been abolished overnight, and that henceforth François would always be Coiske to him as he had always been to Lammie. It was almost as if by using this most intimate family endearment, Mopani in his own subtle, intuitive way was demonstrating that he would be there always to help fill the new vacancy in François's life. But François uttered a curt 'Thank you' and went straight into the kitchen, where Ousie-Johanna, 'Bamuthi and Messenger were in some kind of consultation.

They greeted François effusively. They too wanted François to join them, eager to prove in their own warm, immediate ways how deeply they felt for him and shared his grief. But whatever their vivid instincts might have brought forth was stillborn. François could hardly find it in him to return their greetings properly, not because he meant to be off-hand but because he shied away from the effect any demonstration of sympathy from people he loved so much might have on his overstrained emotions.

Indeed, so abrupt did his manner appear that Ousie-Johanna, for all her understanding of his plight, was instantly hurt. François heard her saying loudly as he vanished through the outside door: 'I know he must be much more upset than we are, but why should he treat us, who want to help him, as if we do not exist?'

Just as his feet found the path into the immense orchard, the multitudes of trees almost brought to their knees with the weight of new fruit and their ardent leaves anointed with fresh morning light, glistening and trembling already under the impact of another urgent, blue day, he heard 'Bamuthi's reply. In a deep, sonorous voice he said, 'I give you a little fountain choked with mud.'

François was not surprised to hear Ousie-Johanna begin to cry because she knew the answer to this just as well as François did. The answer to the riddle was, of course, 'The heart of a fatherless child'.

Such understanding from 'Bamuthi filled François with remorse, and he might well have rushed back to make amends,
were he not now caught up in the necessity of keeping secret
the track to Xhabbo's cave. That could only be done by going
there before the great enterprise of Hunter's Drift was fully
awake, and its many herdsmen and labourers setting out for the
duties of the day. This necessity compelled him to press on to
the cave as fast as he could. Soon, unobserved, he was inside
the cave for the first time since the day after Xhabbo's departure.

It was extraordinary how it looked as if not even time had
stood still for it, but as if the laws of time and change somehow
did not and could never apply. It gave the impression of con-
tinuity which his senses, reeling under the demonstration they
had just received of man's brief, brittle and insecure lot on
earth, clutched at firmly for support.

The imprint of Xhabbo's hand and arm in the gesture of farewell and the sign of the cross Xhabbo had drawn in the sand,
were still there, clear as ever. The paintings on the walls of
Mantis, and all the mystic animals which had accompanied the
Bushmen on their way from the first light of life on earth,
looked down even more vividly than before on him and Hintza.
He squatted beside Xhabbo's sign and looked intently around
the cave, illuminated by those yellow shafts of sunlight striking
so firmly and precisely at the floor that they stood quivering
like the shafts of spears plunged deep into the sand.

The feeling that he was in a naturally sacred place was
stronger than ever. As a result, a fact that had eluded him before
now struck him with force; the cave seemed to be respected
even by the animals, birds and insects of the teeming bush.
Except for that one memorable visit by the Praying Mantis,
there was no indication that any creatures, not even the ubiqui-
tous bats who disliked the sunlight, or the lynxes who normally
loved to lurk in such places, appeared ever to have entered the
cave.

All this added greatly to François's feeling of awe. Yet it was
awe in a positive sense, since out of it flowed reassurance to
join his mood of bereavement. He had no words for expressing
his purpose in being there as Xhabbo most certainly would have

had. He had come without any preconceived idea of how he would 'report' Ouwa's death to the cave. All he could do was to sit still, Hintza stretched out beside him, and let the full tide of sadness, as he put it to himself, 'come at him from all directions'. His feelings, uncensored and raw, had to serve as Ouwa's end-of-term report in this examination room of time, as the cave and the painted invigilators on its walls were for Xhabbo and his people.

The process of just experiencing his own inner feelings in silence, together with the sense of sharing them with countless generations of vanished men, seemed to lighten him within, until finally he was at one with the place. Indeed in the end the feeling of belonging became so intense that it produced a fixed idea that he was charged in Xhabbo's absence to be the cave's custodian. He would visit it regularly in future, not only to commune with it but also to see that it was always tidy and kept ready, so that no matter at what hour of the day or night Xhabbo returned (as he had promised François he would), he would find fresh food and water waiting for him.

This direction of his imagination into the future enabled François to leave the cave in a far less inward-looking mood than the one in which he had entered it. Accordingly he went back to the house sufficiently emancipated from himself to give a thought to what Ousie-Johanna and 'Bamuthi and the others, not to mention Mopani, might be feeling. He was convinced also that he should, without delay, try to set about playing his normal part in the life of Hunter's Drift.

His first chance came at the milking sheds where 'Bamuthi was just saying good-bye to uLangalibalela's messengers. Greeting the messengers politely, François asked 'Bamuthi if he could have a word with him alone, and when out of earshot asked, 'Old Father, you agree don't you, that it was not uLangalibalela's fault that my father died? It's because I went to him too late. Don't you think, therefore, that we should insist that he should accept Night and Day as a token that we know he did all he could for us? And, Old Father, I've not thanked you enough myself for taking me there and for all the trouble you undertook to help me. So I thank you now.'

'The lent knife will return with three,' 'Bamuthi placed his hand on François's shoulder as he spoke, showing how much he approved of what he had said.

He approved so much, indeed, that he would have called for Little Finger to accompany Night and Day, had not François prevented him. This, to François, seemed unfair. It was not 'Bamuthi's fault that they had not gone to uLangalibalela earlier. Had 'Bamuthi and Ousie-Johanna had their way, François would have gone at least a year earlier. It felt right that the penance for this grave error of omission should be his and his alone.

So within a few moments, Night and Day, bewildered by all this apparently senseless marching to and fro on long winding tracks through the singing bush between one great kraal and another, yet placid in temperament from her happy childhood at Hunter's Drift, was able to take it all with a young heifer's equivalent of a shrug of elegant shoulders. She followed uLangalibalela's messengers into the bush with something languid in her carriage, which seems to be a natural prerogative of the feminine in life that knows itself to be beautiful. She looked round only once as if expecting François and Hintza to be following as before. François thought then that something more than astonishment had come to those large, purple eyes, behind their long Hollywood lashes. Was not there a hint in them that she knew herself to have been finally abandoned? Now, on his way to Mopani at home, he could not help feeling something of a traitor.

He forced himself to eat his breakfast with enough appreciation to bring comfort to Ousie-Johanna. But soon after taking his chair at the table beside the hunter, he found himself ready to ask Mopani, 'Uncle, how did Ouwa die?'

Mopani did not answer immediately. He had from the moment Lammie telephoned to him, been assailed by misgivings. These were centred not so much on the obvious impact of Ouwa's death on François's life, as the blow that he feared it would give to the boy's self-confidence. He kept on remembering François's ringing declaration that he would not allow Ouwa to die. There had been nothing but bright determination and certainty in François's pronouncement. Mopani knew, therefore, that Ouwa's death would inflict on François the double burden of a momentous bereavement and also of a sense of intense personal failure. His fears were all the keener when he considered François's singular upbringing. François was not just an only child, but the role of the father in his life was greater, due to their isolation at Hunter's Drift than it would have been if their relationship had been contained within those of a larger community. Mopani's anxieties therefore were acute. His own favourite maxim, 'Never go ahead of the spoor; always maintain the discipline of the spoor', was, at the moment, difficult to follow, although he knew how unwise it was of the mind and heart of man to move ahead of their evidence and experience. Watch your spoor, he had often exhorted François, and the horizon will watch itself. And yet, there he was at breakfast wondering whether François would be able to take up the challenge so startlingly thrust at him? But this direct question, uttered completely without evasion, brought him new hope.

His long experience of life had taught him that one had never done with injury, until the moment came when one could put it into words and speak openly about it. That was the only sign in his experience, that a human being had shed the hurt as a snake sheds its dead skin and that his personality was ready for the future. The emotion produced in him by this simple direct question, therefore, was great. All his faith and love of the boy seemed to be vindicated.

The result was that emotion made him begin rather badly to recite the account of Ouwa's death that Lammie had given him on the telephone. He stressed, as Lammie had stressed to him, that Ouwa's death had come unexpectedly both to her and the doctors. She had repeated to Mopani, as if dazed, still almost unbelieving of the event, that she had left the specialist feeling hopeful. He had assured her that there was nothing organically wrong with Ouwa. He promised her that if Ouwa were brought into his private hospital he would be able to establish to the satisfaction of all that Ouwa was only suffering from physical exhaustion which, with the appropriate tonics he would prescribe and a long change of air and climate on that cool Atlantic coast of the Cape of Good Hope, would soon enough be set right. There was no inkling in what she told Mopani that either she or the specialist had any realization that the kind of change which Ouwa needed, could not be found anywhere in the physical world.

Yet François was convinced that Ouwa had suspected it all along. He remembered the way Ouwa had said goodbye to the sun that last afternoon at Hunter's Drift. His *Langa valela* had carried within it a tone of the ultimate farewell. Was it so surprising, therefore, that in the night, quite alone, Ouwa's ignored spirit had decided that it was time 'to come in out of the open, home', as uLangalibalela had put it so accurately in his message to François and 'Bamuthi. That morning, when Lammie went to call him with a glass of hot milk, she found that he had died quietly in his sleep.

Of course, as Mopani said, all men knew that they had to die. Yet, when it struck at anyone in their immediate vicinity of heart and mind, all men and women were none the less unfailingly surprised. It was unnecessary for him to emphasize Lammie's surprise over her husband's death, for François was already drawing a certain melancholy comfort from this aspect of her account. It fitted in with what he imagined had happened within the heart and mind of Ouwa. It also seemed to confirm uLangalibalela's interpretation that the causes of Ouwa's death had never been physical. This all helped to push the event into the wake of time behind him, and reinforced the resolution with which he had come out of his sleep; to turn his own back on the world which had turned its back on Ouwa. Also, in the forefront of his mind was concern over what Lammie now would do?

This direct question produced the answer. Mopani said Lammie had given him an elaborate message for François. She had asked Mopani to put three alternatives to him. The first was that François should hasten south to join her. Ouwa had never given up his nationality in the south, so legally his will would have to be proved there and a great many affairs settled there in consequence. As his only executor she would have a great deal of work ahead of her. She would do it as speedily as possible but it would take many weeks. She realized that it would be a great interruption of François's self-study prescribed by Ouwa, yet he could either carry on his schooling with her, since she was technically qualified to take Ouwa's place, or perhaps even go to a public school.

264

The second alternative was that François could stay on at Hunter's Drift, carry on his studies as laid down for him by Ouwa and in general take his place at Hunter's Drift, while she completed the settlement of the estate as fast as she could.

Finally, she could herself return to Hunter's Drift for a while and go south again later to deal with Ouwa's estate, but that would be both protracted and expensive. She stressed, of course, how much she longed for them to be together. Yet she also felt that Ouwa would have liked them both to behave as steadily and as sensibly about his death as they possibly could. Also it had to be remembered that however soon François came to her, he would not arrive in time for the funeral.

Mopani found this part of the account much the most difficult to render, indulging in an ambivalent attitude which passed under the euphemism of 'seeing all sides of the question'. He deplored it as part of the profound incapacity of civilized people for single commitment in thought and action. One must admit oneself, indeed, to be somewhat on his side and to suspect that Lammie, in offering these alternatives to François, despite all the necessary allowances for the state of indecision Ouwa's death must have inflicted on her, was subject to at least a shadow of that initial concept of François which was summed up in the by now famous, or notorious, phrase, 'that other little person'. One is disposed to join Mopani in feeling that there are moments in life when it is not helpful to be what the civilized person regards as sensible, and that the suspension, in moments of tragedy, of what is called common sense and controlled reasoning in favour of an indulgence in simple, natural grief and fellow-feeling, is far more sensible and reasonable than being sensible and reasonable in the accepted sense would have been. Nor can one help leaning somewhat to Mopani's conclusion that, despite François's proof of unusual self-reliance, this necessity to choose was imposing upon him a responsibility which was not really his.

Whether François had any of these reservations or not, we cannot say, except that the very first mention of the suggestion that he might have to hasten south to spend weeks, if not months there with Lammie threw him in a condition akin to panic. He felt he no longer had the right to absent himself from Hunter's

265

Drift for so long a time because of his pact with Xhabbo. What if Xhabbo returned to look for him and he were not there to answer Xhabbo's call? If he failed in such an event, he was certain he would never see Xhabbo again, and would have betrayed the first human relationship which was uniquely his own. He knew, conflicting as his feelings were, that this was one risk he was not prepared to take. Yet the confusion inwardly was so great that he was compelled to ask Mopani's advice.

This added to Mopani's predicament. He had always abhorred giving advice to people. He had certainly never advised anybody unless asked to do so and then only with extreme reluctance. For unless one were in someone else's situation so completely that one could be described as being 'inside his skin', one's advice would inevitably be based on an inadequate comprehension of all the facts essential for constructive counsel. Moreover, giving advice in general appeared to him to presuppose a lack of respect – if one may borrow from Lammie's phrase for the 'otherness' of human beings – an intrusion into their personal fate which his experience had proved to be followed usually by undesirable consequences. If there were one person who had a right in this instance to violate the 'otherness' of François, or not even perhaps to violate it so much as to help towards a conclusion by expressing a single, clear command or just a warm and direct living wish in the matter, it seemed to him it could only be Lammie. So he shrank from giving François a direct answer and groped in his mind for a way of bringing the issue back to a straight-forward one between François and Lammie and their feelings for each other. He found this in the suggestion that instead of the two of them taking counsel there and then, François could return with him to his camp, talk to Lammie herself on the telephone and then see what came out of their discussion.

François jumped at the idea. All that was urgent and forward-moving in him longed to come to terms with his grief as soon as possible and the prospect of a journey with Mopani, however short, and the change of scene it would involve, presented itself as a shift of scene in his own heart and mind. One is not surprised, therefore, that he readily agreed, gulped down the rest of his breakfast and rushed out to get ready for the journey.

François of course had done the journey to Mopani's camp many times and there was nothing unusual about it on this particular occasion. There was, however, an event just at the start of the journey, which brought an unexpected reaction from François. He had just come out of the house with Hintza to join Mopani, Nandi and 'Swayo, when he found that 'Bamuthi had saddled up for him not one of the salted ponies but Ouwa's own horse.

Suddenly François was enraged at the thought that Ouwa should hardly be cold in death before he should be taking liberties with Ouwa's favourite horse. Also, perhaps he was rejecting the implicit presumptions that he was already destined to step immediately into the place which Ouwa had vacated. He obviously had no clear concept of his own future except perhaps, one must stress, an instinct to be himself. Confused and dismayed, as he must have been, the instinct apparently was bold and clear enough to insist on defeating any other assumptions at source. Yet he himself was amazed at the violence and distress with which he rejected the horse, and peremptorily ordered 'Bamuthi to bring him one of the other horses in the stable.

The second incident happened early the next morning. Having started so late in the day for Mopani's camp they had to spend the night in the bush. The following morning, after their wayside breakfast of rusks, biltong and coffee Mopani, as usual, conducted François on an examination of the spoor the animals had left in the vicinity of their fire in the night; 'a reading of the diary of the night', as Mopani always called it.

Pausing to look back at the smoke of their fire, and the horses standing patiently close by, saddled up and ready in the dark blue shadows of the trees, Mopani remarked, 'You know, Coiske, wherever a man has camped in the bush, no matter how bleak or uncomfortable the camp, he always leaves something of himself behind, when he goes.'

His words touched a deep response in François for if this were true of a mere camp, how much more true was it for the great cave which had been a 'camp' for Xhabbo and his people for so many thousands of years in their tragic way through life?

It was extraordinary how prominent a role his thoughts and

267

feelings of Xhabbo played on this journey. Perhaps they helped to suppress his own feelings of failure in his mission to uLanga-libalela, removing in the process the temptation that he should try and tell Mopani about the meeting. But in any case he was not certain how much even so understanding a person as Mopani would understand about the mission. He thought, rightly, that on occasions Mopani was near to asking him what precisely he had done to try and prevent Ouwa's death. But happily the old hunter never put the question. As a result the journey to uLangalibalela remained unmentioned, and its record became part of the secret self of François which had been born with the coming of Xhabbo.

It was to have important consequences in François's life, not the least of them being that, in becoming secret, it prevented François from telling Mopani about the strange encounter with the 'men of the spear' on the way to uLangalibalela's kraal. Had he been able to do this and confide it to Mopani, he might have changed the whole of the future for himself and everyone else in and around Hunter's Drift. Through this omission he contributed materially to the sinister pattern of events which, unbeknown, life was inexorably weaving with gathering momentum in the immediate world around them.

Late that night in Mopani's camp François spoke to Lammie on the telephone. The line was by no means clear, nor conversation easy. But it all ended in the conclusion that Lammie would confide Hunter's Drift to François's care and she would stay in the south until she had settled Ouwa's affairs.

She had come to this conclusion not without a certain obvious relief. Though her dutiful self was prepared to take the first train north to join François, her own natural inclination was to keep close to the place where Ouwa had left her. It was as if she could not accept the fact of his death and some archaic belief inclined her to stay on the scene of his death as if by so doing she would still be able to keep in touch with him. She was comforted too, thinking that François, in agreeing so willingly to carry on alone at Hunter's Drift, had implied a readiness to take Ouwa's place in their lives. Consequently she had not hesitated to emphasize how necessary it was for them to carry on the work which Ouwa had begun at Hunter's Drift.

François obviously could not quarrel with such a conclusion although one suspects it made him oddly uncomfortable, as if Lammie were in a sense presenting him, as 'Bamuthi had done at Hunter's Drift the day before, with another of Ouwa's 'horses for his journey through life'. Had he been able to see into Mopani's mind, after he had given the hunter an account of his conversation with Lammie, he would have been surprised how critical of Lammie Mopani had become.

Adding together what François told him, and what he knew of Lammie and Ouwa's life together, Mopani feared that Ouwa, dead, might be even more alive in Lammie's emotions and intentions than he had been in actual life. Yet he said nothing. With the possibility before him of a future with a wounded and slanted mother, however dear, François might well need all the time he could get on his own to grow and gather himself together. Mopani even thought it as well not to insist when François refused to stay on with him for a week or two, much as he, who after all was so much more alone, enjoyed François's company. He compelled himself to approve even when François turned down his offer to accompany him back to Hunter's Drift and merely nodded his quixotic head in acceptance when François said, 'You have already been troubled far too much by us, Uncle. I know the way well enough. If I leave early in the morning, I'll easily be home before sundown.'

So, starting at dawn the next morning François travelled so well and without incident that he reached the Punda-ma-tenka, the great Hunter's Road, which forded the Amanzim-tetse hard by his home, soon after noon. On this road, despite the fact that it was now considerably overgrown through lack of regular use, the going was much easier and François could put his horse into a fast trot. He did this despite the heat, because he longed to be home as if his only hope of re-beginning depended upon his return. Since it was the dead hour of the day, when life in the bush slept soundly, feeling itself for that brief, suspended hour free of fear, François was perhaps not as alert as he normally was, or had been earlier. He too felt free to give himself over to his own tumult of feelings and rode along in a mood of melancholy introspection.

He was abruptly jerked out of his self-absorption by the sound of many voices, shouting and calling out somewhere along the road far ahead. The voices sounded like those of the drivers of wagons exhorting spans of oxen to greater effort, which was not surprising because, in that fiery hour of the day, even animals as patient and accepting as oxen would have expected a rest from their heavy labours. Judging by the fact that the sustained shouting and calling was audible above the shimmer of song of the mopani beetles, François realized that if it were indeed a wagon train ahead, it must be a singularly long one. Even one wagon on that road at that hour was unusual because the coming of railways, and the rapid development of air travel, had brought about a great decline of traffic on Hunter's Road. Now the famous road was little more than a broad footpath on which men of the far interior of Africa travelled from their kraals to look for labour in the great mining and industrial cities in the south. Occasionally, too, it was used by the dilapidated trucks of Indian traders.

As a result François brought his horse to a quiet walk, resolved to approach the source of such unusual commotion with care. One motive for his extreme caution was the lesson he and 'Bamuthi had learned from their recent encounter with 'the men of the spear' in the depression on their way to uLangalibalela. That experience, somehow, had robbed the bush forever of the innocence it had once possessed for him. But so intent was he on the noise ahead that he did not pay sufficient attention to the bush on his flanks. Had it not been for Hintza he might well have missed something of vital importance.

The voices ahead at that critical moment had become so loud and clear that François could hear the occasional electric crack of long, lightning ox-whips followed by the wagoners' cries: *'Trek Staatsman!* [Statesman], Wake up, President! Step out, *Vaderland!* [Fatherland] Pull, you *Swartland* there! [Black country].' These were all the traditional names given by the Cape-coloured people to the oxen which drew the long heavy transport wagons that they alone still used in the interior.

At that precise moment Hintza, who was fully expecting François to stop his horse for a closer scrutiny of the bush on their left, was outraged to discover that François was looking straight ahead. Always a dog of action, he immediately bounded forward to François's side, leapt into the air so high that he could utter his characteristic note of warning right in François's left ear. François with a start of alarm turned quickly to look in the direction in which Hintza's nose and tail, body aquiver like a compass needle, were already aligned.

Some fifty yards to the side, right in the middle of a clump of enormous wild fig trees, rose a steady plume of blue smoke. Between them and the smoke, he could just make out the large canvas top of what he took to be a truck.

Feeling dangerously conspicuous on his horse, quickly he swung out of his saddle, and pulled the bridle reins over the head of his horse, which was trained, as were all his kind, to stand until his rider's return. Unslinging his rifle, he carried it at the ready on his right arm and whispered to Hintza to go carefully ahead of him.

He had not gone far when the sound of unhurried voices in normal conversation reached him. He stopped Hintza and lay down on the ground beside him to listen carefully. He could not distinguish any single word of the conversation but the general tone sounded English; but not the English of people like himself, Lammie and Mopani. None the less, since he was never again taking anything in the bush for granted, he went on stalking the sound as he had stalked Xhabbo in the last phase of their first encounter by the lion trap. In this position he arrived unnoticed on the edge of a small but natural clearing.

To his amazement he saw through a screen of grass and shrub a group of people enjoying a meal in what, to him, appeared to be elaborate luxury for so unfrequented a place. In fact, he thought it the most luxurious camp he had ever seen in the bush, not excluding Mopani's great game reserve where elaborate safaris, complete with caviar and champagne and organized for wealthy European and American tourists, were not uncommon.

Here, for example, was an enormous five-ton truck and trailer, flaps down with the interiors exposed to reveal stacks of canvas chairs, tenting, rugs, blankets, a large paraffin refrigerator, household things and packages of all kinds. Beyond the truck, even more imposing, stood another enormous vehicle, a sort of house on wheels, which François knew to be a caboose.

Cabooses had not been seen in the interior for years but they had been sufficiently common in François's childhood for him instantly to recognize this one. They were built complete with sleeping bunks, tables, wash-basins, fresh-water tanks and chairs, and had been provided in the earlier days of the country by the Government for distinguished officials on tour of their far-flung and sparsely inhabited areas. As a child, they had been things of wonder to François. So now he was, not unnaturally, inclined to conclude that he had stumbled on a Government Commissioner sent out on some new duty.

The thought was encouraged by the sight of the very tall, imposing-looking man who seemed to be in command of the little group. He was sitting at ease in a canvas chair in the shade of both caboose and the spreading branches of the great wild fig tree that topped it. The man was bare-headed. François indeed saw on the ground by his chair his bush hat, some king-fisher feathers stuck in a glowing leopard's skin band around its crown, something that both François and Mopani tended to despise as unnecessarily exhibitionist. Moreover, the man had laid his gun on the grass beside his chair, the point of the barrel resting on the rim of the hat in a way which, by François's exacting standards, was criminally careless. In that position dust and tiny insects could easily get caught in the oiled mechanism, and impair the easy action that one had to take for granted if a gun were to be as accurate as their unpredictable world demanded.

Yet one more look at the man himself gave the lie to any facile interpretation. He had a truly distinguished head with handsome, frank features, as well as an air of natural authority. He was unusually tall, broad-shouldered and a man, François thought of about Ouwa's age. His hair was dark, turning grey around the ears and temples of a broad forehead. Even at that distance, François noticed that his eyes were alert and surprisingly blue. Also he was clean shaven, the sleeves of his khaki bush shirt neatly rolled up to just above the elbow. The shirt was starched, ironed, and obviously fresh since both it and the khaki shorts underneath appeared uncreased. The khaki stockings were neatly rolled down just below the knees, two bright red flashes showing at the sides of muscular calves. His sand-coloured suede ankle-boots looked worn and yet were without stain.

All these things suggested that he must be some distinguished servant of the Government. But the other members of the group appeared to contradict this impression. First, on the chair beside him, chattering brightly, was a young girl. Next to the girl sat an enormous, fat, half-caste lady, dressed entirely and most incongruously in black satin, which shone like starlings' feathers in the noonday sunlight. This ample lady wore not a hat on her head but a tiara of white lace, propped up by high combs of amber, implanted firmly on a head crowned with coils of grey-black hair. She looked like a grander Ousie-Johanna, an impression heightened for François because she appeared to be vehemently reproaching the young girl for something. Though François could not yet hear any specific words, the shrill sound made him suspect that they were not English words.

The young girl, who obviously was a girl of spirit, then turned her head and made a face at the vast, bulging lady. She wore an old-fashioned green chintz sun-bonnet, the kind of bonnet Lammie and all the women of the Joubert family throughout their long history in southern Africa had worn as children, and of which two of Lammie's favourites were still fondly preserved in moth balls and tissue paper in a cupboard at Hunter's Drift. But as she turned, the light reflected from the quicksilver mirror of that heavy high noon lifted the shadow from her face and François saw one of the loveliest faces that he had ever seen.

This did not mean a great deal because he had had little experience of the faces of young European girls. Yet in fairness to him, one must add that his impression was later confirmed by Lammie, who not only had a far wider standard of comparison in these matters, but could obviously bring to her observation a cooler and more critical, even technical appraisal which women are inclined to make of one another. Unlike her father, as François took the man to be, the girl did not have blue eyes. They were, it is true, large and wide, but they were dark, as dark as the two long plaits of hair which flicked across her shoulders as she quickly turned. In that light the plaits

273

seemed to François to have a kind of undertone of red subtly woven into their blackness. As she turned her head she said something so obviously tart to the monumental lady that François was certain that if it had been said in English he would have recognized it.

He was soon proved right because, having spoken her quick piece to her nanny, the girl turned and was on the point of speaking to her father when something unusual caught her eye, an eye, it was to be proved to François's discomfort, as quick and bright as her tongue. It remained fixed in a definite stare in the direction of himself and Hintza for what seemed a long, anxious moment before she cried out in Eng ash, 'Why look, Fa, something strange is happening out there in the bush.'

François had a flash of sympathy that one so slight as the girl, with a father so tall and imposing, would be compelled as it were to discipline the disproportion between them by cutting the 'Father' down to a mere 'Fa'. The feeling, however, immediately gave way to alarm, that he and Hintza might have betrayed all their training and done something silly, like allowing the sun to glance off the barrel of his rifle or taking up position so carelessly that the head and ears of Hintza were outlined above the grass – a possibility that seemed more likely because he felt far from his normal self. Yet he was not going to make things worse now by any readjustments and kept rigidly to his position. He was somewhat relieved, therefore, to find it was neither he nor Hintza who had betrayed their position. Apparently it was an unusually large rhinoceros bird, trained by nature in all possible ways of raising alarms for its neurotic one-horned patrons. Perched on a branch above them, instead of looking around it, alert and suspicious as usual, the bird was in the most undesirable and damnable manner looking down as if hypnotized to where he and Hintza lay spread out on the crimson earth.

The man immediately looked in the direction in which the girl was now pointing, but apparently saw nothing unusual because he turned back to her and asked loudly enough for François to hear each word, even recognizing what had once been described to him as an Oxbridge accent, 'Why, what do you mean Chisai? I don't see anything at all unusual out there.'

François took that strange word Chisai to be some outlandish girl's name, but he was soon to discover that it was a term of endearment used by sailors of the British Navy for children – their esoteric equivalent of 'kid'.

'You're not looking properly, Fa,' the girl protested. 'Look! That bird, just look at it. It's seen something or it wouldn't be sitting like a bit of Mummy's china on that branch out there.'

'I believe you're right. Indeed I do believe you're right Chisai,' the man conceded in a slow, deliberate voice and, as he spoke, bent down to pick up his gun and started to rise from his chair.

François thought it time then that Hintza and he made themselves known, more particularly so because, no sooner was the man on his feet than at the far end of the clearing four Africans, who had been sitting and eating apart, had also stood up and were staring with their experienced eyes full of a specialized interest at the bird on the branch above his head. Rather feebly, François quickly called out in English, 'Hallo there, hallo!' Then, sheepishly, he stood up from behind his screen of brush and grass and stepped forward slowly towards the group.

One look was enough to reassure the man. Instantly he exclaimed, 'Why, it's only a boy!'

The daughter immediately echoed the father's exclamation except that she dropped the *only* and cried out, 'Gosh, yes, it *is* a boy!'

The formidable old nanny also joined in, uttering something quite incomprehensible to François except that he thought it highly emotional and rather over-excited. He was to learn afterwards that it had merely amounted to, 'We must give him something to drink and eat immediately, poor boy. He looks thirsty and hungry and unhappy.'

Before François could say anything, the girl completely won him over because, seeing Hintza step forward beside him, in that rather overdignified slow-motion way he adopted when facing strangers, his sullen, golden coat aflame in the yellow sunlight, she called out, 'Oh, what a beautiful dog!'

The incredible Hintza somehow knew that he had just been paid a great compliment. He was so overcome that not only did his tail start to wag but his whole long hunter's body as well, until he was fawning in the most undignified and obsequious manner as the girl came towards him. François, knowing Hintza so well, was convinced that he was fully aware of the sex of the young person coming towards him and, had he had time, would undoubtedly have teased him as if a revelation of quite a new aspect of Hintza's character had just come to him, remarking something like, 'I fear you have the makings of a great womanizer, Hin!'

Shy and sensitive as François was, his lonely upbringing had made him sufficiently self-contained to realize that he ought to retrieve the rather dubious impression they must have made in the camp. So, calling Hintza to order, he told him to 'shake' just as the girl was about to touch him. With an effort at smiling, which Hintza always tried in moments of exacting formality, and with what François called his 'sloppy look', he held out his right paw. As he did so, François formally introduced them. 'Hin, Miss Chisai, Miss Chisai, Hin.'

The girl had already taken the paw offered to her, but, on hearing the 'Miss Chisai' she dropped it and burst out laughing, rather as Xhabbo had laughed that day in the cave. Like Xhabbo, she was completely taken over by her laughter. Yet she did it in such a natural and appealing way that everybody else in the camp was forced to smile with her, and even François's own underlying feeling of melancholy lightened.

She might have gone on if her father had not lost patience and told her in the voice of someone used to command, 'That's enough Chisai. Stop it at once!'

Even then, as she turned to obey, she stood there doubled over, holding on to her stomach, saying, 'Help, oh help! Oh dear, "Miss Chisai" – Miss "Little one", oh help!'

The cause of her merriment at last translated into English and contained in words, the father stepped forward, held his hand out to François and said, 'Would you like to join us for lunch? My name's Monckton, James Monckton.'

François was about to thank him when Hintza, incorrigibly conventional at such moments, intruded again by sitting down between them and holding out his paw to the man so that François had to repeat, 'Hin, Mr Monckton.'

276

This started the girl laughing again, but not so much that she could not say, 'Not *Mr*, boy, but *Sir*. Sir James Archi-'

She got no further. 'Enough of that,' her father interrupted, 'Help Amelia to get some food and a pot of cha for our visitor. At the double, please.'

François, of course, did not know that *cha* was the British Navy's word for tea, just as 'at the double' was the way of carrying out orders in the ships of war in which the father had served with distinction. All that mattered just then was that the promise of anything to drink was most welcome to him, for he had had nothing since dawn. So, accepting Monckton's offer with gratitude, he asked to be excused first for a moment as he still had one small duty to perform.

With the eyes of everybody in the camp on them, he told Hintza in his clearest Bushman to go back and fetch his horse Hintza, his habits of compliance stimulated by his love of showing off, vanished at speed in the direction from which he and François had come.

As Hintza vanished, François noticed that everybody around him was staring in amazement. The girl exclaimed, 'What on earth was it that you said to your Hin?'

Only then did he realize that those onomatopoeic Bushman sounds, particularly the clicks, must have sounded most strange to the Monckton party. He hastened to answer somewhat evasively, because he did not want to enter into long explanations, 'Oh, it's just a private code Hin and I use between us.'

The irrepressible girl demanded, 'But what did you *say*?'

'Oh, I just told him to go and fetch my horse,' he replied as casually as he could, but not unpleased by the obvious interest that he and Hintza had aroused between them.

He had hardly answered when they heard the sound of a horse trotting towards them. Within a few moments, Hintza appeared on the edge of the clearing with the bridle of François's horse in his mouth, and the horse itself following happily knowing, in the canny way that horses have, that a rest and perhaps food and drink as well, were near.

François had been brought up always to think of the needs of the animals in his charge before he thought of himself. So

277

taking the bridle reins over from Hintza, who was highly pleased at the competent manner in which he had accomplished his mission, he asked, 'I wonder sir, if you could give me some water please, for my horse? We've come a long way since the morning.'

François was immediately asked to bring his pony round to the back of the caboose while his host called to one of the African servants to bring them a bucket. François interrupted to say that he did not need a bucket. With his habit of wearing a hat only in emergencies he had travelled with his khaki bush hat slung by its straps around his neck. Slipping the straps now over his head of thick fair hair, he held it under the tap of the water tank at the rear of the caboose to let his host fill it with a stream of bright water. Once full, he took the hat to his horse who delicately sniffed the water first before drinking it.

François had to repeat the performance five times before his horse had had enough. Then, undoing the girths of the saddle, he lifted it and the blanket from the horse's back, laid the saddle down carefully against the wheel of the caboose, led the horse off deeper into the shade of the wild fig trees where, well away from the luncheon party, he took the bit out of its mouth, slipped the bridle off its head and, to the amazement of the onlookers, left it standing happily out of the heat of the day. That he could leave his horse standing, untethered, seemed to astonish everybody more than had their unusual arrival on the scene.

The girl was impressed, perhaps, most of all. She had never encountered any person remotely like François. The unexpectedness of his arrival, the originality, if not eccentricity, of his behaviour, the almost magical intimacy between him, Hintza and his horse, as well as the fact that he not only appeared completely at home in the bush but was unusually good-looking, all made her feel that he was a character straight out of a legend. Indeed she was in danger of losing her considerable powers of speech but she did just manage to ask, 'But can you leave a horse just like that? Won't it just walk off into the bush on its own?'

François stared at her, amazed. The animals of his world never behaved irresponsibly once they were mature. They felt

278

themselves to be too much a part of the great family that Hunter's Drift was, in essence, ever to want to leave it or its people for the dangers of the bush. Indeed, François took all this so much for granted that he did not know how to explain. All he could do was to assure the girl that the horse would be happy to wait there until it was wanted for the journey, which he would have to resume as soon as possible because he still had a long way to go before nightfall.

Hearing this, his host took him to a chair which had been set out for him and soon François was sitting between father and daughter answering questions, while the fat lady who had been introduced to him as Amelia looked on silently but attentively, refilling his plate the moment it was empty and seeing that his cup was always full of hot, sweet tea and condensed milk.

Much as he enjoyed the food, and generous as his welcome was, he was not altogether at his ease. The moment François had heard the name Monckton he had no doubt that this must be the mysterious person who owned the extremely valuable and large tract of land between Hunter's Drift and the mining city, which Ouwa had always wanted for himself and his Matabele friends. Ouwa, as François knew, had developed an unreasonable and uncharacteristic dislike of the unknown man. Now he felt something of a traitor to Ouwa in being drawn so easily to the Moncktons.

Furthermore, he could not help wondering whether Monckton might not have conceived a similar dislike for Ouwa. François, therefore, was feeling rather uneasy about how Sir James Monckton would react when he discovered François's name which, in the confusion of their introduction had been overlooked, and which his host now, out of politeness and a desire to see that he was made at home, made no effort to extract. François felt almost as if he were accepting their hospitality under false pretences. He wondered more and more whether he should now make himself known when the girl started smiling to herself again before saying, 'You know, *Chisai* is only my father's nickname for me. It's just one of those habits he picked up in the navy. It's the Japanese for *little one*. My real name is Luciana.'

François, embarrassed, nevertheless found himself calmly repeating, 'Luciana'. He found it an unusual and rather attractive name.

'Yes,' the girl nodded her head. 'So please call me by it will you? You see, I'm called Luciana after my Italian godmother. It means Bringer of Light. My patron saint is Santa Lucia. What's yours?'

Here François was completely out of his depth. In that Calvinist world of the interior one did not have patron saints. Indeed the whole concept of saints was somewhat suspect. They tended to be part of the inherited feeling of horror over the Spanish Inquisition, St Bartholomew's Night, the Revocation of the Edict of Nantes and so on, which François's Huguenot ancestors had diligently kept alive in the records of their persecuted past handed down to their descendants.

'I'm afraid I haven't got a patron saint,' he answered politely, but with considerable reserves in his tone.

'You haven't?' the girl exclaimed, as if he had entered their lives improperly dressed.

'No,' he reiterated, somewhat assertively. He was beginning to feel that all this was rather irrelevant.

The girl, however, had not done with him yet. 'But what's your name then? You have *got* a Christian name, haven't you?' she asked, as if not sure of this at all.

'François,' he replied, with great emphasis.

'What does it mean, François?' she asked, indefatigably curious.

'I don't think it means anything except François,' he answered. 'But if it does, I don't know what it is. All I know is that all the first born male children in my family have been called François for centuries.'

The fact that there appeared to be centuries in support of his name seemed to restore him to some state of grace in the wide eyes of this oddly persistent young girl.

'Oh,' she said. Then she paused and asked, 'But what's the rest of your name?'

'Joubert.'

'Joubert!' she exclaimed. 'What kind of a name's that?'

'French, of course,' François replied, for the first time some-

280

what on the offensive over what he took to be unjustified ignorance on her part.

However the girl, seemingly, did not notice his change of tone, because she said with delight: 'French? Oh, that's fun! So you're a Latin, too.'

François did not realize what she meant by Latin. Latin for him was a painful language inflicted on him by Ouwa as a valuable intellectual discipline and nothing else. So understandably he replied, 'I'm afraid my Latin's not much good.'

His answer brought more merriment to the girl before she said, 'I don't mean the Latin language. I mean the Latin people. Italians, Spanish, Portuguese and, of course, French.' Then, in case she might have offended him, she hastened to add, 'I'm partly Latin too because, you see, my mummy was Portuguese.'

That *was* made no impact at all on François at the time. Feeling he had appeared unnecessarily ignorant, he was too busy answering apologetically, 'Oh, I see. I'm sorry. You're right in a way. I suppose we were Latin once, but whether we are still I don't know. We've been in this country for more than three hundred years now, you see.'

'Oh, that doesn't matter at all.' The girl made a face and dismissed the centuries as mere trifles. Her nimble young mind had already moved on to what was far more important to her. 'How old are you?' she asked with the utmost solemnity.

With his slide-rule attitude to time, François had to work out exactly how old he was before answering. He was by training rather slow and deliberate in his speech, as everybody in the Monckton camp had already noticed. He was accustomed to think before he answered. Even more than that, thought tended, as a rule, to lead to action rather than words, and if action were not called for, to silence. Something urgent in his character tended to by-pass words. That, perhaps generically, was one difference between people brought up in a wild pagan world, as he and Mopani had been, and people who came out of a civilized metropolitan context as the Monckton group appeared to have done. In that civilized world, people not only appeared to find it necessary to put thought into words before action, but very often seemed inclined to believe that, once they had expressed their thinking and feeling in words, no further action was necessary. It was the other way round in François's world. Once they had thought and acted accordingly, they tended to leave words aside. Did not the Sindabele after all have the proverb, 'When deeds speak, words are nought'.

Indeed he took so long in answering that the girl became restless. Drawing on one of her father's favourite words, she exclaimed, 'Please, you look as if you were going to quibble, and that would be rather mean you know.'

François knew the meaning of the word perhaps better than she did because it was also one of Ouwa's favourite pedagogic adjectives. He certainly thought it inappropriate but it spurred him into saying, 'I'm sorry, but I was working it out exactly in my mind. I am thirteen years, one month and three days old.'

It was on the tip of the girl's tongue to say that she had taken him to be a good deal older, but she stopped herself, realizing that it would appear too flattering. Flattery, so early in her acquaintance with François, was something her instincts urged her to avoid. Instead she merely uttered a neutral 'Oh'.

François, who thought that he had begun to achieve some eminence in years, was so taken aback by this cool, reserved acceptance that he was at a loss for words. Indeed he looked so confused that the girl, thinking she might have offended him, hastened to add, 'Anyway, I'm glad we're both Latins of a sort.'

By this time the father, who had watched François eating his lunch rather fitfully while dealing with his daughter's relentless interrogation now thought it time to interfere. He had been quite happy to let it go because it seemed that the best way of getting to know something of this boy who had appeared so unexpectedly in their midst, was to have it elicited by someone who was more or less his peer.

He interrupted with a question based on the fact which had interested him most. 'You said your name was Joubert. Are you by any chance related to *the* Joubert?'

François knew that he could only be referring to Ouwa, and the reference tended to restore him to the sense of Ouwa's death which had travelled with him all day and been pushed into the background by this unexpected encounter. He answered rather sombrely: 'If you mean Pierre-Paul Joubert, yes. He was my father.'

282

'Was?'

'Yes,' François answered, trying hard to keep down the emotion which was trying to blur his words. 'My father's dead.'

'You poor boy. Dead. Just like my mummy,' the girl answered in a voice so rounded with sympathy that François's composure was greatly imperilled.

More, as she spoke, the monumental Amelia beside her must have recognized the word 'dead' because she immediately broke in on a high emotional tone asking the girl in Portuguese a number of rapid, high-pitched questions. When the girl confirmed that François had, indeed said what she feared, Amelia broke out into a kind of lamentation, sobbing violently, the tears running down her cheeks. Getting ponderously to her feet, she wobbled towards François, started to stroke him like somebody trying to comfort a wounded animal and uttering many sounds of obvious compassion.

Much to François's relief the girl got up, took Amelia by the arm and led her weeping back to her chair. That done, she turned to François and said: 'She thinks that your father, like my mummy and all her people, was massacred. Was he?'

'No,' François replied, with hesitation. 'He died a – a natural death.'

As he said *natural*, he could not help feeling how odd a word it was for him to use, considering all he knew about his father's death. Also how disdainful uLangalibalela and his own Matabele friends would be could they hear him giving such an inaccurate definition of Ouwa's going.

The girl immediately translated the fact for Amelia who at once calmed down. 'You must please excuse Amelia,' the girl explained. 'She's suffered terribly. All her people were massacred in Angola, where my mummy came from. She doesn't even know where they are buried. She's had no funeral for her family at all. I expect your father had a real funeral.' She said this last as if she believed it would have comforted François greatly.

'My father's funeral is today.'

There was a sudden silence.

Then the man immediately exclaimed, 'How wrong of us to

keep you then. I expect you're on your way to the funeral at this moment. We mustn't delay you any longer.'

François shook his head sombrely and explained that his father was being buried thousands of miles away to the south. He did not add that it would be surprising if anybody other than Lammie and the undertaker would attend the funeral of someone whose official life had been so unpopular.

The girl had gone completely quiet and was watching François with quite a new expression. The father asked a few tactful questions which led to François explaining at length how and why he happened to be there, concluding that he would have to leave soon if he were to get to his home before dark.

Monckton at once stood up remarking: 'Well! We mustn't keep you. But I'm glad we've met so soon because from now on we're going to be neighbours.'

The statement explained a great deal to François, including the noise of the wagons he had heard. It took only one tentative question of Monckton to learn that there were indeed seven wagons full of building materials and other valuable supplies, in charge of a large family of itinerant Cape-coloured artisans and builders travelling on ahead of them and looking for a suitable place to camp before dark. Perhaps, he added, François, who he assumed knew the way well, could advise him where best they could camp?

François immediately answered that it was now too late for vehicles as slow as wagons to make the ancient outspan hard by the ford across the Amanzim-tetse before nightfall. Luckily he knew of a great pan full of water which the wagons could reach before sunset and which would make an ideal intermediary camp for them.

Suddenly it occurred to him, however, that this did not apply to the truck and caboose. Quite naturally he took Ouwa's and Lammie's authority upon himself and suggested that if his host broke camp immediately and followed the road, he would be very glad to invite them to stay at Hunter's Drift until their wagons caught up with them; or for that matter, for as long as it would be helpful to them.

Monckton, knowing they had been on the road for many days would have liked to accept if only for the sake of Amelia and his daughter. But he was not an insensitive person and felt that at such a moment he ought not to impose his whole group on François and his mother. He thanked François warmly but said he thought it too great an imposition.

François, however, insisted. He explained that his mother was in the south and that Hunter's Drift was a large establishment, not only accustomed to giving hospitality to strangers but welcoming it as a break in a singularly lonely routine. He would only beg his host, he elaborated, to follow him as soon as possible, so that they could get to his home before dark.

The girl, who had been listening attentively, if not anxiously, skipped with excitement when she saw that François had overcome the last of her father's reservations. François, who had a special eye for natural movement took instant delight in the ease and grace with which she did her little dance of pleasure. At the same time he marvelled at her quicksilver spirit because already she appeared impatient of the journey ahead, as if anxious to be transported by magic carpet to Hunter's Drift. Eagerly she asked, 'Have we still far to go? I do hope not!'

François did not answer at once, confirming the girl's impression that she was going to find him irritatingly slow in conversation. Then he replied, 'It's another three and a half hours on horseback.'

'On horseback?' the girl exclaimed. 'But how far is that for us?'

'Oh, you'll have some sixteen to eighteen miles to go.'

She looked disappointed and then turned her back on him to call out in Portuguese to Amelia to hurry.

The moment François had answered her questions, he set out to saddle up his horse, leaving the Moncktons to start breaking camp behind him. He hastened because he had promised that he would go ahead to show the wagons where best to camp for the night. That done, he would wait for the rest of the party to join them and then show them a short cut to his home.

He had hardly reached his horse, however, when the girl appeared suddenly at his side to kneel down and fondle Hintza. Hintza, who until this noonday interlude, had never taken kindly to strangers, now was clearly making an exception.

Indeed, he was responding ardently to her advances. All the pet expressions of endearment that the girl used on Hintza caused him to wag and tremble with pleasure at her touch. Even she must have been somewhat surprised at herself because there came a moment when she looked up to say, 'You know, I've never had a dog of my own... I'd so love to have a dog exactly like him.'

François, standing rather tall above her, finished tightening his horse's saddle before he answered. He looked straight down into a pair of eyes open and unreserved and thought he had never seen eyes with such a range of expression. For instance, he had already seen them full of mischief, and all the mischievous eyes he had known up to then had usually been quick, smallish eyes, not nearly as large as those dark, almost weighty ones now looking up at him. Then he had seen eyes full of wonderment, and in his experience eyes that tended to wonder had always been rather vague, unfocused, always inclined to stare as if they did not see a person so much as something invisible beyond him. Yet he knew that these same large eyes, full of their own inner light, were also unusually quick, observant and lively. In fact he had never in his life met a pair of eyes so charged with paradox as those into which he looked, now with yet another expression in them to confuse him, one for which he could for the life of him think of no name at that moment.

'If you could wait long enough, I'm certain I could get you a puppy almost like him,' he told her, touched by the note of longing in her voice and remembering how many years he had had to dream of a dog like Hintza before Ouwa finally realized it for him.

The prospect seemed to overwhelm her into silence before she said in a hushed, almost humbled little voice, 'That would be just too, too wonderful.'

As if afraid that such a prospect might immediately be snatched away, she turned her attention to Hintza, remarking, 'You call him Hin. What a strange name for a dog. What sort of language is that?'

'Oh, it's not his full name. I only call him that for short,' François replied, busying himself with the bridle.

'What's his proper name then? I'd love to know it. It isn't another sort of Chisai, I hope?'

François knew that he couldn't possibly tell her Hintza's proper name then without embarrassing consequences for them all. He could only reply, 'I'm sorry but I can't tell you now.'

At that, the girl's wide eyes grew even wider in amazement.

'Will you tell me soon, please?' she pleaded.

'Of course, one day,' François answered. 'But not just now. I'll explain why tonight.'

That aroused an extraordinary sense of delighted anticipation in Luciana. 'Oh, how lovely. I love secrets, don't you? And I'm good at keeping them too. I'll swap you one of mine if you promise to keep it too.'

The girl's concept of secrets was so foreign to François that he was speechless. The growing pattern of reticence and evasion that life seemed to have imposed upon him, had awoken a sense of guilt in his imagination. Until then the idea that secrecy could ever be justified had never entered his mind; let alone the fact that it could be a source of enjoyment. For the first time his pagan-puritan conscience felt relief. If one as lovely and innocent as this young girl could find the possession of secrets natural, he suspected his own sense of guilt, perhaps, need not press so heavily.

Xhabbo and his cave, and François's visit to uLangalibalela were real secrets. But he had an inkling of relief at the thought that in confiding Hintza's full name to her, and his reason for contracting it into Hin, he might make her in a sense a partner, who, by sharing things he had never shared with anybody else, could in time help to lighten the real weight of secrecy within himself.

This inkling became almost concrete belief as he rode away because, when he looked back just before finally vanishing into the bush, he saw Luciana still standing where he and Hintza had left her. She had removed her sun bonnet and the moment she saw that François was looking back, she waved it vigorously above her head.

As a result of thoughts and incidents like these, François was beginning to feel a different person from the one he had been at dawn. In fact he became so preoccupied that it seemed he had barely left the Monckton camp when he was disturbed once again by the crack of ox-whips and the cries of wagoners on the road ahead of him.

At once he pulled his horse into a fast gallop, and soon caught up the rear wagon of the train ahead. The wagon carried such a heavy load that it was stacked high above the canvas top of the front half. The great load was securely tied down under the traditional 'buck-tarpaulin' of the professional purveyors of this kind of transport in the interior. As a result, he did not see the women and children riding on the driver's bench just underneath the opening in front until he was abreast of them.

They were all Cape-coloured people, dressed in clothes of the brightest colours that gave the remote world of the bush, robbed of its own natural colour just then by the fierce corrosive light of the afternoon sun, an oddly festive if not gypsy appearance. They were all members of one of François's favourite peoples in Africa. Both Ouwa and Lammie, who came from the far south, had grown up with people exactly like these. They had always spoken of them with such affection and lively appreciation that François's whole being was conditioned to feel cheerful at this first passing glimpse of them. He knew them to be the gayest, wittiest, most skilful and least bitter and undismayed people in the whole of the land. And all this in spite of the fact that, considering their origins, their uncared-for upbringing, and their utter rejection by the very Europeans who had created them, they had little cause to be gay.

Yet, even knowing all this, he was still amazed by the cries of surprise, delight and welcome with which the women and children all greeted him as he rode by. Even waving back as vigorously and as cheerfully as he could, his response felt abrupt and inadequate. But he pressed on, so anxious was he to talk to the leader of the team who was walking beside his span of eighteen coal-black oxen, exhorting them to greater effort by constant cries of encouragement, and cracking the lash of his long whip expertly over their long horns, without touching a hair of their gleaming coats in the process.

Leading the team, by a long leather thong tied around the horns of two enormous oxen at the head of the span, was a bare-headed, little coloured boy in ragged clothing, thin and

288

obviously with a long history of malnutrition behind him, yet indefatigable and full of energy, pulling the two immense oxen behind him, either one of which, had they so wished, could have trampled him down at any moment. But instead they seemed to be so dominated by his will and spirit that they responded with the greatest willingness, setting such an example to the rest of the span that the overloaded wagon moved over the road at a pace which François could scarcely have believed possible. The moment he was beside the leader of the team, who had doffed his crumpled hat when he noticed that François was a European, François swung easily out of his saddle to walk beside him.

Then, in the way which Ouwa and Lammie had taught him, he held out his hand in greeting to the man, saying in his own tongue as good manners demanded, 'Good day. I'm François Joubert!'

The man was surprised. But when he saw that François's outstretched hand remained he took it in his own very shyly, with what François thought was a most attractive smile slowly forming on his gaunt and tired face until it became a wide grin of real pleasure.

'Allah, God!' the man exclaimed instinctively, using that combination of both Christian and Muslim gods which the Cape-coloured people draw on in moments of surprise. 'I thought you were a ghost, because who would have thought that a son of a *Blanda* [the Cape Malay word for a European] would pop out like a blerrie Jack-in-the-box in this forsaken place?'

He said all this with such a lack of inhibition and such a pressure of natural cheerfulness that François could not help smiling. Then he told the man why he was there and how he had just come from their employer to show them where they could best camp for the night.

At the same time, noticing the casual way in which the wagon was being conducted through the bush at what was about to become the most dangerous hour of the day, since lion, leopard and all beasts of prey would soon be setting out to hunt for food for the night, he felt compelled to warn the man, saying: 'You know, you're being rather careless. This is very dangerous country you're travelling in. Why haven't you got your gun on your shoulder as I have mine? You can never tell in this part of the world when you might not need it. I promise you, I've lived here all my life and I'm never allowed to walk even a hundred yards from my own home without a gun.'

For a moment the man's gay manner abandoned him. He looked at François. Then shrugging his shoulders he answered, François thought, rather tragically. 'Where do you live then, little master, that you do not know that mere creatures like ourselves are not allowed to possess any guns, even in such a dangerous place? If I had as much as a water pistol on me I would find myself in front of a magistrate before this day is out or my name is not Arrie' – the Cape-coloured abbreviation and endearment for Abraham. Here his natural sense of irony restored his good spirits and he smiled.

Both the 'little master' (a term that François loathed and which had been abolished at his birth from the vocabulary of their servants by Ouwa and Lammie) and the man's explanation, made François feel thoughtless and ashamed. He apologized at once before asking who the leader of the train was so that he could tell him about a camping site for the night.

François's apology and manner restored the man to his natural friendliness. He told François that, of course, the leader of the team was in the front of the wagons. The *of course* was not at all as obvious to François because he had always been told by Ouwa and Mopani that the leader of any wagon train should always travel at the rear, for that was the place where all the trouble tended to collect.

But he did not pause to argue. It all seemed to him typical of the reckless, courageous, everlastingly optimistic abandon with which these people had always hurled themselves at the unknown in Africa and which had enabled them to play such a vital role in pioneering the immense land, though that role was never hinted at in the history books prescribed by the European governments.

Quickly saying goodbye, which elicited a chorus of bright responses from the man's family parked high, bright and full of chatter as Paraguayan parrots, on the driving bench of the wagon, François went on ahead. He passed five more wagons

290

in build and load exactly like the first and each drawn by spans of eighteen oxen. Only the spans were different and expressed the individuality and pride of personal possession, independence and self-respect of the owners. The oxen looked as if they were better fed and cared for than the people. The yokes and leather straps, though worn supple as silk with use, were sound and properly maintained. The wagons, though blistered by sun and weather, rolled on well-greased wheels bound tightly in broad, thick iron bands flashing like silver.

Unlike the first wagon, the span of the second wagon consisted entirely of pillar-box red oxen, the third of tawny-coloured, the fourth was of creamy-white, the fifth was of beautiful strawberry roans, the sixth black-and-white brindled oxen and the seventh span, the leader, was drawn by huge, hump-backed creatures of subtly flashing magenta coats and crescents of gleaming ivory horns. They were to François a brave and exceedingly beautiful sight and he was moved by the look of unreserved acceptance of their arduous lot in their glowing, gentle purple eyes. Even when the muscles on their broad shoulders gathered in huge knots as they lowered their heads to take the extra strain of a steep incline in the rough road, their broad hooves kept up a steady rhythmic beat, as of muffled drums, on the scarlet dust underneath them.

But what excited him most was that on the top of the loads of each wagon ahead were sitting the men who obviously needed rest after their shift of conducting the spans. They had just begun making music as only the Cape-coloured people and the gypsies of Imperial Hungary can do. Strumming the guitars, playing the concertinas and mouth-organs that they carry with them wherever they go and value even more than bread and butter, they were singing the songs of the road which they had evolved for themselves throughout their long, traumatic history.

The songs were at once gay and nostalgic. Moreover they were played and sung with immense spirit and a kind of joyful energy even at their saddest and most nostalgic pitch.

They were all songs that François himself knew well. He never knew whether they made him want to dance or cry, so charged was the music with all the ambivalence of the joyful tidings of the sorrow of the history of man in southern Africa.

291

They were songs one is compelled to render in English since the dialect in which they were sung is not at all widely known nor easily translated. They sang for instance:

> This is a place I can no longer endure
> Because nothing is left for me here.
> The tortoise now is my king,
> The road of the wagon my home!

The mention of the tortoise being their king always touched a special nerve in François's heart, because wherever one went in Africa one saw these little tortoises carrying their great chess-board homes on their backs. Scraggy necks and heads stuck out, paws wide apart, they were always walking from one unknown place behind them towards some even greater unknown ahead; the perfect symbol in fact for people who are compelled by life to be for ever on the move.

They also sang another song with a particular gusto, as if competing with the mopani-beetle eisteddfod, raging in the bush around them. It had for François a rousing pilgrim, almost biblical, note to it and began:

> There comes the wagon,
> The four-horse wagon;
> It has no name as yet,
> It still has to be named.
>   Turn a tillienkie!*
>
> Come about in state!
> There, far away, down by Table Bay.

The last wagon produced perhaps the greatest, most nostalgic one of all:

> Take your goods and trek, Fereira!
> Behind the bush there are some horses;
> Take your goods and trek!
> They are heavy to carry, Fereira,
> They weigh you down on one side, Fereira,
> But pack up and go.

* A particular whirl in a Cape folk dance.

292

Fereira, as Francois knew, was originally a Portuguese name but had become a common family name not only among the Cape-coloured people but also among Europeans in the far South.

Although this encounter was by no means the most significant of the two encounters of the day it was the one that helped most to restore François to his natural context of spirit. As a result it possessed a certain healing quality and he reached the leader of the train feeling almost a member of his team.

The man, although hardly more than another version of the one in charge of the rear wagon, did have a certain air of authority about him. He greeted François effusively, apparently most grateful to him for appearing at a moment when the promise of a camp not far ahead was most needed, saying, 'The blerrie oxen are dead tired. One snort of a lion, little master, and my old bones tell me we might hear the old master [lion] growl at any moment now and the whole blerrie lot of them will drop dead in their yokes.'

'Well, you've not got far to go,' François assured him.

Leading his horse on foot and ordering Hintza to scout ahead, François walked beside the wagoner, hearing all he had to tell him about how they had been engaged by the Moncktons to build a house for them by some river with an unpronounceable 'kaffir' name. The pejorative 'kaffir' was still the discredited term that the Cape-coloured people, out of pride in their measure of European blood, fanatically adhered to when speaking of the Africans of the land. They had not gone far before François not only knew the man's objective, his whole history, his ailments, the names of his wife, children and all his relations alive as well as those who had died of malnutrition and infection, such as dysentery, malaria and bilharzia.

In addition François learned a great deal about the Moncktons, including the most important fact of all (in François's order of priorities), namely that the girl had earned the approval of them all to such an extent that they called her a true 'little old impala lamb', their highest name of praise for a girl. Further, that for a 'rooinek' (literally red neck, and the traditional term for an Englishman) Monckton was a 'white gent, first class, third water and incorruptible by sand'. How these phrases ever came to mean anything François did not know. All he knew was that they amounted to the highest form of approval of which such people were capable in words.

There was only one awkward moment. Round about four in the afternoon where the road crossed a sudden mound of earth in the brush, there was revealed away to the west a large, natural clearing ending against an apparently inviting clump of trees with livid red stems and broad spreading sulphur green tops. The wagon master immediately declared it the ideal camping site and straight away wanted to take his team there so that he could prepare for the night in good time, as did all sensible travellers. But François would have none of it. He told the wagoner quite firmly that he could not have picked on a worse site. The wagoner, who had obviously taken to François, none the less was so concerned for the state of his oxen and the fatigue of his people, arguing that they had been on the road since dawn without a break, that he obstinately rejected François's advice. The exchanges between them were becoming heated on his rather than François's part, because François, in his life with the Matabele, had learned that there was nothing so powerful in argument as patience and courtesy. But the wagoner in the quick, vivid, temperamental way of his people, could not imagine airing any difference of opinion without an appropriate heightening of emotion and was close to a passion of anger, when the sound of the Monckton's truck and caboose hurrying near reached them.

The moment he heard the sound, the wagoner stopped arguing to say to François: 'Well! There is the great master himself at last. We'll let him decide.'

So they stood there uneasily silent until the truck, trailer and caboose drew up beside them. The Moncktons, father and daughter, immediately jumped down, but not Amelia. She was sitting in her padded seat beside the driver, in front of the caboose, like a queen on a throne. She had achieved this position with considerable difficulty and obviously nothing which did not hold out the sure promise of greater sustained comfort and dignity was going to make her abdicate.

The wagon master immediately broke into an excitable account of his difference of opinion with François. François

294

remained silent until he had finished, uncomfortable both over explaining his reasons for objecting to so apparently attractive a camping site; and the possible nature of the reception of his reasons by the great Monckton.

Even when the wagon master had finished, François remained silent until Monckton, who believed in his capacity for knowing his own mind and was by nature and training quick in translating it into decisive action, remarked, not without a stirring of impatience: 'Well, young fellow, that all sounds perfectly reasonable to me, so why do you object?'

François knew precisely why he objected. Even so, as his upbringing demanded, he gave the matter further thought in case he had overlooked something important. This slowness in answering, so starkly in contrast to his swift, accurate physical reflexes in action, did not endear him either to the wagon master or his employer, particularly the latter, for François noticed a tightening of the muscles at the corners of Sir James's blue eyes as if he was beginning to feel irritated.

None the less, François answered only when certain of his words. 'I know sir, that it looks a very attractive place for a camp. But I promise you something bad always happens to people who camp there. We have always avoided it ourselves. You wouldn't get any of our own Matabele people even if you offered them a whole span of these beautiful oxen as a reward, to camp there for a single night.'

'But why?' Sir James asked.

François knew then that there was no help for it. He would have to enter what he knew from sad experience to be dangerous and forbidden territory to the rational, sceptical minds of grown-up Europeans. Speaking even more deliberately than before he said: 'You see, sir, those trees look very nice. But they're not really nice at all. They are not only fever-trees but blood trees as well. Our Matabele people,' he felt an awful coward blaming it on the Matabele and excluding himself, 'say that those trees are inhabited by powerful magicians at night. They say that if you were to cut the bark of those trees at night with an axe, they would run red with human blood. As a result, the other magicians immediately combine to revenge themselves on the people who have caused the injury to one of them. But

even if they are not hurt themselves, they do not like people
near them at night in case they overhear the plans for magic
they gather to discuss there.'

'But surely that is sheer, superstitious rubbish!' Sir James
came as near to what novelists call snorting as so well-bred a
person could. Now he was sure that he had been right from the
start in suspecting François to be superstition-prone. And, like
all persons convinced of the absolute rightness of their judgement, he was somewhat aggressive.

'You don't mean to tell me you really believe such nonsense?'
he asked in a somewhat inquisitorial voice, 'I am certain your
father, from all I have heard of him, would have taught you
better.'

At this the girl, who had been watching this encounter between her father and François with something akin to alarm,
clearly felt that her father was oddly out of character in referring to François's father, who was being buried perhaps at
that very moment. For all his habits of authority, he was a
sensitive and naturally kind person and before she knew why,
she had exclaimed, distressed, 'Oh Fa, please, must you?'

What the *please* was precisely aimed at remained undefined,
but the exclamation obviously neither pleased her father nor
endeared François more to him. François, however, was unaware of the change in climate of the argument. He was far too
busy trying to convey earnestly to his interrogators the truth as
he saw it. He knew, of course, that he was dealing in the idiom
of what he himself had been taught was superstition. But the
pagan influences in his life, his recent experience with uLangalibalela, his own sense of guilt over his omission in the matter of
preventing Ouwa's death, the whole new process of turning his
own back on the world to which he was at the moment emotionally committed, came to a point in something Mopani had said
to him many times. 'Little Cousin, always remember in Africa
that what we Europeans call superstition, is just the wrong explanation for the right truth. It is, in fact, an attempt to draw
attention to mysterious facts and laws of nature which Europeans ignore because they cannot explain them with their
brains.'

Fortified in these recollections, he stood his ground and proceeded to give wagoner and employer a number of dramatic examples of the misfortunes which had overtaken travellers who had camped by those trees. One example in fact was only three months old. A party of European hunters on their way into the interior had insisted on camping there, against the advice of their African servants. In the middle of the night, they had been woken with shouts of alarm. Rushing out of their tents they found their African servants in the act of cutting down one of their number from a branch of one of those trees where he had hanged himself. They had done it just in time to save his life. Asked why he had tried to kill himself, he had answered: 'How could I help myself, my masters, when all night long those trees were ordering me to hang myself in that way from that very branch?'

'The man must have been mad,' Sir James declared, impatiently.

'No sir, he wasn't mad,' François insisted quietly. 'I saw the man myself the next day when they arrived at Hunter's Drift. I heard him tell the story to my father. He was as sane as you or I. But that was not all, sir . . . In the morning one of the white hunters getting out of his sleeping bag was bitten by a puff adder. We only just managed to save his life. All the Africans with the hunters insisted that he, too, had been bitten because the trees had commanded the puff adder to bite him.'

'Sheer coincidence,' Sir James declared. 'If that's all you've to say against the site I really don't see why the wagon master shouldn't pitch camp there here and now, if he wishes to.'

However, at this point François found himself unexpectedly supported by numbers of unlikely allies. While they had been speaking, the women, children and men from the other wagons had come forward and gathered round to listen to the discussions.

At this precise moment, several of them called out simultaneously to François in their own dialect: 'Are you telling us, little master, that the place down there is "be-gooled"?' (be-witched).

Despite their Christian pretensions the Cape-coloured people believed in wizards and an even more sophisticated form of witchcraft than the Africans. François had only to explain to them in their own tongue what he had been saying for them to announce, firmly, that nothing would induce them to camp at such a place.

Moreover, the girl herself at once joined in, to exclaim: 'Oh Fa, why are you always so anti-magic? Even Mummy thought you carried it a bit far, you know.'

She had hardly finished when the wagon master, seeing that a majority of his people were turning against him and perhaps because he also shared something of their submerged belief in 'goolery', settled the matter by announcing that on reconsideration he would agree to follow François to this other camp of water of which he had spoken.

As for Sir James, feeling let down by his own daughter, he was not amused. Also, he was confirmed in his judgement of his employees as being an unpredictable, even fickle, though loveable people. Yet his whole adult life had been spent administering unpredictable people and as a result he accepted their conclusion philosophically. But one suspects that François's role in the matter from then on would not get the benefit of Sir James's philosophical attitude.

An hour later, François leading the way on his horse, the Monckton party close behind him and the wagons lumbering in the rear, they reached the pan of water François had in mind. As they came to the top of another rise in the road, they looked down on a great clearing in the bush to the west. At the end of the clearing, the pan, bright in the afternoon sun, herons already standing on one foot in the water along the shadow-lined edges, wild duck and geese drifting in state on a surface of silk, and great multitudes of other water birds circling over it on trembling, harp-like wings, was a privileged sight.

Yet Sir James could not find it in himself just then to say more than a rather perfunctory, 'Yes, I think that might do rather well.'

For some reason, he had no inclination to examine just then why the argument with François earlier on still rankled. He knew that a trivial episode, particularly with someone so young as François, should not have rankled at all, especially as the boy had done nothing but try to help them since their first encounter. But the realization only made him the more irritable.

298

The wagon master and the rest of the train, however, had no such inhibitions. The moment they set eyes on that pan of water and the trees beyond, they expressed their delight in cries of Halleluyah! Hosannah! and many expressions of pleasure and thanks to François. One young man even started strumming his guitar with sheer joy as he leapt down from his wagon, and as he played, improvised a dance to celebrate the end of the long day behind them, while singing their festive song:

> And tonight our folks
> Are going to cut the cold,
> Cut the corn!
> My beloved clings to the bush,
> Clings to the ipi-hamba bush.

The wagon master would immediately have led his train to camp right down by the water, but once more François objected. He explained how the air there at night was black and loud with mosquitoes. He told them they could not even spend one night by the water without contracting malaria. So he begged the wagon master to camp on the highest ground, and to water his oxen as soon as possible by the pan, because the hour just before dusk was the moment when lion and leopard were already in position to pounce on the animals who came to water there. In fact this pan was the favourite feeding ground for the beasts of prey for some hundreds of miles around. He went on to impress on those incorrigibly carefree and optimistic people, that all travellers with oxen on that road gathered the animals close to their wagons at night, ringed them with large fires and posted fully armed guards on them all night long.

As the phrase 'fully armed' fell from him, he realized that it must have been full of a hurtful irony to their Cape-coloured companions who, as he had been told earlier on, travelled completely without arms. He tried to make immediate amends by asking the wagon master if any of them knew how to shoot.

The wagon master assured him that most of the men did, since they had fought in the war with the Cape-coloured corps in the north of Africa.

François who was carrying Ouwa's heavy gun with him, at once unslung it from his shoulder with the bandolier full of

299

ammunition, and handed it over to the wagon master saying that he could return it to him when they reached Hunter's Drift in the morning.

Sir James, who of course was present all the time, listened to François in an even more divided state of judgement. Only half-an-hour before François had manifested a completely irrational approach by all his talk of magic trees. Yet here, just a few miles farther on the same road, he was handing out advice based on good scientific reasoning. He could not help being struck by the paradox. But since nothing appears to offend logic as much as paradox, it did not improve his opinion of François.

One suspects too that with a long distinguished record in the service of a remote European government, the elimination of belief in witchcraft and magic, and the substitution in their place of reason, logic and scientific knowledge on which the European way of life purports to be founded, must have figured prominently in his concept of duty. The discovery of belief in magic in the son of someone who had a formidable reputation as an Educationalist, was not only totally unexpected but struck him as a kind of betrayal of all he thought good in the European approach to Africa.

One must wonder, moreover, whether the causes of his irritation may not have gone deeper. They could also have arisen out of a subliminal sense of guilt. In dismissing all Africa's claims for superstition and magic as absurd, as they obviously were on a purely rational and scientific level, and by not trying, in fact, to discover what unexplored aspects of reality were keeping the practices alive and vivid in the spirit of natural man, he may have felt a fleeting intimation that he had contributed to western man's failure in Africa.

Was the cause of all this perhaps aptly summed up in what his own daughter, childlike, had just called anti-magic? The mere thought of it was ridiculous, of course, he reassured himself. And yet ... ?

These and many other considerations, however, were cancelled by the immediate duty of supervising the organization of the wagoner's camp for the night. With all that capacity for detail and authority which had made him so eminent a servant of government, he went about the task with great energy.

François, after explaining about the short cut to Hunter's Drift, was already on his horse, pushing on as fast as he could in order to prepare Ousie-Johanna for the reception of the Monckton party. He could not help being somewhat amused by hearing behind him, now that the mopani beetles, not surprisingly, had finally lost their voices in the late afternoon silence of the bush, the calm, authoritative voice of Sir James giving orders to the wagoners, each command ending with a loud, 'At the double!'

Perhaps, more important, had he looked back, he might have noticed Luciana perched on a wagon watching him ride away. He could not possibly have known how the light of afternoon, making the dust raised by his horse and Hintza with the smell of home in his nose, leaping to incredible heights, things of beauty and flame, that his going appeared to her to be even more legendary than his coming.

Yet, happily for François, he had no inkling as to the possible outcome of his encounter with Sir James. He himself was not accustomed to being in the right. Being reproved, not only by Ouwa and Lammie but also by Ousie-Johanna, 'Bamuthi and many of his Matabele playmates, had been a constant factor in his life so that the difference of opinion between him and Sir James was easily forgotten.

All he knew was that it was a perfect evening to bring the eventful day behind him to an end. He had seldom seen an evening more tranquil. He had only one profound regret; not so much that Ouwa was dead, but that he could not have died in such surroundings at such an hour. Then he would have had company. The whole transcendent example of the sinking of the sun and the coming of darkness, the emergence of the stars, would have been there to support his own transition from life into death and into whatever might be beyond.

In a mood of sober resolution he arrived, unobserved, just before sundown at Hunter's Drift. As he dismounted at the entrance to the courtyard, hard by the stables, he could hear from the direction of Ousie-Johanna's rooms, a sound that suggested that she too must have once more found peace with life and the world. She was singing loudly and at her most cheerful best, one of her favourite hymns, 'Nearer my God to Thee'.

Far from having any religious reactions to this sound, François rejoiced in it without shame, for Ousie-Johanna's celebration in song of divine propinquity, gave him a most irreligious lust after food and drink. As he went in to greet her, he thought, 'We shall eat better than ever tonight if she's singing like that.'

Ousie-Johanna did not normally take kindly to any interruption of her do-it-yourself concerts, but this occasion was a joyful exception, until François told her about the Moncktons. The news made her panic, not because she did not like the idea of guests but because she feared she had no time to be at her best. Accordingly she reproved François with a heated: 'You might have let me know before', then declaiming to Heaven that she had nothing appropriate to wear for such a great occasion, and that there was no decent food that could possibly be prepared at such short notice, she ordered François out of her room.

Knowing her as well as he did, François was convinced that even if no one else did, Ousie-Johanna was going to enjoy the occasion to the full. Quick as he himself was in having a bath and changing into clean clothes, Ousie-Johanna was quicker. He found her in the kitchen in her best starched white linen uniform and apron, edged with Madeira lace. On a side-table lay her best hat, with a great clutch of bright red cherries pinned on its side; and a sulphur yellow handbag with massive metal clasps. Neither of which, of course, she would have any opportunity of using but which she invariably displayed prominently in her kitchen so that any stranger who might be brought in to see her, would recognize these as badges of her exalted place in the hierarchy of the household.

He was certain, therefore, that inwardly she was rejoicing at the sense of importance that arose from the arrival of distinguished guests for a whole night. To François's amusement this was making her affectionately truculent and peremptory with him, first by reproving him for taking 'hours' over his bath, and then asking why he had not yet made a single helpful suggestion as to what they could give their guests to eat, seeing that he had left her no time at all for cooking anything worthy of the name of food.

Happily François had suggestions. He had much experience

of the food one longed for at the end of days of travel through so hot and exacting a bushveld. For instance, he himself had been longing all day for some of the wonderful yellow melons they grew so successfully at Hunter's Drift, a melon called 'span-spek' (Span-ham), a name which Ouwa had maintained was a contraction of Spanish-ham, being eaten as an hors-d'oeuvres with ham. At Hunter's Drift this melon could not be equalled at the end of a long, hot day. François therefore offered to go immediately into the garden and select half a dozen of the finest melons. He wanted to rush out there and then, but Ousie-Johanna had not done with him and scornfully upbraided him, 'And do you think that those yellow bath sponges full of scented water you call melons will be enough to satisfy a lot of hungry people?'

Like all born cooks she had a tendency to despise anything put on the table which had not gone through heavenly meta-morphosis in the temple of her kitchen. François had to contain his impatience and finally it was decided that melon would be followed by one of Ousie-Johanna's superb beef-marrow soups, accompanied by crusts of warm, fresh bread, spread thick with the marrow from the bones themselves, and spiced with just enough fresh ground black pepper and the merest sprinkling of young limes to discipline the fat. Then she would immediately get one of the Matabele servants to kill some of their finest fat chickens in order to follow the soup with roast chicken, yellow saffron rice and raisins, and round baby marrows, baked in butter and cinnamon in the oven. Finally, provided François would hasten for once in his life to climb the great trees and pick the berries before dark, she would bake a mulberry tart and serve it with a quart of cream.

François was so happy and hungry at the thought of such a menu that he could not resist giving Ousie-Johanna a quick hug, saying, 'You know, Ousie-Johanna, you ought, if it is at all possible, to sing "Nearer my God to Thee" more often!'

Before she could ask him what on earth he had meant, both he and Hintza were out of the kitchen door and on their way to the garden. By the time he came back he found Ousie-Johanna had all the maids under her command dressed in their best calico clothes and busy opening up the house. Indeed, the great baroque oil lamps, suspended from the ceilings on long, heavy chains like gold in the main rooms and long corridor, were already lit, although the evening still burned like a great bush fire along the horizon and made the wide windows elegiac with light. In the two large so-called spare rooms, which were always kept for unexpected visitors in the tradition of François's people, the windows were open and the beds turned down and, as François found on his quick inspection tour of both rooms, they were equipped with fresh water in thermos containers; tins covered with remnants of some old family chintz and full of rusks standing beside them. Long white candles, made at Hunter's Drift, stood in enamel holders by the beds and on the dressing tables, a box of matches beside each one. Moreover, Ousie-Johanna had seen to it that in each room there were several of the beautiful, old blue and white porcelain Chinese ginger-jars which the East Indiamen, calling in at the Cape of Good Hope centuries ago, had brought from China. These were full of dahlias, zinnias, geraniums and the scarlet wild aloe flowers which were abundant in the summer in the bush around Hunter's Drift.

Indeed it all looked as welcoming and as attractive as it would have done if Lammie herself had supervised the organization, so that François felt extraordinarily confident and rather proud when he went to the kitchen to thank Ousie-Johanna for all she had done. But he did not get far with his thanks, for he was abruptly ordered to take his 'inconsiderate' self away when she and her helpers had so much serious work to do in so short a time.

There was only one item that worried François and which he took it upon himself to change. He found the table had been set as if Ouwa was there to take his place at its head. This presupposed that either he or Sir James would have to sit in Ouwa's place. The thought somehow was too much for him. He immediately asked the maid to re-lay the places, knives and forks of old Cape silver, and yellow mats of Amanzim-tetse reeds with 'Bamuthi's tribal pattern woven into them, at the other end of the table. They had hardly completed the change when he heard the sound of the Moncktons' truck and caboose coming up the road towards the homestead.

Used as he was to arriving at Hunter's Drift after long and exhausting journeys at all hours, François himself had never quite lost the sense of wonder evoked by the sight of his own home. It always looked to him beautiful, welcoming and infinitely reassuring, considering how profoundly it was contained in the wildest, loneliest and widest bushveld in Africa. If it always looked like a thing of wonder to him, one can readily imagine how it must have appeared to the tired members of the Monckton party, seeing it for the first time after their long journey.

Luciana bounded from the truck to cry out with excitement and delight: 'D'you really live here? Do you? Oh, how gorgeous.'

The great Amelia, who had to be helped down from her itinerant throne, did her best to look as if she had seen better things, but to anyone who knew her as Luciana did it was clear that her pose of dignified silence was due to the fact that she was speechless with astonishment. Even Sir James, whose career had not unnaturally inclined him to a certain love of pomp and display was sufficiently impressed to lose some of his reserve, and as a result became more friendly to François than he had yet been, saying sincerely that in spite of all he had heard of the wonders his father had performed in carving Hunter's Drift out of the bush, he had never expected anything quite as beautiful and impressive as this.

As a result, the evening that followed was a happy one. So happy that François had at the end of it, with his Calvinist background, a feeling of self-condemnation that his remorse over Ouwa's death had been temporarily forgotten.

There was only one awkward or, perhaps, funny moment, depending on whose point of view one favours. François had made Sir James sit in the place of honour at the bottom of the table which he had turned into its head for that evening, and asked him to say grace before they started on their cold melons, which lay like half harvest moons on Lammie's best Delft china plates in front of them. François did this because the concept of good manners of his own people demanded that the senior stranger at table should always be invited to say grace. Sir James obviously was not accustomed to saying grace either at his own

305

or any other person's table. François could tell that instantly not only by his evident embarrassment but by the quick look which the girl gave her father out of those large eyes of hers, blacker and more shining than ever under the yellow light of the brass oil lamp suspended in that biblical way over the great dining-room table. It was not at all a reverent look and he was not at all certain that he ought to approve of looks like that in a young girl, or for that matter from anyone else on such an occasion. Whether he approved or not, however, it made no difference to the fact that it was a look of the most sacrilegious merriment suppressed with great effort.

What was worse, it was followed by one of the subtlest and almost imperceptible winks that François had ever seen in the eyes of any living person, a wink so deft, artful and quick that François somehow knew it was the product of long practice. Not the least disconcerting thing for him about both expression and wink was the assumption they seemed to convey that François would be sharing their meaning and that this matter of saying grace by one so awkward at it as Sir James, was an unnecessary and absurd impediment to the important business of eating. François's deduction was confirmed by the fact that Sir James, drawing desperately on remote memories of his past, realizing that the last time he had been called upon to do any-thing of the sort was perhaps as a pimpled prefect at Rugby, had hardly mumbled an embarrassed 'For what we are about to receive' etc., when the girl had her spoon in her hand, dug it into the melon and almost at once, with a full mouth, exclaimed, 'Oh, how scrumptious!'

Her father, his duty done and for the moment comfortable in the knowledge that a whole meal lay between him and that other embarrassing terminal when no doubt he would be called upon to say thanks as well, found the melon so good that he asked François almost with unbelief, 'And do you really grow melons like these yourself?'

On the foundation of several glasses of the cool dry sherry made by François's cousins in the south, as well as a hock of amber, a purple-red wine and some of the oldest of old Cape brandy that followed, Sir James from then on took charge of the conversation. In the process he became so mellow in thought and speech that all abrasion from their earlier encounters vanished from François's emotions. He listened intently to Sir James's eloquent and detailed account of how he had first visited the area as a young District Officer some twenty-five years ago, how even then he had thought it would be the one place in Africa where he would like to spend the days of his retirement. It seemed to him then to offer many precious natural things that were either vanishing or becoming so rare and expensive in Britain and Europe that he was certain they would be out of his reach when retirement came. It was not just the shooting and fishing, and a life of ease with servants who loved serving. It was far more that the people he had met as a District Officer there had made him feel as if his life had meaning because they seemed so grateful for what he could give them of his inheritance of justice, law, order, decency and self-respect. Such a life and such an access to a feeling of purpose and meaning in himself, he had thought, would be available there on the Amanzim-tetse for an indefinite period.

Of course, this was all implied rather than stated literally. Equally, he implied in what he said an extreme distaste of the present and the direction that life seemed to be taking him. He seemed by no means old (even in Francois's reckoning of age), yet his whole imagination, in the best and most honourable way, was still enclosed in the values of the past. It was clear that he had been led to select this remote and isolated part of Africa as a kind of fortress to defend a vanishing way of life against the impetuous future tightening its forces of siege around him.

There even came a moment in the conversation when François had a glimpse of how shocked Sir James had been when rumours reached him that someone else also had taken a liking to his part of Africa and started developing it in a contemporary manner. The shock had been softened only by reports of Ouwa's unusual personality and of his love of the aboriginal life of Africa. Not that he had approved even then of everything that he heard of Ouwa's doings. Sir James's deepest conviction, honourably and truthfully held, was that the sort of Britain he represented had everything to give, and nothing to learn or receive, from the man of Africa except grateful recognition. All these things, however, were conveyed at this most enjoyable of dinners, more by atmosphere than by statement.

In any case, imposing as François found Sir James to be, his own imagination was stimulated far more by the presence of Luciana, who was nearer to his own age. He realized with a shock that never before had he had anybody that was at all sympathetic and close to his own age staying at his home. That it should turn out to be a girl was an event of some significance. It seemed like something straight out of the fairy-tales that he had ceased reading only a year or two before.

One says someone of his own age, because that is what François assumed. Yet one must underline that it had not occurred to him, as it had occurred to the girl at the very first encounter, that he might, if not ought, to ask her age. Thereby, as one will presently see, hangs something not unimportant to this tale.

All one needs to complete the account of the evening is to say that the girl in question, despite the curiosity, excitement, chatter and the bewildering range of expressions on her young renaissance face and in her wide Mediterranean eyes, at which François marvelled continuously, once her meal had ended with a deep, unashamed sigh of contentment, was so worn out that Sir James politely asked François to summon Amelia.

Initially a place had been laid for Amelia on the dining-room table, but she had elected to join Ousie-Johanna in the kitchen. Before François even opened the kitchen door he could tell from the kind of noises coming from behind it that a cordial celebration was in process. He entered to find Ousie-Johanna in the process of filling Amelia's glass from a bottle of red wine, although he knew that Ousie-Johanna never drank at all, and regarded it, as she was fond of saying, as 'a liquid invented by Mephistopheles'. While she was doing this, though she and Amelia did not know a single word of a common language, they were making noises, faces and elaborate gestures with their hands at each other which demonstrated a complete community of spirit as well as great and growing affections.

Pleased as François was at seeing two such monumental ladies of such different backgrounds on such excellent terms, he could not help being astonished. No half-caste person that he had ever known in Africa, least of all members of the Cape-coloured people such as those who were at that moment in their camp above the pan on Hunter's Road, would have dreamed of sitting down at a common table with a black person. It was his first glimpse of how utterly free of colour prejudice were the Portuguese of Africa. Sympathetic as he had been from the start towards Amelia, his heart now warmed to her all the more for taking so immediately to his own beloved Ousie-Johanna, and he hated to interrupt them. However, the moment he indicated that she was needed in the dining-room, Amelia swallowed the rest of her wine in one long gulp, in such a hurry that she sneezed and evoked, to François's amazement, the polite Matabele response from Ousie-Johanna of *'Tutuka!'* that is, Grow!

Dear God, François reflected, if the wish implied in the *tutuka* were granted, it could only be followed by such an explosion that Ousie-Johanna's kitchen would be shattered, because it was quite inconceivable that anybody could ever grow bigger than either Amelia or Ousie-Johanna without imperilling, between them, the laws of safety prescribed by Providence and biology for the legitimate expansion of the human body.

Amelia had hardly gone through the door when Ousie-Johanna, her face shining and eyes beaming, remarked to François, 'What a real lady. A real, stately lady of taste and fashion. Have you ever seen anyone so well dressed in this heathen place? Do you know, her dress shines so beautifully that I could see my own face in the lamplight on her bosom. Do you think our Lammie would let me have a nice, shining dress like that too? We can't have neighbours giving themselves airs and dressing better than we do, can we now? And don't you think my hair would look fine with combs and lace just like that? And do you know, Little Feather, I don't think our Lammie herself, now that she has to go into mourning, could do better than to wear a black dress exactly like that.'

François did not have the heart to tell Ousie-Johanna what he thought about clothes so inappropriate for travelling through the bush as Amelia's, and he skilfully avoided all effort at coming to terms with Ousie-Johanna's highly suggestive praise of Amelia and her appearance, by telling her how much her

309

dinner had been enjoyed and how grateful he would be if they could all be called half-an-hour earlier next morning with coffee and rusks, because the Moncktons were anxious to get to their own place on the river as soon as possible. But Ousie-Johanna was not to be side-tracked. She gave him only a perfunctory word of agreement before she was back on the subject of Amelia.

'And, Little Feather,' she said with such innocent naïveté that François did not know whether to laugh, cry or just hug his own unrivalled Princess of the Pots as 'Bamuthi called her, 'you know she is not only in the mode [South Africans still use in their language the French word for fashion] but she is so well-educated too. She speaks a language even I cannot understand.'

'Why, dear little old Ousie,' François tried to comfort her, 'nor do I understand it.'

'Don't you, Little Feather?' she exclaimed, amazed, before adding after a deep, long pause, 'Dear little Lord in the Heaven, she is better educated than even I thought, ignorant creature that I am.'

François fully expected to find that the great Amelia had whisked the girl off to bed in his absence, but to his astonishment she was still there in her chair, her fatigue forgotten in an argument with her nurse in Portuguese, which appeared based on the simple fact that she just refused to go to bed until she had said good night to her host. She did this, François thought, quite charmingly, in a way he had never seen and yet, as often before with other actions, done with a disconcerting suggestion that the gesture could be both pretended and genuine at the same time.

As he entered the room she broke off arguing, pushed her chair back and jumped lightly to her feet, as if François were not a boy but some dignitary to whom she was compelled to curtsy, as all well brought-up young Portuguese girls are still taught to do before their elders. The curtsy was elegant enough but he did not quite know what to make of her 'Good night sir, thank you for a most wonderful evening.'

Indeed François was so confused by it all that he could only take refuge in the most conventional of all responses, 'Nothing at all to be thanked for, thank you very much indeed,' while

310

inwardly he was irritated with himself for not being more graceful and original in his reply.

The girl swished about like a dancer and was following Amelia dutifully to the door leading into the corridor, when she overheard the conversation starting between François and her father, and stopped.

François was politely suggesting to Sir James that since he had to get up early in the morning, probably he, too, would like an early night. Then, if he would excuse him, François would immediately set about the last of his duties so that the house could be shut up for the night. This was a duty that always fell to him in Ouwa's absence. It was what he called the 'night patrol', a final round of all the buildings, stables and outhouses to see that all were secure against the night, and the Matabele watchman at his post to guard the homestead and the domestic animals it sheltered, against possible marauders.

Sir James readily accepted the suggestion, but explained that he himself always liked a turn about outside before going to his 'bunk', and he announced that he would accompany François.

It was this remark by her father that sparked off in Luciana a fresh act of rebellion. She rushed back into the room and begged: 'Oh Fa, please may I come too? I'd just love to see what it looks like outside on a night like this.'

Despite the objections indignantly raised in profuse Portuguese by Amelia, Sir James, perhaps because he had just had an unexpectedly good dinner or perhaps, more naturally, because despite his air of resolute authority, he could not help spoiling a daughter who, since his wife's death, was the only feminine influence in his life, set about placating Amelia in what appeared to be to François a quite unexpected and diplomatic manner.

As a result, the three of them, with, of course, Hintza, went outside on to the broad stoep, standing still and silent at the sudden transition from the light of lamps into a night without moon. François, who could never get used to the authority of such nights, stood as if to attention before it for a while. He was carrying, as he always did on these occasions, an ancient and beautiful old gun which Mopani had given him. He could never explain why he always carried this particular gun when he went on a night patrol. Yet one suspects that the cause lay far

311

back in his imagination, where an awareness of the antiquity of night, pressing down there at Hunter's Drift, sagging with the weight of stars, suggested that only the oldest in the instincts of the observer matched by what was oldest in his defence against anything that might abuse and exploit the power conferred on it by such darkness, could be appropriate. So they stood there, all four of them, on the edge of the stoep, silent, humbled and solemn in the manner of persons experiencing, after a brief reprieve in the tight ring of artificial light in the dining-room a second before, this impact of African night which one still believes to be the greatest of all the many forms darkness can assume on this insignificant planet.

François was full of gratitude that it was a particularly clear and beautiful night, as though the universe itself were collaborating with his longing for his home and surroundings to be at their best for his visitors. A low exclamation of delight broke from Luciana and moved him to speak to her in whispers. He felt he could never speak otherwise when faced with the night. He pointed out all the main constellations which were so defined and precise on this occasion that one could readily perceive how the Greeks and Romans had imposed particular patterns on them and why they made such singular personifications of their combinations of stars.

For instance, the Milky Way was more even than a way of foam and star-spume. It was a broad river of divine milk. Almost immediately ahead, Orion was a belted, sworded and knightly hunter. The Heavenly Twins were as bright as if, indeed, they were holding up jewelled cups to be filled not with wine so much as the oldest and rarest vintage of light for the gods benighted on Olympus. Sirius, the great Dog star, was at least two double handfuls of silver-green light. Moreover, not only the classical patterns but the patterns of others who had followed in their wake, were just as clear and understandable.

The Southern Cross in particular needed no pointing out to Luciana. Being half Portuguese already her recognition had seized on it. She knew, of course, how it had received its name from the great Portuguese navigators without whom their presence there, in the heart of Africa centuries later, would not have been possible. She appeared to have such strong feelings

312

about it that she did not take kindly to François's predilection for the name the people of Africa gave to it. He explained that they combined it with other stars in the vicinity to call their pattern The Giraffe.

When she asked rather tartly, 'Why Giraffe?' he said it was because the giraffe had the longest neck and perhaps the largest and most glowing eyes of all animals of the bush. As a result it was able to look over the tallest trees to see things that no other animal could see. It was also supposed to possess an insatiable curiosity. This combination of qualities made the Bushmen and others impose on the Southern Cross and its bright fellow-travellers, the image of a giraffe, standing with its feet on the horizon, its long neck stretched high into the sky to look right over the trees of the night so that it could report back on whatever it saw coming up from beyond the dark.

The final explanation, François was happy to note, did something to mollify Luciana's initial objections. But he thought it as well to end his Africanization of the stars and to lead the way all round the house and outhouses. They seemed to find it as natural as he did to pause at the stable doors, listening to the lovely sound of horses crunching their dinner of straw and oats at their manger. They stopped to pat the mongrel watch-dogs who came rushing up to them in what Hintza clearly thought their usual ill-bred manner. They joined François in saying 'good evening' respectfully to the old Matabele watchman who met them at the far corner of the outhouses, just where the great garden and orchards began. He got up from his mat of straw where he sat all night with his back to the wall, a great knob-kerrie and long assegai, a large jug of water and a loaf of bread beside him and a long, self-made wooden pipe in his hand. So accustomed had their eyes become to the darkness that all these and many other details were visible and lovingly noted by François as he took them on past Ousie-Johanna's beloved hen run, where they heard the birds clucking spasmodically over dream eggs hatched in their sleep. At last they finished up once more at the front stoep.

They were just about to go up the steps when down beyond the river a lion roared. It was an exceptionally deep, loud and bass roar. So imperative and powerful was the sound that it startled Luciana, who clutched François's arm asking, 'Oh dear Heaven, what on earth could that be?'

'Oh, that,' François answered nonchalantly. 'That's only old Chaliapin having a good yawn before going to sleep for the night. The old boy has obviously had too good a dinner for once.'

Sir James and his daughter exclaimed in one voice, 'Chaliapin?'

'Yes,' François replied. 'That's our name for him. You see, he has the most musical roar of all our lions.'

'*Our* lions?' Luciana exclaimed.

'Yes,' François replied. 'They're all part of our old faithfuls. They live round about in the bush and have done so for years, so we can tell them by the sounds they make. They're good lions too, because they never give us any trouble. The dangerous ones, our real enemies, and there are hundreds of them, never utter a sound.'

Just then old Chaliapin was answered, as lions often are, by another lion farther down the river. To François it was a younger, and far less impressive sound, for he commented immediately, 'Oh I might have known he would join in too. That's just Caruso trying to show off as usual and pretending that he's in better voice than Chaliapin.'

'Are all your lions named after musicians?' Sir James asked in some amusement.

'Not all,' François told him. 'Only some of them. We have other names for them as well. Some Matabele, some European and even some Bushman.'

He went on to explain, stressing how wrong was the common assumption that all lions were alike. They were highly individualistic animals. No two ever looked or behaved alike and they never did the same things twice. He had hardly finished explaining when another lion roared nearer to the house, as if to illustrate François's theme.

'Now just listen to that,' he exclaimed delighted. 'Did you hear how different that sounded? That was a lioness calling. That was our Garbo answering the men on the other side of the river.'

'Garbo?' Luciana demanded, more interested than ever.

François answered seriously, 'Yes. My parents christened her Garbo because, according to the Matabele, she is the one great exception to the lioness's rule. She always wants to be alone. She was just telling those two fellows you heard across the river that she wants none of their company.'

'She sounds rather anti-social to me,' the girl remarked, then yawned and added, 'I think, if you don't mind Fa, I will now go to bed.'

'Don't mind?' Sir James exclaimed, as if outraged by the implication that his daughter's presence there was of his contriving, and convinced that it was just another example of the irrational and unpredictable in women, even in one so young as his daughter, 'If I had had my way you would have been in your bunk hours ago. Off you go miss, at once, and at the double!'

That night François indeed might have overslept if it had not been for Hintza calling him out of his sleep and drawing his attention to some unusual sounds disturbing what should have been complete silence in that far wing of the house. François was out of bed at once. Opening his door he looked down the corridor and saw Amelia trying in vain to keep her voice down to a whisper as she held on with one hand to the sleeve of Luciana's pyjama jacket, who appeared to be determined to tear herself away.

François discreetly pulled back into his room, shut the door quietly and dressed as fast as he could. Yet, when he and Hintza re-emerged in the corridor, he found it empty and silent and assumed that Amelia had won her battle. But he soon discovered that he had underrated Luciana because, as his hand touched the knob of the heavy kitchen door, he heard her voice joining Ousie-Johanna's in what struck him as a spirited and joyful exchange of sounds, despite the fact that neither of them spoke a common language.

François had a knack of moving quietly; at times people had found it disconcerting. It was perhaps a compliment to Mopani who had impressed upon him the necessity of silent movement for the successful hunter, and had taught him respect for silence to such an extent that he had developed an extreme dislike of unnecessary noise of any kind. As a result, he appeared in the kitchen unnoticed and was able, for a moment, to observe a scene which he found was as stimulating as it was funny.

The great Amelia, with a look of sullen defeat on her face, was sitting in Ousie-Johanna's own chair. In front of her a lovely heavy silver-backed hair-brush, an ivory comb and a rather forlorn little pile of dark blue ribbons, unwanted, lay on the table. While she pretended not to notice, Luciana was helping Ousie-Johanna with almost embarrassing zeal to prepare the trays for the coffee pots, plates, cups, jugs of hot milk and the Delft porcelain bowls of nut-brown rusks for the household.

She was still in her pyjamas, her dark hair, unplaited, came down nearly to her waist. As she darted about from one end of the kitchen to the other, trying to anticipate what Ousie-Johanna needed next, her hair whisked about in such an unruly manner that she seemed to him to be constantly brushing it away from her eyes as well.

François had no desire to interrupt the scene but Hintza had his own ideas on the matter. He dashed towards Luciana, jumped up behind her and placed an affectionate paw on her shoulders, as he normally would have done only to François.

Luciana immediately knew the significance of Hintza's greeting. She turned round. Her face, despite the zeal of her aid to Ousie-Johanna, was still remote with the distance of the wide world of sleep which she had not long left. But her eyes were eloquent with disappointment as she exclaimed: 'Oh, what a pity!'

Amelia who was, of course, also alerted by Hintza, immediately heaved herself out of her comfortable chair with a speed which surprised François, bore down on Luciana like a windjammer under full sail, and began upbraiding her. Judging by the way Luciana suddenly looked down to examine herself from toes to shoulders, François took Amelia's words to be a vigorous expression of her feelings that no female, however young, should ever appear in front of any member of the male sex in a state of undress. It was François's first glimpse into Amelia's almost medieval concept of what was proper in feminine behaviour, and his reading of the situation was immediately confirmed by Luciana, who appeared quite undismayed and unrepentant over Amelia's reproaches.

She turned and said to him, 'Amelia thinks it is very wrong of me to be here in front of you in pyjamas. She thinks that either you or I should leave the kitchen at once – preferably me.'

She had only just finished speaking, when Amelia interposed herself as a solid screen between Luciana and François. In fact Luciana had been compelled to finish her last sentence looking round the side of Amelia's great frame, with only her face, bright with revolt, just visible.

François said at once, 'Tell her my mother and father and I, whenever we had time, always met for morning coffee and rusks in our pyjamas.'

'I'm afraid that's a bit different,' she gasped, as Amelia pulled her out of François's sight.

Far more than the question of the propriety of Luciana's appearance, François was concerned over the look of disappointment with which Luciana had greeted him and the exclamation, 'Oh, what a pity', which he took to refer to himself. Indeed it rankled so much that he was on the point of leaving the kitchen to the incomprehensible women when Ousie-Johanna broke in to ask him in his own language what on earth was wrong. Why, all that nice little Nonna, young lady, had been doing was of the utmost help to her so that she herself could take the trays of coffee to her father and François.

Only then did François realize that the 'Oh, what a pity' perhaps had referred to the fact that Luciana had intended to surprise him and her father in what might have appeared to her a rather mature feminine role, and which his unexpected appearance had cancelled.

He tried to pretend, therefore, that nothing unusual had occurred and politely asked Luciana, and through her Amelia, if they had spent a good night. His inquiries remained unanswered. For once Amelia was determined, apparently as a matter of prime medieval conscience, to win this battle with Luciana. She seized her firmly by the wrist and using her giant strength dragged the protesting Luciana out of the kitchen, to both François's disappointment and Ousie-Johanna's utter incomprehension.

Meanwhile, the battle between the two still raged because soon the kitchen door opened again. Luciana's face showed in the opening and she had just time to call out to François, 'Please tell Mistress Johanna I'll be back in a jiffy to help her again', before she was jerked back out of sight and the door slammed violently by Amelia's elephantine foot.

Luciana, however, was not back in a jiffy. Sir James and François had nearly finished their coffee and rusks before she appeared again, fully dressed, her hair once more plaited, and looking very much as when François had first seen her. But she still looked frustrated and resentful of Amelia who, following her own broad, full bosom like a great ship's mainsail swollen with wind, moved in ahead of her and made straight for the kitchen and Ousie-Johanna. When the door shut behind her, Luciana spoke to her father in a voice bright with anger, which oddly enough made François remember from far back in the past something that Ouwa had once said to Lammie, 'If little girls had the power as they have the will, they would rule the world.'

'You must really speak to Amelia, Fa,' she told, one is tempted to say ordered Sir James, who like the whole of adult-dom had no idea how much the young resent being treated as such in front of their peers, even when they are prepared to accept such treatment in private. 'She *must* stop treating me like a child. The way she carried on in the kitchen just now, you might have thought I was a dancer about to do a striptease.'

The fact that the expression *dancer* and *striptease* suggested access on the part of Luciana to what not only Amelia but Sir James also would have regarded as a world of forbidden know-ledge for a young girl, did not seem to strike him at all. Typically he noticed only what he took as reprehensible and characteristically feminine disregard of logic in Luciana's pro-test. In his authoritarian voice, dangerously close to sarcasm he observed, 'Despite my not inconsiderable experience of the world, I have not yet heard of children doing striptease acts. I would have thought it an occupation reserved for much older women. The obvious conclusion surely is that Amelia was giving you the credit of being far older than you really are.'

'Oh, there you go again, Fa. You never understand how tire-somely old-fashioned Amelia can be.'

'Perhaps I don't,' Sir James observed with a certain affec-tionate condescension, then gave way to a reproof of his own. 'You have not said good morning either to me or your host.'

It seemed to François that the way in which she then held up her cheek to be kissed by her father was more dutiful than spontaneous. When she turned to face him he thought for a moment that she was about to give him a similar salutation and was rather alarmed as to how he should respond.

Luciana herself did not know exactly how to greet him, either, so she chose a proxy for the solution of her conflict. She went to Hintza sitting beside François's chair, saying as she did so, 'Of course, we've already said good morning.' She then knelt down by Hintza and put her arms round his neck and rubbed her head against his, saying in an oddly maternal little voice. 'But you, darling Hin, I've not thanked you yet for the nice way you wished me good morning.'

Could François have read Luciana's innermost mind just then, he would have been amazed that she, too, was involved in the discovery of an unsuspected aspect of herself. She had become aware of a capacity for concealing her real feelings of which, till that moment, she had been ignorant. What is more, she found a certain enjoyment as well as sense of reassurance in this capacity for holding, as it were, her natural hand, despite her usual impulsiveness. Thrilled, as if the discovery had armed her more than ever for future relationships with the men of her world, she fondled Hintza warmly and exulted secretly over the dawning of a feeling of greater power over herself.

Meanwhile, Hintza's responses were so immediate and warm that Luciana was at once restored to her quick, changing self. François thought that he had seldom known a happier early morning coffee. He would have liked it to go on much longer, but was forced to break off when Ousie-Johanna suddenly entered the room to announce that 'Bamuthi was coming to see him.

François, during dinner the night before, had sent a message to 'Bamuthi to ask him to come to the house first thing in the morning. This was because while talking over dinner, Sir James had extracted from François a fairly detailed account of the basis on which the Jouberts had organized Hunter's Drift, and of how Ouwa made it a project of partnership between themselves and their Matabele neighbours. Although there were things about the scheme Sir James obviously disliked, it interested him sufficiently for him to want to know more about it. He too wanted the Matabele linked in some way to what he proposed doing on his own vast tract of land. But he thought that making them partners was going a little too far.

In his heart of hearts, much as he had liked, indeed loved them as a young District Commissioner, he did not think the

Matabele mature enough for so sophisticated a relationship. He proposed paying them generous wages with an annual bonus but he thought that these must be determined entirely by his own judgement. Anything else, he felt, in view of his experience as the last of the great colonial governors in Africa, would be, to say the least, highly irresponsible, if not damaging to the people he employed.

Sir James accordingly was highly delighted when François translated Ousie-Johanna's message that 'Bamuthi, who knew all, had come. He was about to get to his feet to go out to meet 'Bamuthi, when to his amazement, the kitchen door opened and 'Bamuthi, according to the Hunter's Drift custom, stepped quite unself-consciously into the room.

Sir James had hardly time to tell himself that he would never allow such slackness in his own establishment when 'Bamuthi raised his hand above his head in the royal Matabele salute and called out in a loud voice: *'Bayete nKosi, isi-Vuba, bayete!'*

François realized that 'Bamuthi must have met Sir James before, presumably when he had toured the district as a commissioner before the war, when 'Bamuthi himself was a young man. His greeting implied a recognition of Sir James's official status and he also had ready on his lips the Matabele name 'isi-Vuba', which was that of the Great Kingfisher.

Sir James stared at 'Bamuthi in astonishment until the memory which all good governors, like royalty, have to cultivate, came to his rescue. His rather fine administerial face suddenly became young with a smile straight out of the period with which his recollection was concerned, the period when neither Sir James nor the great natural world along the Amanzim-tetse had yet lost their innocence. Sir James even forgot himself to the extent of snapping his fingers, and then said impulsively, 'Wait ... wait ... it was at Osebeni, was it not? Yes, it must have been. Let me see. Yes, you must be 'Bamuthi, the first of the sons of the Keeper of the Ford.'

'Bamuthi's delight at being recognized was as great as François's astonishment that Sir James still spoke, however haltingly, a Sindabele both recognizable and correct.

Sir James, caught up in an exceptionally unguarded mood, might have plunged straight away into a world of reminiscence but he was briefly jerked back into the present by 'Bamuthi. 'Bamuthi, as François knew, was one of the most observant of men, and had not failed to notice Sir James's daughter and the interest, if not undisguised admiration with which she was watching him.

Certainly he looked most impressive at that moment. He had obviously come straight from his early morning round of inspection of the lion traps and unlike Ousie-Johanna and the other African members of the household was still not in European dress. Except for a loin cloth of impala skin and a portion of leopard skin round his middle and divided in front, he wore no clothes. The skin of his body was smooth and shining from the lion-fat he rubbed into it every night before going to sleep. On his chest dangled a necklace of beads, woven in the black, white and green pattern of his tribe. On his right wrist he had two broad ivory bangles; on his left one made of plaited elephant hair with a clasp of copper. One broad hand gripped firmly together both his favourite assegai He-Who-Digs-For-My-Children, and the knobkerrie The-Eater-in-the-Dark.

Although later in the day he would be dressed in khaki slacks, safari jacket and bush hat, just as Ouwa and Mopani always were, this traditional battle dress was the one he chose for doing his dangerous rounds of Hunter's Drift defences in the dim hour between night and day, and no one could have designed a more effective camouflage. Dressed in this fashion he might have stepped straight out of the Africa of the great Rider Haggard.

François was delighted that the girl obviously thought him the creature of wonder that 'Bamuthi had never ceased to be for him, despite the fact that he had known him for so many years and more intimately than any other member of his household.

It was 'Bamuthi who now reminded Sir James that he was, in his estimation, committing a breach of good manners by not introducing him to the girl. 'Bamuthi, politely placing assegai and knobkerrie down against the wall in the corner of the breakfast room and a smile flashing on his dark features, exclaimed in his deep voice: 'And this *'nKosanyana*, this little princess, *n'Kosi*? This little mother-to-be of a thousand generations? Surely she can only be another feather of your wing?'

Sir James, for a moment was somewhat taken aback. He could

not approve of 'Bamuthi walking into the house of his employers, still less doing so fully armed and practically naked. Much as he enjoyed meeting 'Bamuthi again, it was not in keeping with his concept of a civilized establishment. So formally he announced her name to 'Bamuthi who immediately stepped forward and holding out both his broad hands, took Luciana's in them.

Sir James had no option but to look on helplessly while 'Bamuthi exclaimed: *'Auck, 'nKosi!* Beyond all doubt, before many years you will get a thousand and one brindled heifers for her.'

Luciana, knowing no Sindabele, of course, understood nothing of this. She felt only that 'Bamuthi was drawn to her as she was to him. Her lively curiosity prompted her at once to ask her father for a translation of what 'Bamuthi had said.

But Sir James, in his state of ambivalence about the encounter, merely said quickly, 'Will you please leave the room now, Chisai. This man and I have business to discuss. I am certain you and Amelia still have a lot to do. I don't want to be kept waiting again for the journey ahead of us.'

Luciana knew from experience how futile it was to argue with her father, when he used what her mother had called his 'end-of-audience' tone. She would have loved dearly to have stayed and yet immediately, her heart filled with disappointment, she got up and quietly left the room.

She had hardly gone when Sir James and 'Bamuthi plunged back to the past, when first they had met. They did all this so happily and easily that François felt himself rather left out. So, making his excuses, he too went out, followed by Hintza, in order to fetch his rifle from his room before he did his own rounds of the farm.

He was about to make straight for his room when, through the open doorway of the dining-room, he saw Luciana at the far end with her back to him, apparently looking out of the broad, high window into the garden at the side. Her bearing was that of a person who suddenly felt herself unwanted, which François, out of his own experience of these things, could not fail to recognize.

So he changed his plans and went over to join her, so quietly that when he asked suddenly, though in a voice full of concern, 'Why are you standing here alone?' she swung round, startled.

Unfortunately for him she did not answer the question directly, but exclaimed in a voice sharp with frustration: 'I'm sick of men!'

François was rendered speechless by her reply. He thought that if that were indeed her state of mind, the sooner he and Hintza left the room the better.

He may well have done so if she had not recognized his mis-interpretation of her remark, and quickly added: 'Of course I don't mean you and Hin. I really mean Fa. He's just like Amelia, always thinking I'm too young to be told anything that matters, and sending me away when things begin to get really interesting.'

François tried to comfort her, saying: 'You know, 'Bamuthi doesn't speak a word of English. It wouldn't have done you much good to stay on there. I myself thought those business things they had to discuss so uninteresting that I left of my own accord to go out and look round the farm. Perhaps you'd like to come with me instead?'

She hesitated before saying: 'Yes, I think I'd love to.'

There was some faint reservation in her answer which François noticed. 'Perhaps there's something else you'd rather do? You've only to tell me,' he said.

'No ... I'd love to see your farm and garden. But apart from the breakfast-room and dining-room, kitchen and my own room, I haven't seen your home at all and I'd love to see it all before we go ... This may be my last chance.'

'Oh, that's easy. Let's do that first,' François replied, relieved, and at once took her on a tour of the house.

They went over every detail of the establishment, the decoration and the glowing old Cape-Dutch furniture which Lammie kept so lovingly dusted and polished. Luciana showed growing appreciation and delight and not surprisingly, because François's home was a product of all that was best in the experience of Lammie's and Ouwa's two Huguenot families. She had already warmed François's heart by exclaiming, 'Oh! I do so hope our new home can be as nice as yours ...' Then she hesitated and added, 'But ...' she paused.

François had noticed how often the hope in her sentences trailed off into a despondent *but*. Yet out of politeness he had said nothing. But now he could not resist asking, 'Why the but? Surely there's no reason why you shouldn't build something much nicer.'

'Oh, it will be nice enough,' Luciana replied, surprisingly realistic. 'But you see, without Mummy, Fa could easily make it rather like a glorified club full of leather-backed chairs, ashtrays, sporting prints, gun-racks and all the dreary things men seem to like so much.'

Even François, with reservations of his own about Sir James, did not take quite so simplified a view of his tastes. He assumed they would be excellent, even if tainted a little with what Ouwa, whose own taste he trusted implicitly, had always described as 'P.W.D.' (Public Works Department). As a result he interpreted Luciana's remark as a drift of feeling rather than a judgement. With the sense of Ouwa's death so acute and close in his own mind he fastened on to her reference to her own mother and asked, with instinctive fellow-feeling, 'What happened to your mother? Do you mind? Has she been dead long?'

Luciana told him the full story without hesitation in the most straightforward manner. Her father had been stationed, years before, in the far north as a provincial governor on the borders of Angola. There he had become a close friend of his Portuguese opposite number on the other side of the frontier. Her mother was the daughter of this Portuguese Governor. She and her father had met and, despite their differences of upbringing and religion (he was Church of England and she Roman Catholic, as were Luciana and Amelia), they had become engaged. After one of those extremely prolonged and exacting engagements which Portuguese custom still demands, and of which Luciana, young as she was, already clearly disapproved, they had got married.

Three years before, on their way back from England to her father's last post as Governor-General of an entire colony, Luciana's mother had stopped in Angola in order to visit her family in the northernmost province of Carmona. Luciana and Amelia were to follow later from Lisbon where they were staying with an aunt while Sir James went on to the capital of his new Government. Luciana's mother had not been home with her parents for many days when an army of African people calling themselves the Free Angola Forces who had been secretly gathering in the jungles and forests of the Congo near by, unobserved invaded the province at night, and surrounded all the villages, hamlets, settlements and towns. Attacking at dawn, they massacred indiscriminately close on forty thousand people; thirty-seven thousand Africans, and three thousand Portuguese. Among the Portuguese were her mother, her mother's family, Amelia's father, who was Portuguese, and his mulatto wife.

Luciana's gruesome story upset François greatly. He had never before heard of this terrible Night of the Long Knives of Africa and was profoundly shocked to think that the indigenous people of Africa could have behaved in so savage a manner. He was somewhat shocked, too, at Luciana's detached telling of the story. Her voice never faltered and she finished by giving François a direct look and saying firmly: 'And so that was that, and ever since then, Fa seems to have become more of a man than it's necessary even for a man to be. And I don't seem to be able to do anything about it.'

She said this as they came to Ouwa's study full of his great collection of books and the wide desk at which he had always worked, still neatly ordered as he had left it. As the room was in twilight because the shutters had not been opened, François immediately went to fling them wide so that they could take in all the detail of what was for him one of the most exciting rooms in the whole house.

To his amazement Luciana was not looking at the books, nor at the furniture or paintings or rare old Cape prints on the walls. She was staring at the large photograph of Lammie which stood by Ouwa's writing pad on the desk. It was both Ouwa's and François's favourite portrait of Lammie, as she had been when Ouwa first met her. Although taken many years ago, it somehow still seemed to François to represent her essential self. It showed Lammie in a riding habit. With one hand she was holding up the skirt of her habit and her other hand was on the bridle of her horse, Lightfoot, which François had never known except through the tales that Lammie had told him.

She was without a hat. Some obscure village photographer, who had obviously handled his primitive camera with all the reverence the first photographers had for their instruments, as if they were not so much technological devices as instruments of the Holy Ghost itself, had caught her so reverently in an early morning of the temperate south that her abundant hair looked as if woven of strands of the light itself. Her beautiful face looked fresh, young and coolly filled with promise like the dawn of a day in spring.

'And that, I take it,' Luciana said with a matter-of-factness that she was far from feeling, 'must be your mummy. I say, she's a stunner, isn't she?' And then quickly, as if knowing that François might find it difficult to respond in the circumstances, besides being already in her quick, instinctive way on to another trend of thought, she asked, 'How old is she?'

Thinking that this girl appeared to have an obsession about age, he was shocked to realize that he himself did not know Lammie's exact age. He knew her birthday, of course, because they had celebrated it lavishly every year but somehow it had never occurred to him to ask the year in which she had been born, and as far as he could remember nobody had ever bothered to tell him. Feeling annoyed that this girl had such an unfailing knack of making him feel inadequate, he answered, 'I'm afraid I don't exactly know.'

'You don't know?' Luciana exclaimed in a voice of unbelief.

'I'm afraid not,' he reaffirmed, trying to excuse himself but wondering why it mattered anyway. Lammie had been there ever since he could remember, as if before and beyond time, like the bush; one did not think it necessary to ask oneself precisely how old things were that had always been there so why ask it about Lammie? Yet the excuse did not work completely for, with Ouwa now dead, perhaps the girl was right and one should begin to ask oneself such questions.

Luciana, with reasons of her own for thinking that François's apparent lack of interest in matters of people's ages, particularly her own, had a deeper and more disturbing significance, thought it better not to ask any more questions on the subject. She just stood there looking at the photograph repeating how beautiful she thought Lammie was and then, after a long pause, remarked

327

more to herself than to François, 'I wonder what she'll make of Fa?'

François could not have known either from her tone or her manner that her imagination was racing away into the future where she had successfully contrived a match between her father and François's mother.

Indeed the complete blue-print, or perhaps one should say white-print, of an ideal wedding was taking shape in the most minute and loving detail with a speed that sent her heart off at a gallop and filled her eyes with a light as vivid as a dream. Even she, used to her capacity for fantasy, was amazed how all this took shape as if bespoke to the measure of her own needs, for the bridesmaids were chosen, the wedding dress designed, a flower of her own choosing in Sir James's buttonhole, his front glittering with orders, medals and decorations, even the wedding cake baked and the couple, radiant of course, walking down the aisle of the church, no – a church was too humble for so important an occasion – down the aisle of some cathedral with the music of an immense, Gothic organ filling the air up to the loftiest dome like the sound of the swell of the sea breaking on yellow sand. It seemed to her that fate could not possibly have presented two human beings, situated as her father and François's mother were, with a more perfect remedy for the tragedy inflicted on them.

Such a solution, indeed, appeared so Heaven-sent that she had great difficulty in not blurting out there and then what she had in mind. But an inner prompting told her that if she went further she might defeat her own dream before it was born by estranging François, still suffering from his father's death. So with great difficulty she held her peace.

Nevertheless through her preoccupation it was with great satisfaction that she heard François say, 'I'm certain she will like your father very much indeed.'

Luciana, perhaps feeling herself imperilled by the conflict of imagination within her accordingly changed the conversation, announcing that she would now love to go round the outhouses and gardens with François and Hintza, since there was a great deal of the house and its establishment which they had not seen.

They returned just in time for breakfast. There is nothing like a garden in the early morning with the dew heavy upon it and the atmosphere charged with the incense of growth for producing a state of inner harmony, so they returned in the highest of spirits. Amelia, however, was waiting for them with disapproval. She had obviously not forgotten what had happened earlier in the morning, and her sense of grievance must have been heightened by Luciana's disappearance without her permission for some hours and her neglect in helping with the packing.

Sir James, however, dispelled most of her irritation by being in great good humour. His meeting with 'Bamuthi had brought alive in him something of what he had felt when he first arrived in Africa full of ideas, zeal and hope for the future. All the weight of the compromise that the rigid official years had inflicted on his original self, appeared to have dropped from him for the moment. In fact he looked very much younger, even innocent and was obviously excited and impatient to be off back to his own holding. For one brief, warm, privileged moment he was nearer to his daughter and to a certain extent to François, than he had yet been since their first meeting.

By the time he had heard of Hunter's Drift he had already, in the course of a career which had taken him all over the vanished Colonial Empire, seen much of European exploitation of virgin earth and nature and its effect on primitive societies. As a result he had anticipated the worst from Pierre-Paul's intrusion into his own pre-selected world. His astonishment therefore was considerable when he found Hunter's Drift akin to something that he had planned himself. It was true he was not happy about all the features of Hunter's Drift. There was, for instance, the question of over-familiarity with people like Ousie-Johanna and 'Bamuthi which was something to be excluded from the way of life that Sir James proposed for himself and his small family on his own vast tract of land farther up the river. But if he had to have neighbours, he was gracious enough to admit to himself, he could have fared a great deal worse than have the Jouberts.

It was, perhaps, a pity that he could not feel quite as certain in his mind about François. For some strange reason which he had neither the time nor the inclination to examine, the boy was something of a problem to him. And he liked to think that there were no problems to which he did not have an immediate answer. But he seemed to like and yet disapprove of this boy at one and the same time. So, unknown to himself, whenever he looked at François or spoke to him, subtly both his expression and tone would change. The change was not enough to impair his cheerful mood. Yet it was obvious enough to his daughter who, for reasons of her own was watching the way that her father and François were reacting to each other. As breakfast progressed, clearly she became uneasy, for her own high spirits left her and she took almost no part in the conversation.

Something of all this perhaps was apparent even to François in the manner in which Sir James finally took himself and his party away from Hunter's Drift. First of all there was his refusal of François's offer to show them the way to his own tract of land. François had indeed a horse, saddled and bridled and ready to guide Sir James's party. Strictly speaking, however, a guide was not necessary because the road Ouwa had made connecting Hunter's Drift with the railway line went over Sir James's property. The most inexperienced novice could follow it without going wrong. Sir James knew all this already both from François and 'Bamuthi, and used the fact as an excuse peremptorily to turn down François's offer of help.

In fairness to Sir James, however, one must not overlook the fact that the land for which he was making had become, in his long absence, almost a fairy-tale reality. He wanted to see it again as in the first instance, without any strangers present. Indeed, ever since the beginning of this return journey he had found himself silently reciting again and again Stevenson's Requiem, beginning with the lines: *Under the wide and starry sky* and ending:

> *Home is the sailor, home from sea,*
> *And the hunter home from the hill.*

A second incident arose when they all emerged from the breakfast room to find truck, trailer and caboose waiting at the front door. François asked Sir James to delay his departure for a moment. He wanted this because since his first meeting with the party he had been thinking of many things that Hunter's

Drift might contribute to make their life in the camp (which would be their home while Sir James's house was being built and his own land cleared and developed), as agreeable as possible. The most obvious things of course were fresh fruit and vegetables.

So, early that morning, he had ordered two of the Matabele gardeners to pick several bags of bright tomatoes, ripe melons, cucumbers, marrows and pumpkins, all fruit that would keep. He knew that at any moment the gardeners would appear with wheelbarrows full of these things for Sir James to take with him.

But apparently Sir James could not find it in himself to wait any longer. It is true, he thanked François punctiliously, if not graciously. But he added that he thought he ought to be on his way at once, and wondered whether François, if he insisted on such a gift, would hand it over to the wagoners who would be following in his track.

Considering that it was only a matter of delaying the departure for a minute or two, François could not help feeling that in similar circumstances he would have been naturally compelled to wait. Anything else too, by Ouwa's and Lammie's standards, would be taking things too much for granted. By Matabele standards, of course, it would have been inexcusable, considering that no Matabele François had ever known would have accepted the gift of even something so small as a sixpence without holding out both hands cupped together to receive it. But perhaps, he told himself, he was over-sensitive in a way he would not have been if he had felt more secure in Sir James's company. Yet even the expression on Luciana's face suggested that she herself was disturbed by her father's manner.

All the nuances of the occasion, however, were soon lost in the tumult of goodbyes that followed. The tumult was largely of Amelia's creation, who seemed to be emotionally as well as physically a lady of extremes. Unlike François's gardeners, Ousie-Johanna had arrived punctually on the scene of farewell with two large baskets full of gifts for the visitors; some loaves of bread still fresh and warm in their white linen wrappings; half a dozen pounds of fresh butter, bottles of fresh milk, gleaming jars of yellow peaches, apricots, pears and mulberries preserved in their own juice, bottles of the green fig and Cape-gooseberry jams which were among Ousie-Johanna's finest specialities, a fruit cake and, of course, quantities of rusks.

The warm heart of Amelia was immediately inflamed by such munificence. In consequence, she burst into tears and threw both arms round Ousie-Johanna, hugging her tightly, crying and sobbing out words in Portuguese incomprehensible to either François or Ousie-Johanna, but none the less obvious enough in their intent to reduce Ousie-Johanna to crying as well, all the more ardently because it had never occurred to her un-demanding, simple, innocent soul that she could ever have mattered to such a great lady of advanced fashion as Amelia was to her.

It took several of Sir James's most peremptory orders to separate the two of them and to proclaim that he could on no account be kept waiting any longer.

Even then the tumult was not over. Amelia, catching sight of François standing there looking rather more forlorn than he realized, remembered immediately his own bereavement and threw herself at him, submitting him to the same farewell that she had imposed on Ousie-Johanna, tears streaming down her cheeks as she expressed her gratitude and, according to what he understood from Luciana's interpretation of her impassioned farewell, imploring him 'not to let himself be massacred'. She said again and again what a terrible country Africa had become. She did not know what any of them were doing there and she feared that if they stayed there much longer they too would all be massacred ... and that it would have been far better if they had all stayed in Europe ...

No one of course took her tearful protestations at their face value. But just for a moment this reference brought a fitful memory of François's own recent experience with the 'men of the spear' that he and 'Bamuthi had observed on their way to uLangalibalela's kraal. But he said nothing. It was a clear illus-tration of the suppression and secrecy which had invaded Fran-çois's being. During the days and months to come he would review it often in the silent hours of the night. But he was never able to discuss it openly, with anybody else, not even someone he trusted as much as Mopani.

The speed of departure was now all the greater because

Amelia's 'hysteria' as Sir James described it, had provoked him into leaving even sooner than he had intended. François instantly found himself giving assistance in the task of restoring Amelia, inert with misery, to her throne in the front of the caboose. By the time they had accomplished Amelia's coronation, Sir James was already standing ready to get into his own truck and determined to end any further outbreaks of emotion. As a result his 'goodbye' was as brief as it was final. He stood there just long enough to thank François and remark perfunctorily that they would all obviously be seeing one another a great deal in the future. Then he climbed into his seat without as much as a handshake.

In this of course he intended no offence. Perhaps even the reverse was true. It could merely have been Sir James's English way of indicating that by now he knew François so well that shaking hands was no longer a necessity. But to François, to whom greetings either of hail or farewell were much more than mere greetings, this omission was final confirmation of his fears that the great Sir James did not like him at all. But what depressed him even more was that Sir James, in his determination to 'get under weigh' without more delay, had already jammed his daughter in the seat between himself and the driver of his truck.

François was already aware that however dutiful a daughter Luciana might be, fear of her father played no part at all in her behaviour. She seemed singularly free with him and judging from the little of what he could see of her now, her face was vivid with anger. Even as he watched, she seemed to be trying to order her father to let her out but the powerful engines of the convoy of trucks had already been started up and were making such a noise as the drivers warmed them up for the journey that it was impossible to hear any human voices.

Yet it was obvious that Sir James, probably feeling that he had had quite enough of feminine emotionalism for this day, was not going to relent and was signalling to his driver to start. The scene, trivial as it was, suddenly made François angry. For a moment he detested Sir James.

As the truck started off, François jumped on the running board to call out goodbye to Luciana. Hintza jumped with him

333

but the side window had already been shut against the dust. François had just a brief glimpse of her sitting beyond Sir James's distinguished profile. She was about to sink back into her seat but fortunately François appeared at the window just in time for her to see him. Her expression of despair changed into one of brilliant relief. She called out something to François that he could not hear, waved both her hands at him vigorously, tried to smile as well and then suddenly sat back to cover her face in her hands, her shoulders trembling as if she were trying not to cry.

By that time the vehicle had gathered speed so fast that even François, holding on to the handle of the door, had to let go and jump down. He was left there watching the truck go, its dust coming down like smoke of burning sulphur over him and Hintza. Dismayed as he was to see Luciana so upset, he had to admit that he was also oddly comforted. Hintza, however, had no access to such sources of comfort for François suddenly heard a whimper. It was such an oddly young and helpless sound, that it made François look away from the receding convoy and down at Hintza. Hintza was not watching the trucks at all. He was looking up at François, with eyes wide open for an explanation. François immediately knelt down, fondled him, and tried to explain the incident in his best and most affectionate Bushman.

That done, he started back to the house. Ousie-Johanna was still on the steps, wiping her eyes with one of their best dining napkins, as if she were still mourning the departure of her guests. François knew that this was not the entire explanation. Her grief would be real enough but there are among the suppressed and rejected peoples of life those who find not only relief but a certain feeling of importance in affliction. Ousie-Johanna was one of those. The reaction on this occasion however was even more complex than he had expected. As François joined her, he found she was mixing a certain healthy anger with her emotions.

Her first remark to him was: 'If that "red-neck" does not learn to go slowly over the stones, he will soon shatter his blerrie wagon.' The stones, of course, were symbols for her of all the innumerable difficulties that beset the Africans on their way

334

through life and which have taught them that the highest form of wisdom, indeed, the safest way of going through life, is always 'to make haste slowly'.

Something of this reservation too was apparent from François's conversations with 'Bamuthi immediately after. As he had not been present at 'Bamuthi's conference with Sir James, he wanted a detailed account of what had happened. The account began with 'Bamuthi's explanation of how Sir James had acquired the name of isi-Vuba, the Great Kingfisher. 'Bamuthi said that whereas in the past most of the 'red strangers' had come into the interior to shoot game, Sir James, as a young man, seemed to spend all his spare time on his official tours by the Amanzim-tetse, fishing. He was after one of the greatest fighting fish in Africa, the Tiger-fish. As François knew, he said, no Matabele had much interest in fish because it was an accepted fact that eating fish turned a man's heart to water. Yet Sir James seemed to have no greater delight than spending all his leisure fishing. Soon he was known all over the territory as the Great Kingfisher. This bird was an even more ardent and expert fisher than the fish eagle, for it lived right by the edge of the waters in which it fished, making its nests in tunnels dug deep with its long beak into the sides of the river banks. Like it, Sir James camped always close by the water. Like it, he too had powerful medicine to keep his heart from turning to water, for no one could ever have accused him of lack of courage. Yet Sir James had another name too. Of course he, 'Bamuthi, had not mentioned it, out of politeness, because he was not certain that Sir James knew of it. He was known more intimately as *uMetal-Disku*.

François had never encountered this word in Sindabele before and was compelled to exclaim: '*uMetal-Disku!* What sort of a word is that, Old Father?'

'Bamuthi explained that up to the time of Sir James's coming, a great deal of injustice had been caused by the official system of tax collection, entrusted in those days to the police who, as 'Bamuthi recollected with scorn, were so stupid that they could not tell one Matabele face from another. Since the Matabele could not write or sign their names the police made the same man pay his tax not only twice but even three times over.

335

When Sir James heard of this, and as a newcomer knowing himself incapable of telling the Matabele apart, yet anxious to abolish injustice, he had introduced a system whereby every male person of tax-paying age was provided with a metal disc with a number stamped on it and a chain for him to wear around his neck, so that no mistake of identity could be made in future. As a result, he became known far and wide as *uMetal-Disku*, that is, Metal-Disc Esquire.

'But surely, Old Father, there could have been no offence in reminding Sir James of that matter?' François exclaimed.

'Bamuthi gave him a look of pity before he remarked, 'But surely, Little Feather, you must know that isi-Vuba's system failed. As fast as he persuaded the Government to give the people metal discs and chains they were used for barter with the ignorant tribes across the river where metal was scarce. Then if not used for barter, since they were so beautiful they were beaten into ornaments for women. So another system of collecting taxes had to be invented. How could I have reminded isi-Vuba of such a failure when all the time he was trying to help?'

'Bamuthi's story was important to François because, still smarting as he was over the events of the morning, it brought him back to a realization that however much he and Sir James may have failed to understand each other, he must be a person of considerable qualities if people like 'Bamuthi judged that he had redeemed all his mistakes through the concern for decency and fairness which had inspired them. He would return when Lammie was home again so that he could have her permission to enlist 'Bamuthi's cooperation. But already he had told 'Bamuthi enough of his plans to make François realize that although the new establishment basically would be the same as Hunter's Drift, its system of employment would vary. At Hunter's Drift all were partners. At Sir James's place, for which they had as yet heard no name (and this troubled 'Bamuthi because there was magic in a name), they would be workers and paid regular wages. The wages, 'Bamuthi had gathered, would be good but determined entirely by how well the individual persons worked for him.

'D'you think then, Old Father,' François asked, 'that it will be difficult to get people from Osebeni to work for Sir James in this way?'

'Bamuthi's answer was that life was changing so fast that many of the younger people now would prefer to work directly for money and feel themselves free to come and go as they liked and not as at Hunter's Drift, feel themselves to be members of the family.

François asked, 'D'you think that isi-Vuba is wrong, then?'

'Bamuthi hastened to declare that he thought nothing of the sort. He merely took it as a sign of the times in which things were beginning to change faster than he liked. He could tell François such things about the new young men, even among his own sons by his first wife, at Osebeni, that would make François weep. But as far as Sir James was concerned he said firmly: 'Have no doubt, Little Feather, isi-Vuba will be a good master. But will he be a father to his people as the Great White Bird was a father to us?'

Now that the old routine had to be resumed at Hunter's Drift, François made a determined effort to resume the daily round of two hours of study prescribed by Ouwa. He found it difficult if not impossible, because he could not switch his imagination from all the things that had crowded in on him so fast and so deeply in recent days. He was not disappointed, therefore, when within half an hour of trying to study, he was interrupted with the news that the rest of Sir James's convoy had arrived.

François hurried out to meet the Cape-coloured wagoners, their wives and children. The sight of the ample homestead, the atmosphere of civilization and security which seemed to surround it, had done a great deal to restore their natural optimism, but it was obvious to François that they had had some trying hours behind them.

This immediately became clear when the leader of the train approached François with the utmost goodwill to thank him for choosing so good a camping site for them for the night. He was certain that if they had not camped there, they would not have come through the night alive. In the vivid, melodramatic way of Cape-coloured people, who are born story-tellers, he described how all the lions and 'tigers' (their word for leopards) appeared to have been mobilized for war on them during the night. They had spent a sleepless night keeping large fires alight, as one lion or 'tiger' after the other appeared with eyes as large as 'soup-tureens' and green with 'cannibal light' on the fringes of the bush round their camp. Big as the fires were, he was certain that if it had not been for the rifle François had lent him they would have all been devoured, for he had had to shoot at those 'terrible eyes' so often that, even though François had left some fifty rounds of ammunition with him he did not have a single round left! The wagon master had hardly finished his general account when the rest of the party crowded round, each person with a lion or 'tiger' story of his own.

Finally François had to break off the clamour by telling them that they would have to outspan immediately if they were to give their oxen a proper rest, because they still had a long journey to safety in Sir James's camp before nightfall. Another night in the bush clearly was the last thing they wanted and they hastened to outspan, water and feed their oxen.

Meanwhile, François got the gardeners to deliver to the wagon master the fruits from the garden intended for Sir James. That done, he sent them back to gather a similar supply for each of the wagons in the train. The tired, desperate and rather emaciated look on the faces of the women, children and men (so unlike those of the people at Hunter's Drift) upset him a great deal. He got Ousie-Johanna and her staff to make hot coffee by the bucket and sent it down to the convoy with ample supplies of rusks. One of his Matabele men was told to cut up half an ox that had been slaughtered for their own supplies a few days before and was now hanging up in the coolest of their outhouses. This meat he distributed equally among the wagons.

It irritated François somewhat that Ousie-Johanna and 'Bamuthi, so unlike their usual, spontaneous selves, carried out his instructions with extreme formality. As always they seemed to have profound reservations about Cape-coloured people. He knew the Cape-coloured men were not without blame in the matter. They were so proud of the European element in their blood that they tended to regard themselves as superior to the indigenous people of the land. Therefore Africans like Ousie-

Johanna and 'Bamuthi, not unnaturally, countered prejudice with a protective prejudice of their own.

Luckily, their sense of hospitality and respect for travellers was great enough to keep contact between them all on a correct, if not the warmest of levels. Things were greatly helped along by the fact that the coffee was greeted with a great colloquial shout of 'Here comes real "travellers' comfort"!' When the coffee was followed by the gifts of fruit and vegetables from the garden, some buckets of milk, and finally the supply of fresh meat for each wagon, all prejudices had crumbled. The result was a display of gaiety that made carnival of the scene. The feeling was perhaps best expressed in a remark François heard from the head of one wagon group to another: 'I say, *gammietjie* [the Cape-coloured equivalent of the Cockney "my old cock-sparrow"], we must have got the blerrie day wrong and it's Christmas! All we need is a bottle or two of "blitz" to make it New Year as well!'

Blitz was their word for brandy and, hearing it, François was instantly reminded of one of his favourite Matabele proverbs: 'Letting the roof leak for a handful of thatch'. Although it was against the law to give alcohol in any form whatever, whether as wine, spirits or beer to the coloured and black peoples of the land, François had seen Ouwa himself flout it so often that he had no hesitation in going to their huge cellar and returning with a bottle of Cape brandy for each of the wagons.

From that moment on the two hours that the wagon train allowed itself at Hunter's Drift seemed to François like a kind of *Kermesse Héroïque*, a phrase he had picked up from Ouwa. It leapt to his mind partly because *kermis* was still a favourite Cape-coloured word for a feast. Just then he heard it being used all around him. Besides there was something truly heroic in such a capacity for gaiety from a people for whom life was always precarious and the inducements for resentment and bitterness as continuous as they were immense. For the time being, work at Hunter's Drift was brought to a standstill. Everybody, attracted by the laughter, the music, singing and, despite the increasing heat of the day, ultimately the improvised dancing, was drawn to witness so unusual a sight.

Even the departure of the wagons was not the sad anti-climax

339

of François's recollection. Travellers came and went, tending to leave one feeling somewhat abandoned and forlorn. But on this occasion the wagons departed on an ascending note of joyfulness which affected everyone watching.

As that historical and evocative call went up: 'Come on; Trek!' the women and girls in their brightly coloured headcloths and dresses appeared not to climb back to their places on the wagons, so much as flutter over them like a swarm of butterflies. The little boys, standing at the ready between the great crescent horns of the huge oxen, confidently took up their leather leads and pulled the teams one after the other into following them. Seeing well-trained oxen bowing their heads to thrust their broad shoulders against their heavy yokes, while the long steel chains which connected them to the wagon, came glittering out of the dust and went taut with strain, was as always a moving sight to François and the Matabele onlookers.

First came the magenta span of eighteen, to be followed by the brindled ones, the strawberry roans, the cream whites, the Cape-gooseberry yellows, the earth red and, last of all, the coal-black team. At that the Matabele, who love and know cattle as few men do, forgot all reservations and cheered the train on with a reverberating, *'Hamba Gashle!'* Go in happiness.

They were answered in dialect with a shimmer of voices chanting 'Stay joyfully, you farmers there! Stay joyfully!' At the same time, the long whips flashed and crackled like lightning over the heads of the teams and the wagoners exhorted the oxen with cries like: 'Step up, Fatherland! Pull President, you lazy devil, pull! We've drunk tiger-milk now and can do the job ourselves, if you won't!'

As each wagon pulled clear out into the road, a rag and tatter minstrel walked ahead, either strumming a guitar, playing a concertina or mouth-organ, with the people riding on the wagons accompanying him in song. François and everybody else watching, could just hear the wagons creaking mournfully under their heavy loads like ships in a storm at sea. Also they heard the muffled pounding of the earth under the great feet of the long spans of oxen who, watered and well-fed, despite their phlegmatic natures, seemed to be responding positively either to the music or the crackling of the whips.

340

The song varied from wagon to wagon at first, but soon one song, perhaps the greatest of them all, took over and dominated the white, silent noonday. The watchers, sad that such infectious music and gaiety should be creeping by them towards the muted copper bush, heard its chorus passing up and down the line again and again.

> *No! No, my mistress, no!*
> *Here, I have no home.*
> *My time has come to go.*
> *No one knows the way,*
> *But there where the sun*
> *And the moon go down,*
> *Road and home are one.*

'Bamuthi, seeing the last of the wagons and their lines of colourful oxen disappear like stitches of glistening medieval tapestry into the heavy hem of the bush, shook his great head and remarked in Sindabele, 'Those are men who know not that the yoke is never tired.'

François knew that this meant 'Journeys have no end'. And only a fool would have thought, that thereby they meant only journeys by road.

Some two hours later François, accompanied by Hintza, followed the wagons on horseback. François did this because he had promised the wagon master that he would join them for the most dangerous hour of the afternoon. He did this for two reasons. He hoped it would give him a glimpse of Sir James's camp. And he did not feel like lending his gun again to the wagon master because of the thought that another fifty rounds of ammunition might be wasted should he do so. His only regret was that he could not do the journey on foot. Much as he loved horses in the bush where tracks were narrow and where one had to go slowly and silently, he felt infinitely more at home on foot than on a horse. It was remarkable how much one missed when one rode through the bush on horseback. All the dramatic and ever-changing detail of the drama of life enacted by the birds, insects and smaller animals in the bush, which were really just as interesting and subtle to François as the behaviour of the greater animals, somehow got overlooked.

341

However on this occasion he had no option. He had to overtake the wagons, lead them safely to Sir James's land and get home himself before dark and even on horseback he would have to travel fast.

So he set off at a smart gallop, but something seemed to have enabled the wagons to travel at such a pace that François did not overtake them. Some twelve miles from his home he came out of the bush on the edge of Sir James's land to look down from a hump of earth on to the great natural clearing which had originally caught Sir James's fancy. He was just in time to see the last of the wagons about half a mile ahead of him, turning out of the road and making straight for a small hill alone in the level clearing about a mile from the Amanzim-tetse river.

François could not understand why the wagons were not making directly for the river itself. Somehow he assumed that Sir James would do what they had done and build his home near the river so that he had easy access to water both for house and gardens. Indeed so certain was he of this, that his eyes searched the land by the gleaming river banks with the greatest care, but nowhere could he see signs of Sir James's party. It was not until he looked again at the hill for which the wagons were heading that he saw to his amazement the caboose, trailer and truck drawn up at the foot of the hill, some tents already pitched, several fires lit and their smoke standing above them like palms in the mirage of an oasis, before merging with the brilliant afternoon light.

He wished he had brought some binoculars to examine the distant camp because he realized now that, since the wagons would reach their destination well before sundown, he had no excuse for going any further and seeing the camp itself. Why precisely he wanted to see more of the camp just then, he did not know; perhaps because his astonishment at such a choice of site, so far from natural water, was too great ... So he turned his horse and made his way back home.

Unlike Hunter's Drift, Sir James's house was to be built, not on level ground but on the commanding height of that little hill. That hill indeed, imaginatively, had been the inspiration for the name of his property. In his years of exile he had proposed

342

calling it Hunter's Hill; a name derived from the poem by Stevenson already quoted. This poem, not unnaturally, in a person with his Scottish background, had captured his imagination as a boy. Consequently as a result he had a keen feeling of frustration when he discovered that the imagery of the hunter had already been captured in the name for a neighbouring property. That made the idea of calling his own land Hunter's Hill tamely derivative. So, at that very moment, when the amazed François, unbeknown to him, was looking down on the hill from his horse's back, Sir James was announcing to his daughter that he proposed calling their new home: 'Silverton-Hill'.

Luciana was about to ask why but Sir James anticipated the question. He hastened to explain that, since his mother Catriona had been a Hamilton-of-Silverton-Hill, an old loyalist Highland family, he thought nothing could be nicer than connecting this hill in Africa with that other hill in Scotland which had been their original home. Besides, he added, if she deigned to look around there were other justifications for the name ... In the brilliant light at that hour in that setting, he pointed out, surrounded as they were by a great forest, all copper and gold, the grass in the clearing, the brush on the hill and even the water of the flashing river in the distance, were all in one way or another just variations in tone of the brightest silver. Their new land, he concluded, was nothing if not 'silverton'.

Luciana stared at him in amazement as if what she had just heard were evidence of a return of her resolute father to a state of grace. Her whole expression lightened, and she exclaimed, 'Gosh Fa, I didn't think you still knew how to pun.' And then, to Sir James's relief, she burst out laughing for the first time that day.

'Bamuthi's reaction was as characteristic as that of Sir James's daughter. When François first heard the name Silverton-Hill, he hastened to inform 'Bamuthi, because 'Bamuthi had almost daily asked him what their neighbours had decided to call their new property. 'Bamuthi was obviously convinced that the place would not be properly protected against all the negative aspects of the forces of magic which invested the vast bushveld, until it had been well and truly named. However, even after a breakdown of the word Silverton, François found that its two-edged significance remained beyond 'Bamuthi's grasp, largely because 'Bamuthi had no idea what silver was. He knew iron, steel, copper and even gold, but silver was not an African metal.

So François decided that only the sight of silver could make the meaning clear. He rushed into the house on impulse to seize the nearest piece of silver. By an extraordinary coincidence he found one of the maids polishing the household silver, including the heavy fish knives and forks Lammie had brought with her from the south. Taking a knife (because he knew that a knife would impress 'Bamuthi more than a fork), he dashed back to hand it to 'Bamuthi, saying: 'There, Old Father, is the metal we call silver.'

'Bamuthi turned the knife over and over again between the fingers of his hands, the metal flashing like a mirror in the sun, before he felt the edge with a broad thumb. Instantly his face showed how he despised it for not being razor-sharp and piercing as all good Matabele knives were supposed to be. After contemplating it silently for quite a long time, as if searching his mind for some obscure association of his own with the knife, a shrewd look took possession of his features and he asked, 'Tell me, Little Feather, is this not a thing used for the eating of fish?'

Up to that moment François had not given a thought to the use of the knife but now he admitted readily enough that 'Bamuthi was right.

'Bamuthi gave a profound grunt of satisfaction, as if he might have known it all from the start and remarked, 'The place is well named then, for who can doubt that in the kraal of the Great Kingfisher on the hill, more fish will be eaten than has ever been eaten in this land before.'

François's impulse was to laugh at 'Bamuthi's comment but out of politeness he restrained himself. But out of this partial understanding a new name was born. Sir James's home was from then on to be known far and wide among the peoples of Africa, not as Silverton-Hill, but Fish-Metal Hill, a fact which all persons instinctively conspired to keep hidden from Sir James, for knowing Matabele feelings in all matters concerned with fish, they would not have liked him to be hurt by the highly derogatory name.

François himself was not informed officially of the name, Silverton-Hill, until a fortnight after his abrupt parting with Sir James and his daughter. Busy as he had been with his studies and trying to fill in the gap created by Lammie and Ouwa's absence, he still would have had time to ride over and visit his new neighbours. Indeed, all the engrained customs of a pioneering people like his own, would have compelled him to go to Silverton-Hill within a few days to see what he could do to help. But some instinct held him back. His willingness to help had been so implicit in his reception of Sir James and his party that it needed no re-emphasis. But he had been left uncertain about Sir James's attitude to him. So, undecided, he drifted from day to day hoping a positive move would come from Sir James himself.

Nonetheless, François could not help reminding Sir James of his existence at least every other day of the week. Every other day, he included in the loads of fresh vegetables and meat sent nightly by mule-wagon to Hunter's Drift siding, more fresh produce for Sir James and his party. The gifts always drew prompt acknowledgement from Sir James written on the most expensive writing paper in an elegant flowing hand. This puzzled François until he learned one day that even there in the bush Sir James conducted all his correspondence by writing with goose quills which he cut and trimmed himself. This, like shaving meticulously in the morning, having a canvas-bucket bath at the end of the day and changing into fresh, starched clothes laid out for him in his tent by the African valet he had brought with him, it seemed, were all essentials for preserving both letter and spirit of the example that he felt people like himself had been born to set in Africa. The letters always began, 'Dear François Joubert'. The envelopes were always addressed to Master François Joubert. Despite all the expressions of gratitude, these slight nuances in matters of address continued to form a signal to François that it were better for the moment to keep his distance.

No one, least of all François himself, could have told how long he would have been able to keep his distance. Since the coming of Xhabbo into his life forty-four days before he had had a surfeit of distances, physical, emotional and psychological, imposed upon him. The departure of Ouwa and Lammie,

Xhabbo's going and the death of Ouwa; this last the most diffi-cult distance of all since it was infinite. Now there was this gratuitous distance in 'feeling' between new neighbours who could have helped to bridge the widest gap he had ever ex-perienced between himself and the society of people of his own. It was all right during the day when he had lots to do and people like 'Bamuthi and Ousie-Johanna doing all they could to give him a warm feeling of companionship. But at night, alone in his room, he had to admit that much as he loved Ousie-Johanna and 'Bamuthi, they could not help as much as they would have been able to help forty-four days before.

One is compelled to measure this distance in days. In the exacting slide-rule of time built into François the days had be-come like months, and too approximate to measure the swift swollen current of events in a period of life he could have calculated almost to the minute. More important and subtler still, a new kind of distance, a distance within himself had un-fairly been added to the old familiar distances without. A new kind of François had come into being. Looking back, in the darkness of his room, it was astonishing to him how far he had travelled from that other François and how fast he was re-ceding from it, just as a figure on a quay, waving farewell, diminishes in the darkened eyes of the migrant of whom he had read in books and seen in paintings, setting out to sea on a fast ship in search of a new life in a new world. Most painful of all perhaps, was the fact that as fast as he was finding persons who might be companions to his migrating self, like Xhabbo and (the intimation was all the more acute when it came because it took him completely by surprise) even a mere girl like Sir James's daughter, fate seemed to have no scruple in separating him from them. Rationally, there was no connection to be seen between Xhabbo and Luciana. Not only was one a man and the other 'just' a girl, but their origins were apparently irreconcilable; one being, as it were, a product of pure nature; the other of a most refined and sophisticated culture. Yet in his imagination in the dark of night, they were a pair, almost one and indivisible to him in their significance, so much that he was confident he would only have to bring them together for them to mean as much to each other as they already meant to him.

The only thing that troubled him was that, just as Xhabbo had found it necessary to give François a name of his own, so François felt compelled to search his imagination for a name for Luciana. As names went, Luciana was apt enough in its own family context, particularly because it meant 'Bringer of Light'. Yet the name seemed to him to have a trace of presumption which made it inappropriate. He never thought of her as Luciana but merely as 'the girl'. Just as 'Bamuthi was unhappy because Sir James's land had not the magic of a name to protect it, so he felt he would not be content until the girl, too, was encircled in a name of his own. But what name? Surprisingly, he was able to settle on a compromise inspired by Ousie-Johanna.

Ousie-Johanna had taken greatly to Luciana, all the more because she was in the care and protection of Amelia, who in her absence grew to be the absolute of fashion and good form. Ousie-Johanna invariably referred to Luciana as 'the little Nonnie'. Nonnie was a diminutive of *Nonna*, the polite word for mistress used by the servants in François's world. The daughters of the houses inevitably became *Nonnie* (little mistress), and Ousie-Johanna's addition of *little* to Nonnie was an extra endearment. In François's world, unlike the world of Luciana's Italian godmother, where affection takes the form of exaggerating the stature of its subject, the more one loved a person the smaller one made it in one's feelings. One elaborates this fact because it was an integral element of François's character, derived from the Bushman influences of old Koba, since what distinguished the Bushman spirit so singularly from others was its uncompromising rejection of the physically great in favour of the small as if, long before the poet Blake, it had discovered infinity in the grains of sand of the desert that was its last home on earth.

François, indeed, knew that many girls among his own people were christened Nonnie and he felt that by calling Luciana Nonnie he had, as it were, given her a valid passport to the world of his own Africa. In all his conversations with Hintza she was now always referred to by this name and it was significant that Hintza from the start wagged his tail whenever the name was mentioned.

It was astonishing how much easier it was now for François

to think of her as a future companion and how urgent became his desire to show her all the thousand and one things he loved and cherished in the bush and had never shared with any living creature except Hintza. Even Sir James's hurtfully ambiguous attitude rapidly lost importance and it became increasingly difficult for him not to ride over to visit his new neighbours. It became more so when 'Bamuthi and Ousie-Johanna began to reprimand him for not behaving at all like a good neighbour. They reiterated daily that he should have been over long since to see Sir James and find out what they could do to help, apart from sending them, as 'Bamuthi put it, 'scraps of food' from the kitchen. That phrase was most unfortunate, because it offended Ousie-Johanna who had put a great deal of imagination into the gifts she included in their parcels to the newcomers.

Fortunately on the thirteenth day after Sir James's departure, when François's irresolution was at its greatest, two things happened to decide the issue for him. One was another letter of thanks from Sir James. The contents of the letter itself seemed to François most ominous because, after the usual gracious expressions of thanks and an admission that the sort of things provided by Hunter's Drift were things that his commissariat could not yet do without, Sir James announced that he could no longer impose on their generosity and would have to insist on paying François for all future supplies.

François had only to communicate this part of the letter to Ousie-Johanna and 'Bamuthi for them both to be as horrified as he was. In fact they were not only horrified but deeply insulted. 'Bamuthi, in particular, thought it a sign that Sir James saw himself as superior. He asked François rhetorically, as if he were asking it of the vanished millions of Bantu men who had created their traditions in these matters, 'Does he not know then that only a chief of chiefs has the right to make much of such trifles and reward a man for them? Does he not know that to take payment for food from strangers and travellers is to steal?'

Ousie-Johanna was hardly less scathing, declaring, 'I knew it from the day I first set eyes on him that that great *Rooinek* has not been properly brought up.'

Her remark, if it could have been repeated to Cheam, Rugby, Caius and the other hallowed places of his education, not to mention the wardrooms of His Britannic Majesty's ships of war in which Sir James had served with gallantry and distinction, as an officer in the Royal Naval Volunteer Reserve, might not have created the alarm and despondency which Ousie-Johanna would have thought appropriate, but certainly would have caused a great deal of amusement at Sir James's expense. As the person responsible for telling François's story, one has to hold a balance of just understanding between everyone concerned in it, and recognize that the predictable reaction to Ousie-Johanna's remark in Sir James's world reflected more on the limitations of its own values than on those of the big kitchen at Hunter's Drift.

However François, determined not to accept payment merely for doing a neighbourly duty, knew enough of the sort of world from which Sir James had come to understand why the man could have been genuinely embarrassed by receiving so much from strangers. Whether he would have understood quite so easily if it had not been for a postscript at the foot of Sir James's letter is another matter. It consisted of a few lines in a roundish, somewhat irregular hand and appeared to François to have been written furtively and in haste immediately below Sir James's flourishing official signature. It read. 'Please tell Ousie-Johanna, Amelia finds her bread gorgeous and I think her cakes scrumptious. We all love your fruit and melons. But aren't we ever to see you again? Darling Hin by this time will have completely forgotten me.' The lines ended in a large blot and no signature which reinforced François's impression that they had been added without Sir James's knowledge.

While Ousie-Johanna and 'Bamuthi continued to indulge in their feelings of outrage, he lost all interest in that aspect of the matter. His only concern from then on was that if Nonnie felt brave enough to go against her father and hint that it was time they saw him again, he would be a coward not to respond.

The second important event was the arrival of Mopani that evening. Since Mopani had promised Lammie, Ouwa and François that he would visit Hunter's Drift as often as possible, his arrival was not unexpected. What was unexpected was a subtle change in the mood of his coming which had a significant bearing on the future.

As usual, it was Hintza who gave François warning of

Mopani's coming. Hintza had been watching the track where it broke with the bush for some time, as if suspecting that something might be stirring within it, and so he spotted Nandi and 'Swayo the moment they emerged. Nandi and 'Swayo, who regarded Hunter's Drift as a second home, had long since come to feel free to dismiss themselves from the discipline of the trail which kept them at the side of Mopani's horse and to race ahead as heralds of their own and their master's coming. Hintza, too, immediately left François's side, determined to meet them halfway and leave no doubt as to his warmth of welcome. By the time Mopani appeared in a more leisurely manner François himself was waiting in front of the homestead to meet him.

It was a mark of the strain through which he had been since their last meeting, as well as his need for help in containing the complex of feelings that had swollen into a flood within him, that the moment he set eyes on a person he loved as much as Mopani, he found it suddenly extremely difficult not to burst into tears. Somehow he managed to restrain himself but he did embrace Mopani with such warmth that the wise and sensitive old man was fully aware of the turmoil within François. Therefore, he did not immediately give François the messages received from Lammie on the telephone the night before. He limited himself to returning François's embrace with equal warmth. Then, with the bridle in his right hand, he kept his left arm firmly round François's shoulders, thereby conveying the kind of sympathy and reassurance he wanted François to feel.

Walking forward slowly, he asked in as normal a tone as possible, 'Would you mind, Coiske, if we don't go immediately into the house? I would like to cool down and water Noble myself this evening before we do. I have pushed him very hard today.'

Noble was the favourite among Mopani's small stable of salted horses. When François heard its name, he realized how absorbed he must have been, because for the first time in his life he had not noticed which horse Mopani was riding. The moment he realized this the reason for Mopani's request appeared obvious and, as Mopani had hoped, helped to normalize the occasion. Mopani, as a rule, was quite willing to let one of the Matabele stable hands take over horses from him when he arrived. Noble was the one exception. Mopani was so devoted to Noble that he always insisted himself on seeing to the all-important process of cooling down after a long journey. This consisted of walking horses slowly back and forth for about half an hour until their hearts beat normally and the sweat had dried on their coats. François did not need telling how dangerous it was to give horses cold water to drink before they had properly cooled down. They themselves in the past had lost a number of horses because they had been watered too soon by their Matabele helpers, who did not have the same instinctive understanding of horses as they had of their native cattle.

What he did not know was that on this occasion Mopani's concern for Noble was also a means of postponing the moment when they would have to go inside and, inevitably, begin to talk about matters that were bound to increase the emotional strain on François. The longer the moment could be postponed, Mopani felt, the easier it would be for François and himself to talk calmly and fully as they would have to do. So, while Hintza, Nandi and 'Swayo played together, chasing one another in wide circles and then breaking off to rush up to man and boy in order to be patted and fondled, François and Mopani led Noble slowly up and down the wide open space between the homestead and its long line of stables and outhouses.

It was a scene that stood out because there was something singularly moving in its impression of complete communion, between dogs and horse, age and youth, experience and innocence. The evening light of Africa, as always at that hour, was a Biblical one, the scene was illuminated to present itself as a parable not in word but deed, implying that perhaps the one unpardonable error of men is to withdraw from communion with one another, no matter how good the reason for withdrawal. If dogs and horses, young and old, could be so lovingly and utterly at one as that little group, the occasion was explosive with the question of whether life would not cease from inflicting disaster upon disaster, could men only use their great gift of words not for dividing, but for confirming and enriching an act of communion for which they were born.

No wonder those dogs in that light looked to be dogs of gold, and Noble, long-maned, long-tailed, black all over except for a white star on his forehead, one white forefoot and one white hind-hock, looked not just a horse but the plenipotentiary of all horses in the life of men, as he walked with all the delicacy of fatigue beside man and boy, the evening wrapped like Indian silk about him, its tone all the brighter for the sense of communion between them.

For François, the fact that Mopani was there and had accomplished the long journey in one day just in order to see him said more than any words could conceive. He was utterly content just to pace back and forwards listening to the odd comments Mopani had to make about his journey because, no matter how often Mopani had done it, he always appeared to have accomplished it as if it were for the first time. His comments were always new, strange and rewarding.

Moreover, at that hour of the day for him, too, there was an extra dimension. It was a dimension into which access was made easy by the hour of the day. People who are born, grow up and die in the metropolitan context of our time have, perhaps, lost awareness of what this hour can do to human perception. Out there in the natural world of the bush around Hunter's Drift, this moment was always like a magic mirror on the walls of François's mind, making things visible that had not been visible before. It produced subjects of conversation, observation and a kind of interchange of mind and heart almost as if that moment were an immense junction for the reality of life, where all the traffic from the past, the immediate present and the most distant future, met. It was a moment of perception lifted all the higher by reason of the fact that the whole of nature seemed to participate actively within it. Night and day joined to produce a kind of beauty that was an expression of both, and all living creatures were marshalled to take part in the scene, as in a theatre of fate.

It was, for instance, the one moment when the great baboons of the day in their keeps on the cliffs by the river, barked at the same time as the lions roared. The jackals janked, the hyenas howled and the leopards coughed before they set out on their nightly prowl. The bats of the night too were already on their zigzag wing, the night plovers sounding their bosun's pipes and the great ghost owls hooting, while all the millions of birds of day would still be illuminating the silence, each with its own brilliant cry, to set the conflagration of evening song aflame. Geese, duck, goliath herons, fish hawks and the great portentous hammerheads, the messengers of tidings of death for the Bushmen simultaneously would all be still in flight. It is, perhaps, the most imposing natural moment of resolution of which life on earth is capable because, within its still centre, the earth forgives the sun for the heat of the day. All death, which the fight for survival has inflicted, is understood, and a brief state of innocence for all is poignantly established, before another battle for survival under cover of darkness comes into being. It is a moment so naturally transcendental that for people like Mopani and François, it never bred contempt through familiarity, but with repetition actually gained in force of impact.

Something of all this was apparent in the first remark that Mopani made to bring to an end the long silence which had followed their first greeting. The remark came at a moment when the noises of night and day, especially the song of the birds by the river, had achieved their summit.

Mopani, stopping, declared almost as much to himself as to François, 'Have you ever known a more beautiful evening? I've heard it said somewhere that human beings should look on all things lovely as though for the last time. But this is the kind of evening which makes me want to look on it as if for the first time. Just listen to those birds, *Coiske*! Have you ever heard them quite like that? I certainly never have.'

François listened carefully, responding as he always did spontaneously when exhorted by Mopani to do anything, because of the lack of any inclination ever to criticize him, something which had not passed unnoticed in the grown-up world around him and had been a cause of envy in many otherwise ungrudging hearts. Yes, Mopani was right. He had never heard birds make quite that kind of noise. Lovely as it was, however, something about the noise made him uncomfortable, almost as if the birds (to use what Ouwa had once described to him as one of the most ominous phrases in English) were protesting too much. There was an element of frenzy and desperation in the singing, as if the birds might be afraid that they were saluting such loveliness for the last time.

353

Just for a moment François himself was frightened. He shivered as if cold and unconsciously held on more firmly to Mopani before he managed to reply, 'You're right, Uncle. I've never heard the birds sing like that before. It's lovely, but isn't there something unhappy about it all? It frightens me rather.'

'Why frightened?' Mopani, returning François's grip, asked the question not because he had not understood its meaning at once, but because already in his intuitive way, his imagination was dealing with the meaning to which François's question was inevitably leading, and he wanted time to find the exact words for shaping his response.

'It sounds as if they were feeling themselves that it was the last time ever that they would be able to sing just like that,' François replied in a whisper as if the words he had just used had increased his fear.

Mopani might have refused to discuss so vast and intangible a subject with most other people, but not with François. The world outside he knew tended to be too busy to live, confusing being with having, and would have been impervious to anything so light and strange as the thing pleading for admission at a back door of François's mind. The world, as he had learned, rarely recognized any new reality in its beginnings. Reality seemed to have to grow great and terrible, like an angry giant hammering on the doors of closed minds, before people would take notice and then, alas, it was almost invariably too late.

But Mopani was troubled because François's response and question showed that he, too, was already on the frontier of some new aspect of reality. And he had never been tempted to give anything but a true and full answer to François's questions, however much the conventions governing the behaviour of old and young might have argued against him.

His hesitation, therefore, was brief before he said, 'I don't mind telling you, Coiske, that I'm a little bit frightened myself.'

This admission, from one of the bravest men François had ever met, raised Mopani immeasurably in his estimation. Nothing feeds fear so much as the pretence that it has no valid cause to exist. Mopani's admission not only confirmed the validity of François's own fear but also by abolishing all pretence between them, made them partners in fear, removing the greatest dread of all: that one would be left to deal with fear on one's own. What so many people would have regarded as a confession of grown-up failure François took as an immense compliment to himself. He experienced such an inrush of re-assurance and affection that all he could manage to say was, 'You frightened too, Uncle? Why?'

Mopani's answer was typically indirect because, as always when confronted with anything important, he obeyed his favourite maxim that 'the longest way round was the shortest way there'. He began by telling François how this occasion and the nature of the hour reminded him of something that had happened to him when he was little more than François's age. He described in great detail how, at just such an hour, he was in camp with his father deep in the bush farther north. His father, too, had exhorted him then to listen to the birds and, after they had listened attentively, he had asked Mopani the same question that he had just asked François. His own response had been very much like François's,

From then on, both he and his father studied the sounds of the birds in the bush with the greatest attention. Their premoni-tions of the night before, that they had been listening to the final chorale in a great cycle of birdsong, was confirmed. They never again heard birds sing quite as on that night. Theme and tune of their song at evening had subtly changed and the an-nunciation of change become progressively more elaborate and emphatic. Even by day the noises sounded different. Until that moment, diverse as they were, they had followed a certain common pattern which he and his father had taken so much for granted that they had never really noticed it. Only then, when it appeared to have vanished for good and was replaced by a series of unrelated sounds and expressions of irrevocable discord, did they miss the rhythm.

Some time after that, Mopani went on, the news reached them there in the bush that the first World War had broken out. It might seem very fanciful but neither he nor his father were surprised because, in some strange way that he, Mopani, could not pretend to understand, they were both convinced that it was this event which had forced the birds to change their tune. By changing their tune they could perhaps have prepared the hearts and minds of those who had ears to listen. More specifically, it had prepared Mopani for the fact that, when he saw his father ride off to war, he knew it was for the last time, because he was riding to his death in battle. But that was not all.

In the manner of our time, Mopani went on, he might have perhaps come to the point where he would have dismissed this apparent change of tune by the birds of Africa as 'pure coincidence' for what, he asked, could be more characteristic of our time than its obstinate refusal to admit the reality of the singular? Fortunately his life in the reserve and his life as a hunter had called him back to his natural senses and to his natural belief. Namely, that in some mysterious way there was some profound inter-relationship existing with the life of the great world beyond, and that nothing so unnatural and monstrous as war could be growing great in the calculations of men without disrupting the natural rhythm of the universe, and so communicating discord also to the natural life of the bush.

Mopani went on that he had read somewhere that one of the church fathers had once said that the soul of man was naturally religious. He would add to that that the birds and animals, indeed, all the flora and fauna of Africa, were naturally devout because no other living things obeyed so implicitly the laws of their own creation. As François knew, the war had taken him to many different places in the world and he had come back from them all convinced that Africa was the last continent in the world that still had a soul of its own. François could understand, therefore, how troubled he had been during the last year when he began to notice in the sounds of the bush the same elements of disruption which had invaded it on that other occasion. He had said nothing about it before because he was not sure that he was not perhaps inflicting his own apprehensions on the natural noises of the land.

François, who had been listening with such attention that he had completely forgotten his own troubles, nodded his head and said, 'I know what you mean, Uncle. I'm afraid that's what Ouwa would have said had you told him. I remember once when I told him I thought the land there on the edge of the desert looked sad, he pulled me up rather sharply saying, "The sadness is never in the landscape, but only in oneself." '

356

That, Mopani said, was precisely the reservation that he had had in mind and which had made him keep his fears secret. Yet, just recently, he had grown convinced that something strange and terrible for the life of Africa, if not the world, was already throwing its shadow before it to darken the singing of the birds. He was glad that he was there to share this with François. He was getting old and might not be with him much longer and he would like François to know the truth in these respects. François might need not only the knowledge but also the time for preparation. There would be many people who would try to prove to François that this kind of thinking was nonsense. Their condemnation would be all the more convincing because the world was full of know-alls who knew only what they knew and no longer what they did not know. To them, that there could be proof of any relationship between the mind and spirit of civilized man and the mind of the natural world, would be ridiculous. But this, Mopani said, was in his view the sickness in so-called civilized people. In the final analysis one had to stand by one's own experience of life and refuse to allow any one-sided specialist to discredit it.

He himself would not hesitate to stand by his own experience of these things. He would like François, therefore, to remember that in his opinion there was the most delicate relationship between what went on in their own minds and the awareness of the animal world of Africa. He had found, for instance, that when he and his father had gone out into the bush to kill, the behaviour of birds and animals was totally different from those occasions when they rode out without any intention of killing. He had been indiscreet enough to mention this once to an eminent zoologist whom the Government had asked him to conduct on an expedition into the bush. The zoologist had laughed, and claimed that the explanation could only be that observant animals would have learned to be suspicious of man when they went forth with guns on their shoulders. But he and his father had proved repeatedly that this was just not true. As François knew, they never travelled anywhere without guns. Yet riding fully armed, for instance, towards a herd of buck with no intention of shooting, the animals would make little attempt to get out of their way. The next day, perhaps, they

357

would be compelled to ride out towards the same group of buck intending to shoot one for the pot, and the moment they appeared the animals immediately scattered.

He could give François countless illustrations of this kind of intercommunication between men and the life of the bush, between the intent of one animal and another, until it all wove itself into a pattern of universal inter-communication, fashioning, among many other things the bird-song and change of tune flaring among the trembling reeds by the river and over the shivering tree-tops of the bush around them. Yes, he feared that it all added up to the sad fact that, like François, he did not like this change of tune at all and was convinced that some new element had entered the life of the bush.

Mopani's reference to a 'new element' made François think of the Moncktons. He did not for a moment mean to put it forward as an explanation of the changes that Mopani had been describing. But, as Mopani paused after this singularly long exposition, François blurted out the news of Sir James's arrival.

'Yes,' Mopani said, 'I know about Sir James's coming. In fact I have an urgent message which the Government telephoned to me last night and asked me to deliver to him. More important, I have messages for you from Lammie as well. We will talk about these things presently, but at the moment . . .'

What Mopani had intended to say was interrupted by Noble. A pitiful nicker came from the horse. He put his great head into Mopani's shoulder and nudged him as if to remind him of his existence and the fact that, whatever the views of Mopani and François on the famous cooling-off process, Noble was certain that its virtues could be grossly overrated. Mopani smiled a smile at himself which François knew would have been a great and inappropriate laugh in anybody else, shattering the delicacy of the moment. While he ruffled Noble he remarked fondly, 'Yes, boy, yes. I agree most emphatically, it's high time we gave you your liquor and your food.'

Soon they had Noble in his favourite stall in the corner of the stable, hard by the double door. A deep, warm bed of clean yellow straw glowed around him like lamplight in the evening shadows. His crib was full of their best clover and maize. As always at Hunter's Drift it was soaked in water for some twenty hours before it was fed to the horses. By this time Noble was so hungry that he lowered his head and pushed Mopani aside almost roughly in order to get at his food. One wonders, therefore, whether he appreciated, or even heard, one of Mopani's rare jokes.

Mopani, as François knew better than most, despite his reputation for being a serious, some thought over-serious person, had his own quiet sense of humour. It was essentially a personal and private aspect of himself which he was shy to reveal to anyone not close to him. When he did so, it was invariably the greatest expression of affection and trust of which he perhaps was capable. The manner of it always touched François so much that he didn't know whether to laugh, cry or do both together, for it was the sort of humour which is bred only by extreme loneliness in the hearts of men, all the more touching for being utterly child-like and simple.

All it amounted to on this occasion was that, as Mopani fondly rubbed his hand along the bowed neck of Noble, crunching his maize and clover, he said, 'Good night Noble boy, sleep well, and no nightmares please.' Having said this, he looked shyly at François to see whether his little joke had been observed.

François was so touched that he used the strongest exclamation of surprise borrowed long ago by his people from their Mohammedan slaves: '*Allah-Wereld* [Lord-of-the-World] Uncle, I wish I could pun as well.'

Outside the stable they found Hintza, Nandi and 'Swayo sitting on their haunches, all exuberance gone and a certain reproachful expectancy on their alert faces, as if they, too, felt they had been neglected too long, a feeling perhaps made all the keener by the most wonderful of all sounds reaching them from the stable: that of a hungry horse crunching his well-earned supper between strong jaws. So they all made immediately for the nearest entrance to the great house which happened to be the kitchen door.

The windows of the house were already shuttered and the house prepared for the night like a great ship battened down for a storm. The only light showing was the glow from the kitchen

oil lamp. As they approached they saw the large figure of
'Bamuthi, standing silhouetted beside the door. From inside the
kitchen they heard Ousie-Johanna, speaking in an unusually
earnest tone, followed immediately by 'Bamuthi's bidding her an
unusually ceremonious farewell. Then the silhouette vanished
from the shining door and they heard the muffled sound of
'Bamuthi's massive bare feet on the earth as they moved fast
along the pathway which led to the Matabele kraals. Added to
all he was feeling about the natural sounds of the bush and the
heavy fall of night, that scene of brief farewell by the door
seemed to François suddenly extremely odd and the hour too
late for comfort.

Ousie-Johanna barely greeted Mopani and François when
they entered the kitchen, and it needed only one look at her
face to make François realize that something had upset her.
'Why, little old Ousie, what's the matter? Is there anything I
can do to help you?' he asked.

Ousie-Johanna's response to this proof of sympathy was
immediate. It was, she explained, something 'Bamuthi had said
to her, not even what he had said as the manner in which he had
said it, which had upset her. She hastened to add that 'Bamuthi
was a heathen and had many superstitions with which she herself could never hold, but there was no doubt, as her Little
Feather knew, that he was also a very smart person and knew a
thing or two that other people, far better educated, could learn
to their advantage.

Knowing how long Ousie-Johanna could be in coming to the
point, François pressed her again to say what troubled her.

'*Auck,* Little Feather,' she confessed, as if afraid now that it
amounted to very little. 'It was just that when I reproached
'Bamuthi for being so late in bringing me the cream I had asked
him for when I knew we had a visitor, he said that something
had made them late with their milking. When I asked him what
it was, he told me – would you believe it? – that it had been the
birds down by the river.'

She paused, as if she feared that such an unusual excuse
would strike François and Mopani as being as absurd as it had
struck her. To her astonishment she saw the two of them exchange a very odd, knowing glance and then her Little Feather,

looking at her, with his eyes large with interest, asked, 'And what did you say to him then, little old Ousie?'

'I told him straight it was a blerrie lot of childish nonsense, allowing birds to get in the way of so important a matter as milking!'

Something of the original heat of her remonstrance came into her voice, but quickly receded as she went on to ask, 'But do you know what he said to me then?' Too caught up now in the emotions of the impending revelation, she did not wait for an answer, but hurried on, 'He told me that they had always to listen in to the birds, because always the birds were the first to know.'

She paused again, convinced that now, surely, François and Mopani would comment on the absurdity of it all, but, as they remained silent and apparently as interested as ever, she went on, 'So I asked him straight, what important thing it was that the birds were the first to know tonight?'

Some of the sarcasm which had accompanied her question was back in her voice and she asked rhetorically, to give herself a plausible excuse to pause for the full effect of the answer, 'And what do you think he said? He looked at me with those great eyes of his and said in a voice that made my heart go black on me, "It is too soon to tell for certain. But all are agreed that the birds have changed their tune."'

All traces of sarcasm vanished now from her voice and, to François's dismay Ousie-Johanna's own dark, large eyes seemed full and overflowing with the light of wordless apprehension.

François had never been more grateful for Mopani's company than he was that night, nor more grateful for having Lammie's messages explaining, at great and affectionate length, the reasons for her delay in the south. There was also the coming of the Moncktons and Mopani's intention to call on Sir James early the next day, as well as a score or more of relatively objective matters to discuss. They had both experienced the fact often enough, that it took only a small tent and a fire to exclude the mystery and abolish the darkness of the universe enthroned glittering and high in the exalted African night. So one can imagine how successfully the dining-room, full of the light of oil lamps as a comb in a beehive is with translucent honey, banished the darkness outside. Excluded, too, was the sea of sounds that had joined the acute fall of night and sharpened not just François's and Mopani's apprehension but, judging by Ousie-Johanna's account, also that of everyone else at Hunter's Drift. Was it pure coincidence (although if it were so one is certain François would not have found it any the less meaningful), that Mopani chose for his after-dinner reading from the Joubert family Bible, the psalm which begins: 'The Lord is my Shepherd'?

It was indicative of François's new state that it was not the fact that the Lord was his shepherd (Mopani read it as if it were one of the great unchanging, unchangeable and everlasting facts of life) which impressed him most now, as it had always done in the past, but rather the verse: 'Though I walk through the valley of the shadow of death'.

Ouwa's death, some eighteen days before, no doubt was partly responsible but, whatever the cause, this verse for the first time held his imagination so firmly that he could not share the psalmist's emotion expressed in the triumphant assertion:

'I fear no evil', and so on to the final resolution of both fear and evil which had always made such music in his heart; 'I will dwell in the house of the Lord for ever'.

He did not analyse the process of reservation which held him back. All he knew now was that those lines were ringing a kind of prophetic warning in his imagination, like a church bell in a deep medieval valley warning unsuspecting man of invasion and that, in a way he could not explain, he was indeed afraid of the future. He felt not at all sure that he would dwell indefinitely in the great house in which he was sitting at that moment, apparently so secure in such an atmosphere of well-being, surrounded by striking evidence of the love of many generations of his family.

All within him suddenly felt horribly and dangerously ephemeral. It was only by concentrating on Mopani's presence, and on what he stood for, and by remembering all the many long, dangerous and unpredictable vicissitudes through which Mopani had come without ever losing any of the feeling that the Lord had unfailingly been and remained *his* shepherd, that François managed to recover some measure of courage within.

But later, alone with Hintza in the darkness of his room, he was back in a turmoil of uncertainty. This new fear was aided and abetted by an element of guilt over the secrets he had kept, particularly his encounter with the 'men of the spear' and his failure to report it to Mopani as 'Bamuthi had counselled at the time. Why had he not mentioned the coming of these men? Of course it was because he feared it might lead to the disclosure of his visit to uLangalibalela's kraal and his reasons for going there. Much as he loved and trusted Mopani, he did not think that even he would entirely understand. He knew he could be wrong, but he could not just then face the thought of any misunderstanding between himself and the old hunter, whose unqualified support was more important to him than ever. So wherever his review of himself took François, it always led to the one conclusion that not only had the birds changed their tune but so had he. He was not at all certain that he liked the change, whatever it was, only that it left him feeling frighteningly alone.

He found himself looking back with inexpressible longing to

that evening when Hintza had first come into his life. It was as if that moment had marked off a frontier in his experience, rather like the border of the great garden which is the image of man's beginning, when he was still without knowledge of good or evil, surrounded by trees full of yellow fruit, a light that was of neither night nor day dripping like water from leaves as they shook and trembled still from the movement of the hand which had just fashioned them. And it seemed to him now that he had been expelled from all such a garden symbolized, and that he could never go back. Indeed the awareness of a new, imperative self appeared to be urging him on like an archangelic presence with a flaming sword mounted over the garden gate, now firmly shut between immense trees of figs, great and purple and aglow against a hard, new amethyst day. This feeling of being alone was assuming the proportions of self-pity when a sound from Hintza corrected him, Hintza was trying to tell him in his quivering whimper that his dreaming self had at last located the hunter's quarry in some wide and starry dimension of sleep. So why was François as always so slow in locating it too?

François stretched out his hand to stroke Hintza gently. At the touch of his hand Hintza's whimper instantly ceased, a sigh of relief broke from him to be followed immediately by a great spasm of muscles as all four legs tried (difficult as it was for a dog asleep on a mat) to go through the motions of racing as fast as he could straight for the place where his quarry had just vanished.

The spasm was so long and violent that François had to stroke Hintza repeatedly and say in Bushman softly in his ear, 'There now, Hin boy, there now ... well done! You've got him ... you've got him! Home, boy now, home ...'

A sigh of contentment broke from Hintza and he was once more still and relaxed beside François's bed. Slight as the incident was, it brought an inclination to smile within François which carried with it a rebuke. The act of sleep is nothing if not an act of trust and a re-commitment of one's daytime self to the unfathomable depth of the urges that have raised life from clay. It was this example of an animal finding life confirmed in sleep by pursuing a great dream which now consoled François. He thought of Mopani's remarks earlier in the evening on the animals of Africa. He remembered once in a discussion between Ouwa and Lammie, that Ouwa had quoted something from a new Dead Sea Scroll about how to find the way to the Great Kingdom. It said in effect: 'Follow the birds, the beasts and the fishes and they will lead you in.'

Perhaps he could do no better than to follow the example of trust being set him by Hintza? As he thought that, he remembered something else. It had been by following Hintza that he had found Xhabbo. He was not really so alone as he had been feeling. He had not only Hintza, but the promise of a companionship of his own choosing in Xhabbo. A swift calculation made him realize that Xhabbo could now be back with his people. Soon, therefore, it would become possible for Xhabbo to keep his promise to return to see François. This thought led to another. He must make sure that he was never away from Hunter's Drift for too long in case he was not there to answer Xhabbo's pre-arranged call.

His imagination thus drawn into the future, he increased his expectation of companionship in contemplation of another fact: that for the first time in the history of Hunter's Drift they had European neighbours, and that there was the probability of companionship with a girl of approximately his own age, whom he had already nicknamed Nonnie. At this point his own dreaming self took over so successfully that it was impossible to tell who was sleeping more soundly, Hintza or François.

It seemed only a moment between his falling asleep and his departure, with Mopani and the three dogs, for the Monckton camp. Much to Ousie-Johanna's disgust, they left before breakfast. Ousie-Johanna in her emotions was entirely subjective; to reject her food was to reject her. She had a capacity for being hurt that amounted to genius, matched only by the capacity for being instantly consoled. So François knew he had only to make an extra fuss of her for all to be well. Before leaving, he directed her feelings towards the future by stressing how both he and Mopani would be getting hungry all day for the dinner they knew she would have ready for them on their return. He was able to heighten her expectations by repeating a remark Mopani had made to him. 'I think, Coiske, we ought to reckon with the possibility that after reading the message I have for him, Sir

365

James might well have to come back to my camp and spend the night here first on the way. Do you mind?'

Ousie-Johanna's mood cleared quickly at the thought of guests and she ordered François imperiously not to come without that satined figure of romance, the great Amelia, and her sweet and pretty little Nonnie, beside the 'English Lord', as Sir James had become in the process of anticipation, instead of a 'badly brought-up *Rooinek*'.

The journey on horseback was uneventful, yet it was of great importance to François. Full of the thought that he had given to Xhabbo the night before, he questioned Mopani a great deal about the desert to the west, where the last remnants of Xhabbo's people had found sanctuary. Mopani himself did not know the desert well, but he described in minute and fascinating detail how, even in the worst of droughts, his father had found it possible to live in the desert with the help of friendly Bushman guides. He told François that he did not know the Bushmen and the desert as well as his father had done, because all his leisure time had been taken up exploring an immense swamp which impinged deeply into the desert. This swamp was created by a great river which started high up in the mountains far away in Angola and ended as a vast desert delta. In it, Mopani said, there was a scattering of one of the most rare of all the branches of the Bushmen race, the River, or Water Bushmen. He had never himself encountered them because among the great papyrus reaches and everglades, and on low islands covered with dense copses and clusters of great soaring trees, tightly interlaced as any black, Victorian boot with fastening of monkey rope and other creepers, the Bushmen hid successfully from the strangers who in the past had brought nothing but destruction to them.

One reason why he, Mopani, had been so interested in the swamps was because of the strange myth believed implicitly by all the African peoples for some thousands of miles to the west and north. Namely, that in this swamp grew the original tree of life. This tree of life, according to the legend, had originally been in the keeping of 'a white feminine presence'. Mopani did not know what else to call it. It was always difficult to find European parallels for African concepts, but he would be inclined to say that this legendary presence was a kind of white high priestess, or goddess. Mopani had even met Africans who claimed that there was a painting on a rock on the other side of the swamps and desert of this young white woman, standing on the smooth, steep flank of a sheltered rock among barren mountains, with a flower in her hand. The tree, he believed, was the nearest approach in the belief of all these millions of black people to a common religious temple, an equivalent of Sinai, from which originally they had received their commandments and to which their prophets and seers, in the past, went in times of trouble for consultation and guidance. According to the legend, these commandments issued always from the tree in song and, therefore, it would not surprise François to know the tree was also spoken of as the Singing Tree.

However, since the coming of the Matabele, who had so brutally invaded the interior, and hard after the Matabele the appearance of the all-powerful Europeans, who disrupted their way of life even more, the tree was reported to have ceased singing. Yet the legend persisted that a day would come when the tree would sing again and that the singing then would be a sign to all Africans, far and wide, that the time had come for them to unite again and drive both Matabele and European back to the Great Water from where they had come.

Mopani could not explain why, but he had longed to find this tree. He had tried repeatedly but never succeeded. All he had done was to prove to his own satisfaction that the people who lived closest to the great swamp still believed firmly in it and in its prophetic truth. He suspected that they knew exactly where the tree was, but would on no account share their knowledge with strangers, particularly a 'red stranger'. Considering their terrible history, no one could blame them for their refusal.

It was most strange, he went on, that they should happen to be talking just then about this tree, and the River Bushmen, because only a week before the legend again had been brought to his notice. One night, out on patrol, he had overheard an African ranger talking. He was married to a woman of the Makoba, the tribe which lived around and within the fringes of the swamp. The ranger's wife had recently returned from a long, round-about journey to her people, and Mopani heard her husband telling the other rangers that she had come back with a rumour that the Singing Tree was singing again. He thought that the Matabele who formed the majority of his staff would laugh off so foreign a rumour. To his amazement they all took it so seriously that they became unusually silent and grave.

Mopani, no doubt, would have carried on his account, and François had a mob of eager questions clamouring for answers in his mind, but already the conversation had taken so long that they found themselves at this point emerging from the bush and looking down on the wide Monckton clearing. All this was, perhaps, a pity, since the conversation is included in François's story not for the light it can undoubtedly throw on the wide aboriginal soul of Africa dreaming of things to come, but solely for the reason that it was extremely relevant to what happened to him. In fact, the particular moment was already mobilized among the secret forces of the future, where this incomplete piece of knowledge would suddenly become relevant and fall, as if made to measure, into place in the complex pattern of François's life.

At that moment, however, any elaboration of this significant legend was rendered impossible because Mopani broke off talking, pulled Noble to a halt and exclaimed, unbelievingly: '*Allah Wereld!* Now, there, *darem*, is a thing. Yes-no Coiske, it looks very much to me as if your Sir James is building right on top of that hill.' He paused, as if even then he did not accept what he saw, patting Noble's sweating neck as he did so. He then ended a long train of thought with an enigmatic, 'But I dare say he knows his own business best.'

François had already of his own accord noticed what Sir James was up to, but in a sense had been prepared for it by his previous glimpse of the camp. In some curious way the impression he had of Sir James's character made it obvious to him that he should build by preference on a hill. Sir James was a man who would feel compelled to 'surmount' any difficulties which confronted him. François knew, in the way only the young and the primitive can know their elders and betters, that Sir James would not, like Ouwa or their Matabele, try to seek a way round his difficulties. Hunter's Drift was such a reassuring place in François's mind, just because it did not set itself above or apart from the surrounding bush, but was a companion and contributor to it. But there now in front of them was the emerging blue-print of another kind of approach and intent, that of a man who would command the land on which he was settling, and so logically and inevitably would choose a commanding height from which to do so.

Mopani had hardly finished speaking when his conclusion was confirmed in the most convincing fashion. A great spurt of red dust suddenly shot up from the hill, to form a dense cloud all over it. A few seconds later it was followed by the thud of a heavy explosion. When the dust cleared, the skyline on both sides of the hill was dark with the silhouettes of men climbing to the top, obviously Sir James's Cape-coloured builders coming out from behind the stones where they had sheltered during the blasting.

'They're not wasting any time down there,' Mopani remarked, rather wryly. 'And we'd better follow their example and waste no time either.'

At that Mopani pulled Noble into a gallop. François did the same with his horse, while Hintza, Nandi and 'Swayo fanned out in front of the cavalry patrol like scouts on point duty. They rode fast down the clearing, sloping towards hill and river.

Their coming was not observed until they were in Sir James's camp. He had pitched it on the far side of the hill, and Mopani and François had to pull up their horses into a slow walk when they reached the great ironstone boulders, which were strewn all over the ground at the foot of the hill. They made their way round its base so silently that they were almost among the tents before they were seen. Indeed, they just had time, before they were noticed, to take in the whole of the layout of the camp, and François was struck by the strict, mathematical pattern in which it had been organized.

He had never seen a camp quite as elaborate and, to his eyes, quite so acutely deliberate. Even their three dogs appeared to him to be somewhat overawed by its strangeness, for, instead of rushing at the camp to herald their coming as they would almost certainly have done with any other in François's experience, they all three promptly sat down on their haunches, their long pink tongues flickering in and out of their mouths. They prudently exchanged first impressions with each other before looking over their shoulders to make certain that Mopani and François were there in close support, in case of unexpected eventualities.

Immediately in front of them was, presumably, Sir James's headquarters, laid out in a square with large bell tents at each corner, and a huge, rectangular marquee in the middle. This was obviously the camp kitchen, because from behind it rose a slow flutter of blue smoke. All round the tents, but also in straight lines meeting at right angles, the grass and brush had been cleared away, a measure which clearly spoke well for Sir James's experience of life in the bush, since this was a highly necessary precaution in a world so full of scorpions, poisonous snakes and spiders. Yet, much as François approved of the measure, his eyes remained full of reserve because he knew that round tents like those, as well as those of the Matabele, demanded that any necessary clearing was done in a wide conforming circle and not an arbitrary square.

Moreover, from this square there ran, again at right angles, a straight path, meticulously cleared, to where a good furlong away the wagons of the Cape-coloured people had also been made to form not the normal defensive circle but another huge square with the space in between roofed over by the great buck tarpaulins of the wagons roped together. The squared wagons would have looked like a formidable itinerant fortress, had it not been for another redeeming circus touch brought to it by the brilliant dresses of the women and girls, who were laughing, talking and singing like speckled African starlings as they moved about, with the vivid splashes of colour of their laundry spread out on the bushes along the fringes of another immense square clearing.

François warmed, perhaps disproportionately, to this splash of colour and the shimmering sound in the distance, so much did they humanize the abstract pattern that Sir James had imposed on his native scene. He did not know that he was looking on the display of colour for the last time because, barely a quarter of an hour before, Sir James had rebuked the wagon master for such untidiness and proclaimed that on the far side of the wagons, out of sight of his own camp, proper laundry lines should be set up so that the washing of what was now quite a sizeable community could be dried in a more orderly, efficient and hygienic manner.

Mopani, however, was not surprised. He must have experienced this sort of camp many times before, because he quickly interrupted François's as yet incomplete survey of the scene by exclaiming: 'Huh! Planned and ordered and performed ... latrines and all. The writer of the Queen's own Service Manual could not have improved upon it. Yes-no, Coiske. There now is a real British service fellow's idea of a camp. And make no mistake about it, I have known many far worse.'

Speaking, he nudged Noble gently forward and he and François rounded the first tent just in time to see Sir James coming towards them from the far side of the square with the Cape-coloured wagon master, who was also the head builder. Sir James, as always, was immaculately dressed, exactly in the manner François had first seen him except that, on this occasion, he had a long, fat roll of white papers, presumably plans for building, tucked under one arm. In his right hand he wielded a stout, brightly varnished shooting stick.

He was obviously taken aback at being confronted so abruptly by two horsemen on the fringe of his camp for he stopped in his tracks. His first instinct had been to command them to halt, but François and Mopani were already dismounting, debarred by their own sense of fitness from going uninvited with their horses into the middle of somebody else's camp, a rule of behaviour they would have rigidly observed in the humblest of camps or poorest of kraals. His first impulse proving unnecessary, Sir James just stared at them with a certain militant astonishment until he recognized François. His aggression vanished, but he observed rather flatly, as if this visitation were the last straw to other irritations of the morning, 'Oh, it's you young fellow, m'lad. A good day to you,' before adding, quite unnecessarily, seeing that they had already done so, 'Perhaps you'd like to get down.'

Sir James's tone merely implied to François that as far as he was concerned Sir James was in business as usual. Neither he nor Mopani could know that the thought of François had singularly rankled with him on this particular morning, because of something his daughter had done. Neither did Mopani fail to notice something perfunctory in their greeting, nor be surprised by the extent to which it differed from what was customary among people, even utter strangers, when meeting in that lonely world of Africa. He exchanged a quick look with François which made no secret of his reaction.

François, however, forgetful of Sir James's reservations about shaking hands, had already left his horse standing with the reins trailing in the dust at its feet and stepped forward with his hand outstretched, saying: 'Good morning, sir. I've brought Uncle Mopani over to see you.'

As he said 'Uncle Mopani' he suddenly felt foolish, because obviously Sir James could not possibly know who Mopani was. Confused, as well as irritated by a fact that Sir James, just by what he was, could make him feel awkward, he blushed and forced himself to add, 'Of course, I mean Uncle Mopani Théron.'

François, however, had underrated Sir James's knowledge of Africa. The instant he heard the word Mopani, his governor's memory had swung majestically into action and, by the time François had produced the relevant surname, it told him precisely who his other visitor was.

Full of delighted surprise he dropped François's hand and held out his own to Mopani, clasping it warmly and exclaiming, 'Not *the* Théron? Surely not Colonel H. H. Théron?'

François nodded emphatically on behalf of Mopani, who was too embarrassed by the unexpected note of appreciation and the raising from the dead of a military rank, long buried decently in the graveyard of his memory, to do more than mumble a sound which was an equivalent of 'I suppose so'.

From there on there was nothing too much that Sir James could do to make Mopani welcome. His attentions seemed to by-pass François. His Royal Naval shout directed at the kitchen had produced a servant to open out some comfortable canvas chairs and a table, to set them up in the shade of his large dining-tent, to cover the table with porcelain cups of a white, blue and gold Foreign Office design, with hot milk in a jug and coffee in pot to match, and Huntley and Palmer biscuits in a tin covered with a delicate Victorian chintz material.

372

François, however, felt so out of place that he said, 'If you don't mind, Uncle, I think I'll go and see to our horses before I have any coffee.'

Mopani, without knowing the reason, was already aware of François's embarrassment and, accordingly, welcomed the suggestion, deliberately making much of François's thoughtfulness so that Sir James could not fail to notice how high was his regard for the boy. Indeed, Mopani's intention got through to Sir James immediately. He gave François a glance which showed a glimmering of forethought that he might have to re-appraise his attitude to the boy, not only in fairness, but also so as not to alienate someone whom he himself had always secretly hero-worshipped in an anachronistic Victorian fashion.

Leaving them deep in conversation, François remounted and led Noble slowly out of the camp, careful not to raise any dust, while the three dogs happily trotted and skirmished playfully round the horses. Once in the saddle, he remembered that he had as yet seen nothing of Amelia and her charge, and used his convenient vantage point to look all over camp and clearing. But he saw no sign of either. He wondered what could have become of them, for certainly they must be in or very near the camp. Disappointed, he walked the horses away from the camp, but he had hardly reached the edge of the wide clearing around the tents when a sudden spiral of wind, which the bushveld day raises when the black earth begins to go white with heat under the sun, carried a flutter of large sheets of white paper across the horses' path.

Both Noble and François's own horse, trained to be on the watch for signs of anything strange, halted immediately. Their nostrils widened and quivered and their skin under the saddles shuddered under the strange flutterings of sheet upon sheet of paper blowing round them. Thinking that they could well be some of Sir James's official documents, François swung out of the saddle and proceeded with difficulty to collect the sheets one by one until he had about twenty in his hand. He then found himself looking, not at documents of state, but a series of drawings.

He did not know which aspect of these drawings amazed him

most, their abundance or their unity of subject matter. Sheet after sheet was covered with nothing but drawings of the same horse in various aspects, cantering, standing still and even bucking. Only in three or four drawings was there a suggestion that the horse had a rider on its back, but the figure was very vaguely sketched in. It was the discovery of these drawings, although François, of course, could not know it, that had irritated Sir James just before his and Mopani's arrival. He had called them 'idiotic doodling', and ordered Amelia to take his daughter out of the camp before it was too hot and walk some sense into her.

Thoughtfully rolling the sheets of paper into a neat scroll, François slipped them into one of his two saddle-bags, remounted and walked the horses on slowly towards the river, where he sat, preoccupied, in the saddle. It was not until all three dogs came running back fast through the grass ahead of him, and all three began leaping up and down in excitement at his horse's head, that he was forced out of his preoccupation.

He looked sharply around him and saw a wide-brimmed khaki hat waving wildly above the silver-tipped grass, and heard a faint but clear young voice trying to attract his attention. The moment the dogs observed that their mission had been successfully accomplished they swished about and, with Hintza in the lead, made straight for the owner of the hat, while François put his horses into a canter. He perceived at once that the owner of the hat was racing towards them, while the dark, satin figure of Amelia followed slowly some fifty yards behind, wobbling in the sea of grass like a cumbersome barge caught in a speed-boat's wake.

François's surprise and delight gave way almost immediately to acute concern that these two should be wandering so far from the safety of their camp without protection of any kind. Much as he loved and trusted the Africa in which he lived, he had been taught that the trust was only justified if matched by an equal respect for danger to which the normal and natural life of the bush was also subject. He had never forgotten how angry Mopani had been when he found him without a gun only a short distance away from his own home. Yet here, in a totally untamed part of the bushveld, a young girl and a fat old lady had been allowed to wander about as if they were in one of Sir

James's mild ancestral meadows. His concern flared into bright anger.

While he was dismounting from his horse to greet Luciana, the three dogs had already reached her. Dressed now in suede ankle-boots, khaki slacks, bush jacket and khaki hat like his own, the chin straps of her hat let out to their full length so that it could hang suspended round her neck and behind her shoulders, she sank to her knees, her arms stretched out to Hintza who was first to greet her. After a long, warm hug Hintza became the automatic medium for presenting Nandi and 'Swayo to Luciana.

Luciana's exclamations of pleasure and affection made Hintza retreat. Nandi was the first, sniffing, to move forward. But there was nothing effusive about her advances to Luciana. Despite the fact that Luciana looked like a young boy, Nandi had at once recognized her as a girl, and was obviously submitting her to a thorough examination. 'Swayo, however, with no such inhibitions, pushed Nandi aside and threw himself at Luciana in order not to be outdone by Hintza in his zeal for welcome and ingratiation. But he was not allowed to succeed, for both to his and François's amazement, a strange, deep growl of warning, which none of them had ever heard before, rumbled deep down in Hintza's throat, while he bared his teeth between stretched and quivering lips, jealous of his own father.

At any other time and place François would have been amused by Hintza's behaviour, but today he was not his usual, composed self. Luciana rose to her feet, smiling and delighted to see him again but she noticed, to her utter bewilderment, that there was not the slightest indication in François's manner that he was pleased to see her. His set young face was old with anger and the strange, hard look in his eyes dismayed her.

She had no time to question him for François had taken her roughly by the arm, asking, 'What d'you think you're doing here like this out on your own?'

There is something so authoritative about pure anger that for the moment Luciana was overawed. She answered defensively: 'Why, I've just been for a stroll with Amelia.'

'For a stroll with Amelia!' The *naïveté* of it made François pompous with fury as he swept on. 'Don't you know that one just doesn't go for walks on one's own in country like this unless one is properly armed or accompanied? Don't you know yet how wild this country is? All sorts of dangerous and unexpected things can happen to you here at any moment. Where, tell me, is your snake bite outfit? Have you and Amelia not been told that one goes nowhere without one here? And where . . .?'

He got no further with his violent cross-examination, because he was interrupted by her abashed admission, 'I'm afraid we don't have things like that with us.' Then, with a more spirited reaction, she demanded, 'And why should we, so close to home?'

But her question seemed to inflame François all the more. He had, out of the corner of his left eye, seen a significant movement near a termite mound some seven yards away from the track. A quick, sideways glance told him both what it was and that Providence could not have provided him with a greater justification for his behaviour. He was still gripping her by the arm and so could pull her round sharply to face the mound, and, while pointing with his other hand, he said gruffly: 'You ask why? Just look at that ant-heap there and tell me what you see.'

She looked, and in the barren space common around termite heaps in that part of the world saw, sitting upright on its tail, black as ebony and shining as with oil, a seven-foot rinkhals cobra. For a moment it was still, erect as an antique black tulip, rooted in the earth. But suddenly the hood inflated, the ring of white became a band of ivory round the long neck, the eyes glittered like sequins and a long, thin tongue flickered like forked lightning at its lips. As it lay in the dust, warming itself in the sun, it had been alarmed by the thud of horses' hooves and the close sound of human voices. It had shed all languor and shot up like a jet of midnight darkness to survey the surroundings.

Although a spasm of fear and revulsion made her shudder, Luciana was also strangely thrilled by the sight and gasped, 'But I say! Isn't he a beauty?'

François was so amazed at her reaction that he was rendered speechless. All his anger vanished and a totally unexpected joy possessed him. He could not have had more convincing proof that she could love his world as much as he did. The proof was

376

all the more effective because, despite all his experience, he had never been able to overcome a loathing and fear of snakes. Certainly he had never been able to think of them as beautiful.

He looked at Luciana in undisguised admiration and respect and then looked back at the cobra. It was still there, swaying slowly as if keeping time to the rhythm of the wheeling sun and the sound raised, quivering by the rim of its metal light, from the harp-like grass around them. Swaying, it recovered that bright dream of the first earth that had made it a jewelled coil and collapsed into sleep at the foot of the magenta mound.

Any tendency to resentment in Luciana had gone even before François's glance. From the moment he had pointed out the cobra, everything about his behaviour was clear to her. The explanation was simple. It was all due to his concern about her. But what had really thrilled her was that he could be so angry. Instinctively she found herself wondering: he was terribly fierce with me; could he be as fierce with Fa?

All possibility of misunderstanding resolved, they stared at each other until Luciana asked, 'Where were you going when you saw us?'

François gave her a full account of his and Mopani's visit before explaining that he was on the way to water the horses at the river. She jumped with excitement, begging him to take her along. At this moment Amelia, labouring like a ship in a heavy sea, her corsets creaking like strained timbers, puffed and somewhat huffed, joined them. She arrived with the intention of relieving her soul of its tensions by upbraiding both Luciana and François.

These had been building up in her ever since Sir James had dispatched her on this mission, for which neither her build nor her temperament was suited. Long before François had shown up in the distance she had reached the stage where she never wanted to see another horse in real life, since it was the proliferation of horses in ink and horses alone that had brought about this minor disaster to shatter the placid routine of a normal day.

Wallowing in the wake of Luciana, who was utterly unabashed by Sir James's decree of banishment and was setting far too brisk a pace for her, Amelia had muttered to herself, sullen as sulphur, 'Dear Mother of Christ, Good blood of the wood, why must it always be like this? I know they all have to grow up, but why should they always begin by falling in love with horses? Her sainted mother was exactly the same ... first just horses in general, any old horse ... cart-horse, milkmen's ponies, cavalry gigs, any old broken down nag sends them off besotted and starry-eyed. Then suddenly, there's one particular horse. You can manage them for a while because that one horse and no other one will do and you think the search is over and peace has come. But one underrates the cunning of the creatures! For you wake up, one fine morning, and you find even *that* horse is not enough. It suddenly has to have a rider; all sorts of riders to start with and the search is on again until the rider, like the horse, becomes a particular one, not just any old boy; then they are all utterly unmanageable and the child you have known and nursed is gone for ever, less than this terrible dust to which we are told we must return.'

Here some tears had rolled down her sallow cheeks and she crossed herself before sighing, 'If only we were in some civilized place and one could have the Mother Superior of a good convent and all her nuns to help one, the problem would not be so bad. But, dear Mother in Heaven, what is one to do in such a place, with such a father? Great gentleman that he is, he's only a man and like all men knows little enough about women, let alone young girls. And he has set us all down here where, Heaven knows, at any moment we will either be eaten up by lions or massacred! I ask, dear Heaven, whether it is not as sinful as it is mad, and what is to become of us?'

However, the picture of the two of them looked, at that moment, so innocent that her carefully prepared contribution lost all its impetus.

She might have been able to resist the appeal of Luciana because, devoted as she was to her, she did, after all, see more than enough of her. But there was something about François which from the moment she had first seen him, produced a quite unexpected fellow-feeling within her. Seeing him looking at her in a rather serious, almost solemn way, out of wide, calm blue eyes (an attribute of which she felt Providence had unfairly deprived her Iberian race), she was possessed by powerful emotions. For all his obvious self-reliance and appearance of being well able to take care of himself, she felt that underneath there was a person almost as deprived as she, unmarried, and with her memories of disasters and massacres, felt herself to be.

So she now found herself sailing down, her front billowing above the sea of grass, towards François, clasping him in her arms and hugging him. Embarrassed as he was, he knew he could not disengage himself abruptly without hurting the feelings of so warm-hearted a person, and so in measure returned her welcome in kind.

Fortunately Luciana put an end to it by saying something to Amelia in rapid Portuguese. Then, by way of explanation, she said to François, 'You mustn't mind her. She thinks you look unhappy sometimes and just wants to comfort you.'

The idea that he looked unhappy had never occurred to François. Until Ouwa's death it had never seemed to him that he had ever had cause to be unhappy. Amazed and rather upset he just gaped at the pair of them.

Luciana continued, 'You look surprised, but you must admit you don't laugh much, do you?'

It was again news to François that he did not laugh much. Yet, as the remark went home with far more point than Luciana intended, his natural sense of fairness suggested some reason for it. He knew it was not that he wasn't as full of laughter and fun as other people, but he had to admit that, leading a life so much on his own, he perhaps was compelled to experience laughter and fun in other ways.

Indeed one has to support him in this by pointing out that laughing aloud is very largely a social phenomenon and that, unless one has others to share it with, it loses much of its point. The result was that, had one experienced the impulse to laugh in François's circumstances, one would have probably done what he did and laugh, as it were, inwardly. Besides, what could have been more disastrous, François asked himself, than to laugh out loud when one was watching close by a whole tribe of baboons playing the craftiest and subtlest of jokes on one another? He had been filled with laughter to bursting point on countless occasions but never given way, since the first sound would have brought the joyful scene to an abrupt end and sent the baboons scampering away into the bush. He might, it is true, have laughed with Lammie and Ouwa, but there was a snag to that too. In spite of a great deal of amusement experienced in their company, it was amusement of a kind that did not produce sheer animal laughter so much as a smile, often the strange Mona Lisa sort of smile which is the unique expression of intellectual superiority, occasioned as a rule by wit or irony. His home, much as he loved it, had not been a school for laughter. That, perhaps, was why he had been so envious of the way Xhabbo had laughed the first time in the cave, and why he had been so impressed by the way this girl, apparently so devastatingly critical of him just then, had laughed at their first meeting. Somewhat subdued by this reflection he heard himself saying, 'You're wrong, I laugh a great deal, inwardly.'

His explanation produced an outbreak of merriment equal to that at their first meeting. But noticing that François had no inkling that she was not laughing at him but with him, delighted at so original a concept of laughter, she stopped and faced him apologetically, saying, 'But seriously, I do wish, even if you must laugh so much inwardly, you would smile at us more often. It rather suits you, you know.' Then, tactfully changing the subject, she said, 'And please, let's go to the river.'

François hesitated. 'It's rather a long way for you to walk. Can you ride?'

Her instinct, as a young person who had ridden ever since she could remember, was to laugh again. However, instead she made straight for Noble as if to get into the saddle. But François restrained her. As far as he knew, he was the only other person allowed to ride Noble, just as he had been the only person who had ever been allowed to shoot with any of Mopani's guns. Besides, his own horse, often ridden by Lammie, seemed a more obvious choice. Accordingly, he quickly shortened his own stirrups, made sure the girth had not slackened, and the horse was ready for Luciana. She was so impatient to be off now, however, that she did not even wait for him to help, but took a run at the horse, jumped, threw herself across the saddle, scrambled upright, quickly found the stirrups, took the reins from François and exclaimed, 'Lead on, MacDuff!'

For a moment François thought Amelia would protest, but

the temptation of now being able to withdraw from an uncomfortable excursion under a hot sun to the comfort and coolness of the camp was too much for her. After some ambiguous noises and a perfunctory gesture of disapproval, she swung slowly about and retreated with great dignity towards Sir James's tents.

For François, the most important thing about the journey to the river and back was perhaps the extent to which it revealed differences in their temperaments, which at times excited and at others dismayed him. He had had no experience to enable him to decide to what extent the differences were due to the fact that she was a girl and he a boy. All he knew was that she did seem to have a knack of making him feel an awfully slow, plodding sort of person when he had always taken it for granted that he had quick reflexes and reactions. Even their pace of thought and feeling appeared different. His seemed slow, single and persistent; hers quick, varied, changeable and no sooner announced or felt than impatient to be realized without delay.

She was hardly in the saddle before she called out, 'I dare you to race me to the river!'

'I'm afraid we can't do that,' François replied, annoyed that he had to say no. 'We have to walk them so the horses can cool down properly before we water them.'

She made a face full of disappointment before her expression brightened and she countered, 'Well then, I'll race you back to the camp. I bet I beat you to it!'

She said it with such confidence that François could not possibly suspect that this mystique of horses which had invaded her like an attack of scarlet fever, as Amelia would have had it, demanded that the rider who had featured so prominently in the drawings which had incurred Sir James's disapproval, had to be expert at racing, particularly races with young women.

However, she was disappointed again. François, in his slow, deliberate way, explained that nothing could be worse for horses than racing them with their stomachs full of cold water.

'Oh bother!' she answered, irritated again and needing all the self-control of which she was capable, to alter the 'Why must you always be so maddeningly sensible?' that was on the tip of her tongue, to an oblique, impatient and scathing, 'Why must one always be so sensible? I do hate having to be sensible all the time, don't you?'

This was a favourite theme, but with a secret aspect to it. It may have been pure reaction against the eminently practical sense of her father, or the peasant, shrewd sense of Amelia, raised in the Portuguese governess's case to a point which transformed Luciana from a sort of female Sancho Panza to an incorrigibly quixotic charge. But, whatever the reason, part of her had come to dislike what was called 'being sensible' to such an extent that she had already informed Amelia that when she grew up she would never dream of marrying anyone who, in addition to the exacting range of other qualities expected of him, was not also utterly incapable of being sensible about her.

François did not quite know how to answer. He hesitated in fact so long that his silence was misinterpreted and he was unfairly upbraided with a scornful, 'Ah, I might have known it. There you go searching again for a sensible answer. I wish you would say the first thing that came into your head.'

Even then François did not answer. He was thinking, as so often since Ouwa's death, of something he had once said on this subject. It was extraordinary how in some way Ouwa had now become a more clearly defined and real person to François than when alive. Most vividly he could now hear Ouwa's rather tired, slightly ironical voice saying, 'The art of living, François, is nothing if it does not consist of being sensible on completely non-sensible grounds. It is, if I dare suggest so flagrant a defiance of collective precepts for wisdom, nothing if not a leap into the dark; a finding of alternatives to what common sense holds to be inevitable. Those who look before they leap, never leap.'

François would have liked to explain all this, but apart from the fact that being more a feeling than a process of reasoning, it was difficult to put into words, the time and place seemed wrong. All he could do was to protest, 'It isn't that at all. I often do wild, impulsive things. Perhaps I can tell you when we have more time. Only the other day I did something that frightened everyone at home.'

He uttered this last sentence rather proudly; for he was, of course, thinking of the way he had allowed Hintza to lead him out into the dangerous first light of day to find Xhabbo and rescue him from the lion trap, the leopard and all the other dangerous things which had threatened him at the time. He had not been at all 'sensible' then, and he had an instinct that he could trust her with the full story, without imperilling Xhabbo. He longed to do so but knew he would have to wait.

However, not what he had said so much as the tone in which he had said it, had apparently been enough to restore him to grace, for Luciana exclaimed eagerly, 'I smell another secret. You promise to tell me one day, if I promise not to tell?' She laughed, and drew the edge of her hand sharply like a knife across her throat and clicked her tongue against her teeth, before reminding him, 'And what of that secret about Hin? You've not told me about that yet.'

Hintza and his parents were scouting far ahead at the moment, so François could tell her, without chance of being overheard, why *Hintza* had been contracted into *Hin*, as well as the origin of *tsa* as he had had it from old Koba, and how old Koba and her people had had it from the stars.

He was rewarded not only by the fact that she listened with the utmost attention, but also by her final exclamation, 'Oh, I love it so when things have stories to them. And they all seem to have here in this place where you live.'

And on this occasion the sharing of the secret was made more dynamic by the fact that chance provided François with the opportunity of illustrating the need for the contraction of Hintza's name. Perched high on his horse, he spotted about fifty yards away to the left of them, behind an ant-heap, the tip of the nose and pointed ear of a jackal which the Matabele call the 'turn-about' jackal because of its adroit way of twisting, turning and doubling back on its tracks in order to avoid its many and far more powerful enemies.

Calling Hintza to him, François had only to point in the direction of the jackal in the long grass which was invisible from Hintza's level, and proclaim a loud *'Tsa!'* Instantly Hintza, followed by Nandi and 'Swayo, set out at great speed to flush the jackal within a few seconds and pursue it with incredible speed and determination.

Luciana appeared to be equally divided between two longings; one to see François's Hintza succeed in his mission, the other to spare the life of the nimble jackal. Running races with death in the animal world of Africa produces the greatest and most poignant of all eurhythmic graces. It was utterly impossible to watch the lithe body of the jackal, elongated with the extremity of speed, its dark coat streaked with gold and silver, flashing in and out of occasional bare patches of the vast clearing, and to see it soar effortlessly over some thorn bush into a sheet of sunlight like an animal breaking a silver hoop in the limelight of a circus, not to want such perfection of movement and beauty of form to out-run death.

Fortunately François had no love of unnecessary killing. Also he had another, perhaps more egotistical motive: he wanted to spare Hintza loss of face in front of the girl for it was just possible that he and his parents could fail to catch so expert a quarry.

The moment the point of his demonstration appeared effectively made, he put two fingers in his mouth and a whistle, loud and clear, broke the silence of the day. Hintza at once swung about and, followed by his parents, came back as fast as he could towards the horses.

'Heavens, what a whistle!' Luciana exclaimed. 'Do you think you could teach me how to do it too? And how perfectly wizard of Hin. What a magic word that *tsa* is!' (To François's delight she pronounced the *tsa* perfectly.)

A few minutes later they came to the edge of the broad belt of reeds and rushes along the banks of the river, its sound reaching them like that of the wind which produces the slow build-up of clouds before rain in François's world. There, to Luciana's amazement, François turned off the track to ride straight into the grass and reeds, so tall that they brushed her lips, even when sitting on her horse.

François, looking round to see if she was following, noticed her surprise and exclaimed, 'The river's full of crocodiles making their living by waiting for the game who never learn how stupid it is always to use the same track to drink at the same place. It's easier of course ... but sheer laziness on their part. And nothing could suit the crocodiles better. They study their habits and so know exactly where to lie in wait for them.

You should hear 'Bamuthi on the subject! He says that there's nothing more dangerous for man in the bush than regular habits.'

By the time he'd finished, they saw the smooth broad water of the river, flashing beyond the tall rushes and reeds. When François at last found an opening in them produced by a large flat slab of an outcrop of ironstone, he walked his horse across it to the water lapping at the edge and dismounted.

Luciana, whose first close glimpse of the Amanzim-tetse this was, seeing it so broad, smooth, purposeful in its urge to find the far-off Zambezi which was the royal way of all their rivers to the sea, noticed how the water against the far bank was like a Chinese painting on silk. There was the reflection not only of the sky but also of the taut, river-bamboo, sprung grass and rushes bent low with birds' nests that hung like round paper lanterns on them.

Luciana swung out of her saddle to come and stand silently, deeply stirred, beside François. François had already released Noble from his bit and snaffle and allowed him to step forward to drink, or rather sip at the water because, like all their horses, he did so with the delicacy of a gourmet, first blowing away any film of dust or grass seeds which might have collected on the surface of that sluggish backwater and then, thirsty as he was, taking only the smallest of mouthfuls to see whether the water was of a vintage to his liking, before drinking it more steadily.

François, perhaps, should have responded to the girl's appreciation of the scene. But he appeared to her to be insensitive to it all and more interested in unslinging his gun, unlocking the magazine and deftly undoing the bolt to push a bullet into the breech. The harsh, metallic sound jarred sharply on Luciana. She looked at François, feeling reproachful that he should introduce so discordant a sound and be so impervious to what seemed to her the most harmonious and peaceful sight she had ever seen. Worse, he seemed not only totally unaware of the beauty of the place but completely unaware of her presence. He was just standing there with his gun held at the ready in front of him, utterly absorbed in examining, first their bank of the river, then the water immediately in front of them and finally the far bank, and that shining sheet covered all over with the inscriptions of the vegetation looming over it. Had it not been for that humbling episode of the black cobra earlier on, she would have suspected François of playing at some kind of Boy Scout heroics.

Her attention came back to the river and nothing, she realized, had ever looked lovelier to her. It was not only the cool, purposeful sound of the river, nostalgic for its own great sea-level, and the noise of the trustful horses drinking up water like wine. She was also hearing in concert, woven into the wind-instrument music of the river, the calling of all sorts of birds among the reeds. She saw them in all shapes and colours, fluttering from one dense clump to another, until the green and gold tops were a confetti of crimson bee-eaters, bronze sun-birds, glistening green-black starlings, with stippled breasts; chrome yellow and olive green finches; blue Ethiopian rollers; cool, purple little doves with warm voices; water plovers with flutes in their throats and vivid little weaver birds, coming in and out of the side entrance of their round green homes suspended low over the water from the tip of bent reeds and rushes. Indeed, it all looked such a secluded place that François, standing there with his gun at the ready, struck her as unnecessarily melodramatic.

It was suddenly too much for her. Despite her stirred-up feeling, she found herself whispering again as if she were in some great concert hall, wherein one is listening to a performance of universal music which the human voice, however still or small, could spoil, 'You're mean to stand with your back to me. Can't you tell me the names of those lovely birds?'

François was not aware of doing anything unusual. He had done what he had done unconsciously, so much had his earliest training to be always on guard become a habit. Surprised not only that his behaviour was not understood but also by the vehemence of feeling which had blurred the whisper, he said without turning round in, to her, a maddeningly unperturbed tone, 'I'm sorry to look rude, but I'm keeping an eye on that crocodile there.'

She made a sound of unbelief because it was odd, if not a little suspicious, that always there appeared to be some animal conveniently at hand to excuse this infuriatingly imperturbable and deliberate boy. 'Oh come,' she said, 'you're just trying to frighten me. Fa, and he's seen more of Africa than you have, says there are more crocodiles and snakes in a person's mind than there are in the whole of Africa.'

The remark did not raise Sir James at all in François's estimation. If he really was simple enough to believe that, he thought, Africa sooner or later would have an alarming last word to say about it. But at that moment he was too intent on the business in hand to let it trouble him. He merely pointed at a patch of water some twenty feet to their left and, still in a whisper, asked, 'Look, can't you see? There's old Rameses-the-Great himself, trying to decide whether he should have a go at us or our horses.'

Ever since François had read somewhere that crocodiles were sacred in ancient Egypt, Rameses had become his own private name for any of the male old crocodiles who ruled a particular stretch of river. Since the one there now was one of the biggest in his experience, the name came out naturally. It was just another instance of how, in a sense, like old Koba's people of the early race, the animals of his world were highly personal.

Luciana was too interested in the present to ask any more. The least she could do was look in earnest in the direction in which François was pointing. But, try as she might, she saw only what looked to her like a piece of dead wood in the river. Then she realized, with a twist of alarm, that if it were a dead piece of wood, it certainly would not keep perfect station in one position like that and would long since have drifted in the current past them. She looked closer and, at the tip of the log of wood, wearing ripples of water like a ruff of lace, she saw a pair of very large, exceedingly black and terribly impersonal ice-cold eyes watching them.

'Oh Heavens!' she exclaimed with a touch of alarm.

François stooped, picked up a stone in his right hand and said, 'I don't want to frighten everyone by shooting. Let's see what a stone will do to his Egyptian Majesty.'

He threw the stone with an accuracy which surprised even him. It hit the water just under the tip of Rameses's nose. Instantly there was a tremendous, convulsive swirl in the water, a huge long tail flashed like the lash of a whip in the air and sent Rameses-the-Great vanishing into the deeps of the river.

Luciana watched it all with mixed feelings. She said nothing, realizing François had not done yet with the episode. Almost immediately, as much to himself as to her, he said, 'When you see a thing like that you have to admit, as my father always said, that it was rather ironical to call this the Amanzim-tetse.'

Luciana fastened on to the word and asked, 'What does this Amanzim-tetse mean?'

'It's the Sindabele for "Sweet Water",' he answered non-chalantly: 'But my father could never resist translating it for the benefit of European visitors as Lady Precious Stream.' Then quickly, as if afraid that yet another recollection of Ouwa could darken what was now an exceedingly happy day for him, he added, 'I'm glad I didn't have to shoot. I don't think that old Pharaoh will trouble us again, and for all that, it *is* a sweet and precious stream.'

Perhaps the whole episode had disturbed Luciana more than she realized, for she reacted quickly: 'Sweet? With that beast in it?'

This, perhaps, puzzled François most of all, since everything in the world of the bush, provided it kept to its time and place, had always seemed to belong and to add to the richness of their lives.

'Oh, he's all right in his way,' he replied, 'and he has, as Mopani says, his own right to be here and keep alive. Just look at that spit of sand on the far side over there, and you'll see how even crocodiles have their domestic moments. D'you see what I see? They're in the process of having their teeth brushed.'

The notion of anything so ridiculous as a crocodile brushing its teeth made Luciana giggle, so it was a long time before François could get her to concentrate. Then he enabled her unexperienced eyes to penetrate the natural camouflage of the river world and see seven huge crocodiles, stretched out rigid with languor in the sun, eyes ecstatically shut and mouths wide open, while numbers of little birds perched on their lips and darted inside their jaws. They were, François explained wryly in a way that made her laugh, dentists, carefully using their sharp,

388

deft little beaks to remove fragments of decayed meat, lodged in the crevices between the double rows of crocodile teeth.

There was, he added, a story from old Koba about it all. The first great Grandmother Mother Ostrich (the highest Bushman title of authority, their equivalent of Empress) was dismayed by the extent to which the crocodiles were devouring the birds who depended on the pools and rivers of Africa for their living. She had appealed to Mantis, who gave her the idea of making a pact with the original Rameses-the-Great who, in his turn, was greatly worried by the growing number of toothless crocodiles. Crocodiles, as everyone knew, lived so long that finally they were practically toothless. The pact was simple. All the birds with the finest beaks would be appointed royal toothpicks-in-waiting to the crocodiles, in return for a pledge from them to leave all the other birds unmolested.

Such a clear gush of laughter burst from Luciana at this Alice-in-Wonderland vision with which François had just presented her, that all the birds in their vicinity went silent. The thought that she had spoilt the concert among the reeds and rushes made her put her hand quickly to her mouth to stifle her merriment. Soon the world round about them once more recovered its rhythm and both sounded and looked more beautiful than ever. Indeed for some moments neither of them spoke. François, still in as watchful attitude as ever, was so pleased that old Koba's story appeared to have drawn them closer together, that he now risked glancing sideways at her from time to time.

Whenever he did so, she was squatting beside her horse, looking deep into the water immediately in front of her as if into a clairvoyant's crystal. Then an extraordinary thing happened to him. The water there was as smooth and still as a mirror, and in that mirror there lay the trembling reflection of his horse, and beside his horse, the face of the girl caught up in thoughts without name, and for once all her lively, yet delicate features were at one and still. In some odd way the reflection looked more real, permanent and convincing than even the orginal posed above in bright sunlight. It was an intense dream reflection, yet something which seemed to have been always intact and unchanging in the depths of his imagination. So startlingly convincing was it that it was easy to look on the reflection as the lasting reality, and the horse and girl above as merely transient. Moreover, as he stared, the impression grew that as long as such a dream carried him on like a river, the reflection would keep him company as a point of direction. The only troubling thing was that it had taken so many long days and years to find the right place and right river to provide such a magic mirror to make visible the essential compass image of themselves.

François became so hypnotized by the reflection that he was in danger of forgetting his sentinel duties, and may even have been guilty of negligence if suddenly there had not been thrown into the centre of the magnetic reflection a blaze of colour as if from some Arabian jewel.

It was the reflection of one of the loveliest of all river birds, the one the English call a malachite kingfisher. It had obviously seen a chance of some food in the river near by and was fearlessly hovering in the air in front of them, its wings moving so fast that, quivering and trembling, they appeared always in the same position. The head, a bright feather in its peaked cap and with a scarlet beak, was staring down into the depths of the river. The blazing tail also was trembling as it worked to steady the burning little body in between.

François and the girl looked up simultaneously. François thought the expression on her face then about the most beautiful he had ever seen as she called out, 'Oh, how beautiful! How perfectly stunning!'

The expression of wonder instantly changed to astonishment, for the little bird folded its wings, fell like a stone into the river with barely a splash and almost at once rose easily out of it, a gleaming little silver fish in its beak. Astonishment changed to horror on her face as they watched the bird leave a rainbow trail in the platinum air, on its way to the branch of a dead tree just a few yards away. It perched there for a moment or two, holding the fish bright and gleaming in the light. When presumably it had recovered its breath, it deftly beat the little fish to death against the branch on which it was sitting and then swallowed it whole.

'Oh dear,' Luciana sounded distressed to the point of tears.

'Why must it spoil everything like that? Why was it made so beautifully if it has to do such things? You can expect it of those ugly black old crows and those awful old vultures we saw on our way up here, but not from such a lovely little thing as that.'

François did not reply, because just then another and greater kingfisher appeared, which was not as bright and jewelled as its malachite colleague. It was bigger, more functional and not nearly so selective or tentative in its behaviour, for its mind seemed made up well in advance. It just plunged headlong into the river and came out with a much bigger fish in its beak, and flew, sagging with the weight, low over the reeds and rushes to the far bank and out of their sight.

'Oh no, not another, please. It's really too much,' the girl cried.

But François still did not answer. She had barely finished speaking when an enormous fish eagle appeared, and, as if inflamed by the lesser examples they had just seen, hurled his black and white body like a harpoon into the stream, to rise from it with the biggest catch of all, a gold and silver mullet, held firmly, squirming in vain, between the eagle's crampon talons. The fish indeed was so heavy that the eagle had the greatest difficulty in lifting it clear of the water and carrying it off, straining every gleaming feather in its broad, vibrating wings to make its distant nest.

'Does it go on all day long like this?' Luciana demanded. 'Is there nothing but killing and eating, eating and killing from sunrise to sunset?' To François's dismay, she now appeared thoroughly disenchanted with his world.

'Only until they've had enough to keep themselves and their youngsters alive,' François replied in his best peace-making tone, learned from 'Bamuthi who was an artist at it. Yet he could not resist adding, in defence of the paradox of living beauty and ugly death in the bush, 'None of them ever fishes just for fun, like human beings.'

It was on the tip of his tongue to add 'as your father does' but he was still so much in love and at one with their surroundings that there was no room in his mind for discord. He eagerly anwered, when she had asked him the names of the three birds,

'The first one was what your people call a malachite crested kingfisher, but what Mopani and I call "Little-Joseph-feather-in-cap".'

She looked at him with such incomprehension that he added, ' "Little Joseph" because it has a coat of many colours, and besides the Bushmen say he is a great dreamer, as the Bible says Joseph was. The biggest one of all was a fish eagle. If you listen carefully you can hear it bark with pleasure after delivering some much-needed food to its nest. Then the in-between one is the giant kingfisher. We all think it the most expert fisherman of the lot. Even the Matabele, who don't think much of fish anyway, can't help admiring it. You should just hear the rumble of admiration in their voices when they call him by his Sinda-bele name: *isi-Vubu* ... It's because of that that they've given your father the praise name, *isi-Vuba*.'

This last bit of secret Matabele information escaped him before he realized that he might have chosen a more suitable time and place for telling her. He went scarlet with annoyance at himself, but fortunately the girl was not looking at him.

'They call Fa after such a bird? Why, I wonder?' Then, re-membering her father's love of fishing she added, as if in defence of him, 'I can't believe that all the birds and animals in this world don't also kill just because they like killing, or else they wouldn't be at it all day and night.'

This was such a remote view of nature that if he had heard it from anybody else François would have dismissed it with scorn. But coming from a person whose feelings he feared he had hurt, he answered her at great length. He explained that it seemed to be a law of the bush that no bird, animal, insect or reptile was killed for any reason other than for food or in self-defence. It was true that jackals, hyenas and wild dogs, given the chance, sometimes killed more than they needed, but they did so because they were in many ways the most insecure of all animals, and more than any other had to endure such long periods of hunger that when they had a chance of killing they tended to do so unnecessarily as a kind of insurance against the long periods of hunger that experience had taught them could be ahead.

Even so, the significant thing was that, however understand-able their bouts of over-killing might be, the rest of the animal

392

world despised them for it. It was noticeable, he remarked, how the other animals avoided even looking at them as they did at one another. He could tell her many Bushman stories of how the despised creatures resented the scorn of the respectable, middle-class society of the bush.

To François's delight Luciana laughed so much at the thought of 'middle-class animals' that he had to quieten her. He went on to say that he hoped one day he would be able to show her an example of what he meant, a hyena coming home in the half-light of morning, limping sideways as if ashamed and constantly looking fearfully over its shoulder. At that hour of the day he himself, from behind some bush, had often looked straight into the eyes of a hyena and the expression induced in them by the feeling of being an outcast from the wonderfully rich, law-abiding animal world of Africa was so intense that they blinked with anguish at the growing light of the day that they shunned. It had made him feel almost equally stricken. That is why, François added, he always thought of the hyena as Ishmael.

There was, too, another remarkable thing in this connection. The more powerful and brave the animal, like the elephant or even lion, the more gentle and tender were its natural ways, however quick and ruthless the act of killing in self defence or for food had to be. He would love to show them to her in the midst of their families, considerate, delicate and wise, purring sounds of experience to their young. The instinct of the fearless and strong to live and let live was strongest in such powerful animals.

He would like, too, to show her one day also the other side of *isi-Vuba* and how, for instance, it was a great architect and engineer. How it built a cunning, impregnable home in the banks of the river, tunnelling anything from eight to twelve feet deep into them, in an expert manner which would make her proud of it, and see that it was not an unworthy image for a father who was building so formidably on a hill.

François's explanation, long for him, did something to restore Luciana's natural high spirits. She had been watching the river while he had been speaking and now it did not mean entirely what it had meant to her in the beginning. Now it was her turn to feel as if the river also had a current inside herself, carrying

393

her on like that great log from somewhere far back in the bush, turning helplessly round and round as if trying to escape from the clutches of the powerful stream but always failing, being sucked back into the mainstream and swept remorselessly along. Suddenly she longed for the river to stop just for a second. And as suddenly she was afraid.

She shivered and jumped to her feet, turned her back on the river and asked, 'Don't you ever get frightened of all this water just streaming by as if nothing mattered except for it to go on and on, and it making no difference whether we were here or not?'

François shook his head, although he understood her reference to fear. 'I'm often afraid. Every day there's something to make me afraid. But Mopani has taught me to fear nothing more than fear. He says all bad things come out of failure to stand up to fear.' The confession that he, too, knew fear, of which she had as yet seen no visible signs, comforted Luciana deeply. Then François went on more slowly, 'I even have one fear I don't know what to do about; that one day I might be forced to leave all this for ever.'

He sounded so shaken that she made an effort to change the subject. She said. 'You seem to have names for everybody and everyone, except me. Why?'

François asked lamely, 'Why d'you say that?'

'Well, you never call me by my name although you've heard me called Luciana dozens of times.'

'I'm sorry,' François replied, 'I didn't realize that I didn't call you by a name ... I suppose I always have my own names for people and even if I haven't said so to you, I do call you a name to myself.'

'Oh, so you talk inwardly as well as laugh inwardly, do you? I see I must get a stethoscope to have a proper talk with you.'

The fact that François's failure to call her by a name did not mean that he was neglecting her immediately restored her to her bright teasing self, causing François to give one of his rare smiles. 'Indeed I do, a great deal, living so much by myself,' he answered. 'But Hintza already knows my name for you as well as his own.'

She obviously thought he was about to reveal what he called

her. However, he paused too long for her impatient, quick self, and she had to ask, 'Well, go on ... what do you call me? *isi-Vuba*'s daughter, or some other equally unflattering, fluttering thing?'

François suddenly lost his shyness. He said firmly, 'I call you Nonnie to myself.'

'And, pray, what sort of a bird is that?' she asked, eyes bright with provocation.

'It's not a bird at all,' François answered, precisely, beginning to feel unfairly assaulted. 'It's a diminutive of Nonna; a word brought to my country from the Far East by the original Javanese slaves. According to Ouwa, they made it up from some Portuguese word meaning mistress. Nonnie is a diminutive of this corrupted Portuguese word, and we all use it to mean "little mistress of our home". It's not unusual for daughters of my people to be called Nonnie.'

The implication that there were other Nonnies apart from herself seemed to Luciana the only undesirable element in the name François had given her. But the idea of being regarded as the little mistress of a home seemed so attractive that she became unusually serious and said, 'Promise, François, never call me anything else.'

And then all at once it seemed to her that the morning was complete. Nothing else could be added to it now without spoiling it. She felt urgently that, as quickly as possible, they must leave this river hurrying on its own way to the sea and find a place less changeable in which to continue. So she begged François, 'Look, even Noble has had enough to drink. Please let's go home now, at once please.'

As she spoke, there came suddenly from across the river the call of a bird, sounding as if it were indeed ordering them away. The meaning was so unmistakable to her that even before François could speak, Nonnie's eyes grew great with surprise and she exclaimed, 'Why, I believe that bird is ordering us to clear out too!'

François, happier than he had been for days, hastened to explain. 'That is exactly what it is saying. We call it the Go-away bird. I can't tell you how many times it's stopped us from shooting food for the pot. Suddenly, just when we're creeping up on game, it'll fly straight up in the air, calling out at the top of its complaining voice to draw attention to us. It's a conceited little bird, with a crown of feathers on its head, a Roman nose and a proper magistrate's beak, just ordering everybody about. Listen ... it's one of the few birds I know who speaks English ... can you hear?'

Yes, she heard it plainly and with satisfaction, ordering them off with a judge's weary enunciation: 'Oh go-go-go-away! Go away!'

10 • Finishing School of the Bush

They arrived back in camp rather late for lunch. Had it not been for the fact that Sir James had not only thoroughly enjoyed his morning with Mopani, but been given much cause for deliberation over the message Mopani had brought him, he would have scolded his daughter for keeping them waiting, and would have been correspondingly distant in his manner with François. His good humour, however, had been encouraged by several glasses of his favourite sherry straight from the large white refrigerator looming in his dining-tent. As a result, he could not have been more gracious in the way he presided at table. He helped them to the most precious delicacies from the hamper which was sent regularly to him from a great London store that had specialized for centuries in administering to the tastes of Englishmen condemned to exile in the service of the Empire.

Besides, there was a new element at work in Sir James's mind, and it was of particular importance to François. Mopani's love of François, and the way he had spoken of him not as a young boy but as an equal and a respected partner, had had a considerable impact on Sir James, who was at heart a thoroughly honourable and decent person.

So for the first time François was addressed straightforwardly as François, an event so unexpected that he nearly choked over a spoonful of hot turtle soup. Nor did the change fail to escape Sir James's daughter. Her spirits were already so bright and high that one would have thought them raised to the ultimate, since nothing confirms friendship so much as a feeling of having done something together, apart from a mere exchange of ideas, however congenial. Even so, this slight sign that her father now might lift the mental sanctions which he had applied to François and see him as she was seeing him, was almost too much for her.

The stimulus indeed was so great that for once she sat and ate in silence, not listening to the conversation but watching, as one watches the faces of actors in a theatre, the expressions of the men as they talked, obviously finding in the wise way of children and primitive people, that the look in the human eye ultimately says far more than any words devised by the most articulate of men. So unusual was her silence that Sir James misinterpreted it, and reproached her for having done too much by going on the long excursion to the river and tiring herself unnecessarily.

This reproach only increased Amelia's criticism of her employer. To her, it was further evidence of how much Sir James still had to learn about her sex, provided he still had it in him to learn, which she was inclined to doubt. For her, the meaning of the silence could not have been plainer. Already she was beginning to believe that the most difficult moment of all in her relationship with Luciana was approaching, when, as she put it to herself, even the horse which had figured so prominently in her early morning soliloquy, would be put permanently out to grass in the young girl's spirit, and only its rider would be left in the centre of a storm of fantasy.

But the greatest surprise of all came towards the end of the meal. Sir James was pressing Mopani to more Stilton, Bath olivers and coffee. Mopani, whom François thought had just about as great a natural sense of the importance of good manners as 'Bamuthi, declined politely, explaining that if they were to get to Hunter's Drift before Sir James and his party, he and François should really be on their way.

François's surprise was great and he certainly showed it. For Sir James had been so lively, dominating the conversation at table almost as if he was once more in the cuddy of one of Her Majesty's ships, that Mopani had not had a chance to tell François of the plan which he and Sir James had made. This was that they should hasten to Mopani's camp in order to telephone the Government in the capital. For the message which Mopani had brought was an urgent summons requesting Sir James's immediate return to London to head a Royal Commission appointed to examine aid for what were now called the developing countries in Africa. The summons could not have come at a more inconvenient moment from Sir James's point of view. Yet he would not have been so successful in his career if he had not, in a sense, been born to it. Although he would go through all the motions of asking for more information about the appointment offered to him, he already knew instinctively that he would be compelled to accept it.

So, at Mopani's suggestion, he was going to leave Amelia and his daughter at Hunter's Drift for the three or four days that it would take him to travel to Mopani's camp and back.

Seeing François's surprise, Mopani, now somewhat aggrieved that the news had had to be broken in this way, immediately apologized for not first telling him of the arrangement. Happily the look on François's face made any explanation of how much he welcomed the decision superfluous. But the most unexpected reaction of all came from Luciana. She jumped from her chair, skipped round the table and stopping beside François's chair said in a bright, clear and rather bird-like voice, 'Oh go-go-go-away! Go away!' She laughed unashamedly, certain that François would understand even if no one else did. And that was all that mattered.

But Sir James took her outburst literally and reproved her sharply, 'Attention Chisai, attention! You must be very tired to speak like that to one of our guests.'

Unabashed, she came to attention, giving him a mock salute and saying, 'Aye-aye sir.'

To François, the time between the arrival of Sir James, Amelia and Luciana at Hunter's Drift that evening and the return of Sir James and Mopani three and a half days later, passed far too quickly. Although he rose early on the morning after the arrival of his guests, to make certain that Mopani and Sir James had a proper breakfast before they left on their journey, he found Luciana already in the kitchen helping Ousie-Johanna, while Amelia, serene and august, was in Ousie-Johanna's place of honour at the head of the table with a large pot of coffee to herself. Her state of mind about her Luciana seemed to have changed, for she showed no trace of concern now in the fact that Luciana was darting around in the kitchen in her pyjamas.

The moment François walked in, Luciana, without bothering

to say 'Good morning' announced, as if it were a message of the greatest importance, 'Do you know, your Ousie's calling me Nonnie, too?'

François, feeling that if Ousie-Johanna had not done just that, he would have been compelled to remonstrate over such a lack of good manners (since 'little mistress' was the polite form of address for her in the circumstances), merely answered, 'I should hope so!'

Disappointed that he apparently did not see how significant it was for her, she could only gape at him and exclaim, 'Oh!'

She may even have stayed abashed for a full minute, were she not feeling far too happy to let anything distress her. So she quickly said what a pity it was that she couldn't speak Ousie-Johanna's language, because she was certain that the 'Lady of the Kitchen' was trying to tell her things of the greatest interest.

François explained all this faithfully to Ousie-Johanna whose cup of joy, already full by having Amelia at the head of her table, flowed over at such amply merited appreciation of her experience and wisdom. Tears came to her eyes and she asked François, 'Please tell the Little old Nonnie that I was merely explaining to her how important it was to know exactly how to pour coffee into a pot. It is not only a question of having the pot hot first but of getting the right amount into it. Now take your Lammie. We all know she is no fool, but you know it is impossible to get her to get a pint of coffee into that pot. It takes experience to do it and in this house, I am the only one who has ever been able to do so.'

François explained this to Luciana and took the precaution of saying, 'You must please be careful not to laugh. And look properly impressed. She was trying to tell you that she is the only person who can get a pint of coffee into that pot which will not hold a pint for anybody else. But really she has no idea what a pint is.'

Ousie-Johanna, thus encouraged, told him to tell Nonnie that she must not worry about her father going off with Mopani. 'Tell her, please,' she begged François, 'that Mopani will take good care of her father. He has more backbone in his little finger than most people have in the whole of their hand ... And tell her that the moment I have done breakfast, I'll pray for them and play "God be with you till we meet again" on the gramophone.'

François, after another precautionary warning to Nonnie, translated word for word what she had said. Somehow, sharing these secret sources of amusement added immeasurably to François's and Nonnie's relationship.

During the whole of the period that Sir James and Mopani were absent François felt his duties as a host justified him in suspending his own schooling. Every morning after breakfast, before the heat of the day, he would set out with Nonnie to show her some of the many things in the bush that were dear to him. He did this not on horseback as Nonnie, if consulted, perhaps might have preferred, but on foot. For him, going on foot out into the bush with Hintza was by far the best way of discovering the world of the small, the shy and the defenceless, which were for him the true glory of his world. It was all part of the Bushman concept of things that his beloved Old Koba had, for good or ill, induced in him, so that the importance of the small mattered far more to him than the physically great. Old Koba had had charge of François's imagination for the first nine years of his life, and in one profound aspect of himself, she had transformed him into a Bushman. That is one of the many complex reasons why the coming of Xhabbo had meant so much to him. And it was like an inspired Bushman that he took Nonnie on excursions to see the secret life of the bush. He never thought of her now as Luciana. He was, indeed, so surprised when somebody called her by that name that he would look around him as if for a stranger.

On their first excursion he had some opposition from Amelia to overcome, and he might not have been successful had not Ousie-Johanna come to his support. Although Ousie-Johanna and Amelia had hardly a dozen words in common, painfully coined, they had acquired an impressive Esperanto of noises, looks and gestures more meaningful, immediate and satisfying than any fragmentary exchange of words could have been.

Despite the acute anxieties Ousie-Johanna had suffered on François's account in the past, she secretly had the utmost confidence in him as a hunter and woodsman. Also it was only natural to her that François and Nonnie, like all the young of her own and 'Bamuthi's people, should go out into the bush to enjoy themselves, like those she had known in the far south, where all the young were allowed to swim and play freely in the blue Indian Ocean.

Significantly enough, Amelia's greatest worry appeared to be that on these excursions François took Luciana on foot. Seeing the three of them, Hintza in the lead, then François and finally Luciana, vanishing into that great bush, was almost too much for her. For one thing the bush was always so disquieting, murmuring and whispering, its green, copper and burnished leaves quivering and trembling, sun-shattering and light-tapping, even in the airless hours of day as if they were registering the beat of the heart of a hidden, powerful and potentially antagonistic force. That alone frightened her. Then at heart she was always homesick for one of those little Portuguese towns which, remembered even in exile, pre-suppose a tranquil square, a small bandstand in the centre, music at night-fall and the smell of scarlet geraniums heavy on the air to invest it, as it were, with incense for the communion of man at the end of a day of labour with the sanctity of starry and God-like nights.

Also it was for her the final proof that the great innocent epoch of horses had for ever come to an end. Now, for good or ill, Luciana was at the frontier of the enigmatic age of man, where heart and mind have to dismount inwardly and go on foot, slowly, step by step, into the unknown future. No governess could give assistance. Only life and always (here she would cross herself very quickly) such guidance as the Church and the saints in Heaven had provided could protect them. But since the massacre, although Amelia would have been the last person to admit it, her belief in such guidance was no longer what once it had been.

This reasoning, which was not thought but pure peasant intuition was so profound that, after arguing in vain against François's first excursion when she saw them all vanishing into the bush, she burst into tears. Quickly she was taken into Ousie-Johanna's arms, and later consoled by coffee and fluffy buns. When in doubt, Ousie-Johanna firmly believed, food and drink came first, and then prayer and song.

Meanwhile, François and Luciana, with Hintza as their new

frontier scout, would move from bush to river, river to hill and back from the hill to the river again, seeing life in a new way that was a reading of that first magic saga that is called nature.

François, of course, longed for nothing more then than to take Nonnie to Xhabbo's cave. He would have liked to have made it their first excursion because he had a feeling that she was another vital part of the development in his life started by the coming of Xhabbo. In fact he came very near to doing so, so near that, when alone in his room on the night after their first outing, the thought of how he had nearly betrayed Xhabbo's secret made him extremely uneasy.

It had happened when they were walking out into the sparkling morning, still some distance from the bush. Nonnie seemed to have taken to the way of Matabele women, walking naturally behind the male and carrying on a conversation without expecting François to turn round as she spoke.

François, who in the past had had trouble with European visitors on such occasions, was considerably impressed by this fact. He himself, of course, was accustomed to carrying on conversations under these circumstances without for a minute taking his eyes off the trail ahead. But the fact that a newcomer like Nonnie could do this naturally from the first moment, struck him as so remarkable that when a moment came for him to call Hintza back and he had to kneel down beside his dog to give him some instructions in Bushman, he could not resist adding, 'Do your best Hin, because you know, she's one of us.'

He had hardly finished his exhortation to Hintza when, from behind him, he heard Nonnie say: 'You told me you'd done some terribly wild things, so awful that you've frightened everybody at home. You promised to tell me. Please tell me now, what's the worst thing you've ever done?'

Of course, the most striking example was his adventure with Xhabbo, and the request filled him immediately with acute tension between his growing desire to share everything with Nonnie and also to keep faith with Xhabbo.

For a moment he walked on silently, until Nonnie begged again from behind: 'Oh, do tell me. People aren't real friends until they share all one another's secrets, are they? Besides, I feel a friend is only a friend if you're sure you *could* do something wicked with them, not that you would necessarily *want* to.'

This last observation so troubled the Calvinist sediment in François that he had another source of tension to add to a struggle that was already great enough. Yet he managed to reply with deliberation: 'I'd love to tell you about the wildest thing I've done, and I promise you I'll do so one day. But I don't think I can now, because it's a secret I share with someone else.'

The words 'someone else' sparked off such a fire of jealousy in Luciana that she herself was surprised. It was a good thing that François could not see the expression of anger that made her eyes brighter than ever, although the tone of her voice was uncompromising enough as she said: 'Oh very well. When she's been good enough to give you her permission to tell me what it is I may be prepared to listen.'

'She?' François exclaimed, surprised. 'There's no she about it. It's something I share with a young man whom you don't know. I gave him my word of honour that I'd not reveal it to anybody else. It's a very exciting secret but until I've asked him I can't tell a soul about it.'

Nonnie immediately was ashamed of her involuntary reaction and said quickly, 'Of course you can't break your word. But will you ask him tonight and tell me tomorrow? I can hardly bear to wait.'

François shook his head at the bush and the trail ahead. All the longing he had to see Xhabbo again as soon as possible made his voice forlorn and low, as he answered, 'I'm afraid I can't ask him tonight. I'm afraid at this moment he's very far away from here and probably in great danger. I really don't know when, if ever, I shall see him again. But until I have seen him, or know that he's dead, I can't tell even you.'

Touched by François's tone and reassured now that she knew that it was a man and not a woman who had extracted this pledge of secrecy, Nonnie wanted to console him immediately. 'Don't worry,' she said quickly, 'I'm certain your friend will be back. Then the moment he is, you must please let us meet and you both can tell me the secret. And by that time you'll know that there's nobody who's better at keeping secrets than I am, even from Amelia. I can't tell you how I love having secrets to share and I've never shared one with a boy before. But surely you can at least tell me his name? And his age ... how old is he?'

François repeated his promise to tell her when he could but concluded defensively, 'I'm afraid I can't even tell you his name because that would give the whole show away.'

François could not have been more grateful when all she said was, 'Gosh, I think it must be the greatest secret ever. I don't know how I'm going to wait until you tell me!'

François would have been even more impressed had he realized that all this air of gay acceptance had not been achieved without a struggle. The fact that once more he had totally ignored in her remarks the importance she attached to age dismayed her afresh. 'Why, oh why doesn't he seem to want to know how old I am?' her heart implored her reason, 'I've given him scores of hints and he's just done nothing at all about them. I don't think he can be really interested if he doesn't care how old I am.'

As a result she heard François say, as from a great distance, 'But I'll show you something very secret in a few minutes if you promise to keep as quiet as possible please. I'll show you a real, high-class baboon finishing school.'

Nonnie may have preferred to start her initiation into the mysteries of the bush with something more glamorous than baboons. But, by the time she had accompanied François and Hintza to the edge of a deep, natural theatre sunk into the summit of one of the rocky hills in the bush, and spent an hour or more lying flat on her stomach close beside François and Hintza, watching a great family of baboons teaching their young how to behave, she could not have been more delighted.

François himself was rather proud of the skill with which he and Hintza had brought her without being seen. They had crawled into position despite the fact that the baboons, on this happy day, while they played and taught, had confided the vital duty of keeping watch on the bush to the greatest of their elder statesmen.

François knew him well. He was at the centre of one of François's first clear animal memories. There was not a moment when he had not been to François's recollection a great power in the land of baboons. He had aged, and François, lying there as observant as he had ever been, could clearly see how his auburn hair had gone white at the black temples. But his authority was greater than ever. He sat there on his haunches, high on the rock above the din of the other baboons below, as if he were a baboon Buddha, calmly and serenely surveying the floating world of leaves below him, utterly encircled in a long-term view of life and fate.

'Look!' – François nudged Nonnie with his elbow as he whispered, 'You've been greatly honoured. Adonis himself has turned up to preside in person over this passing-out ceremony of the young in the academy down there.'

'Adonis?' Nonnie asked, putting her head closer to his to hear his whisper. 'You call him Adonis? Surely Adonis was the most beautiful person? I'd hardly call that old brute beautiful.'

It hurt François to have the old baboon referred to as a brute. But it was not unexpected. He had often suffered from people who had this prejudiced reaction to the creatures of the bush. As far as he was concerned, the greatest 'brutes' he had ever known had been the humans who came on safari tours to shoot and kill those same animals. They were the same people too who had killed Ouwa by 'the turning of their backs'.

He drew back from the thought and hastened to explain the name to Nonnie.

'You're right to find it funny,' he whispered. 'The name was meant to be funny in the beginning. It was what my father always called "a name given ironically" to male baboons by our early ancestors in Africa. We have been calling all the greatest male baboons Adonis for more than three hundred years now. But it's no longer a joke. When you live as close to baboons as we do here in the bush, you come to know and see them from a baboon's point of view. Soon you realize that the old fellow you found so ugly is really a very beautiful baboon man.'

He was so grave that Nonnie felt herself so corrected. Nevertheless she teased him a little to restore the balance between them. 'You're talking almost like a baboon yourself. Why, now that I think of it, you could even *be* an honorary baboon!'

The idea so pleased her that she was ready for laughter. But François spoilt her amusement by taking it all seriously.

406

He replied: 'You'd be surprised how great a sense of dignity as well as beauty these Adonises have ... Look at that young one down there and you'll see him beating up that young fellow for playing pranks on him. Look. You'll realize how wise it is to treat them with great respect and even flatter them. You know, 'Bamuthi himself will not pass them in the bush when he knows they've seen him without giving them the royal Matabele salute and calling: "I see you, great and most excellent baboons. Oh, I have seen you." But look there!'

François was pointing out a fine, upstanding young baboon belabouring a youngster with his fists and nipping him smartly with his teeth.

All this, combined with the many curious happenings in the scene below her, was tempting Nonnie to explode again into laughter. But the authority with which François spoke restrained her. François from the start had impressed them all as being an unusual mixture of youth and experience; innocence and maturity. Yet none of it could be compared with the natural authority which invested him here in his own element in the bush.

So instinctively Nonnie accepted it and obeyed characteristically, making a face at him as she did so, whispering, 'I see you, most excellent baboon. I see you and I hear.'

She wriggled closer to him and listened with growing fascination to his account of why he had never thought of baboons as mere animals but always, as his own nurse Old Koba had taught him, 'The People who sit on their Heels'. He told her of their great natural intelligence, their capacity for reasoning, for remembering the past, linking it with the present and behaving in the present out of their experience of the past with forethought of the future.

He surprised her by telling her that he thought that they, rather than the lion, leopard, elephant or buffalo, were the truly heroic people of the bush. They were the bravest of all because they knew so acutely what fear was. Once one looked at baboons in that way, and treated them always with respect, there came occasions when they themselves could look straight into the human eye without fear or enmity, and one saw in those hazel eyes, dark with antiquity, a glimmer of awareness of how much nearer they were to one than any of the other animals of Africa. They themselves were highly sensitive in regard to this element of human dignity which they possessed and were therefore easily hurt in their feelings. So that it was not just ironical but extremely wise to call them Adonis and to go on thinking of them as possessed of Adonis-like qualities.

Indeed they were so human, François stressed, that one of his most terrible memories was of the early years at Hunter's Drift when they were forced to shoot the baboons who would not leave off raiding their gardens and could be taught only through war. Everybody was extremely distressed then because the wounded and dying baboons made noises exactly like wounded human beings and seemed to die like real people. He could not think of anything more horrible than having to shoot at a baboon himself and he was certain that when old Adonis on that rock up there died, the world round about Hunter's Drift would look singularly empty.

He glanced sideways at her to see if this all-important fact had been noted and found that she was staring at him instead of at the scene below. He took it as a sign that she was absorbed in listening and prepared to continue, but something in her eyes made him wary of her. He continued to speak but her eyes appeared concentrated on his face. He could not know that his face and quick changing expressions as he talked had become matters of all-consuming importance to her, far more important than the baboons and their school.

'Why Nonnie,' he exclaimed, 'I believe you've not been listening to a word I've said. You're not the least bit interested in the baboons down there.'

Ashamed, she came out of the centre of her world to join him in the present, instantly contrite and reassuring. 'Oh, please. I've not missed a single word . . . I've never been so interested in my life or enjoyed myself so much . . . Please carry on, comrade baboon!'

Reassured, François urged her: 'If you don't perhaps believe what I was saying about the baboons being brainy, just look down below. They're teaching their young ones there how to count.'

Nonnie, however reluctantly, looked as directed. Believe it or not, a number of father baboons were sitting in front of their young with fistfuls of pebbles from which they took one pebble at a time to place it in front of the youngsters: one, two, three at a time, and then taking the pebbles away again: three, two, one, until the earth in front of them was bare again. At each stage of the demonstration they made a different clicking noise to go with it. When a youngster failed to reply with the corresponding noise, the fathers would take them by their necks, whip them round and beat them with their fists until they were shrieking just like children.

'But why only three pebbles?' Nonnie asked.

'Because,' François answered, 'they can only count up to three. That's the difference between their brain and yours. Everything over three is, to them, as you will hear if you listen, "a hell of a lot".'

And indeed from down below, when the stage of more than three pebbles was demonstrated, came a chorus sounding very much like an orchestration of: 'a hell of a lot'.

Meanwhile, in other parts of the school, some other young baboons were corrected for having tried to cross the path of their elders and betters, the correction again taking the form of more spankings. At the farthest corner two young female baboons were watching exactly how baby baboons should be spruced up and fed by their mothers, and above all how important it was to see that they were adequately de-flead and de-loused.

According to Mopani, François said at that point, learned scientists who knew only baboons in Zoos claimed that this was not an unselfish action on the part of the baboons. The scientists held that they were not disinterested but did it meticulously all day long purely in order to gather specks of much needed salt left in the coats of their fellow baboons in dried-up sweat. But that, Mopani had told François bitterly, was typical of the way scientists tried to reduce human beings as well as animals to something less than they were in actual living fact. One could not live with baboons as close neighbours in the bush without knowing they had what Ouwa had called, 'the highly developed social conscience of the baboons'.

He wished that Nonnie could have seen, as he had on a few

rare occasions, how baboons could die for one another. For instance, the worst enemy of the baboons was the leopard. Twice he had seen leopards pouncing on unsuspecting young baboons who had 'strayed too far from their fellows. The leopards had dragged them off screaming into the trees but old Adonis had immediately rallied all his grown-up followers with a series of the most exciting and manly barks François had ever heard. What was so impressive, he said, was that the baboons had responded and come to him immediately although they were obviously terribly frightened and wanting to do nothing more than run away to save their own skins. Yet despite all, with old Adonis in charge, they had charged after the leopards screaming in voices that were a most moving mixture of fear and courage. He had stalked after them to find them surrounding the leopards, screaming insults at them, barking at them, dashing in to snatch at their heels, thus forcing them finally to turn round in all directions so fast and so often that, dazed and bewildered, they had dropped their victims and allowed themselves to be driven away into the undergrowth. But unhappily, not before three of the baboons were dying, moaning in a most human way from terrible wounds.

There was only one fear which they seemed incapable of mastering, a fear with which he, François, sympathized deeply, and that was their fear of snakes. When they came across snakes they seemed to lose all control of their senses. For instance, he had seen old Adonis himself sitting on that very rock where he was sitting now, unaware of the fact that because it was such a hot place in the sun, an enormous copper-coloured Cape cobra had uncoiled itself at the foot of the rock to warm itself in the sun. The cobra and baboon had sunned themselves happily, unaware of each other's presence, until some noise in the vicinity disturbed them both and the cobra swiftly threw itself up some seven feet into the air, eyes glittering, tongue flickering and its broad hood fully expanded to see what might be threatening it. With all that uncoiling and flashing of superb movement, the copper body lassooing the sunlight, old Adonis's eyes were drawn downwards. The moment they recognized the cobra, a great cry of despair broke from him, sounding exactly like 'Oh God!' in Dutch, and he fell from the rock to land on the earth just beside the cobra. Fortunately the cobra was so alarmed by this descent of a god from Heaven that it shot away sideways into the thorns.

François broke off, feeling really carried away by the tale. He glanced sideways quickly, so quickly that Nonnie only just had time to look down at the baboons below.

She managed to exclaim however: 'I wish I'd been with you to see it too. But how clever of you to discover such a wonderful place. It must have been awfully difficult to find, wasn't it?'

Reassured, François explained how for years, even at Hunter's Drift, each morning punctually at half past ten he had heard from far off the pitiful sound of young baboons wailing, sobbing and crying. Whenever he asked 'Bamuthi and the others what this sound meant, they would just shrug their shoulders and answer with indifference that it was merely the baboons as usual punishing their young and teaching them how to behave. Pressed, they would add that the moment the sun showed above the bush, the baboons would come down from cliffs and tree-tops to look for food in the cool of the morning. Once they had had their breakfast they would set about educating their young before it got too hot for thought. When that was done, they would find a sheltered place for their siesta during the dead hour of the day, leaving a proven citizen on guard, as Adonis was just then. Then, in the afternoon they would go out again for more food and get back into the trees and cliff-tops well before dark.

When François had asked them if anyone had ever been to look at them, the Matabele had always said disdainfully, implying they had better things to do: 'We are not *Baghatla* [Men-of-the-Baboon] that such matters should be of any concern to us.'

And there the matter had rested until a day came when François was out on his own in the bush, and this sound of whimpering had broken out very close to him. After that it had been just a question of stalking patiently in the direction of the sound, to arrive at the very place where they were now lying. From that time he had come regularly to watch the baboons. It was a favourite pastime and taught him more about the baboons and life in the bush than any book he had ever read.

411

At this point François saw that old Adonis was suddenly extremely restless. He was taking funny little jumps straight up into the air, in order to be able to look down from a greater height in their direction. Between each jump he would sit down, still staring hard, and bring his long black arm and delicate wrist to arch over his greying hair while he scratched his head with one long black finger, just like an old Matabele counsellor confronted by a grave and problematical affair of state.

At first François hoped this was just one of Adonis's routine precautions. But when Adonis did it four times and each time strained his eyes at the fringe of the bush where they lay, he feared something was giving them away. He re-examined the place where they lay and was about to conclude that nothing could possibly be wrong, and that all they had to do was to keep still, when he noticed that a shaft of sunlight, now striking through the bushes among which they were lying, had found Nonnie's left hand and the little gold signet ring which she wore on her finger. Then, of course, he knew that it must be this sparkle in the shadows which had drawn old Adonis's attention to them and that it was only a matter of moments now before he would take action.

He arrived at this conclusion just as Adonis took the highest leap of all and then, most ominously, did not go back to sitting on his haunches but returned to walking up and down the high sentinel cliff, never for a moment taking his eyes from their hiding place.

'I'm afraid he knows now that something strange is here,' François informed Nonnie. 'So I'll have to show Hin and myself to him, or he'll come over and investigate, and that could have unpleasant consequences for all of us. I don't want to have to shoot any of them.'

'Can't we quietly go away?' Nonnie asked.

'I fear that won't do now,' François replied. 'I don't want to spoil this place for them and that is precisely what might happen if we just run away and leave it to their imaginations. That way they'll certainly come to all the wrong conclusions, and abandon this place altogether. They might think the leopards are back on their track again. No, Hin and I will have to show ourselves to them openly.'

'Can't I show myself too?' Nonnie pleaded.

'No,' François answered, rather severely and abruptly she thought, not realizing that it was only because he himself was tense with need for speed. 'He doesn't know you. You just go on lying there and please, please tuck that little finger with the ring on it under your bush jacket, because it's that that has given us away. And keep as still as you can.'

François took it utterly for granted that Nonnie would do as he told her. He didn't even look to see that she did. He just called Hintza softly to come to him and rose slowly to his feet. With his gun at the trail and Hintza beside him he stepped leisurely out on to his rim of the theatre, in full view of Adonis and all the enormous gathering of baboons below.

From the theatre came the sound of a hundred and more baboons whisking into position to stare, alarmed, at the intruders. Then the day went completely silent. Old Adonis stopped in the middle of his sideways-walk and turned about, facing François with only the dip in the ridge and a space of some thirty yards between the two of them. For a moment François thought he was too late and that Adonis would let out his great war bark which always precedes attack. So quickly and calmly, a difficult combination which only his natural reflexes, conditioned to that end by 'Bamuthi and Mopani's training, could achieve, he raised his hand high above his head and called out part of the traditional greeting old Koba had taught him. The Bushman clicks of the consonants crackled like electricity on the still noonday air, 'I saw you looming up from afar, oh you man there who sits on his heels.'

Hard on that he commanded Hintza in Bushman, 'The grandfather greeting, Hin . . . quick. The grandfather greeting.'

Hintza immediately obeyed. He stepped out beside François, the sun a ridge of flame on his healthy tawny coat, aligned his long, elastic body on Adonis, and then stretched out both long front legs forward together as far as they would go and bent down towards the great baboon, so that his head and jaw were level with the ground.

Nonnie watched all this in apprehension. But suddenly the tension went out of the situation and she was amazed to see old Adonis go slack with relief and hear a couple of barks, great and round though not unfriendly, come from him, sounding very much like a gruff, 'Oh, it's only the pair of you again. Well, how do you do?'

She realized he had recognized François and Hintza, not surprisingly since he must have seen them a hundred and one times together in the bush. After waving an authoritative hand at the gathering below, as if to indicate, 'Now get on with your schooling. It's getting hotter by the minute', he behaved as if the matter were of no further account.

François, followed by Hintza, then retreated into the cover of the brush, knelt beside Nonnie and asked her to crawl backwards with him until their heads were well below the rim of the theatre. As he helped her on to her feet later he said with obvious relief, 'Phew! Yes-no, as Mopani would say, that was *darem* a near thing. Thank goodness we can behave normally again.'

He would have set off immediately for home, had not Nonnie rushed at Hintza and put her arms round his neck. 'Oh Hin,' she fussed over him, 'whoever taught you to curtsy so beautifully? You're certainly the most wonderful dog ever. I wish I could curtsy half as well.'

François, who knew that Hintza, in his heart of hearts, felt it just a little beneath his dignity to curtsy to baboons when he gave only one royal paw to the far superior human beings of his world, thought it most understanding of Nonnie to help restore Hintza's self-respect. He thanked her and explained, 'You know, poor old Hin rather resents having to kow-tow to anyone or anything, particularly baboons. He believes a little bit as you do, that they're not at all as beautiful and wonderful as they themselves think; that they're inclined to give themselves unnecessary airs and be far too pretentious and too fond of playing tricks. But *that* will make him really feel a good deal better, and more inclined to curtsy in future.'

Nonnie immediately rallied to the defence of Hintza, declaring passionately, 'Oh, I think you're being most unfair! I don't think that curtsy of his was at all unwilling or could have been bettered. I'm certain he did his utmost, didn't you Hin?'

Hintza with all this became so obsequious that François could not help saying, half in earnest but with one of his rare smiles,

'I do believe Hin, you've forsaken me and come to prefer Nonnie.' Both Nonnie and Hintza answered him with glances full, dark and wide with reproach. Hintza, indeed, had a subtle suggestion in the eyes implying that not only had he understood but also that he found François's observation completely illogical. 'What's the difference?' his look asked. 'Sure, if I love one, I must love the other one as much, or would you want me to lead a dog's life for ever, torn between the two of you?'

The episode of the baboons is perhaps the most complex example of the secret life of his world which François shared with Nonnie during that too brief period at Hunter's Drift. There were many others, slight, fragmentary and apparently isolated. Yet in the final count all joined together to form a single experience which glowed in Nonnie's spirit like the colourful detail of one of those great French medieval tapestries of *La Grande Chasse* which Nonnie had seen with her mother in the museums of Paris. These, too, had been seen as in a dream through the dark woods and opaque forests of an oblivious Europe long before its great awakening from an age of darkness.

There was, too, the occasion when they came across the hunting spider. Spiders normally frightened Nonnie. Yet in François's company on a track in the bush, with the grass and the leaves around them all mother-of-pearl with dew and the opal dawn, she actually found the spider beautiful. François, as usual in front, stopped and beckoned her to his side to whisper, 'Look there.'

She came up quickly, but in the densely camouflaged bush at first saw nothing.

'Can't you see?' François whispered.

Dismayed, Nonnie shook her head, certain that she had missed something stupendous.

Then she heard him put a name to the creature, 'A trapdoor spider.'

With a great effort she managed to see it at last; a hunting spider, spread out ready for the sun beside its home. The spider was still and its long legs silver with dew. Its body was centred upon them, sparkling like an Indian ruby. It was brilliant in that prismatic first light of morning. For the moment she forgot, indeed, that it was a spider. Willingly she obeyed François's suggestion to stand still and not to move because the vibrations of the ground under their feet, however silently they moved, might make the spider vanish.

'Look just beyond it and you'll see its home,' François told her.

She looked, and there, near by in the bare earth, was what looked like a miniature man-hole with a round cover raised on a hinge straight above it. Only this cover was not made of metal but appeared to be of some soft mauve material which glowed like raw silk. At that moment the day exploded into sunlight, and a bright shaft splintered on the track beside them, so that she could look into the hole itself. To her amazement it appeared to be lined with velvet. She had never seen anything made by human hand and needle that looked so neat, well-chosen and well fitting. The science, cunning, and the sheer perfection of it impressed her far more than the baboons. She was sorry therefore when François announced: 'Now watch. You'll see how carefully this little Red-Riding Hood locks her door after her.'

With that François gently rustled the grass beside the spider. For all its inert appearance, the spider at once shot sideways into its hole with such speed that Luciana's eyes could barely follow it. At one minute it had been there like a jewel: the next, it had gone down that close-fitting cylinder of velvet, the lid pulled down on top of it with such force that a tiny trace of dust stood in the track to mark the place where it had disappeared. Without that pool of light and dust smoking in the track, she would not have known where the spider lived, because the uppermost part of that beautifully silk-lined lid was made of dried mud, looking exactly like the rest of the ground around it.

She found herself holding her breath, overcome by the weight of the mystery of things pressing upon her. For the first time, perhaps, she fully understood François's deference, if not reverence, for the life of the bush, which perhaps, not surprisingly with her metropolitan background, had at times appeared exaggerated. Standing there with the day exploding in flame and dew-smoke around them, the coming of light welcomed by a

416

bird-hymn of glittering intensity and volume, the mysteries of life acquired new dimensions. It was no longer confined to sky and bush where she could eagerly acknowledge it, but was suddenly shown to be also deep in the darkness of the earth out of which that little spider had issued as an ambassador of another world. Yet all belonged together as did also both she and François.

So great and sudden was the extension of awareness and so vast the view disclosed that she was apprehensive, and in order to stifle her fear, she resorted to the next best thing. Her eyes on the place where the spider had vanished, she raised her hand as François had raised his to Adonis. In an almost joking manner that sometimes comes to people who are fearfully in earnest she called, 'Oh brave and most excellent little housekeeper. I have seen you and I greet you.'

Quickly, still keeping her face averted from François for she was shy of what he might see in her eyes just then, she tried to speak normally, 'Oh blast! I would never have thought I could find anything so revolting as a spider quite so beautiful.'

The frontiersman in François was still young enough to recognize the moment when others arrived at a new frontier in themselves. He understood what was happening to Nonnie better than she could possibly realize because he had been at just such a place inside himself many times before, and was beginning to know the predicament well. At such moments he knew how much it helped him to recall those who had been there before him.

Therefore he told her quietly: 'You know, Old Koba told me that the People of the Early Race claimed that they owed the first light in the darkness of the beginning to a female spider. Tonight I will show you the place in the Milky Way where they say she went to sit, and still weaves a great web to catch the light hiding in darkness and to force it to shine so that the people on earth can see the way they had to go. It is the place in the Milky Way which my father's books on astronomy say is known popularly by many other names, such as the "Entrance to Hell" or the "Coal Sack" and so on. But, according to Old Koba, it's just a vast female spider sitting there, for ever spinning and re-spinning her web in order to catch all that light that we see in what is to us just a terrifyingly empty black hole in the sky. You know, Old Koba always used to say that there was nothing on earth that you cannot find in the sky; and nothing in the sky above that cannot be found below on earth.'

Then there were their experiences with birds. In general, they were important not only because of the delight they gave Nonnie but because of the revelation that they were really the greatest and most passionate interest among François's overwhelming range of interests in the life of the bush. She discovered that to him they were miracles. He always spoke of them as if he had just come across them for the first time. He must have introduced her in those three lightning-swift days to a hundred or more different kinds of birds, whose names, even when presented prosaically as names in a catalogue, read like a paraphrase of a sonnet composed in honour of all the joy that went on wing through the bush. There were glossy, plum-coloured, red-winged and wattled starlings, blue Ethiopian rollers, golden and black-headed orioles; copper, bronze, dusky, scarlet-throated, olive, malachite, double-collared and purple-banded sun birds and broad-tailed and grey-throated paradise fly catchers. Thert were scarlet and gold parakeets, scores of larks and multi-coloured finches, dozens of different thrush-bush warblers, each with an oratorio of its own in its throat, honey-guides and kingfishers, bar-throated and yellow apalises, 'court singers' and gorgeous bush-shrikes, Angola and Kalahari tits, buff-streaked and mocking chats, each without exception with a separate voice, theme and colour scheme.

Two experiences, however, need conversion from the general to the particular, because of the special impact they made on Nonnie and the significance they possessed for François. Strangely enough they were connected perhaps with the drabbest-looking birds of all. The first was a strange little grey bird. François said he had not yet found a scientific name for it because in none of his books on African birds did it even appear. He knew it only by its Sindabele name, the Isala bird.

This little bird announced itself in the most mournful voice Nonnie had ever heard. They were resting in the shade of a wild fig tree when suddenly the Isala bird called out from a clump of thorn close by. The sound was so bleak and devastating that

418

Nonnie cried in alarm, 'What on earth is the matter? Why does that bird sound so sad, as if everything had gone wrong for it?'

This brought a smile to François which Nonnie misunderstood and she protested, 'I don't think it's anything to smile about, Master François.'

'It was only your use of the word "wrong" that made me smile, I promise,' François answered quickly. ' "Wrong" is the key-note of that little fellow's call,' he continued. 'It has only one tune and one message. No matter where it goes or where you find it in the bush, it always sings, "Oh wro-ong, wro-ong, wro-ong, so, so wrong." It's the bird 'Bamuthi calls Isala but I call the Conscience Bird.'

'Conscience bird?'

'Yes,' François reaffirmed. 'Isala is a Sindabele word for a decoration of feathers Matabele women used to wear on their heads. They have a legend that a greedy and evil Sindabele man once murdered a woman whom he met on an isolated track for her possessions. The Isala of feathers on her head fell to the ground and immediately turned into that little bird. Wherever he went from then on the bird appeared at odd moments on the way in front of him, crying, "Oh wro-ong, wro-ong, wro-ong, so – so – wrong." He trapped and killed it and buried it deep many times, but it just resurrected itself and reappeared like this. At last people began to wonder why he was haunted by a bird like this, made inquiries, discovered his crime and punished him for it. Ever since then, they say that wherever a man or woman goes through the bush, not necessarily having done anything bad, but with what the Matabele call "black thoughts" in their hearts, this bird appears and warns them with that call. I've seen a whole Matabele kraal terribly shaken by the intrusion of that little bird in their lives.'

Nonnie asked logically, 'D'you think either of us have done anything wrong, or are thinking of it, that this bird should put itself in our way and draw our attention to it?'

She had no sooner asked than she regretted the question because François answered rather forlornly, 'Not you Nonnie, but it could be me.'

'I'm certain it couldn't be you!' was her robust response. 'You've never done anything wrong, or could be thinking of doing anything wrong for that horrid little bird to accuse you of it.'

'No,' François persisted, 'I'm afraid it could be me.'

'But why?' she asked, puzzled and unbelieving.

'I'm afraid I can't tell you exactly why. But I think it's got something to do with that secret I've promised to tell you one day.'

'Oh nonsense,' Nonnie answered with immense scorn, 'the only thing wrong about that secret is that you haven't shared it with me yet, and the sooner you do that the better it will be.'

Her protestation was spontaneous and clear-cut with anger, and it had an immediate effect on François. But it was not soon enough to prevent her taking, from that moment on, an extreme dislike to the bird, and to compel her, whenever they heard it, to answer it, first by sticking out her tongue at it and then loudly imitating the go-away bird, ordering it, 'Oh-go-go-go-away!' The strange thing was that invariably her method worked and promptly the Isala bird would spread its wings and fly away.

The other experience was the encounter with a very rare form of dust-buff African partridge with legs in red hose and feet in yellow running shoes, which is known as francolin. Nonnie and François had flushed many of its kind from the brush in their comings and goings in the bush, but this one was remarkable because it refused to be flushed.

They would not have discovered it at all had it not been for Hintza, who had a 'thing' about birds. It was not that he disliked them, but one suspects that he secretly envied them, feeling that if any form of life on earth really deserved wings it was the species of dog in general and the breed to which he belonged in particular. Perhaps he took a particular delight, therefore, in seeing birds earth-bound and, as it were, in his own dimension, so that he could exploit the situation, rushing at them not with any intention to kill but forcing them into the sky as if to say, 'You've got quite enough space of your own up there without coming down here to add to *our* population explosion.'

On this particular day he went rigid in what François called his 'bird watcher's stance', trying to indicate to François, 'There's another one of those birds taking liberties down here.'

420

François stopped Nonnie, and both pairs of eyes searched the bush and grass around them with the utmost care, but saw nothing. Yet it was clear from Hintza's attitude that there was something and that by the minute he was becoming more exasperated over François's and Nonnie's failure to see it too.

In the circumstances François did what he always did and whispered to Nonnie, 'Come and kneel here beside Hin. And don't try looking any more. Just sit very still . . . It's amazing, but if you wait, you'll feel not only what he's feeling but what the thing he's looking at is feeling, and the two things between them will draw your eyes to it.'

So they sat for perhaps a minute or two on either side of Hintza, each with a hand on his magnetic back, letting the day and its hidden life flow like a stream through them, trying to feel without will or thought, until there came an extraordinary moment when François and Nonnie simultaneously felt and saw, barely ten feet away, deep under a thatched roof of grass, a pair of dark birds' eyes, bright with terror.

'Good Heavens!' François exclaimed softly. 'I believe it's a francolin partridge brooding.'

As he said it, he noticed that the grass immediately above the eyes was trembling and knew immediately why. He whispered to Nonnie, 'Look at that grass over the eyes. Poor little thing. Its heart is beating so fast and so violently with fear that we might discover its nest and kill it, that the grass around is shaken by it . . . It longs to fly away; there's nothing in the whole bush so defenceless as a little bird sitting on earth. She's the mother bird you see, so she's got to stay and hatch her eggs . . . I often wonder what I'd do if I felt so threatened. But she'll never allow herself to be pushed off her eggs. In fact, I've found the skeletons of many francolin birds who've sat it out to the point of being killed on their nests. If you come quietly with me I'll show you just why I think birds are the bravest of all things in the bush.'

'Oh no!' The protest from Nonnie was immediate. 'That would be too cruel. You call off Hin and let's go as quickly as possible.'

François had never seen her so vehement and it compelled him to whisper a command to Hintza and quietly lead the three of them back into the main track. There he was amazed how flushed Nonnie's face was. Although she thanked him she added with rising emotion, 'But you must admit, it *would* have been cruel to prolong that poor little thing's agony.'

This side of it had not occurred to him. He had only wanted to show Nonnie how beautifully the francolin made its nest in the grass; how skilfully it hid itself from its many powerful enemies; how it sat there in a world of danger, with its little head cocked on one side as if it were listening for the first sounds of life stirring within its six white, brown and pink eggs underneath it, and how it would, if necessary, give up its life for the new life growing within them.

He tried to say this to Nonnie but for the first time she dismissed his explanations, saying impatiently, 'Oh bother you men and all your talk of courage and bravery. You're just like Fa, always trying to prove to himself how brave he is and that bravery in himself and other things, even fish, is all that matters. Even *you* are always talking to me about fear and courage as if they were the all-important things in life. Why?'

François did not like the comparison with Sir James at all. Besides, he was not without a feeling of guilt for never having thought of the francolin's side of the matter. All he could finally say was, 'Nonnie, you misunderstand me. If I talk a lot about fear and courage it's only because I'm so often afraid myself and badly in need of courage.'

This confession of weakness fired a strange new flame of protectiveness in Luciana. She instantly forgot her own agitation and protested with some remorse, 'I don't believe you. If there's anybody who doesn't know what fear is I would have thought it was you.'

'You're wrong ... You couldn't be more wrong,' François said in turn with tragic emphasis. 'I'm so often afraid that I need to look constantly at creatures like old Adonis and that partridge to reassure myself that there's enough courage in life for all, as Mopani so often tells me. I don't know what I would have done, perhaps run away to some awful old town long ago, if it hadn't been for the example of the birds and animals, that are so much less powerful than us. If it were not for them always reminding me, I might forget there's as much courage as we need, if only we know how to ask for it. Mopani said that the smaller and stiller the voice is within oneself, the more one should listen to them. He says it's like that with courage too.'

'Well, Master François,' Nonnie was driven to banter, dismayed at having produced so serious an atmosphere between them, when at heart she had been feeling so happy, 'if it's any help to you, I can tell you that the very next time I'm badly frightened I'm not going to think of your old Adonis, or even that partridge, but of you, to get me out of it.'

The moment when she would need all the examples of courage she could think of, however, came sooner than either of them expected. It came at a particularly delicate moment when both she and François were singularly vulnerable.

On their return they sat on the edge of the stoep outside the kitchen, side by side, Hintza lying happily at their feet in the twilight and 'Bamuthi standing in front of them, tall and indistinct like some dark archaic statue outlined against the west. François was translating questions and answers for Nonnie and 'Bamuthi. François thought he had never seen 'Bamuthi in a more sensitive and solicitous mood. He had just answered Nonnie's question as to whether he knew that baboons counted up to three, and thought of everything beyond that number as a 'hell-of-a-lot', with the oracular reply, 'And who then is there here who would say that this is not a matter of common knowledge?'

'Bamuthi would obviously have wanted to elaborate the theme but at that moment the moon rose. He instantly stopped and paused, deep in thought, before he looked at François to say, 'Little Feather, you always ask me about the singing crested cobra and because you have never seen it, although you have been too polite to say so, I know you have always thought it to be just a tale told by the old women to our children. But if you go, asking with your heart, to that circle of rock beyond the kraals on the edge of the bush on such a night as this, you will have a good chance of seeing the singing crested cobra for yourself because, for some months now, it has been reported that such a cobra has been visiting just that place.'

François translated all this faithfully to Nonnie and told her this singing cobra was the strangest and most persistent legend of the peoples of the bush. Who could imagine a cobra with a plume of feathers and a voice that went beyond a hiss to sing in the irresistible sea-siren way in which 'Bamuthi claimed it sang? He had always longed to see it but had never succeeded. Mopani, too, had encountered the legend all over Africa and tried to find the singing crested cobra but he, too, had failed. There was nothing that François would have liked more than to go now with Nonnie to see whether the mysterious serpent really existed. And Nonnie and Hintza simultaneously sprang to their feet, Nonnie exclaiming, 'Oh, how exciting – let's go at once!'

But just at that moment the mongrel watch dogs started to bark furiously and François knew at once that Sir James and Mopani were coming home. It was odd how effectively that barking and the sound of well-shod horses abolished the sense of mystery. The thought of a singing crested cobra somewhere out there on the edge of the bush, serenading the moon on behalf of all the secret life within the earth, was reduced in a flash to what 'Bamuthi had called 'an old wives' tale'. For François it was as if some great antique city of wonder and magic had suddenly crumbled to dust around them, just as the walls of Jericho had once fallen to the sound of tocsins.

The detail of what followed is irrelevant. But the one over-whelming fact was that the summons from Sir James's Government overseas seemed so important to him that he was going away almost immediately and, of course, taking Nonnie and Amelia with him. Mopani had agreed to supervise in general the construction of house and buildings at Silverton-Hill which, since they were being built of stone quarried and cut on the place, would take at least a year to complete. Mopani had also assumed the right (certain that it would help François) to promise that, in between his own visits, François would act as his deputy and inspect the site at least once a week to help the Cape-coloured builders.

François, of course, was as grateful to Mopani as anyone could possibly be in a moment of disaster so brutally and un-expectedly introduced in his life, since he had assumed that in Nonnie, at last, he would have a friend of his own close by, indefinitely. But he was too miserable to give his mind to either the food or the conversation at dinner that evening, and he lay awake for a long time in his room, the hypersensitive Hintza whimpering at odd moments in his sleep as if he, too, knew of the impending separation.

François seemed to have hardly fallen asleep at last when suddenly he was woken by what sounded like someone fumbling at his door. Wide awake at once, he grabbed his gun, always at the ready by his bed, and faced the door fully pre-pared, although, since it was an inside door, he could not im-agine any real danger. Moreover Hintza, instead of warning him, was standing beside his bed and wagging his tail in the most friendly and ardent manner, thumping it against the bed-clothes. Then suddenly the door opened, a torch shone on him and a clear, low whisper he knew well, trembling more with shyness than nerves, said, 'Please don't shoot ... It's only me. May I come in? And shush, please ... Amelia would murder me if she knew I was here.'

'Of course, Nonnie, please come in,' he answered, amazed. 'But what's the matter? Just hold the torch steady for a minute while I light my candle.' He did so and over its pentecostal little flame he saw Luciana standing there, wrapped in a warm dressing gown, yet shivering like someone come in straight from a storm.

'Why, you're frozen,' he exclaimed alarmed. 'Where have you been? What's gone wrong?'

'Oh just everything is wrong, and I'm not shivering because I'm cold,' she said, sitting down uninvited on the side of his bed and continuing out of her shyness and nerves to be accusing, 'Don't you realize I'm going away, that I shan't see you for another year, if ever, again? You ... you ask me so calmly what's the matter, as if it didn't matter to you at all whether we ever saw each other again.'

'Nonnie, how can you say that?' François protested warmly and quickly, for she sounded near to crying. 'D'you know, I've lain awake half the night thinking about you going away today and how awful it all was.'

'Oh, have you? Have you really? Please be honest with me.' Nonnie sounded comforted by the thought that he had suffered a sleepless night on her account and exclaimed, 'François, I wonder if you know how tired I am of being younger than everybody else?'

She peered closely into his eyes to see whether he knew what she meant and apparently was not entirely satisfied because she continued, 'But I dare say that's another thing you just don't care about. You aren't interested in ages are you? You're above such petty things, aren't you?'

He answered back more indignantly than he would have done if he had understood the need for reassurance behind it all. 'Nonsense . . . It's only that I'm not bothered by these things as you are. What on earth does it matter how old people are, as long as you like them?'

'But it *does* matter, François,' Nonnie on her dignity argued in turn. 'I don't think you can really be interested in people unless you're interested in how old they are. Take me, for instance. I asked you the first day I met you how old you were, and you've never once yet showed the least little bit of interest in how old I am.'

'But it's not at all important to me how old you are, can't you see?' François's reiteration was perhaps as truthful as it was tactless because it increased both Nonnie's bewilderment and her dismay.

She jumped from the bed and whisked about as if to make for the door. 'You see,' she said, 'you just *don't* understand and you don't care and a fat lot of good my coming here has done. I may as well go back to my room and Amelia.'

François instinctively caught her by the sleeve of her dressing gown, and told her sharply, 'Oh, Nonnie, you couldn't be more wrong. The only reason I never asked you is because, whatever your age, it's always seemed just right to me. From the moment we met it felt as if I had always known you . . .'

He stopped himself abruptly. He was about to refer to the great secret and the impact Xhabbo had had upon him. Fortunately she did not seem to notice, for she faced François and asked in a very small voice, 'Oh François, is that really so?'

François looked steadily at her and nodded his head emphatically. From far across the river old Chaliapin gave one of his greatest roars, the sound reverberating in the silence all around them like the final Amen on a cathedral organ. The

426

silence that followed, the look on François's face and his nodding, did far more than any words could have ever done to convince Nonnie.

She took his hand in both of hers, clasped them tightly and said, 'Coiske, will you promise, please, always to think of me as being just right for you. Please always think just that.' And then more lightly, because she was deeply stirred. 'For your private information I beg to inform you that I'm four months and seven days younger than you are.'

François pressed her hand so hard that she came near to wincing. He would have said more but he was prevented by the sound of shutters being thrown open in the kitchen, where Ousie-Johanna, with a private despair of her own because she was losing her great lady of fashion that morning, was getting ready to prepare the farewell breakfasts. They both knew that the great house would soon be waking. Indeed the sound brought a rare look of alarm to Nonnie's face. It moved François deeply for it made her look so defenceless.

She called out, 'Oh my God – Amelia. But thank you Coiske, thank you. You will always be the right age for me too. Thank you, and goodbye . . . and I'll write to you.'

Quickly she vanished through the door as silently as she had come. It was their own private and personal hail and farewell, as complete as life could for the moment allow it to be.

One need not give an account of the formal farewells that followed, except to mention one small thing. Just before stepping into her father's truck, Luciana, after cuddling Hintza, suddenly produced a handkerchief. She held it loosely round his neck and tied a knot in it where the ends met. It was many weeks before either François or Hintza knew why she had done it.

11 • And So to the Washing of
u-Simsela-Banta-Bami

It is not necessary to emphasize how profoundly Nonnie's going affected François, nor how slowly the days and nights turned over for him in that exacting measure of time to which one drew attention at the beginning. It was like the wheels of a great mill grinding out the detail of life as bucket after bucket was slowly filled with a trickle from the dark waters of time.

Once more he took refuge in his well-established routine of study in the early hours of the morning, and work and hunting for the pot for the rest of the day, with one welcome variation: once a week there was now an excursion to Silverton-Hill. Always he went armed with presents of fresh meat, fruit and vegetables and was made more and more welcome, making real friends with that gay and colourful little community building a great house to the sound of endless music in the lost world of the bush. He found himself looking forward to these excursions more eagerly as the days went by and blessed Mopani in his heart for having persuaded Sir James, who he was certain would have needed a great deal of persuasion, to entrust him with so mature a task. As Mopani had obviously foreseen, it helped to make him feel in touch with Nonnie and, as he saw the yellow walls of the building grow on the hill, to reinforce the belief that despite his feelings time was passing and the day would inevitably come when the house would be complete and ready for Sir James and his daughter's permanent occupation.

What was reassuring to him too was how well his experience of Nonnie seemed to fit into the company of himself and Xhabbo, so much so that he revised all his plans for preparing Mantis's cave for the day of Xhabbo's return. He revised them so that the cave could be ready for the moment when he could share his secret with Nonnie and it could be a place of welcome not just for two but for three.

428

Knowing that once Lammie returned, his freedom of movement would be more restricted, he immediately set about equipping the cave as if for a siege. In full control of the ample stores they kept at Hunter's Drift he hastened, before Lammie returned, to resume his ultimate authority over them, and so to remove little by little supplies which he thought essential for turning the cave into a kind of fortress. For example, he extracted from surplus military equipment that Ouwa had bought up years before from the government three of the largest haversacks, three of the largest field flasks, three pairs of webbing anklets (designed specially to protect human legs from the iron barbs of thorn of the bush), and three metal dixies for cooking. These he deposited in the cave. He took one of the many guns in the gun room, a gun which according to Mopani was the best all-purpose rifle for use in Africa, and two hundred rounds of ammunition, and hid them also in the cave. He had no fear that the absence of any of these pieces, even the rifle, would ever be detected, because it was a department in which neither Lammie nor Ousie-Johanna had ever displayed the slightest interest. In addition, he managed, by setting out before first light, to carry unseen four empty four-gallon petrol tins to the cave and from then on he skilfully contrived to keep them full of fresh water.

After that, acting on the basic precept of the military law of his country that every male between the ages of fourteen and sixty-five must always have available enough food for a fortnight in case of an emergency mobilization, he saw to it that there were always in the cave enough rusks, biltong, sugar, coffee, dried fruit and even as a special refinement of his own, packets of dehydrated soup, to last three people for two weeks. In all this he took great care never to approach the cave by the same route, and once his emergency commissariat was established, he went only when necessary to replace the stale rusks with fresh supplies. It meant that he himself had to eat the stale ones in the larder but since these rusks were renowned for keeping fresh this was one of the least of his difficulties.

As time went, he added all sorts of other basic substances such as tins of condensed milk, tins of bully beef and sardines, a large tinned plum-pudding, and slabs of bitter chocolate. Above all, he did not forget a complete snake-bite outfit and a small Red Cross stock, complete with quinine and the latest sulpha-drugs.

He could give no rational explanation to himself why he did all this. The plan was based entirely on some instinct that had been stimulated by his favourite story of Robinson Crusoe, and Defoe's detailed account of how his hero had been compelled, wisely, to create a secret fortress for himself when alone on a desert island.

Yet sometimes he thought that he was being ridiculous; playing a retarded boy-scout game with himself. These misgivings were usually most acute at the end of the day when he was tired. But it was significant to him how a good night's sleep would send him into the day happy at the thought of the cave, close at hand and now completely self-contained to give Xhabbo a safe place of return at any moment that he might choose to come.

It was indeed fantastic what reassurance equipping the cave and maintaining it in a constant state of readiness brought to his deprived spirit, in the feeling that he was providing Xhabbo with a secret larder and a place where first the two of them and perhaps later even Nonnie could one day meet and talk unobserved.

Considering how careful he had to be not to arouse the suspicions of their observant Matabele partners, and that all his experience had taught him that one never was anywhere in even the densest bush without some 'eye' upon one (not to mention Ousie-Johanna who normally seemed to know if only one grain of sugar had been illegally extracted from her pantry), his difficulties were formidable. But somehow his new, cunning self accomplished the task in perfect secrecy. Only it took so long that he had hardly completed it when, some two months after the departure of Nonnie and Sir James, Mopani arrived with the news of Lammie's return.

François, as always, was overjoyed to see Mopani and delighted, moreover, that Mopani had come a few days before Lammie's return at Hunter's Drift Siding to be with him and to visit Silverton-Hill. It brought to François the first hint of a feeling that time had moved on, and would perhaps increase its sluggish pace. The feeling was confirmed when he and Mopani rode over to Silverton-Hill and saw how high the walls of stone of Sir James's buildings were rising above their foundations. That made him happier. But one slight incident there reproduced that odd upsurge of inexplicable and acute alarm which had afflicted both him and Mopani ever since that fateful evening when they had concluded that, for good or ill, the birds in the bush had changed their tune.

In fact this particular cause of alarm had not vanished for François. Not a twilight or a dawn or, for that matter, the dead hour of the day, had gone by without the birds announcing to his sensitive ears that something in the universe had occurred to trouble the rhythm of their singing. By comparison, the incident which produced this new flare-up of anxiety was prosaic enough – it happened merely over a large consignment of enormous crates which had been brought by ox-wagon from the railway. Some of the Cape-coloured workmen were busy opening them and, to François's amazement and unbelief, extracting one red roof-tile after the other.

'But surely, Uncle,' he found himself exclaiming loudly, 'surely Sir James ought to know Africa well enough to realize that a tiled roof in this part of the world won't last a single summer. Surely he knows we get at least three or four bad hail-storms a year. Only one would be enough to smash his tiles to pieces! Besides, he has miles of river reeds for a perfect roof of thatch.'

Mopani nodded before answering, with the air of resignation of someone accustomed for years to having himself and his experience of Africa rejected, 'I know, Coiske, I know. I warned him about it when we went over the plans. But you must know by now that this house he is building will be almost an exact copy of his old home in England. It's meant to be as much a cure for homesickness as a practical piece of building, and he made light of my warnings. He merely said that a few broken tiles were a trifle and that there were plenty more where they came from. I told him that replacing tiles in a bad season, perhaps two or three times a year, might strain anyone's purse, but he just waved my arguments away and there was nothing more I could do about it.'

'But Uncle, that's stupid, and surely he's not a stupid man?' François protested, more troubled by this example of unreason and obstinacy in Sir James than even Mopani, perhaps because he feared the power of such inflexible characteristics in his own regard in the particular as well as in the general area of personal relationships between Hunter's Drift and Silverton-Hill. So he pressed on, hoping for some reassurance, 'Do you think he hasn't got it in him any more to learn? Surely he'll have a lot more to learn if he's going to be happy and successful out here.'

'You must not worry unduly,' Mopani replied philosophically. 'He will learn in time all right, I'm sure.' Mopani paused, for as the word *time* fell from his lips, a strange, far-away look came as always to his eyes as when seeing, as he so often did, a sign in the bush that others could not see; a look that François knew well. Then he went on as if to himself, 'That is, provided there is still time to learn.'

There was something so ominous in Mopani's tone that François, dismayed, called out, 'Oh Uncle, why do you say it like that? It sounds as if you feel that time is just about up for everyone, and everything around us here.'

Mopani was annoyed with himself. It was one of his favourite maxims that it was ignoble of human beings to trouble others with their own private apprehensions before they were verified, and even then, only if necessary for the well-being of all. So he hastened to qualify himself, 'I don't mean that at all, Coiske. I was just thinking aloud to the effect that in life it is always somehow later than we think.'

The following day they were early at Hunter's Drift Siding to welcome Lammie back. François could not be certain but he suspected that the old hunter assumed Lammie would arrive, as the saying went, in deep mourning. In any case it was obvious that Mopani was somewhat taken aback to see her step out of the train dressed in an exceedingly smart travelling suit, as if returning not from a funeral but a holiday; a bright kerchief round her throat and a small, gay, jaunty, almost defiantly young little hat on her head. François knew his mother well enough to realize that this could be entirely a form of bravado, and he found her effort to keep up a bright and gay appearance in dress far more moving than any conventional black would have been. He had only to look at her beautiful face and notice that her large, cool, steady eyes appeared somewhat deeper set, the fine bone in her delicate face showing just slightly more precisely under the smooth skin than before, to have an inkling of what she had been enduring. He was so moved that he had to draw in full on this discipline of calm and ordered emotion which Lammie had imposed upon herself, so that he could greet her with enough composure to calm his feelings.

She herself, much as all this was in keeping with the main trend of her clear spirit, might have found it difficult to maintain such an ordered attitude to the new life which faced her, because one look at François was enough to tell her that he had suffered too and in a way that had complications of which she was totally unaware. He looked older, taller and in an odd way remote, as if he had in fact become a stranger to what he had been when she had last seen him as well as perhaps to herself. The impression dismayed her but vanished quickly because a new kind of mechanism which had established itself in her from the moment of Ouwa's death, took over, and it turned her from herself into a continuation of what Ouwa himself would have been had he been there beside her, to such an extent that she saw François not through her own heart but entirely as she imagined Ouwa would have done.

It was as if she could hear his voice in her ear as she said to François in that teasing, ironic way of his, 'Ah, I see you've not wasted any time in my absence to promote what I always suspected was a scheme of yours. I always thought you were bent in your secret self on being taller and better-looking than your father. Obviously you have made full use of the absence of competition to forge ahead and be so disrespectful as to grow taller than your gullible parent. I would not have thought that you would welcome one by heaping coals of such fire on a well-meaning head!'

Somehow this imagined, unspoken voice out of a past more vivid still than the present, helped her to maintain her calm. She greeted Mopani affectionately, yet without a blur of emotion in eye or tone. She talked in a lively and factual way on the journey home of the battles she had fought with lawyers and authorities to get Ouwa's estate settled and of how well she felt she had succeeded, in the end, so that she would not have to leave Hunter's Drift again but could get on with the main task of developing it as Ouwa had wished, as well as taking his place as François's tutor in order to hasten the time when he could go to a university to complete his education.

François did not think it appropriate then to announce that he had turned his back on that world from which Lammie had just come, and that he was determined never to leave Hunter's Drift or go near anything as pernicious as a university in a system of education which had brutally rejected Ouwa. Like Mopani, he thought it best that Lammie should do the talking and somehow through it expend the turmoil of emotion which her approach to a place which she had created with Ouwa out of nothing must be increasing by the minute. And somehow the unspoken plan worked so well that, although Ousie-Johanna took Lammie in her arms, sobbing bitterly, and 'Bamuthi, his head men and their principal wives all wept openly and bitterly on seeing her, Lammie's calm never failed her.

She remained strangely royal in circumstances that François was certain any other woman would have found intolerable. In a way it made him proud of Lammie. Yet at the same time, he was sad that her control should cover so large an empire of her life. Whenever he looked at Mopani, he thought something similar was simmering in the old hunter's heart.

Some of Lammie's controlled warmth came out in the imagination with which she had planned her return. That very evening everyone who worked at Hunter's Drift, from the oldest to the youngest child, was summoned an hour before sunset to the great courtyard between kitchen and stables. There Lammie announced that Ouwa in his will had left something to each of them. All the time he had been at Hunter's Drift he had kept a list of everybody who shared in the enterprise. The moment a new child was born, the name, date of birth and all were carefully entered on the list. From year to year, according to the age and length of employment, the gifts that Ouwa wanted to go on his death to each person were brought up to date.

So, with 'Bamuthi and François at her side, Lammie now called out the names from the list, working up finally to Ousie-

Johanna and 'Bamuthi, and told them what each of them had been left. One of their best young bulls was for 'Bamuthi. Ouwa's legacy to Ousie-Johanna, because she was the only one sophisticated to understand it, was a legacy of £3 a week for life.

All this Lammie followed up with personal presents of her own to all persons on the list; carefully chosen bracelets and necklaces of the finest beads for the young girls, silk shawls and headcloths of the loveliest colours for the young women, rolls of cloth for the old ladies, knives for the young boys, bush suits of cavalry twill for the older ones and so on and on. Ousie-Johanna, however, thanks to hints contained in François's letters to Lammie, wherein he had described the relationship between Ousie-Johanna and Amelia, was presented with a heavy, shining, black satin dress and white silk apron, as well as a fat album of all the latest recordings of the most famous hymns, including one new to her, 'John Brown's Body', which was soon to threaten to replace 'Nearer my God to thee' at the top of her religious pop list.

'Bamuthi, as head of them all, received a long army greatcoat of majestic proportions, with a double row of gilt buttons bearing the crest of the regiment in which Ouwa had served in the war, a large military bush hat with a lion skin round the crown and an ostrich plume to go with it, so that in the end, far from the first day of her return ending in the sorrowful occasion which everyone had instinctively assumed it would, it became a feast of transfiguration and rejoicing which Lammie somehow thought was exactly what Ouwa would have wished. It was not for nothing, she recollected, that his favourite Shakespearean sonnet, which she herself had played on the piano and sung for him many times began, 'No longer mourn for me when I am dead'.

Yet, great as the rejoicing was, and moved as everybody was by their dead employer's and his widow's solicitude on their behalf, there was something about it all which troubled the wise and vigilant intuition of so profoundly instinctive and natural a people. There seemed to be a feeling that Lammie was being too good to be true and that she was exceeding their sense of the natural proportions of life. This kind of unease, an unease one hastens to add purely and unselfishly on Lammie's behalf, showed itself in many different ways, but all amounted in the end to the same conclusion, which is perhaps best exemplified by the reactions of Ousie-Johanna and 'Bamuthi.

Ousie-Johanna, who for days could not begin the day without bursting into tears the moment she saw Lammie and François alone at the great table, would afterwards take François aside and whisper: 'I can't understand our Lammie not joining in the weeping too.' Then, as the days passed, she came to the point of anger, announcing in judgement to François: 'I don't know what is blerrie-well the matter with that Lammie of yours. Why has the good God in Heaven given people grief if not to weep over it? Can't she see that she owes it to our Ouwa to weep for him? If she is not careful she will turn him into a ghost that will haunt all of us.'

'Bamuthi had the same concern but put it less violently. With the ingrained poetic beauty of his sonorous native language he asked rhetorically, 'Is it to be then, Little Feather, that the Lammie of our house is never to string the beads? Does she not know that grief grows great and terrible if beads are not strung for it? Since when has grief become a stranger that we should shut our kraals against it and not welcome it to our fires and warm it with our tears? Is it not a sister to our joy that has a right of its own, even in the huts of kings?'

But despite all this concern which François himself secretly shared as far as Lammie was concerned, there was no 'stringing of beads' in the presence of others. What may have been done in the dark when she was alone in her bed at night is unknown. The only indication lies in a remark she made once to François. Clutching his arm one evening at sundown she heard herself saying, 'I'm grateful that Ouwa never knew what it meant to lose a life-long partner.'

There then followed a period of some fourteen months which was the longest, most difficult and the least happy that François had yet experienced. There was not only this weight of Lammie's undeclared sorrow which seemed daily to grow greater and which he, as the person closest to her, had to carry as well as his own burdens. In addition, there was the constant tension caused between them by the need to parry Lammie's declared determination to get him ready as soon as possible for completion of his education in the university where both she and Ouwa had graduated.

François was as determined not to go as Lammie was that he should. He was wise enough to protest openly as little as possible but to follow one of Mopani's maxims: to keep quiet and not attempt to cross that particular bridge until they came to it. But in the depths of himself, he knew Lammie was aware of his resistance and that an all-out battle was being mounted in her spirit to be fought when the moment came. The battle, François knew, would be the more formidable because Lammie would fight it with the strength of two; her own and also that borrowed from her own private image of what she imagined Ouwa would have done in the situation.

What made this prospect worse for François was that, for the first time, he was doubtful of Mopani's support. Whenever he tried to discuss the matter with Mopani on his now frequent visits to Hunter's Drift, Mopani, though saying that they had plenty of time for considering the matter, indicated that it might be a good thing if François did consider going to a university. He would add remarks to the effect that they were living in an extremely privileged world there in the bush and that life abhorred nothing more than privilege. He himself knew from his work as a conservationist that their way of life had powerful and well-organized enemies in the world outside – greedy men who were increasingly attracted to so large a tract of virgin Africa with a mounting determination to have it thrown open for economic exploitation. He told François of his own private doubts as to whether he would be able to maintain intact his own great reserve. He thought that if people like himself and François were to fight the battle effectively for preserving the things that they loved in the bush they could do so only if they understood their enemies thoroughly; and knew the sort of weapons and forces that they could bring up against them. For these reasons alone if for no others, he thought it would be as well if François did go out to a university.

François, as far as all this was concerned, was in the grip of emotions too compulsive to make him accessible for the

437

moment to the wisdom in Mopani's reasoning. He was dominated by a feeling that if Mopani really supported Lammie for such excellent reasons, he might well lose his campaign. Yet there was one battle he was not going to lose on any account, even if he lost the campaign. He was not leaving before he had seen Xhabbo again; or knew him to be dead.

As the long months dragged by, he found himself listening with increasing desperation for Xhabbo's call sign. There were countless occasions by night and day when the call of the plover or the mournful yanking of a jackal would start up just as if it were the beginning of the call Xhabbo had promised for announcing his return. François's heart would beat faster. Yet, in the end, the right combination of plover and jackal sounds was never achieved, and he would sink back into a dark mood of disappointment, if not despair.

All this added greatly to the powerful undercurrent of tensions between Lammie and himself. Unfortunately, even these did not make up the full sum of dislocation and discord which seemed to confront him every day. There were outside elements, too, to broaden these areas of discontent.

For instance, for the first time the Matabele at Hunter's Drift seemed out of tune with themselves and their surroundings. It was no longer just a matter of general alarm, set to music with increasing intensity by the birds at dawn and sunset. There was an increasing anxiety abroad which made itself known to everyone with gathering urgency by the news travelling through the bush from far and wide. It was that the great and Right Honourable Sun-Is-Hot himself was said to be exceedingly troubled by omens. It was widely reported that he no longer allowed people to consult him on private matters; he said that the moment had come when he had to give himself over entirely, for the good of all, to following the voice of the great first spirit of their people, Umkulunkulu. It was declared that Umkulunkulu himself had appeared to uLangalibalela in a dream to tell him that a time of great trouble was upon the land. Could they not all see, the dream asked, how the young men had forgotten the praise names of Umkulunkulu and no longer spoke of him but only of things that were useful to them? Unless they could be brought back to praise him and to fear

438

with awe the first spirit of all things, then disaster would fall upon them. This was bad enough, but worse was to follow.

One day the dread news arrived that uLangalibalela had been on a journey to the sacred hill of his people more than a thousand miles away in the south-east. There a vision had told him that disaster was now inevitable. It was said openly that as uLangalibalela stood on the sacred hill, asking with his heart, even he, uLangalibalela, was frightened because in the clear night sky above him, star after star fell out of position in the ordered procession of the Milky Way. Instead of travelling from east to west as Umkulunkulu had willed them to travel ever since his first praise name was called, the delinquent stars went against their lawful courses, and travelled from west to east, until they were lost in darkness.

Of course there were many who argued that even uLangalibalela could be wrong. But to François the arguments only proved that all men at heart were now deeply afraid.

Even Ousie-Johanna was affected by these rumours of uLangalibalela's vision. Never before in the history of Hunter's Drift had her gramophone called on God so often and so deeply into the silence of the night, which now was so heavy and profound that the branches of the bush seemed bent low with its weight.

Then suddenly the Punda-Ma-Tenka, the great old Hunter's Road, became busy again in a way that none of them could remember. It started being used not just by men making their way in small groups between the remote interior in the north and the mines and industries in the south, but by a steady procession of the most modern trucks. No one could tell what these trucks carried or where precisely they came from, or where they were bound. They were usually driven by Africans of other nations, dressed in smart khaki overalls, apparently as well trained as they were well-stocked with provisions and supplies. Moreover, they seemed to know this long, rarely used route well, or perhaps had been fully informed in advance of how to follow it. They usually arrived at the great outspan by the ford just before dark and left just before sunrise, so that it looked as if they had deliberately arranged their journeys so that they could reduce to the minimum the risk of encounters with curious men.

'Bamuthi and some of his senior people, with their traditional sense of hospitality, had gone down to see if there were anything they could do to help these travellers. They returned increasingly resentful over the cold, if not hostile reception that they received from the men who drove the trucks, so much so that they finally abandoned their efforts of help.

'Bamuthi even went so far as to tell François that he would like to prohibit such men from using the facilities of the Hunter's Drift outspan, moving them on before they took as a right what, after all, was only made possible for them by the generosity of the owners of Hunter's Drift. But neither François nor Lammie would agree. They thought such men were no more than a sign of the lack of grace of the times, and best ignored. Yet François, nearly a year after Nonnie's departure, had cause to wonder whether 'Bamuthi had not been right after all.

It came during the rainy season. There happened to be down by the ford for some two hundred yards on either bank of the Amanzim-tetse a stretch of black cotton soil which it was almost impossible for vehicles to cross after heavy rain. In fact François had often seen elephants sink up to their stomachs in this black soil. The short crossing from river bank to firm ground was so difficult that when they finally emerged from the black glue they would stand for an hour or two, limp with exhaustion, to recover their breath before continuing their journey to the bush. On this occasion he was watching seven trucks arriving at the ford in a heavy downpour of rain just at sundown. He was not surprised, therefore, on his way to the milking sheds at dawn the next day to hear the engines of the trucks racing noisily and see the vehicles stuck fast, although numbers of black men were pushing to try and help them along.

All the time François was at the milking sheds, the futile grating noise of engines and the shouting of men at one another, increasingly angry over an ineffective struggle against the intractable African mud, continued. At last François suggested to 'Bamuthi that perhaps they ought to go and do what they would automatically have done a year earlier, and offer to pull the trucks out of the mud with teams of oxen.

To his surprise 'Bamuthi argued vehemently against it, saying that since they knew by now what sort of men they were,

440

'dogs of the wind' and 'feet of baboons' (all Sindabele terms of scorn for feckless and treacherous persons) it was not for them to offer help but to wait until the men themselves came to ask for it. However François persuaded him, in the end, to accompany him down to the drift.

The moment the men at the ford saw them approaching they stopped racing their engines. The drivers clambered quickly out of their seats and joined their supporters, about thirty in all, to come walking to meet them in such a truculent manner, that 'Bamuthi warned, 'See that you have your gun ready, Little Feather. I did wrong to bring you here without *u-Simsela-Banta-Bami* in my hand. Let us stand calmly here and wait prepared for them to come if they will come.'

François did as 'Bamuthi told him and while doing so he noticed that Hintza had stepped out in front. The hair on his coat was rigid and erect and something close to a snarl quivered on his long black lips and from time to time he bared his strong white teeth. They stood there silently while the menacing strangers came closer in a body, until they were only some ten yards away.

Then one man stepped forward and called out in English: 'Go away, settler boy. Go away. What d'you mean by poking your bloody white nose into our business?'

It was just as well that 'Bamuthi did not understand any English for it is doubtful if his reaction would have been as controlled as was François's. He, thanks again to Mopani's training, tended to become calmer the more menacing the situation.

'We merely came to see whether we could help you,' François replied. 'We used to have an expression here that "the road is king" but obviously you would not know what it means. Go back to your trucks and get out of your troubles yourselves. I will only remind you that you are here on our land and this is the last time that I will allow ungrateful men like you to camp for any reason whatsoever on our property.'

'Your property, you bloody little white settler?' the spokesman retorted angrily. 'We'll see how much longer it'll remain your property. But just you get back and keep out of our business.'

François felt that a vital principle was at stake. 'It is not for you to tell me what to do on our land. Just get back to your trucks and see you get away as soon as possible.'

For a moment it looked as if the spokesman would order his men to force François and 'Bamuthi to turn back. Indeed 'Bamuthi was not in need of any translations to know what was going on. The tones and attitudes were quite enough to keep him posted. He turned his back on the men and let out a great Matabele shout, the equivalent of a knight's, 'To me! To me!'

The volume of sound alone was impressive. Instantly, from gardens and kraals, men and boys, hurdling over fences and bushes, came running as if their lives depended upon it, sticks, spears and knives in hand, straight towards 'Bamuthi and François.

The shock and dismay on the faces of the men confronting François and 'Bamuthi was so great as to make 'Bamuthi laugh with scorn and to call them some good, old-fashioned Sinda-bele names, like 'dogs willing to snarl but afraid to bite'. Then he shouted at them: 'You, less than men who breed like ants and proliferate like rats in holes among the cliffs.'

The greatest insult of all, however, was hurled after the spokesman, who, regrettably, probably did not understand enough Sindabele to appreciate it. Its incomparable Sindabele sound, *u-Sinque-Siname-Kasane* means literally 'Old-tick-covered-buttocks', and is a phrase of the utmost scorn for a born trickster. However, whether they understood or not, the men turned and ran for the shelter of their convoy.

Later, however, there was some sort of triumph. At eleven o'clock in the morning the same spokesman who had faced François and 'Bamuthi arrived, khaki cap in hand, at Ousie-Johanna's kitchen door. She, oblivious of what had happened down by the river at sunrise, was already entertaining the confused and bewildered man, who had obviously expected more insults if not blows, and was treating him to coffee and rusks when François appeared.

The man could not have been more slick or more apologetic. He begged François to excuse him. They had only behaved as they had done because of hostile receptions from other 'settlers', as he insisted on calling the farmers whose property they had crossed some hundred miles farther south. He excused himself at great length before he begged François to help them with his teams of oxen.

François trusted this aspect of the man even less than he did the first. He had an odd feeling that 'Bamuthi would never be forgiven by these people for his reaction in siding with him. But, of course, he felt they had no option but to help. In any case François was anxious to see the last of such truculent people as soon as possible.

So a reluctant 'Bamuthi and his helpers were made to produce six teams of oxen and to haul the trucks out of the mire into which their wheels had sunk. Then they had to pull them across the swollen ford of the river and out of the black cotton soil on to firm ground beyond. François was there to help with the operation and it all went smoothly and well, except that none of the picturesque banter or vivid conversation which is usual, rich and fluent on these occasions between African travellers, took place at all. The whole operation, beyond the orders necessary for carrying it out, was conducted in a singularly sullen and ominous silence.

None of this would have mattered very much to François had it not been for a slight incident when he unhooked the last team of oxen to return to the homestead. He himself was leading the team past the truck that they had just drawn on to firm ground. He was level with the dashboard at the rear when he noticed that the tarpaulin laced over the truck was being held apart by what looked to him like a pair of exceedingly pale African hands. Instinctively he looked closer and quickly made out, just above the hands, first the eyes and then face of a man who was obviously assuming that he was invisible in the shadows. The man was watching him intently. François nearly gave himself away, so violent was his start of surprise. He had no doubt that the face he looked at was that of a Chinese, the same face moreover which he had first seen on that outcrop of rock in the depression of the Mist of Death when he and 'Bamuthi were on their way to uLangalibalela.

He said nothing of this to 'Bamuthi for he was overcome by the realization of how wrong he had been not to speak of it all

443

to Mopani before as, at the time, he had promised 'Bamuthi that he would do. He resolved then that, no matter how much it endangered his own special secret life, he was going to confess everything to Mopani, just as soon as he could. He might even have ridden over to his camp that day, did he not know that Mopani was away for another six weeks in Europe, representing the Government of the country at an international conference called for the preservation of world wild life.

There was another incident, on the face of it not so disquieting and yet for François almost more unpleasant because of the distress that it caused Lammie. It came only five weeks after his second glimpse of the mysterious Chinese. The rain and that cotton soil at the ford were again responsible. One evening a solitary truck was stuck in the mud and this time the occupants of the truck did not wait for Hunter's Drift to offer help, but came soliciting for it. There were four of them, an African driver and three men in clerical dress. They had, François thought, in spite of their clothes, the same grim expressions that he had seen on the faces of the 'men of the spear' in the depression, despite the fact that the faces of those men had been Bantu and the faces with them that night at the dining-room were pink, well-fed European ones.

He felt keenly that the dispositions of the men were singularly unresponsive, although they were being provided with some of Ousie-Johanna's best food and drinking Ouwa's best wine, and being offered hospitality extended in Lammie's most gracious way. No matter what conversation François and Lammie tried, their responses remained perfunctory. They offered nothing of their own. Even the oldest of the three, having been invited to say grace and thanks and to read a passage from an English Bible, considerately produced for them by Lammie, did so as if he had been trapped into aiding and abetting his hosts in an act of hypocrisy.

Lammie, vulnerable as only François knew her to be at the moment, at first could hardly believe what was happening at her table. But when the senior member of the mission announced finally that they had been sent out by the World Council of Christian Churches to look into 'the exploitation of the innocent black people of Africa by you settlers, and to

444

advise on the extent to which it was a Christian duty to help the "freedom fighters" of Africa in their battle against Imperialism and neo-Colonialism', François could tell from the colour that came to her delicate face that at last she was angry.

It was almost the first natural impulsive reaction that he had seen in her since her return and he was almost grateful to those tight-lipped men for producing it. But it did not endear him to their manners.

He was sorry indeed that he thought them too insensitive to notice the dismissal implicit in the extreme politeness with which Lammie said good night to them and asked François to show them to their rooms, or too unaware to notice that she did not appear when they left in the morning. François, however, who had come rather late from the milking sheds, paused at the breakfast-room door before entering. He was amazed that men who had been so taciturn at dinner the night before could now, among themselves, be so lively and full of things to say. They were remarking how disgraceful it was that one woman and one boy should be living in such great wealth and extravagance in the bush, when all their servants lived so miserably in huts and were obviously overworked and poorly paid. Could they, one of them even asked rhetorically, just before François's entrance silenced them, have found anything in the twentieth century quite so feudal and so wicked? The sooner they got to the real field of battle, they said, and found out what the men who were fighting against such injustice needed, the better.

François had always been astonished how well 'Bamuthi and the other Matabele could determine what was quintessential in the character of the Europeans who came to Hunter's Drift, although they did not understand a word of their languages. Yet he had never been so impressed as he was an hour or two later. They stood watching the three priests climb into their trucks, safely hauled by oxen to firm ground, and 'Bamuthi, shaking his monumental head, announced from the pit of his stomach, 'Auck! I do not like it, Little Feather. I do not like it. There they go, three black crows, and three black crows together, our ancestors warned us, means a killing somewhere, some time.'

Even Ousie-Johanna had something to say about the visitation. She understood a few key words of English and lost no time in taking François by the arm to lead him aside. In a voice of total bewilderment she asked, 'I wonder what those three men are up to? You know, I think they tried to tell me that I must not think that all Europeans are like you and Lammie, as if I didn't wish they were! They had the blerrie cheek to tell me the world was full of people who were sorry for me and would soon come to my help. Help for what? Do they think then I did not cook well enough for them, to need more help? I tell you I didn't trust them, although they were dressed like men of God. Do you know, they offered me a sixpence each and I told them straight what they blerrie-well could do with their money and asked them if they thought we were a boarding house to make travellers pay for a few crumbs of bread?'

The scorn with which Ousie-Johanna uttered 'sixpence' nearly made François smile. He knew how their attitude must have hurt such a generous soul, who resolutely rejected all tips, some even amounting to pounds. But he controlled himself with an effort as she concluded, 'But they're so badly brought up they didn't understand a word I said.'

All this time François had three sources of real comfort. Two have already been mentioned: his active role in supervising the building of Nonnie's future home, and equipping the secret cave in which he hoped that one day Xhabbo, Nonnie and he could all meet. The third was that Nonnie kept her promise and wrote to him. For the first time in his life, he had someone of his own age to write to. The correspondence, although irregular, was maintained and showed no decline in interest on either side.

More tangible than the letters were two parcels which arrived for François some time after Sir James's departure. One contained a dog collar made of very soft leather. It was obviously designed with considerable imagination. The top was closely studded with brass spikes that shone like gold.* Underneath, where the brass spikes were riveted into the leather, another band of soft leather had been sewn over it, to prevent the metal from rubbing against the skin. Inserted in the centre of the studs was a neat, flat little bronze plate with the inscription, 'For darling Hin from his loving Nonnie'.

* The weather quickly removed their lustre imposing a greenish patina upon them which relieved François of the necessity of removing the collar when out hunting.

The gift, of course, explained the episode with the handkerchief which had lingered vividly in François's mind. Moreover it was accompanied by a letter. In it Nonnie wrote how she knew that François detested dog collars, but she hoped he would please accept this one, since it was no ordinary dog collar. It was not meant as 'a slave collar', an outrage to Hintza's dignity. Nor was it just a token of her love for Hintza. It was mostly a product of her concern that Hintza should be protected by the collar in what everybody told her was the most vulnerable part of a dog's body and the place for which all its enemies, like leopards, lions and even snakes, would strike first. She had designed this collar, she wrote, especially for Hintza, to make him immune against such perils.

François was not at all certain how Hintza would take to such an encumbrance. As far as he was concerned, the fact that the collar was an expression of imaginative concern more than reconciled him to the teasing he had to endure from Lammie, Ousie-Johanna and 'Bamuthi, all of whom had for years been trying to persuade him to fit Hintza with a proper dog collar like all the other dogs in the land.

When he produced the collar to show it to Hintza, he was utterly astonished. Perhaps some of Nonnie's scent when she handled and packed the collar must still have clung to the leather. At first Hintza sniffed it ardently, almost as if he could not believe his own nose. Then he started to wag his tail and look round about him. After that, he took to the collar itself without reservation. Indeed François burst out laughing when, a day or so later, he came upon Hintza actually standing looking at himself in the mirror of his room. Unlike other dogs, Hintza appeared to have understood the mystery of reflection, whether in the waters of the Amanzim-tetse or in François's mirror.

The second present was for François himself. It was considerably larger than Hintza's and when unwrapped proved to be a painting. It was a French colour reproduction of a Flemish primitive picture. François thought he knew something about painting because Ouwa's study was full of books containing numerous coloured illustrations. But this particular painting was new to him. He quickened to it immediately, for it seemed

447

as if painted by some extraordinarily gifted young person while the sense of wonder was still intact and his feeling for the mystery in all the ordinary things of life had not yet been educated out of him. In the most sensitive and loving detail were flowers, stones, trees, leaves and birds, everything in background and foreground painted as if each were infinite in its own right. All led tenderly up to the central theme which was that of a man in medieval hunting clothes, arrested on the edge of this embroidered forest. He stood there, spear in hand, staring motionless with wonder at a great stag some short distance away in a little clearing. The large, dark eyes of the stag were without fear or reproach and between its antlers, it carried a model of the crucifixion.

François had no clear idea what this strange encounter signified until he read Nonnie's letter. He would remember, she wrote, how much she had wished that he had a patron saint to protect him. Therefore she and Amelia had searched through the calendar of saints. By some extraordinary coincidence she had found that François's birthday was on the day devoted to Saint Hubert; the patron saint of all hunters. This picture was depicting how Saint Hubert, who had been an inveterate hunter, had seen one day, between the horns of a stag he was about to kill, the vision depicted in the painting. From that day on he became not only patron saint of hunters but also of the hunted. Would François therefore please keep it in his room?

For once François's Huguenot prejudices appeared inactive. He loved the painting and was strengthened in his love of it by Mopani. Though Mopani had never heard of Saint Hubert either, he seemed even more impressed, if that were possible, than François, for he remarked, after considerable thought, 'Yes-no Coiske, this is *darem* a wonderful thing. You remember some months ago when we talked about what Ouwa told you of that remark in the Dead Sea Scrolls, that men only had to follow the birds and beasts and the fishes to find the way to Heaven? Look ... here's the same thought in this picture. A man shown the way by a European buck centuries ago. It is *darem* remarkable, you know. I have always thought us hunters a bit like Paul in the Bible. You remember that he came to Christianity by persecuting Christians. It seems to me a lot of us come to it through killing the animals we one day learn to protect and, in protecting them, save ourselves.'

Grateful as he was, François ignored Nonnie's suggestion that he should hang the painting in his room. He thought about it for days but the painting somehow did not belong there. And then, on one of his visits to the cave, he discovered why. It seemed made for Mantis's cave, which felt like a kind of hunter's temple to him. So with a vain, becollared Hintza to observe him, he built a little 'altar' of white river pebbles against the part of the honey-coloured walls of the cave where there was a cross painted in red by some long-forgotten Stone Age hand. He stood the painting on the stones and in time he smuggled some packets of their best, long table candles into the cave and saw to it that two always stood sentinel-wise on either side of the painting. On each visit he would light them, each flame as clear and clean as the blade of a spear in that still air. His sense of the cave being some special sacred place was now complete.

And here one might, perhaps, cite as an example of how much of 'the other little person' he was in Lammie's life, that the absence of the painting from the walls of his own room, where it might have been expected to hang, was neither noticed nor commented upon.

In comparison with these gifts and the effect they had on François and Hintza, his own presents to Nonnie appeared to him rather feeble. All he could do was to enlist the help of 'Bamuthi's oldest daughter, who was the greatest expert not only at Hunter's Drift but at Osebeni, in the making of colourful necklets of beads. Like the girls of her clan, she made a different one at each turn of the moon, as if in obedience to the same instinct which makes Europeans give each month its own precious stone. These beads were dedicated to their ideal of man and were the most precious form of jewellery in their culture. They contained, not in words but in the symbolism of the design itself, different nuances of the love and admiration natural between young men and women. For this reason, cruder forms of the art were sold in the cities of the land under the name of Bantu 'love letters'. Not only François, but everybody else at Hunter's Drift would have scorned so crude and simple a label,

449

for the patterns were far older than any letter of any alphabet or Chinese character, issuing sheer and immediate from the depths of life where dreams and their meaning are fashioned.

François would have had to be in Europe, in the convent in which Nonnie was being educated while Sir James was engaged on affairs of state, to see the expression on her face in order to know that he could not have sent her anything more to her liking. That being impossible, he could never believe altogether that her profuse words of gratitude in the letters that followed the gift could be more than an over-generous acknowledgement of such humble offerings.

Yet through these contacts with Nonnie, and an increasingly precise feeling that Xhabbo would at any moment now reappear in his life, François somehow got through the long months, until some weeks after the arrival and departure of the 'crows of God' (as the priests had now become in Ousie-Johanna's vocabulary), there came a letter from Nonnie announcing that Sir James's mission was accomplished. Within a week or two they would all be on their way back to Hunter's Drift and Silverton-Hill 'at the double'.

The twenty-four hours before their arrival at Hunter's Drift, almost eighteen months to the day after that early-morning warning from Hintza which had taken François out on his perilous journey to the lion trap, were some of the most unpleasant he had ever experienced. If only he could have put a mental finger on the cause for the unpleasantness and found some name, sentence or even paragraph to describe it, he would have felt more able to cope. But it was nothing tangible, just an incredibly sullen, depressive atmosphere, a kind of cosmic unease. It not only affected everyone like the coming of a thunderstorm, but, of course, the birds down by the gleaming, remorselessly onflowing Amanzim-tetse that, according to the Matabele, were always the first to know, now sang as if a prelude to a play in the sombre cycle of the Eumenides. It was this period of twenty-four hours which produced perhaps the most singular omen of all.

Mtunywa (Messenger) had a daughter called Langazana (Miss Earnest-Longing), who was regarded by everyone as simple-minded and, as such, possessed close bonds with natural things,

450

particularly the birds of the bush. She appeared at the milking sheds, in the evening which began this last twenty-four hours, screaming and so distressed that all the men stopped milking and crowded round her in case they were compelled, as they were when people's souls threatened to leave their bodies, to enclose her in a healing circle, pressing tightly against her to dance her fleeing spirit back into her body. But it soon became clear that this girl was not concerned about herself. She was screaming because she had a message of urgent impact for them all.

Sobbing, she said that all afternoon, wherever she had gone in the bush to gather dry wood for the evening fires, a black crow (which everyone knew was an omen of sorrow) had pursued her. It had insisted on sitting on a branch of a tree directly in her path, looking at her, and whenever she tried to ignore it, it had screamed at her, '*Mamah-Weh!*' (My mother, oh!). She had ordered the crow over and over again to go away but it had refused and pursued her with this sound until just twenty minutes before sunset. The crow then had suddenly started to upbraid her in an almost human voice, screaming, 'It's not me, it's you who should go away. All, all go away for if you stay in this place much longer you will all be killed.'

There were many sources of natural intelligence which even the omen-minded men at Hunter's Drift doubted. But they knew this girl to be too simple-minded ever to say or do anything which she did not absolutely believe. Indeed, such a state to them was in some sort a gift of grace, and so altogether they took Langazana so seriously that 'Bamuthi himself set about calming her. He thanked her and promised her that he would call a council the next day to choose someone to go to uLangali-balela himself to interpret the omen for them. By that time, of course, it was so dark that even so portentous a crow would be in its nest and not there to suggest (as it may well have done, considering the urgency of the message), that when a messenger came back with uLangalibalela's interpretation of its intelli-gence, it could well be too late.

This omen alone was the nearest thing to a fact in François's possession to help him account for the extraordinary night of apprehension through which he slept fitfully, with Hintza whimpering as if in a succession of nightmares by his side. Again it was the only fact available to explain the feeling of unease and the brooding silence which descended on the little community the next day and which affected everybody from Ousie-Johanna and Lammie to the young boys making cattle of clay by the irrigation ditch at the far end of the garden.

With such a night behind him and such a long, depressing day drawing to an end, François viewed the coming night with growing dismay, until suddenly the five mongrel watch-dogs, coming on duty, started their tell-tale barking and, in between the barks, there became audible the sound of a truck approaching along the Punda-Ma-Tenka. At first François thought it was just another of those unwelcome trucks using the old Hunter's Road, typically timed to arrive at the ford at dusk, but this truck, instead of making for the outspan by the ford, sounded as if it had left the main road and was making straight for the homestead, where the windows were already on fire with the sunset, and the white walls and eurhythmic gables stained with colour. 'Thank God!' he cried, 'Nonnie.'

Hintza had reached the same conclusion and was already running as François had never seen him run before, his body elongated and glistening in a twist of evening light and speed, towards the truck labouring towards them.

He himself had just the presence of mind to put his head through the kitchen door and shout at Ousie-Johanna, 'Little old Ousie – visitors . . . quick, tell Lammie. Visitors!' Then, gun at the trail, he followed Hintza.

Of course it was Sir James's truck, with Amelia, more monumental than ever, suitably enthroned on high beside the driver, and Nonnie, looking older but reassuringly dressed as she had been when he had last seen her, in bush jacket, slacks and calf-skin boots. Only this time she wore a wide-brimmed khaki bush hat lined with a pillar-box red material, that brought out all the colour and light on her face. She was first out of the truck. The moment she landed on her feet in the grass Hintza threw himself into her arms, and at once both in his own right and in the role he played unknowingly as a proxy for François, he received a double ration of welcome.

While Sir James and Amelia were descending in dignified

452

state from the truck and expecting to be received with due respect themselves, Nonnie instinctively found it safer to go on fondling and stroking Hintza as she knelt in the track, while looking up at François with expressive, dark Iberian eyes now shining with happiness. She managed to say at last, 'Oh, it's been such a long, long time.'

François, with the greatest difficulty, could only manage a mere, 'It's been no time at all.'

'You haven't changed a bit,' Nonnie retorted gaily, far too happy to be critical. In any case she had gone away finally understanding François's highly personal attitude to time. But she teased him instinctively as a way of by-passing the storm of emotion in herself. 'I see. You still have that sublime indifference to time and age. So all these long months have been just no time at all to you, Master François?'

Thinking he had never been so misunderstood, François protested, 'I don't mean anything of the kind, Nonnie. I just meant, it was the kind of time I would have preferred not even to have existed.'

As he said it, there was a glimmer at the back of his mind of one of the basic realizations of the imagination brave enough to look into the mysterious role of time in the life of man: the fact that the very time which passes so slowly and reluctantly because of separation or unhappiness, seems, on looking back, to have vanished in a flash almost as if it had never been. Yet time which is charged with meaning and joy goes so swiftly that one longs to stop it. Once over, it has this paradoxical compensation that, in recollection, it seems to have lasted longer. The intimation made François repeat, 'I promise you, Nonnie, it was just no time at all.'

Her eyes clearly showed that she understood. She may even have responded in a far from teasing way had not the voice of her father, perhaps even a little more official than before if that were possible, due to his recent voyage in enigmatic waters of state, broken in with an 'Ah, we meet again, young fellow, m'lad. Good evening to you, and I hope not too inconvenient a moment to beg you and your mother hospitality for just one night?'

François, however awkwardly, managed to make it convinc-

453

ingly clear that everyone at Hunter's Drift had been looking forward to just such a visit from them, and would have been most disappointed had they not come. He would have elaborated if he had not then been abruptly enclosed in Amelia's arms and hugged and kissed ardently, and informed, over and over again, in a Portuguese he could not understand, how delighted she was and how much she thanked God and the saints in Heaven, to whom she had regularly prayed in their absence, that no one at Hunter's Drift or in the vicinity had been massacred, yet. That *yet* was uttered in such a tone as to make it quite clear that in Amelia's heart, Africa and the inevitability of the ultimate massacre of everyone not African in it were still a sombre unity.

It was a wonderful evening in the homestead that followed. François rejoiced, not only that Nonnie was back but also that Lammie had not for many years been so gay, or looked so beautiful. Sir James, too, having been prepared by the many things he had heard about Lammie to find her not only extreme.y beautiful but also possessing so lively a mind, imagination and a great range of interests in regions in which he himself was at home, was at his most gracious best. He revealed aspects of himself which did something to soften the impact of François's previous experience of him.

François and Nonnie faced each other across the table, set with the old Joubert family silver, their best plate and old wine glasses from France, decanters full of Ouwa's best wine and bowls of fresh fruit glowing like jewels under the light of the great oil lamps. They were content to communicate with each other with looks rather than words and wisely to leave the conversation to the capable tongues of their highly articulate parents.

Nonnie indeed had a private inducement of her own to keep silent and listen carefully so as not to miss a nuance of voice or expression as she saw her father and Lammie getting on so well together. Nor was she travelling alone in this wide dimension of anticipation. Whenever the door at the far end of the dining-room was opened she could just make out two vast ladies in the dim light beyond, one Portuguese, one African, their arms round each other, heads close together discreetly observing the

454

table, their eyes moving from one expression on Lammie's face to the corresponding one on Sir James's.

One cannot describe what Nonnie would have said, might she have seen through the walls to the kitchen when the door shut between courses, for in the intervals those two ladies were busy using that Esperanto of signs and sounds they had evolved at their first meeting, to make it quite clear to each other that they had not only indubitably reached the same conclusion but approved in equal measure and with a rapidly accelerating degree of warmth. They celebrated the various degrees of their conclusion with more embraces and expressions of joy at the vast prospect of accord opened up in their imagination. And on each occasion Ousie-Johanna, when she reluctantly withdrew from Amelia's arms, filled a glass to the brim for her with the good red wine which, for all her opinion of it as a brew of the devil, she felt free to offer to Amelia as Lammie had specially ordained it for that very purpose. As the wine warmed blood and hope within Amelia, and the communion of hope and warmth created an excuse for more wine, it soon became perhaps the one moment in years in which even her bruised mind was free of any thought of disaster and massacre.

The evening ended somewhat abruptly for Nonnie. Sir James suddenly broke off in his conversation with Lammie, during coffee in the drawing-room, and ordered his daughter in his best quarter-deck manner, 'Bedtime, Chisai. Off you go below deck, at the double!'

Although the command was not without some camouflage of playfulness, Luciana knew her father had never been more in earnest. The woman in her was already old enough to suspect that this display of discipline and firmness on his part may well have been put on for Lammie's benefit, since women perhaps tend to be impressed by a man's capacity for being firm with all members of their sex except themselves. 'Why Fa,' she thought to herself, 'I never knew you could be so cunning.'

However she was ready to do anything just then to serve her father's cause of impressing Lammie. Also, she had her own reasons for instant compliance. She had already arranged with François that she would accompany him on a dawn patrol to the place where they had had their first complete experience in the bush together, watching the baboons. So an early night suited her secret purpose admirably.

Accordingly, she immediately left her chair, curtsied gracefully to Lammie, waved her hand lightly to François, touched an imaginary able-seaman's hat to her father and with an 'Aye-aye sir and a good night to all', she vanished from the room.

Although it took François a long time to go to sleep, once asleep he slept soundly, until he found himself suddenly sitting up in his bed, reaching for his rifle and listening to the sound of first one long night-plover call like that on a bosun's pipe, followed immediately by the mournful bark of a jackal – all emitted so faultlessly that only François could have known that they were human. Dear God, he thought, it was the pre-arranged call sign. Xhabbo had come. Xhabbo at last was out there in the bush and the dark.

He had hardly admitted the conclusion and lit the candle, when Hintza set his paws on the bed, almost uncontrollable with excitement and eagerness to be off. 'Shush, I know, he's back. I know. Quiet, please keep quiet.' François calmed Hintza and started dressing as fast as he could. However he had not even got his trousers on properly when again there came exactly the same series of calls, this time closer and even more urgent than before. The urgency was immediately stressed because, after hardly a minute's pause, the second call was followed by a third reiteration at a faster and even more imperative pitch.

'Something's wrong, something's terribly wrong. Dear God, we must hurry. But please Hin, quiet! We *must* be quiet.' He told himself and Hintza this in Bushman, as Hintza seemed beyond himself with his own reading of the need to haste towards the call. He was now scratching fiercely at the door in a manner which could wake up the whole household.

Completing his dressing in record time and quickly blowing out the candle, François opened the door quietly, exhorting Hintza to greater calm, and tiptoed along the passage towards the nearest outside door.

But he had not gone far when suddenly a torch flashed in his face and a voice whispered, 'It's you, François. I didn't realize we were going to set out quite so early. What a good thing ...

456

I was so excited that I woke up early and couldn't resist getting ready. I seem to have been waiting here for hours not daring to breathe.'

It was Nonnie of course and a complication that François would have given anything to avoid. He could not tell what Xhabbo would think of him if he came with another person to their meeting after so long. Nor could be explain to Nonnie why he could not allow her to come.

As he stood there hesitating what to do, the call sign was repeated for a fourth time. François knew then that he had no option.

He said to Nonnie rather fiercely, 'Come quickly then. But for Heaven's sake come quietly. There's something very strange going on outside. You must promise to be silent . . . not to speak unless spoken to and not ever to tell anyone about what happens.'

Without waiting for Nonnie's answer he made immediately for the door, opened it soundlessly and led the way on to the broad stoep. From there he saw that the morning star, Xhabbo's Dawn Heart, was already risen, the dawn obviously not far behind and the bush for the first time that he could remember, was completely and most ominously silent. All is well, Xhabbo has come, one half of his heart called out to him. The other called out as loudly, all is not well.

François thought Xhabbo's call had come roughly from the direction of the place where he and Hintza had originally found him caught in the lion-trap some eighteen months before. But he was not certain. He would have liked another call from Xhabbo just then to help him get his bearings more precisely. But another call in so short a space of time might alert even the experienced Matabele senses, however sleepy. So he whispered to Hintza to take the lead, knowing that his sensitive nose would be even better than a compass for the shortest way through the dark to Xhabbo.

It was just as well that he handed over command to Hintza. To his astonishment, Hintza led off on a different path through the garden which led to a track bearing away between the Matabele kraals and the river, to a point where the crescent of hills behind his home met the river, almost immediately underneath the place of Mantis's cave. Hintza, despite François's efforts to restrain him, for once appeared to find it necessary to match their pace to his own reading of the urgency of the situation. He went ahead in the darkness so fast that François had to break into a quick trot to keep close to him. François feared the pace might be too fast either for observing the necessary silence or for a city-bred person like Nonnie. But every time he looked round he was impressed to find her close behind him.

They went on like this for close on a mile, leaving the Matabele kraals well behind, without attracting any attention. Then François thought he saw at an acute angle to their direction, half-left behind them, not far from where the Punda-Ma-Tenka road reached the ford on the river, a blur of some dark mass which he could not explain, moving silently but fast across the starlit clearing towards his home. Indeed Hintza must have recognized the same unusual phenomenon because François nearly bumped into him, halted in the track, his head turned sideways in its direction and an ominous sort of murmur in his throat.

François may well have stopped too and turned round to investigate that dark blur of movement if, almost directly ahead of him and now very close indeed, Xhabbo's call sign had not gone up in the silence. Not only the pitch and the speed at which it was uttered but just the fact that it had been emitted at all, implied an extreme sort of desperation in Xhabbo.

The need for the greatest silence as well as haste made François go down on his knees in the track and command Hintza: 'No Hin, no looking back, that's Xhabbo calling. Forget everything else ... find Xhabbo, quick. Search and find. You must be quick as never before.'

Getting to his feet, he turned round and whispered in turn to Nonnie, standing silently behind him using her utmost self-control not to give away to her own curiosity and spurred on now by a feeling of alarm. It was an immense triumph of will and loyalty to François, that she asked no questions and remained silent, although she was certain that the beating of her heart, both from the long, fast run and the fear within her, must be audible to both him and Hintza.

François could not see her face in the darkness, despite the brilliant starlight, but her nearness and her silence were enough somehow to move him extremely, and for the first time to be truly glad that she was there with him. 'Well done, Nonnie,' he found himself saying softly. 'Well done. I only hope I was right to bring you along. There's something terribly wrong, perhaps extremely dangerous about. We can't be careful or quick enough. But just follow us like this and we'll soon know.'

The warning may have been unnecessary and uttered only because by now his own feeling of danger had become almost overwhelming. There were, as he had emphasized to Nonnie, foreign, dangerous and hostile presences in the bush and all around them, because if that were not so, he was certain that just now Caruso would have called out his soaring Halleluyah to the first light, just drawing a red pencil line along the black sheet of the fast receding night; Garbo would have immediately added her own ardent Hosannah and old Chaliapin would have proclaimed on behalf of all the life of the bush that had come safely through so great and troubled a night, his profound Amen. Also old Adonis, perched high on the cliffs with a clear view of the explosion of night into a red dawn, would have commanded his nation with a series of booming barks to 'rise and shine, as our great god, the sun, was about to rise and shine'. Only something terrible could have made these great heraldic officers of the bush suspend their duties of sounding their fanfare for the arrival of another day.

All these thoughts went through François like the shadow of a torn, storm-battered cloud driven by a high wind over the hill, as he started running forward again after Hintza, who was already lost in the darkness ahead. At the very place where the hills met the river they caught up not only with Hintza but also with another dark shape whom François recognized at first more by smell than sight as it came hurrying towards them. It was Xhabbo.

Overjoyed, François was about to utter the traditional greeting but Xhabbo gave him no time. Indeed he gave himself no time even to wonder why François was not alone, but he immediately seized him by the hand, pressed it hard and whispered, hoarse with haste, 'Come quickly, utterly quickly, Foot of the Day. Come because we are all utterly in terrible danger.'

François had no time to question, or even to remonstrate for Xhabbo had sped, bounding up the hill so fast that he was already a blur up ahead despite the lifting of the dark. Hintza was at his heels, leading them up the side of the cliff. All François could do was to follow with Nonnie as fast as they could until they arrived, breathless, on top, some hundreds of feet above the river just as the dawn exploded in a turquoise sky to stand briefly like a Chinese fan of the brightest lacquer held in the hand of the day from just below the horizon. Xhabbo went down at once on his stomach behind a rock, signalled to François and Nonnie to do the same. Once certain that they were properly hidden, he began to explain.

'They are coming, Foot of the Day, in their thousands,' he said. 'For thirty days now Nuin-Tara and I have seen them coming in their thousands in this direction. Although we have utterly hastened to come to you and warn you, we could not get to you before, as we could easily have done had they not been there. Oh, Foot of the Day, neither Xhabbo nor Xhabbo's people have ever seen anything like it! There were so many of them and they were so utterly everywhere that we had to hide by day and travel only by night.'

François had no idea who 'Nuin-Tara' could possibly be. He recognized the word only as Bushman for 'Daughter of a Star', and one of the most exalted names a Bushman could bestow on a woman. Also, he was far more concerned with the 'thousands' who were coming and were everywhere in the bush. 'But the thousands you mention Xhabbo, who are they and what are they coming for?'

Xhabbo's low voice, raised just above a whisper answered sombrely: 'Thousands of kaffirs, carrying arms just like the one that you are carrying, and many spears, knives and things that I do not know myself ... All I know is that our kinsmen who come and go between the desert and the world outside have now for many moons told us that the kaffirs were massing in the mountain valleys and bush on the far side of the desert and coming to kill everyone who is not a kaffir in the place of

Foot of the Day and all the other places of the white men yonder.'

François, who knew the word kaffir (which is derived from the Arabic for unbeliever, and was one that the slave traders from Zanzibar imposed upon the long-suffering indigenous Bantu peoples of Africa), would never himself have used the term on any black man, since it had long since become an insult to them. Yet he knew from Old Koba that the Bushmen, who had been even more cruelly persecuted by the black people than by the white, had adopted this term for the black man as their own name of scorn for them. He was about to ask Xhabbo for more information when about a half a mile away to the west of where they were lying, there came a great shout.

It was a shout of all that stood for courage in man who, however great the inducement to fear and no matter how hopeless his cause, maintained his stand to the point of death. As such it was the purest human sound François had ever heard. Everything in him responded to it and urged him to go instantly to the man who had uttered it. But Xhabbo, feeling the muscles in François's body beside him gathering to rise, held him down by force, saying fiercely, 'No, Foot of the Day. We *cannot* help. It is utterly too late.'

The cry, of course, was that of 'Bamuthi calling that 'To me!' to what must, by now, be the awakening Matabele kraals and homestead. The call had barely died away, François was still struggling wildly with Xhabbo, and Hintza was beginning to whimper with confusion as to why François and he were not speeding down already to that beloved voice calling to all that was free of fear in man and dog, when the quick staccato stutter of a burst of fire from an automatic rifle shattered the heavy silence below.

As the stutter of sound ended abruptly in the bush, some-where near the lion-trap, it was followed from the direction of the kraals, Hunter's Drift, the clearing, the ford and the river by the blast of military whistles.

The blast sounded ridiculously normal, as if it were doing no more than setting some Cup Final in motion, until it was suc-ceeded by an immense war cry coming from far down in the throats of hundreds of men and, hard upon the cry, an eruption of automatic fire from a thousand or more rifles sending burst after burst of controlled fire to end the calm of morning.

François for the moment stopped struggling. It was too late to do anything about Hunter's Drift. Sick in heart and body at what he knew for certain was happening down below to all those people whom he loved so dearly and to whom he owed so much, too stricken even for tears, he assured Xhabbo he would not do anything foolish. But he had to go and look. Xhabbo's grip relaxed and he nodded his agreement.

Then the two of them together, very carefully, raised themselves to look over the boulder behind which they had been lying. The light was good enough for them to see that the vast clearing around the homestead was filled with men in uniform, obviously well-trained and disciplined, surrounding the kraals, gardens and homestead in organized platoons. They were directing their volley of automatic rifle fire into the buildings and kraals and apparently at whatever and whoever might be coming out of them.

There was indeed nothing François could do to help, although if alone he might perhaps have been driven by the extremity of the tragedy and outrage in him to rush down the hill and shoot until he had no ammunition left. But the thought of Nonnie and Xhabbo stopped him.

He looked at Nonnie and found that she too was looking over the boulder, her head close beside him, her face white and tense and her eyes full of horror. She turned to François. 'Oh Coiske, what's happening? What can we do?'

To his astonishment and intense admiration there were no tears in her eyes as she spoke, only horror and anger, naked and unafraid, over the cause of the horror. He was about to reply when he became aware of someone crawling up behind them. Alarmed, he looked quickly over his shoulder and found himself staring into a beautiful Bushman girl face, all the more poignant because the eyes were so young.

He heard Xhabbo explain: 'Nuin-Tara. She is utterly my woman.'

François, boorish with haste, greeted her abruptly and found himself saying urgently, 'Xhabbo, it may not be possible to go down into the clearing and do anything against those men shooting my people. But here, from the hill, we have bushes and trees enough for cover to enable us to go to the aid of the man whose shout we heard down by the lion-trap.'

'But that too was only the shout of a kaffir!' Xhabbo objected, amazed.

François did not need to forgive Xhabbo the remark, because how could Xhabbo possibly have known the facts? He just answered sadly, 'It may have been a call from what you call a kaffir, Xhabbo. But for me it was a call from a man who ever since I can remember was a father, brother, friend and sometimes even a mother to me ... While there is a chance that I can help, I must go. There is a great tapping inside me, Xhabbo, which you yourself would tell me it would be foolish to ignore. It says, Foot of the Day, you must go to him.'

François finished. Suddenly he remembered the moment when he had heard Mopani's quiet voice beside him, 'You take him, Cousin', and he had had to shoot Uprooter-of-Great-Trees. Indeed, just for a second the image of that other morning was bright in his mind. All that was happening around them suddenly became another Uprooter-of-Great-Trees, mad on marula spirit, which perhaps only he could take.

Xhabbo protested no more. He merely said: 'Foot of the Day, if you go, Xhabbo goes. All Xhabbo asks is that this your woman goes immediately with Nuin-Tara to Mantis's cave and waits there, not to come out again, but to wait and wait until we come back, if ever we come back.'

As far as Nonnie was concerned, this corresponded with François's own deepest wishes. However much Nonnie pleaded he ordered her with authority to go with Nuin-Tara. So with Nuin-Tara not uttering a word of protest but setting the example, Nonnie was compelled to crouch low, and follow her to Mantis's cave which happily was near at hand. Deeply afraid that this might be the last time she would see François alive, Nonnie looked back just before she went down to crawl through the narrow entrance to the cave, but François had vanished.

He and Xhabbo, with Hintza in front, were already some way down the hill making their way carefully under cover of the brush to where 'Bamuthi's 'To me!' had thundered out.

There was no longer any regular automatic fire to be heard

from the homestead and kraals, but every now and then a single shot would still thud in their ears, as if the attackers were inspecting their field of battle and finishing off the wounded who were not killed outright in the main attack.

Except for those odd sounds of distant rifle fire, the silence in the bush was complete as if all that had lived and made their homes there over the long millennia were overcome with horror and lost. The voices which would have filled the blue and delicate silver of any other autumn morning with music were silent. So great a silence made it all the more imperative that none of them should make a sound because any noise, however small, just then, could easily bring disaster.

Fortunately, young as they were, Xhabbo and François were old and rich in the experience of going noiselessly and unseen through the bush. They came, without being heard or seen, to that great ledge close by the track where François had hidden the sorely wounded Xhabbo eighteen months before. Xhabbo recognized the place instantly and his archaic face, just briefly, was illuminated with a glimmer of a smile, as a sign to François of how vivid still was his gratitude to what François had done for him that day.

François immediately responded, moved as people are when the nearness of death banishes all that is false and illusory. He put his hand on Xhabbo's shoulder and was amazed how all differences and distance from another person, physically, culturally and in every rational way so removed from him, indeed how even all his own inner 'otherness' was abolished by that touch. It was as if they were not two but one in the same skin. He would have lingered, perhaps, to draw on such a feeling of togetherness to add to his courage for the way into the world of fear and death ahead of them, had not Hintza suddenly uttered a sharp warning. He was standing still, the hair on his magnetic ridge erect, nose and tail aligned in the direction of the lion-trap.

Xhabbo and François both stared at where Hintza was pointing but saw nothing. At a sign from Xhabbo they both went down flat on their stomachs. Hintza following their example, they all three slowly wriggled silently forward until François saw, through the bush immediately ahead of him, what looked

464

like an extremely blotchy piece of jungle-green linen. He crawled closer. In a minute he found himself looking at a dead African in camouflaged uniform, lying on his back, an enormous jagged wound over his heart where the blood had barely congealed, and the latest automatic rifle with a short little modern bayonet fixed to it, resting on top of a bush beside him. The wound that had killed the man, he was certain then, had been inflicted by 'Bamuthi. Far from being horrified at the sight of the dead man, a bright light of a strange joy flared fiercely in the darkness within him. 'Oh, pray God you killed them all before they could kill you, Old Father.'

Xhabbo must have reached a similar conclusion because already he and Hintza were wriggling on beyond. Some five yards away they found another dead man. He was stabbed between the shoulders as if surprised by 'Bamuthi from behind and beyond this body they came at last to the lion-trap. There, another dead uniformed African lay, held firmly in the trap by the leg as Xhabbo had been.

François was now sure that 'Bamuthi, on his early morning round of the traps, must have come across this group of armed men, probably an advance patrol under orders not to betray the main party behind by any shooting. They had been put in a terrible predicament by getting this man caught in the great trap. While struggling to release him they must have been surprised by 'Bamuthi. Under orders not to shoot, they obviously had tried immediately to attack him with their bayonets and 'Bamuthi, trained and wise in the darkness, would have defended himself so well that he killed the three of them in the process.

The conclusion raised François's hopes higher still. Oh, what a battle there must have been, he thought, and if only 'Bamuthi could be alive so that, by the side of a fire in another hut in another and greater Hunter's Drift, he could still tell the tale to the end of his days to other children and grandchildren, as an example of what life can ask of men and what a man's answer can be.

At that moment of quickening hope, however, Hintza came back from a precautionary reconnaissance of the bush in the vicinity. He was whimpering softly and pitifully and immediately started tugging at François's slacks. François signed to Xhabbo that they would do well to heed Hintza and to follow without delay.

Some twenty yards on through the bush Hintza brought them to another dead African lying on his back but this time with the shaft of an assegai sticking in his body and standing up straight high above him. The length and nature of the shaft told François immediately that the spear was 'Bamuthi's beloved *u-Simsela-Banta-Bami*. So they had come to witness the washing of He-Who-Digs-For-My-Children at last and all hope died within François because, if that great assegai was left standing there in the dead body of an enemy, it could only mean that it had 'dug' for 'Bamuthi's children for the last time; and that his own dead body could not be far away.

Hintza almost at once took them to 'Bamuthi. He was lying some four yards away just round a curve in the track, with six bullets in his body. That, no doubt, had been the first burst of fire which François had heard from the rim of the hill. It had been also the final testimony to 'Bamuthi's courage and skill as a warrior because the fourth African, finding himself the only survivor of the patrol, clearly had felt compelled to break his orders and open fire on 'Bamuthi, thus forcing the main attack on the homestead and kraals to begin sooner than planned. Despite the terrible burst of fire into 'Bamuthi's body, judging by the trail of blood between him and the dead man, his courage and spirit had been so great that he had still managed miraculously to kill his own killer before he died.

Unlike his attackers, moreover, he had died like a man completely at one and at peace with himself, for he was lying there with his eyes shut as if merely asleep, like a black marble statue of Homeric man in Africa, thrown from its pedestal in the bush that was his Athens, to lie there waiting for the re-emergence of men of true worth to raise it upright from the dust for the future to mark and observe. François knelt down in the dust beside him. He found himself taking 'Bamuthi's hand, which felt still warm, and putting it to his lips he remembered with what tenderness 'Bamuthi had looked down on the dead body of Uprooter-of-Great-Trees, and what a black hole the elephant's going had made in the day. The hole, in that far-off magic lantern morning, diminished to a pin-prick compared to the void facing him now and he murmured, 'Old Father, beloved Old Father, you were a great lord, and in this dark hour, He-Who-Dug-for-your-Children was your hand. Oh, I thank you for dying for us as you did. I thank you and bless you.'

And then Xhabbo was pulling him by the sleeve and saying, 'Quick, Foot of the Day! There is someone else out there moaning. Listen, can't you hear it?' And François, his eyes blurred with tears, had to allow Xhabbo to lead him by the hand in the direction of the moaning, which he could not even hear because of his pain. Some sixty yards deeper into the bush, they came to a man who was making the moaning.

It was Mtunywa, Messenger, bleeding from several bullet wounds, and in desperate, if not dying, condition. The need for immediate action brought François back to all his practical senses. As he went down on his knees beside Mtunywa, he pulled out the field dressings he always carried in the pockets of his bush jacket, immediately tied them on round the two worst wounds, produced the two handkerchiefs he had on him and used them for two more bad wounds. That left only a fifth on the side of Messenger's head, fortunately not so serious and one that could be left until François could tear a strip of clothing for dressing it.

The great and immediate need was to get Mtunywa somewhere away from the track because there was no doubt that the men who had organized the patrol would soon have people there to find out what had happened and why their patrol had broken their orders not to open fire.

Asking Xhabbo to take Mtunywa by the legs, François held one hand to the wound in the head to prevent the blood from leaving any marks on the grass, leaves and brush which might betray them. Then with his rifle slung over his shoulder and right arm round Mtunywa's shoulder, they carried him as fast as they could to the ledge under which Xhabbo had once found shelter. They had barely got him there when they heard sounds of men laughing, shouting and carelessly trampling about the bush as if they owned it, coming towards the lion-trap from the direction of the homestead.

François knew their only chance now of escaping detection

was to stop Mtunywa's pitiful moaning, which was increasing as
he got colder with shock and pain. Fortunately François also
carried as well as his field dressings, some aureo-mycin and
morphia tablets. Quickly he slipped a tablet of morphia and
two of aureo-mycin to prevent infection of his wounds between
Mtunywa's lips and put his flask of water to the wounded man's
mouth. Instinctively Mtunywa, parched as the human being
becomes from pain, loss of blood and shock, gulped up the
water. In less than a minute, the moaning stopped. Suddenly
released from pain, Mtunywa opened his eyes. Seeing François
crouching beside him in the shelter, he smiled wide with relief
as if he were not wounded at all and no longer in danger.

The impression, however, was immediately belied for the
smile vanished as he remembered. He clutched François's hand,
murmuring slowly with many a pause and hesitation: 'Oh,
Little Feather, you must go and leave me to die as I must die ...
They know that you are not dead and somewhere near and
alive ... They are determined to find you in case you get away
to tell others of what has happened here and warn them they
are coming ... I heard them talking as they left me for dead by
the milking sheds. They said all must go out and search to find
you. They are the same men we pulled out of the mud with the
oxen that day. They know you and they want you dead. Leave
me please, Little Feather, and go, go to our other father Mopani
before it is too late. All ... all in our kraals are dead from the
smallest baby to the oldest lady. The Lammie of our house, the
Princess of the Pots, the lady of the little mother-to-be of a
thousand generations, all, all are dead ... even *isi-Vuba* is
killed. Ah there was a man! He was shot in the door of your
home but even so he killed before he was killed and left us,
with all dead except you and me ... As for me, my shadow is
lengthening for the journey to Amageba and I thank the Amatonga for letting me live to see you. For I see you, Little
Feather, yes I see you and greet you!'

The Amatonga, of course, were the spirits of his people, and
often openly called upon, but that ancient word Amageba was
another matter and nearly unmanned François, because it was
used only on the gravest of occasions in the Matabele spirit,
being their sacred name for the land of their origin, and mean-

468

ing the place in the far mountains where the evening shadows gather.

Moreover all the time Mtunywa spoke, his speech became slower and the words slurred, and François hoped against hope that he was not dying, but that the morphia was taking increasing effect. Soon, indeed, he appeared to fall into a deep sleep. It was just as well, because the careless talking and laughing of the men crashing through the bush had stopped. There was a long silence before one great cry of horror and anger after the other, broke from them, as they found first one dead African companion and then the other three. Their rage was so great that when they came across the body of 'Bamuthi, they expressed it by firing burst after burst of bullets into his body as if they thought themselves capable of improving on death.

That done, they scattered and could be heard running up and down the track, crashing through the bush all round them, as if they did not believe 'Bamuthi alone could have inflicted so much killing, and must have helpers near at hand. At one moment they came within three yards of the ledge, so close that François had to put a hand over Hintza's mouth and nose, afraid that the snarl forming on his lips might turn into a fatal growl. Then he took his gun in his right hand ready to shoot.

But in time the men went away. Once more there was complete silence in the bush, for so long that François seriously considered whether he and Xhabbo should not take the unconscious Mtunywa, however difficult, stage by stage under cover of the bush up to the shelter of Mantis's cave. But Xhabbo would not hear of it. François had never known him so firm. He just said that he had a tapping that told him that the men were searching everywhere and that they had to stay where they were until the evening.

Xhabbo's wisdom and the veracity of his tapping were soon made manifest. For it was not long before they heard the sound of many men returning. This time happily they came not to search but to bury their dead. When they came to the lion-trap François plainly heard the sounds of picks and shovels digging. The digging went on until the early hours of the afternoon when it stopped, to be followed soon after by the sound of earth being shovelled back to cover in the graves they had dug.

It was not, François estimated, until nearly four in the afternoon that the burial party at last withdrew. Once the burying was over, they obviously relaxed in the shade of that great wild fig tree in order to eat the food they had brought. When they had gone, François was on the point of suggesting that they could perhaps risk taking Mtunywa with them up the hill, when he felt Mtunywa's hand, which he had been holding all the time in his own and stroking for comfort as he had stroked Hintza when still a bewildered puppy, stiffen. He looked down and Mtunywa, too, was dead, carrying perhaps as his last act and deed as a messenger, a report to the Amatonga of the apparent triumph of evil over goodness and courage, their especial gift to man, despite the exertions of their servant 'Bamuthi.

He looked at Xhabbo and whispered, 'He's dead.'

Xhabbo did not answer in words. Instead he put out his right hand and hooked its little finger round François's own, the Bushman act of expressing a feeling of oneness with another. And through this contact, more than any words could possibly have conveyed, there flowed into François a stream of strength and understanding, coming not only from Xhabbo but through him from hundreds and thousands of others who, in long centuries of their remorseless history had been hunted down first in the far north, then on in the south, generation after generation had been pursued and slaughtered by more powerful men, until now only a tiny fragment remained in that desert towards which the sun was sinking.

The strength was all the purer because, despite that inexorable succession of killing, they had never lost their love of life, nor the will to live, nor the capacity to love even those others coming, like François, from a breed of men who had joined in their persecution. If there were in life a specialist in knowing precisely what the tragedy which had just been inflicted on François and Nonnie meant, none could have been greater than Xhabbo. Feeling this, François was freed as much as one caught up in such a torrent of horror and tragedy could be, to think of Nonnie. He wanted to go to her at once in the cave but again Xhabbo refused. He insisted that they wait there until the sun was about to touch the trees. Even then he led the way up the hill with as great a care as they had come in the morning.

How wise he was in this was proved when near the rim of the cliff on which they had sheltered in the morning, there suddenly emerged on the skyline almost larger than life in the glass of evening, the dark silhouettes of men with rifles and fixed bayonets on their shoulders, going vigilantly towards Hunter's Drift. For a moment François feared he would see Nonnie and Nuin-Tara prisoner in the midst of the men, since they were coming from the direction of the cave. But they were just another platoon which had obviously been searching far and wide in the bush for him, and returning, unsuccessful, to their base. He and Xhabbo and Hintza waited, hidden in the brush long after the men had vanished. The sun was about to go below the horizon before they went on to arrive safely at the entrance to Mantis's cave. As they arrived the sun vanished and left a vast fire, flickering, flaming and turning the dust of the desert that was Xhabbo's home and which filled the sky, into sparks soaring into the darkening blue.

Xhabbo was about to go down on his knees to crawl through the entrance when Nuin-Tara emerged. François knew enough of Bushman eyes by now to see the acute relief which came to her. But that was all that he could measure it by, because she made no sound and merely went up to Xhabbo, dignified with her certainty that words were unnecessary and all that needed doing was for her to take his hand in hers and hold it.

She was followed by Nonnie who, the moment she saw François, ran to him and threw her arms round him, not saying anything but crying with relief as if she would never be able to stop. Finally she managed to blurt out, 'You see, I was sure you were killed as well when we heard the shooting below ... Thank God you've come ... Oh Coiske, Coiske, you've come, that's all that matters. You've come and I don't care what happens now. But what are we going to do?'

François stood there, stroking her head as gently as he had stroked Messenger's hand. There was nothing more to be said and no answers in his heart or mind to any questions, even the simplest ones. Then a whimper made him look down and he saw Hintza staring up at them, his own great eyes glowing with concern, in that light the full purple they had been when he had opened them first on François as a cold little puppy.

'Look, Nonnie,' he begged her. 'Please look at poor old Hin. Say something to him. Without him we wouldn't be here and he's as unhappy as you and me.'

It was the best thing he could have done because it summoned the mother latent in Nonnie. She went down on her knees and held Hintza in her arms, no longer in tears as she murmured words of gratitude, love and comfort over him.

Xhabbo, however, did even better. He knew, out of his endless history of persecution which had created its own immediate instincts, what must be in her heart. He said quietly, 'Foot of the Day, tell this utterly your woman, not to let her heart be troubled. Xhabbo will find a way.'

François told her, and the strangest of all things to give him hope was that she seemed to accept this promise from someone she had never known and could not even have imagined existed. She looked up, her eyes bright, her hand resting on Hintza's neck and asked François to thank Xhabbo and to tell him she believed that he would indeed find a way.

For a moment the four of them, no five, for the dog that had been the first animal to become the friend of man; a man and a woman of the people who had been the first representative of man in Africa, and a boy and a girl who were of the people most recently come to the Dark Continent, stood there. Two of the remotest beginning and two of the most immediate now stood as one and watched the fire die down in the west. As it died they saw star after star come into the sky until the last red glimmer of light vanished. Then, as Xhabbo said, it was 'utterly dark, the night feeling itself to be utterly dark'. From east to west, north to south, from the rim of an horizon round and perfect as a ripple on a tranquil, limpid pond travelling into the smooth night, to the greatest deep of the sky above them, Heaven was packed with stars bright as only the stars of Africa can be.

All these stars had thrown away the arrows and spears with which the Bushman imagination arms them, and gone over to watering the night with their tears. They were indeed, as the Matabele would have said, 'stringing the beads' for all the many good and dear people who had died that day, stringing them indeed for a whole heroic age of man and his empire of natural

472

spirit that had crumbled to nothing in one brief red dawn and was now beyond recall. Somehow, this feeling that the stars in their lawful courses were weeping for them, informed the four on that rock high above the precious, onflowing river which they heard beneath them like a great wind in the dark as if it were the river of time itself, that they were not alone but facing the future in infinite company.

It was a moment of such brave and perfect illumination of night that Nonnie, one hand on Hintza, took François's in the other, her heart crying out to her mind, 'Oh, how beautiful, how absolutely beautiful. With such beauty, how *can* men be so ugly as they have been today?'

At that moment first one and then a succession of great stars came shooting red out of the sky over the river and fell in a slow, heavy arc towards the horizon, almost touching it before vanishing. For the first time that day a voice spoke up in the bush, the voice of the great, lonely old lion.

The one voice and the echo of its calling vanished, and in the stillness they heard Xhabbo sigh a profound sigh of fulfilment as he declared quietly: 'Xhabbo knew that the stars who hide in light as other things hide in darkness were there to see all today. For the stars do fall in this manner when our hearts fall down. The time when the stars also fall down is while the stars feel that our hearts fall over, because those who had been walking upright, leaving their footprints in the sand, have fallen over on to their sides. Therefore the stars fall down on account of them, knowing the time when men die and that they must, falling, go to tell other people that a bad thing has happened at another place. Tell this utterly your woman, Foot of the Day, that the stars are acting thus on account of us and that we are not alone.'

Xhabbo paused until François had told Nonnie and in the telling noticed how the tension went out of the hand in his. Hintza, too, was still, his head on one side listening. Then, so accustomed were their eyes to the darkness and the starlight so bright and quick that they could see Xhabbo's arm pointing high while he went on: 'Look, Foot of the Day, how those stars which have not fallen over are full of a tapping as I, Xhabbo, am full of a tapping. And their tapping is joined to

Xhabbo's tapping, seeking to tell me of the way we must go. I must go into the cave and sit apart, listening utterly to this tapping, in order to learn of this way we must go.'

After that he put his arm on Nuin-Tara's shoulder in a way that was a sign to her. She instantly went down on her knees and crawled into the cave. Xhabbo followed at once and François, putting his hand on Nonnie's shoulder as Xhabbo had done on Nuin-Tara's, sent her down on her knees carefully after them. Hintza followed her, and finally François, as someone from far back in time turning for help to the last temple left on earth.

More about Penguins
and Pelicans

Laurens van der Post

The Lost World of the Kalahari

In this enthralling book a distinguished explorer and
writer describes his rediscovery of the Bushmen, outcast
survivors from Stone Age Africa. Laurens van der Post
was fascinated and appalled at the fate of this remarkable
people, who seemed to him a reminder of our own
'legitimate beginnings'.

Attacked by all the races that came after them in Africa,
the last of the Bushmen have in modern times been driven
deep into the Kalahari Desert. It was there, in the
scorching heat of an African August, that Colonel van der
Post led his famous expedition. His search for these small,
hardy aboriginals, with their physical peculiarities, their
cave art, and their music-making, provides the author
with material for a dramatic and compassionate book.

'He is even better in print than he was on T V' –
J. B. Priestley in *Reynolds News*

'No one can write more feelingly of Africa . . . an
experience not to be missed' – Elspeth Huxley in the
Evening Standard

Laurens van der Post

Journey into Russia

'The next best thing to seeing the place for oneself . . .
is to read *Journey into Russia* . . . sceptical, well-informed,
unprejudiced and amusing. A truly civilized, discriminating
observer' – *Guardian*

'He went to Russia for the first time in 1961 with an open
mind; he travelled all over the Soviet Union in four
separate journeys, and spoke to thousands of people,
from almost every walk of life . . . As a general picture of
Russia today there can hardly be a better book' – *Listener*

'An honest account . . . full of delightful vignettes of
Soviet life brought out with a subtle sense of humour' –
Daily Worker

Laurens van der Post

Venture to the Interior

This is the story of a journey made in 1949, at the request of the British Government, to investigate little-known territory in Nyasaland, the remote Mlanje, and the inacessible Nyika plateau. Laurens van der Post brilliantly evokes for us such events as a charge of zebras, an auction of Victorian furnishings in the heart of Africa, the psychological effects of an African drum, or the catastrophe which befell his party on Mount Mlanje.

'The reflective passages are very important and the idea of framing them in the journeys is inspired, and some of the poetic descriptions of the scenery are most beautiful and fill me with envy. I think the book is magnificent' – Stephen Spender

Also published

A Far-Off Place
The Heart of the Hunter

Alan Moorehead

The White Nile

In reviewing *The White Nile* in the *Observer* Sir Harold
Nicolson spoke of the gigantic ghosts that haunt the
Sudan. They are ghosts of many nationalities: the
Khedive Ismail, the Mahdi, savage King Mutesa of
Buganda, and a bevy of Arab slave traders. There is
Richard Burton, the restless, inscrutable scholar; his dull
but vindicated opponent, Speke; Livingstone, the
indomitable Scot; Baker and his beautiful Hungarian wife;
the bumptious American journalist, Stanley, who searched
for Livingstone and later for the German scientist, Emin
Pasha. And finally there is Gordon, the strange heroic
martyr of Khartoum.

These, in their full stature, Alan Moorehead parades
before us this account of the opening of the Nile. It is a
story which enforces respect for the Victorians' faith
in civilization and their hatred of slavery.

'He appears to have visited every inch of the scene himself
and puts it before us with simplicity and power' –
V. S. Pritchett in the *New Statesman*

Also published

The Fatal Impact
A Late Education